HELIX

EXPERIENCING TRUE PURPLE
BOOK 2

L. S. SILVERTHORNE

L.S. SILVERTHORNE

HELIX

EXPERIENCING TRUE PURPLE

Sting taught him how to fight.

Peter taught Sting how to hope.

Together, they taught each other how to survive.

And Peter will risk everything

To change Ku'Tal's outcome.

Peter Mitchell returned from Ku'Tal to a life he ached to live. To the woman he loved. But after escaping the military, he can't settle into this incredible new life. *Because he can't forget his best friend.* Struggling to fit into Diana Temple's world, Peter attempts to reach the forbidden alien outpost where Antarans take captured recombinants—for experimentation.

Until the night Antarans attack Civilization's training base.
D'Angelo, Sergeant David Temple's unhinged commanding officer, leads a covert op to the Antaran outpost, forcing David and his fiery pilot sister, Diana to join this descent into madness.
To protect Diana and Sarge—and find Sting—Peter dons another recombinant's uniform and joins the suicide mission.
Risking D'Angelo recognizing him. Risking execution as an escaped recombinant... to save Sting.

Helix

Book 2 of the *Experiencing True Purple* series

Lisa Silverthorne

Copyright © 2021 by Lisa Silverthorne

Published by ElusiveBlueFiction.com

Elusive Blue Fiction Logo designed by Samantha Romage

Cover Design by Lost Souls Studio

Additional Cover Elements licensed by Creative Market, DepositPhotos, Shutterstock

ISBN-13: 978-1-955197-21—2 (Hard cover)
ISBN-10: 1-955197-21-0

ISBN-13: 978-1-955197-20-5 (Trade paperback)
ISBN-10: 1-955197-20-2

ACKNOWLEDGMENTS

A big thank you to my dear friend, PATRICIA DUFFY NOVAK who generously provided her time and copyediting expertise to this book. And I am grateful. Thank you.

Novels by L.S. Silverthorne

Experiencing True Purple series:

RECOMBINANT, Book 1

HELIX, Book 2

SPLICE, Book 3

Standalone:

REDISCOVERY

Writing as Lisa Silverthorne

A Game of Lost Souls series:

Contemporary Romantasy

THE CINDERELLA HOUR

THE PRINCE CHARMING HOUR

THE EVER AFTER HOUR

THE FALLEN HEARTS SEASON

THE RISING SPIRITS SEASON

THE ETERNAL SOULS SEASON

THE ROYAL WEDDING HOUR

THE HEAVENLY HONEYMOON HOUR

THE DIVINE NEWLYWEDS SHOW

THE CELESTIAL COUPLES SHOW

THE ENOCHIAN APOCALYPSE SHOW

THE ANGELIC ANNIVERSARY SHOW

THE PERDITION PICTURE SHOW

Complete Series!

Curse and Crown series:

Epic Court Intrigue Romantasy

THORN & BLADE

STORM & STEEL

The Spiral series:

Dark Contemporary Fantasy

BETWEEN

REPRISE

AVENGE

The Resurrectionist Papers

Paranormal Romystery

GRAVE RECKONING

Standalones:

ISABEL'S TEARS

LANDFALL

PACIFIC BLUE TATTOO

Short Story Collections

THE SOUND OF ANGELS

THE MAGIC OF ORDINARY THINGS

TIMELESS

WINTER'S EMBRACE

1

FOR THE FIRST time in a long while, Ex-Private Peter Mitchell wished for the datadump headgear. The sanitized images and crafted memories weren't his and he couldn't control them, but the headgear had been the only thing that ever shut out the nightmares.

And the painful memories not caught by his MRC, the chip replacing his memories with those carefully chosen by the Recombinant Defense Program. Recombinant soldiers weren't allowed to think or dream on their own, so being free of that control gave him a feeling of lightness and strength he'd never had before.

Until he lost Sting to the Antarans.

Something his MRC hadn't parsed out. It hadn't had time and without the data dumps to replace those memories, it was the most painful memory in his head.

He sat on the edge of the mattress, clutching crisp blue sheets, gasping for air, his white T-shirt clinging to his sweat-slicked body. It took a few moments for the sleep to leave his eyes and that horrible feeling of not knowing where he was to dissipate.

The dreams had been so strange. So foreign. Not his own. But how could that be? Mimi's underground personnel had removed the MRC from his neck. He should be dreaming his own dreams now.

Like the nightmares—they were his.

Slowly, the little narrow room behind Mimi Constantine's restaurant on Civilization came into focus. He'd been here six weeks yesterday. Six weeks since he'd escaped UCOE's Armed Forces. Six weeks since he'd carried Sarge out of the Ku'Tal swamps. He swallowed a sigh. Six weeks since he'd been forced to say goodbye to Sting, the best friend he'd ever known.

Even now, the cost of his escape had been too high.

The tiny room was small but comfortable. In the thin, pale light trickling under the white latrine door, the silvery metal cooking and cooling units looked almost new. Things he'd never used before coming here, just recognized from the datadumps.

Pale grey walls and wood-planked floor blended together, but he didn't mind. He'd never had a room to himself before.

To his right, wispy blue curtains hung above the small orange shipping trunk and flapped against the open window. Peter loved the smell of fresh air, even if tart with ore dust and tanged with onions from last night's meal. He loved onions. And tomatoes. Things he'd never tasted before. It all felt alive and fluid and new. Changing. And real unlike the sum total of his life. Most of it was just vapor that existed in his head.

He was never certain what was real and what was memory.

The familiar confines of the room helped push away the strange dreams—and the nightmares. Horrid images of Sting being endlessly tortured by Antarans. Images of dark, cavernous rooms flickering with lights, equipment, circuits—machinery—from floor to ceiling. And the rows and rows of glass-like bubbles filling the expanse. Hundreds. Thousands. Maybe more. Each one containing figures. Blue and grey and tan bodies. Human and inhuman. Tangled limbs and distorted features changing as the lights flickered.

Suspended. Floating. Waiting.

He groaned at the images. His hands glowed, burning as strange currents ran through him. Into his chest. Down his legs as he stood on a round disk in the center of the dark space, traces of lights shooting toward him. Into him. Through him.

He rubbed his face. And then there was the nightmare.

The same one over and over, always ending with Sting being eviscerated by the caregivers. No, the one with the white hair.

He shivered, eyes stinging. And it was all his fault.

Guilt was a bitter taste in his dry mouth as he flipped on the light and huddled against the creaking wooden headboard, pillow against his chest. His light blond hair was damp and clung to his face and he brushed the heavy locks out of his eyes. He'd replaced the training base bunks and the swamps of Ku'Tal's war front with a regular civilian room and bed. No longer did his daily routine revolve around a sergeant's orders and UCOE's threat of returning him to the Recombinant Development Center for washout.

Just the threat of discovery. Of being an escaped recombinant.

No more patrols, hands numb against a rifle, muscles corded waiting for the sensor grid to whine disaster. Feet froze and soaked in fetid swamp water.

UCOE thought he was dead.

He'd left all of that behind, but here on the planet that Diana called Civilization (where the training base orbited) he felt so lost and out of place. The memories and the pain remained even though he was far from the battlefield. And he couldn't shake them.

The recycled soldier had become a recycled citizen. Who'd lost one of the most precious things in his life—his best friend.

He glanced at the clock on the wooden nightstand. 04:30 A.M. in glaring red numbers. A half full glass of water sat next to it. He reached for it, throat dry, tongue sticking to the roof of his mouth, and drank a warm mouthful of water. With shaking hands, he set the glass on the nightstand. Sometimes, citizen time confused him. When they said four o'clock and said it was afternoon. He only knew that as 16:00 hours.

He sighed. Sometimes, citizens in general confused him.

He did his best to move freely about the small mining town as if he were a real citizen, but fear shadowed him everywhere. The fear of discovery. Fear of standing out. Fear of giving himself away as a recombinant.

Everything he'd hoped for had come true, but not in the way he'd wanted it. He understood one of Diana's phrases very well now.

Be careful what you wish for.

Despite Diana and Sarge assuring him he had a right to citizenship, he still felt like an imposter. All of this pretense at his best friend, Private John Stingley's expense. It wasn't fair.

Sting was like a brother to him.

They'd gone through training together and the hell of Ku'Tal's swampy war front, fighting Antaran biodrones—and most of the Antaris Nation. Just trying to stay alive. Sting taught him how to fight. He taught Sting how to hope. Together, they taught each other how to survive. A recombinant's average life expectancy, training and at the front, was one year and that was fairly accurate. Most either washed out in training or died on Ku'Tal. Or wherever the new front was now.

Yet, here he sat, just past his one-year life expectancy. He'd just turned twenty-three, achieving consciousness at twenty-two. His head ached. So much of it he didn't understand. And he still hurt all over.

Dammit! It wasn't fair! Sting should have been here, too. He'd earned the right to a new life on Civilization. He'd been to the front and lived through it—until he met Peter.

Sting's absence tore at him.

Rain streaked down the windowpane and Peter watched the colored lights ooze across the watery trails. Rainstorms were frequent on Civilization's arid plains, but the heat swallowed up the moisture by morning. He reached for his water glass again and sucked down another big drink to soothe his dry throat before setting it back on the nightstand.

Still, the question haunted him. *Why? Why had Sting taken his place and gone with the Antarans? Why had he allowed it?*

The Antarans wanted him. He was the advanced UCOE recombinant with the traits they sought. He was the type of cloned soldier that the Antarans wanted to study.

Why did they take Sting in his place? His stomach burned. *Why did he let them take Sting?* For weeks, he'd tried to understand.

He clenched his hands into fists. He should have stopped Sting somehow! He should have fought the Antaran caregivers. All three. Shot them with the plasma rifle he'd carried that night and led Sarge and Sting out of the Antaran repository. To the safe house. He shouldn't have let them take Sting. He didn't even fight for his best friend.

He bit his lip, pounding the mattress. *Why hadn't he fought for Sting? Why?*

Rising stiffly from the bed, moisture stinging his eyes, he moved toward the window. Still shaking from the dreams, he sucked in a breath and stared out at the dark horizon, his hand against the god symbol Sting had given him that night. He clutched the half black half white medallion in his fist, chain rasping against his neck, remembering that long-ago moment when Sting disappeared inside the Antaran ship. Watching its silver hull shoot across the horizon and disappear into the cold white stars beyond Ku'Tal.

He smashed his eyes closed.

Where was Sting right now? Was he even still alive?

For weeks, Peter tried to put it all out of his mind, to concentrate on becoming a citizen, to live this new life. Sting wanted him to live. But to do that was to forget his best friend. Something he could never do. Sting had gotten him through all of his training, especially the sims. Saved him from washing out. Without Sting, he'd have died a thousand times over.

No, Sting was family. He couldn't live a life he didn't deserve, not without Sting sharing in the escape. He winced. *But what if they'd already killed Sting?*

He began to shake.

Purples, blues, and greens splashed across the windowpane and he traced their shapes against the cool glass, his eyes filling with tears. All the colors and shapes blended together, creating glossy patterns across the pane.

He felt so out of place here, burdening Mimi. The last thing Mimi Constantine needed at her restaurant was a clumsy recombinant that broke more dishes than he washed. She'd rescued several recombinants from UCOE, but she didn't employ them forever. Or board them in this spare room. Besides, it wasn't right for her to support him forever. But she refused to let him leave yet. Or let him stay with Diana in her apartment. He didn't understand why and neither did Diana. She'd asked Mimi several times, but Mimi always said he wasn't ready to charge into a relationship yet.

Maybe she was right?

Everyone was doing him favors, treating him like an orphaned desert mouse. Didn't they understand that he needed to find his own way? To earn his keep. To serve a purpose. He sighed, longing for a sense of place. He didn't want to stand out. Just blend in, like the array of colors smearing the window.

But the guilt remained, aching in the pit of his stomach. He missed his best friend. He'd thought it over for weeks and knew there was only one way he could live a real life here.

And that meant rescuing Sting. Finish what he started.

Bleary-eyed, Peter dressed and wandered out of his room, into the hallway leading toward the restaurant. The warm smells of spiced sausage, eggs, and bacon filled the air, surprising him. His stomach twisted. No one usually haunted the kitchen this early but him.

He paused in the darkness, listening. In the short hallway that led past End of the Line's kitchen toward the dining room's double doors, plates clanged and voices murmured low and soft. Many times, Mimi cooked meals in the restaurant kitchen for those who worked in her other business, the ones minding the underground operation of rescuing recombinants. An operation that didn't keep restaurant hours.

But not this early.

Especially since it had been such a busy night at the restaurant, miners celebrating payday and UCOE forces using day passes from the training base that orbited the planet.

Two shadows crossed the hall and passed through the double doors into the dining room.

"Peter? Is that you?"

Mimi Constantine's voice echoed down the hallway. She'd heard his footsteps on the tile. He entered the brightly lit kitchen, a long, galley-like setup with cream-colored walls and three rows of silver wire shelving lined with bright silver equipment and brick red floor tiles. Along the back wall were three tall, metal doors, two leading into cool storage and one Mimi called a freezer. It was icy inside, boxes and containers covered white with a frosty film that clung to everything. Even the walls. And stung. He liked to draw pictures with his fingers in the frosty white layer on the metal walls. Or step inside after a long, hot run to the spaceport.

Even though it sometimes reminded him of the Ku'Tal swamps in winter.

Mimi stood in front of a large griddle off to his right, amber and glistening with oil where eggs and bacon blistered and sausage patties browned. She piled the sunny yellow eggs, sizzling bacon, and hot sausages onto a white platter beside her and slid it under the heat lamp.

"Yes, it's me," he answered in a quiet voice.

She smiled and moved toward him. Her strawberry blond hair was a tangle of curls. A crisp white apron draped over her green leggings (as Diana called them) and a long burgundy shirt. She looked much, much younger than her age. She never failed to impress him with her unusual brand of wisdom, her upbeat outlook, and her command of her own life.

Mimi did what she thought right and didn't care what anyone else thought. Not as fiery as Diana, but she spoke the truth. From all the people he'd met here, she was different. She didn't have the *two faces* he'd seen most everywhere else. Like Diana and Sarge, Mimi never said one thing and did another.

"I made breakfast for some of my underground employees on their way here. Hungry?"

He shrugged. Not at all.

She took him by the shoulders and scrutinized him for a moment. "You look exhausted, Peter." Concern burned in her soft brown eyes.

"Couldn't sleep," he muttered.

"You've said that a lot lately. Are you sure you're all right?"

Peter shrugged. "I'll be okay," he answered.

"Well, at least have some coffee."

She let go of him, moving past to retrieve two coffee cups from a cabinet behind him. She carried the heavy white mugs over to the coffeemaker on the far-left side of the room, beside the doors leading into the dining room. She stood there a moment, a hand on her hip, coffee cups balanced in her hand, and waited until the coffeemaker gurgled steaming, dark coffee into the waiting glass pot.

It smelled rich and warm, like a toasty blanket on a cold morning. When the pot had filled halfway, she slid the empty pot beside it under the stream of coffee. From the half full pot, she filled the two cups. She handed one to Peter.

"Thanks Mimi," he said, pausing to take in the warm scent with its hint of nut-like spice. It was Karaban. He'd smelled enough of it, fresh-brewed and stale, while cleaning that machine. "But I did want to talk to you about something."

Mimi motioned him to follow. With cup in hand, Peter crept across the black rubber, honeycombed mats that squeaked against the freshly mopped, dark red tile, through the swinging doors, and into the dark dining room. The dark red tiles glistened against the faded rubber mats.

Mimi's office was past the kitchen, at the opposite end of the restaurant. She turned right out of the kitchen into another short hallway. This small section was Mimi's office. Four stairs at the end of the hallway led up to her living quarters above the restaurant.

The door to her office was open and the lights flicked on when she entered. The office was sparse and clean, white walls and green-colored tiles, a messy wooden desk covered in papers and half full cups of tea. Mimi only drank coffee in the mornings. The room smelled of day-old tea, peppermints, and something earthy that Diana called patchouli. The walls were that same deep red as the floor tiles with green accents trimming the wall and a huge holo painting depicting an alien landscape hung on the wall behind the desk. Every moment or so, the image bled into another landscape. None that he recognized.

Mimi frequently changed the colors in the room, but the same holo painting always remained. Mimi's slender fingers took hold of his arm and guided him into a soft, deep red chair beside the desk. She sat down in the office chair beside him and took hold of his wrist, holding his hand up to the light.

"The purple in your aura has deepened," said Mimi as if it was fact. "But the color is so fragmented."

He managed a slight smile and set down his coffee cup. That was Mimi's quirky way of telling him he was unhappy. Diana said that auras and mystics were part of Mimi's beliefs. He would respect that even if he didn't know what they were. She held on for another moment and then let go.

Peter struggled for words. How could he explain everything he'd been feeling for six weeks? "I-I—" With a sigh, he rubbed his hand across his face. "I just don't—belong here, Mimi."

Frowning, she stared at him and it felt like she'd looked into his soul. He didn't care what the others said. Recombinants *did* have souls. But he wondered how she saw any purple left in his. Or any color at all.

Blackness? What color was a coward's aura? A sell-out's aura?

"Of course, you do, Peter," she said in a quiet, certain voice.

"Don't you understand? I sold out my best friend!" He blurted out the words and gripped the arms of the chair. "I should have stopped him and I didn't. I was too scared. *I* was supposed to be on that ship, not Sting—*me!*"

Her hands gently cupped his. "But you weren't. Sting wanted you to be with Diana Temple. He wanted you to get her brother, David, home. Peter...he wanted you to have what he couldn't."

Peter shook his head. "He wanted those things, too!" He pulled his hands free and rose from the chair. "Sting wanted to watch the skimmers on the river and see Civilization's colored lights! He wanted to walk out of the military and never go back." He kicked the chair. "Why didn't *he* get a shot? He survived two tours on Ku'Tal, Mimi. He deserved that chance! Much more than I did."

Her chair rasped against the tile and she was standing beside him. She wanted to help, he knew that, but there was only one thing she could do for him now.

Get him to Ballese. He had to make this right. He had to...

"No, Peter. You deserved that chance just as much as Sting did."

He turned to her, nodding. "Okay, then doesn't Sting deserve the chance to escape from Ballese?"

"Of course," she answered, a wary look on her face. Worry sprang to her brown eyes.

"Then help him! Send your underground team into Ballese and get him out of there before they kill him!"

Mimi shook her head. "It's just not possible, Peter. If it were, I'd have suggested it six weeks ago."

He started to protest, but she cut him off.

"Peter! They've dug into Ballese. They've made their bases and facilities there. After killing over twelve thousand colonists."

"They dug into Ku'Tal, too, but you got me out of there. And a bunch of other recombinants!"

Mimi sighed. "That was different. There were plenty of UCOE

forces covering our movements on Ku'Tal. Ballese is completely controlled by the Antaris Nation, Peter. UCOE doesn't even have a toehold. I know because my brother was killed there. Our arrival would be like shooting off a flare gun. Fireworks!"

She stared at him for several long moments, finally reaching out a hand to touch his face. "You look so much like him, Peter. It's like looking into the past. Just takes my breath."

"Mimi, what if we sent just one shuttle? In and out—under radar?"

Even before he'd finished the first sentence, Mimi was shaking her head. "It just won't work, Peter! Without specialized jamming equipment, they'd capture us before we even stepped off the shuttle. Or kill us outright."

"Then we find the equipment we need!" Peter felt the desperation creep into his voice, but he couldn't hold it inside. "Please, Mimi. They'll kill him...just like your brother!"

She shook her head. "Peter, you're not listening."

"They said they'd pull out of Ku'Tal," he said, his voice rushing ahead, his volume rising, "but Antaran ships still land and UCOE still sends recombinants there. The Antarans said they just wanted to save their people, but the killing continues and they move deeper into this system." He took hold of her shoulders. "They said they wouldn't kill him, Mimi, but it's just another lie. It's my fault and I can't leave him there like this. I can't!"

A swampy landscape materialized on the holo print.

He froze.

The old fear welled up in him, all those months of death and uncertainty on Ku'Tal rushing back. His breath quickened. Heart began to pound. Cold dread burned through his stomach, the images stark, the memories flooding back.

Gotta get out! Now! Before they trapped him.

He glanced past her. At the door. Over his shoulder. Expecting biodrones to swing down from the trees and cut him in half.

Get out! Now! NOW!

Flash of explosions. Cascade mines igniting around him. Feel of Sting's body against his back as he carried him back to camp.

His hands shook. Eyes wide. Glazed with fear.

Can't move! Can't escape. No escape!

"Peter? Peter!"

Her voice snapped him out of the memory. He sucked in a breath, turning to gaze at her again, sadness filling his eyes with moisture. He wiped it away with the back of his arm.

"Please, Mimi, please—help me get Sting out."

Her hand caressed his cheek. "If there were any way, Peter, you know I wouldn't hesitate."

He pulled away. "Then I'll find another way."

Peter fled from the office, running toward his room. If Mimi wouldn't help him, he'd find a way on his own. He wouldn't leave Sting—his best buddy—on Ballese to rot. To be torn apart and analyzed.

LATER IN THE DAY, Peter left the restaurant in Mimi's skimmer bound for the shuttle port. Four recombinants made it to the Karaban safe house and had arrived on Civilization this afternoon. Mimi sent him alone this time, but he'd been along on enough of these rides to know what to do.

He ran alongside the river for a few minutes, but decided to see how the skimmer performed in the river. He'd always wanted to skim the river. Mimi wouldn't mind. Besides, it would take his mind off things. The parched air smelled tart with ore and musty with silt from the river. He'd been reading all about it on the handheld Diana carried.

Veering over a stand of yellow brush, he gently eased the skimmer onto the river's murky brown surface. It reminded him of cream-laden coffee.

Cool air brushed over him, smelling of fish and algae, the

sunlight so bright. He opened up the throttle and the skimmer lurched ahead, whispering across the river's surface. Wind and spray rushed over the nose, the hull humming. Frothy wakes swirled behind him, spilling onto the banks. He wished it had been night, so he could have seen the colored lights glitter in his wake. Bridge shadows zipped past as he skimmed faster underneath the arched structures.

Only when he approached the shuttle port bridge did he slow down the skimmer and jump it over a line of gellenberry bushes, the dusty white berries ripening gold in the heat. Sweating, he zipped onto a side road that led to the shuttle port's loading docks.

He glanced over his shoulder at the river still churning brown and white in his wake. Grinning, he returned his attention to picking up the recombinants.

He followed the long, winding service road toward the rounded silver overhang of the shuttle port hangars. Slipping past the first set of long, arched hangars, he stopped and backed the skimmer into bay six. Where four tall, lanky recombinants, dressed uncomfortably in a jumbled array of civilian clothes, stood near the bay door. They looked lost and out of sorts.

Like he still felt after six weeks on Civilization.

Peter motioned them toward the skimmer. They ran toward it and climbed inside. He made sure they were seated and buckled in before he sped out of the bay and back onto the service road.

"What's the situation on Karaba?" Peter asked the recombinant seated beside him.

The black-haired private shrugged. "Dunno. Bad, I guess. Lots of us dead or missing. Biodrone patrols are more frequent. They're evacuating a lot of people. Somebody said the coffee crops were going to be in trouble soon."

"Karaba is going to fall," said a recombinant from the back.

Peter glanced back at him. His hair was light and curly, reminding Peter of Sting. He listened for his friend's familiar voice, but this recombinant sounded nothing like Sting.

"The Antarans are starting to dig in there. The coffee plantations will go next. It's over."

"Once they dig in, it's too late," Peter echoed.

"What do you know about Antarans?" one of the recombinants said with a snarl over the skimmer's movement. His tone was challenging and Peter bristled.

He rubbed his hand against the back of his neck, remembering the tricky procedure that had removed his UCOE MRC chip. He stopped the skimmer and turned to stare at the recombinants in the back seat.

"After training, I did six months on Ku'Tal before I got out. And I barely got out."

"You were on Ku'Tal?" one recombinant said with a whistle. "Those fucking swamps? Daaamn."

The other recombinants stared at him with wide eyes. "How far past life expectancy are you?" one asked anxiously.

Peter smiled proudly. "I just turned twenty-three. They said I had a year at best and here I am. Six weeks past and still going."

"Twenty-three?" Silence hung over the recombinants.

"Do you have citizen papers?" another asked in a hushed voice.

Peter's gaze fell. Mimi was still working on that. It would be another few months before he had official citizenship papers. "That takes time, but I'm close," he answered.

The recombinants seemed to relax a bit as Peter set the skimmer in motion again. He slid across the river and behind Mimi's restaurant, End of the Line. Someone opened the restaurant's back door, motioning to the recombinants. They piled out of the skimmer and scurried inside. Peter parked and locked the skimmer, then hurried inside with the ignition card.

Mimi stood in the dining room doorway, quickly directing recombinants and personnel through the restaurant hallway to the storeroom off the kitchen. Peter handed her the skimmer's ignition card.

"Thanks, Peter. Good work. Could you get started on the dishes now? And next time, make sure they're clean before your shift is over."

"Yes, ma'am. Sorry. I will."

She smiled at him, arms crossed. "You seem to be feeling better than you were this morning."

Nodding, he turned away, not wanting to discuss it right now. He grabbed a white cloth apron and hurried into the dish room. He grimaced. Soured tomato sauce, grease, and stale garlic odors wafted toward him. Four grey plastic bus tubs awaited him.

He groaned. He'd washed dishes last night with Wyen, one of Mimi's regular employees. A citizen. Wyen had been the one closing and said he'd finish the rest of the dishes when Peter's shift was over.

Apparently, Wyen didn't say when that would be.

Sighing, Peter emptied the first tub onto the long silver tabletop and sink beside the slide-through dishwasher. With the high-powered sprayer, he rinsed the dried crust of tomato sauce. Someone had also dumped a bunch of grease from the stations into the tub, coating everything in a thick, yellow waxy film.

He sighed. This would take several rinses to clean.

He worked feverishly for over an hour until all four tubs of dishes were spotless. Then he slid up the dishwasher door and slid out the rack of burning hot dishes and glasses. He stacked the hot glasses and cups on the nearby plastic trays and quickly transferred the molten hot silverware into containers. He carried stacks of bowls and plates into the kitchen and placed them on the shelves at all the prep stations. And the silverware next to burgundy cloth napkins in an alcove in the hallway.

As he bent down to stock the sauté station, four plates slipped out of his hands. They crashed to the floor and exploded into burgundy and white shards.

He hung his head, hating himself.

Setting down the remaining plates, he began picking up the shards and cleaning up the mess he'd made.

Mimi rushed into the kitchen.

"Oh, Peter," she groaned. "Not again."

"I'm so sorry, Mimi," he said in a small voice, his face flushed. "They slipped out of my hands."

"How many this time?" she asked, a hand to her head.

"Four."

She inhaled sharply, as if trying to restrain her anger. "Please, be more careful."

"Yes, ma'am. I'm really sorry. Please, let me pay for them this time. Or at least let me work them off."

Sighing, Mimi turned toward the kitchen door. "That won't be necessary, Peter." She hurried out of the kitchen.

Behind him, at the grill station, two of the line cooks chattered as they scrubbed the grill with wire brushes.

"Why doesn't she get rid of him? He can't even wash dishes without breaking something."

"*If* he washes them. What do you expect from a recombinant?"

Peter quickly tossed the plate shards into the bin, throwing them away. He stacked the rest of the plates and carefully put away the rest of the dishes and cups. He passed one of the cooks on his way back to the dish room.

"Keep up the good work, Mitchell," said the short, balding man.

Peter scowled. They say one thing to him and another when Mimi was in the room. He didn't understand citizens. He left the kitchen and went into the dining room to setup tables for the supper rush.

THAT EVENING, Diana and her brother, David arrived at End of the Line for supper. End of the Line was the southernmost establishment in Civilization, so it was truly the end of the shuttle line.

Still operating on only a few hours' sleep, Peter met Diana and Sarge at the table. He felt tired and distracted, but Diana insisted that he eat with her and Sarge tonight. He'd expected her to be with him when he returned, but she seemed to be keeping her distance.

And it hurt.

Maybe Mimi was keeping her away, giving him time to adjust this new life? He didn't understand why she'd been so distant. If Mimi wanted her to do that, then why hadn't she told him?

He had so much to learn, so much to understand.

As expected, Sarge chose a traditional table instead of the Middle Eastern styled low tables with pillows that Diana preferred. Peter liked the pillows because he'd never seen anyone sit on them instead of chairs. Sometimes, he just liked things because they were different.

"Peter!" Diana cried and put her arms around his neck. "At last, I get to see you."

His heart raced. Diana!

Smiling, he slid his arms around her and kissed her. She looked so beautiful in that metallic silver skirt and purple blouse. Her hair, the color of rich chocolate, was so shiny and her big gold-brown eyes melted him. Every time he looked at him. Diana Temple always looked cheerful with bright eyes and soft features. He envied her that.

Just knowing it was him that she loved lightened his mood.

He grinned at her familiar purple scarf tied around her neck. It was tattered and a little faded from the months he'd carried it against his chest throughout his tour on Ku'Tal. Diana's scarf had been her grandmother's (three whole generations!) and had always been a symbol of long life to her. Diana had given him that scarf with the hope that he'd survive the front and return it to her. She'd worn it tonight just for him.

"You feel so good, Diana," he said softly and ran his hand through her thick, silky hair. He brushed his fingers across the scarf, smelling warm with vanilla, like Diana. The world made a little more sense around her. He wrapped his arms tighter around her, holding her to his chest until he felt the beat of her heart. Her warmth calmed him, even if it was just a moment or two. It was something he needed right now.

Finally, she let go of him, frowning a bit. "You look so tired, Peter. You're working too hard."

He shrugged. "Didn't sleep well last night."

Sergeant David Temple extended his left hand to Peter and Peter shook it. Sarge's right arm was still in a cast, a remnant of his tour on Ku'Tal. Sergeant Temple came back from Ku'Tal a war hero after carrying explosives into the Antaran munitions depot and single-handedly destroying it. Officially, Private John "Sting" Stingley was credited with blowing up the depot, but Peter knew Sarge was still a hero. And the brass knew he'd assisted.

Sarge was nearing the end of his medical leave and due back at the training base that orbited Civilization in a day or two.

"Good to see you, Mitchell," he said with a smile. "I was hoping that slave driver, Mimi, would let you out of work tonight, so you could celebrate with us."

Peter laughed. Mimi was anything but a slave driver. "Are we celebrating your imminent return to duty?"

Sarge nodded. "Partly." He plopped down onto the black padded chair and slid it toward the table.

"I have some news," said Diana in a quiet voice. She sat down across from her brother.

Peter slid into the chair beside her and put his arm around her shoulders.

"What news?" he asked.

Mimi moved toward the table in an ocean blue tunic, richly embroidered silver with sea creatures. Her strawberry hair was swept back from her face.

"David and Diana, it's been much too long! I've missed seeing you in this place. To eat, that is." She glanced at Peter. "I've seen quite a bit of Diana these past few weeks." She set a large green bottle on the table. "I've been saving this pear cider for a while. Had a guy bring this to me all the way from Earth."

Peter studied the bottle. He didn't know what cider was—or a pear, for that matter.

Diana's eyes widened. "Pear cider? It's been years since I've had that! How'd you know, Mimi!"

Mimi winked at her. "I just knew," she said and set three wine glasses on the table.

"She read it in your aura, Diana," Sarge said with a grin.

Diana rolled her eyes. Peter laughed. Sarge had always been puzzled by Mimi's outlook on life.

Mimi filled three glasses. She cast a lingering stare at Peter, but after a moment, he avoided her gaze. She'd been treating him strangely since this morning. He turned his attention to Diana. She had a way of calming him, soothing his turmoil.

Shortly, Mimi left them to attend to customers waiting at the reservations desk, a little dim-lit alcove with dark woods and colored silks draped like curtains in front of the dining room entrance that she parted every time she seated anyone in the large dining room. All the shades around the expanse had been opened after sunset, allowing an incredible view of the colored lights glimmering in the dark river.

Peter studied the bubbles percolating through the cold, golden liquid. He picked up the glass and sniffed it. Smelled like some of the cargo he'd unloaded from Mimi's skimmer. Round red and green things, sometimes with leaves. Smelled not exactly sweet, but pleasing, like fresh flowers and plants.

Diana giggled. "You look so perplexed, Peter," she said, picking up a glass. "It's an alcoholic drink. Made from pears."

"From whats?" he asked, glancing from her to the glass.

"Pears. Remember the apple I gave you a couple of weeks back?"

He nodded, watching the bubbles rise in the glass.

"It's a fruit, like an apple—only it's a pear," Diana explained.

"With a kick," David added, a wry grin on his face as he picked up the third glass. "We drank this all the time back home on Earth. In Washington State."

With a grin, Sarge hoisted his glass into the air.

"To friendships and cease fires," he said.

"To long life," Diana said and clinked her glass of golden pear cider against Sarge's glass.

Peter sighed and raised his glass. "For everyone," he added and tapped his glass against their glasses.

The cider was cold and rich with the apple-like pears. It had a milder, sunny taste, almost sweet, and a mellow lightness that hinted of alcohol. He smiled. If he closed his eyes and let the cider roll over his tongue, he saw a green meadow with tall, waving grasses and crisp blue sky.

"Do you like it, Peter?" she asked, smiling at him.

"I've never tasted anything quite like this," he answered, returning her smile. "It's like they bottled a summer sky."

This brought a smile to Sarge's face. "Pete, you have a way of making everything a refreshingly new experience."

Peter's face burned at the sound of *Pete*. Only Sting called him that and he couldn't bear to hear anyone else say it—not even Sarge.

"Please don't call me that," he said in a low voice and set down his glass.

"But that's all Stingley ever called you. I thought you preferred it."

Peter shook his head. "No. I don't."

Sarge cast an odd glance at Diana and took another sip of cider.

Peter wanted to kick himself. He hadn't meant to snap at Sarge like that. For nearly a year, the man had been his training sergeant at the base and then his field sergeant on Ku'Tal. Next to Sting, Sergeant Temple was the best friend he'd ever had.

Except for Diana, of course.

"Does anyone want to hear my news?" Diana asked. She leaned forward.

"Of course," Peter answered, managing a smile.

Her face glowed with excitement as she studied Peter's face for a moment and then Sarge's. "UCOE begged me to fly again for the base at a whole level higher pay grade. I accepted this morning! Isn't that great news?"

Peter's stomach twisted into a knot at the thought of Diana flying recombinants out to Ku'Tal and Karaba, risking her life for planets that would probably fall soon to the Antaris Nation.

"Diana, you can't!" Peter cried, wide-eyed.

"What's wrong, Peter?" she asked. Her warm gaze quieted his panic.

"Can't stand thinking about you flying to Ku'Tal with the Antarans gearing up like they are."

Sarge set down his glass. "Mitchell's got a point, sis. Flying recombinants to and from training sims is fine, but not into the Taus system's hot zone. Flying anywhere from Ku'Tal to the edge of the Antaris System is riskier than swallowing plutonium right now. Please, rethink your decision. Mitchell and I don't want to see anything happen to you, okay?"

"I've already lost one of my best friends," said Peter, his voice unsteady. He bowed his head. "I can't lose you."

"Oh, Peter," she whispered. She leaned over and kissed his lips. "Nothing's going to happen."

He rose from his chair, his face contorting. "How do you live like that?" he asked, feeling sick inside.

"Mitchell?" said Sarge with a frown. He gave Diana a worried glance.

"Every day I wake up, I'm amazed that I'm still drawing breath, but citizens—they think they're invincible. That their days are endless. How can you risk your days so lightly when each one is so precious? Excuse me."

Peter rushed out of the dining room and into the hallway. He thrust open the door to his room, almost falling inside. Closing the door, he collapsed, shaking, onto his bed. His chest heaved as he fought for breath.

Can't breathe. Why can't Diana see that it isn't worth the risk? Why?

Memories of the Recombinant Development Center shivered through him, how they washed out newly conscious recombinants with barely a thought or a reason.

Too aggressive. Not aggressive enough. Too volatile. Too docile. Too angry.

He clutched the god symbol at his neck, a half black half white circle, wishing he'd given it back to Sting. Sting needed it now more than anyone. Tears slipped down his face as he prayed for Sting and a place where he belonged.

2

STUNNED, Diana sat back in the chair and stared blankly at David.

"David, what just happened?" she asked finally. "I've never seen him like that before."

David shook his head. Unlike her, David seemed as if he'd somehow anticipated this outburst from Peter.

"I'm not sure. He hasn't been the same since he returned from Ku'Tal. Not that I expected him to be." David took a long drink from his cider. He set down the glass. "He needs our help, Diana. Mitchell went through a lot out there and he's going through a lot here."

Diana nodded. "Trying to fit in, trying to understand citizen behavior. It doesn't make much sense to him, I'm afraid."

She saw his confusion every time someone said one thing and did another. How people valued things and then risked them for little—if any—gain or reason. She'd heard him say that more than once. She'd known for some time that he was unhappy here. She thought Peter had accepted what happened to Sting—not that any of them *wanted* to accept it. But until tonight, she hadn't realized how Sting's fate had eaten away at him.

"I didn't want to see that hell hole change him and his incredible sense of wonder at the world," said David.

Diana nodded. "I know. Sometimes, he just gives me chills at how he sees the simplest things. He makes me see the world differently. And appreciate it." She tapped her glass. "Like the cider."

Looking tense, David rubbed his chin. He still looked thin and Ku'Tal had changed him, too, but he hadn't lost his good-hearted, practical nature. The David she knew had come home with his hope and compassion intact. But Peter—he'd lost some of his wonder at the world. That saddened her. It was one of the things she loved about him.

"Same here, sis. Think about it though. Besides Mimi, we're the only people he knows. He's in hiding and he's already lost his best friend in the whole world. Now, he's been hidden away in the restaurant, alone, while we go back to our lives. He needs to make a life for himself, but he's probably afraid we'll follow Sting."

Diana fiddled with her burgundy and white bread plate. "I'm really worried about him. I can only imagine what you and he went through out there. We went through enough at the safe house. I have no desire to repeat that experience. Shuttling to and from the base is enough for me."

The tension seemed to drain out of David's limbs. He settled back in his chair and picked up his glass of cider. She smiled. He wasn't going to tell her what to do. David had changed.

"To boredom," he said with a smile.

Grinning, Diana clinked her glass against David's. "To boredom." She was content with having a little boredom in her life and she looked forward to introducing Peter to the concept.

"I'm going to go talk to him, David." She leaned across the table, lowering her voice. "Do you think maybe he's suffering from PTSD?"

David's eyes widened. "Hadn't even considered that, sis. God, do recombinants suffer PTSD like the rest of us?"

"Find out," said Diana.

"No problem," said David. "But first I'll start practicing my new lifestyle. Of boredom."

Diana started to rise from her chair when Mimi walked toward the table.

"Where's Peter?" Mimi asked.

"He excused himself," she said, not wanting to worry Mimi.

"He feels so guilty about what happened to Sting," said Mimi. She sat down in Peter's chair and Diana took her seat again.

"Guilty?" *Of course! Why hadn't she realized that?*

He felt responsible. He was here and safe and Sting was—out there somewhere. Suffering. Or maybe dead. Mimi was right, but sometimes her bluntness was startling.

David's face darkened, his brow furrowing. "My memory of that night is so hazy, but I recall Mitchell making some kind of deal with the Antarans. Mine and Sting's safe passage in exchange for him as a test subject."

"What?" Diana cried, her heart racing.

How close had she come to losing him?

"When the exhaustion caught up with Mitchell and he fell asleep, Sting changed the deal. He went with the Antarans. Mitchell got out."

"I can see the huge scars on his heart chakra," said Mimi.

David frowned and shook his head in confusion. "His what?"

"Never mind that, David," Diana snapped. "Please continue, Mimi."

Mimi tended to talk in metaphysical terms that were unfamiliar to her and David. Mimi's mystical outlook on things had never troubled her, but David bristled at the terminology.

"Peter can't live with what's happened," said Mimi, "and he's trying to make it right somehow. Yesterday, he begged me to send my underground team into Ballese and get Sting out."

An uneasy silence fell over them.

Go into Ballese? And face the ruined Earth colony?

For years, Diana had been haunted by the horror stories of what happened on Ballese, how the Antarans destroyed the colony. A group of over twelve thousand scientists, engineers, teachers, farmers, and merchants and their families were massacred. And the thriving new colony was leveled. No one knew the full story, but the rumors had been enough to terrify her.

Part of her longed to know the story, just to put that old childhood fear to rest. Another part of her never wanted to know what happened to those poor people. UCOE forces had never been able to gain a threshold on Ballese, either. It had been hard enough gaining the precarious one on Ku'Tal.

But Ballese—? She was scared now. For Peter.

"Ballese?" David shouted. "He's not thinking straight!" David's eyes burned, a mixture of fear and fury. "It'd be suicide to send civilians in there! Does he think he can just walk in and grab Sting?" David smacked his hand against the table. "If Sting's lucky, they killed him quick six weeks ago. God only knows what Mitchell might find if Sting is even still alive."

A palpable silence hung over the table. Diana sighed.

Was Sting still alive?

Thousands of horrors sprang to her mind of what they could have already done to the bright-spirited young man with his curly blond hair and intense green eyes. Peter idolized Sting. He was a brother to Peter. Her eyes welled with tears. The uncertainty and the guilt must be overwhelming him.

"I'm going to go talk to him," said Diana. She rose from the chair again and moved slowly across the dining room. Behind her, David's frantic whispers rose. He was worried, too.

At the end of the hall, Diana stopped in front of Peter's closed door. Inhaling sharply, she knocked.

No response.

"Peter, it's Diana. Please let me in."

"Please come back later," he answered in a thin, raspy voice.

"I can't do that, Peter. We need to talk. Please, open the door."

"Please go away—"

"Peter, I love you and I'm worried. Open the door."

The room fell silent until finally, a lock clicked.

Gently, she pushed on the door until it creaked open. She slipped inside. Grey walls and floors gave the small room an austere look, only the blue curtains and blanket adding any color to the room with its tiny white bathroom off to the left.

He sat on his bed, staring out the window as he rubbed thumb and forefinger against the yin yang symbol hanging from a silver chain around his neck. Sting gave him that. Just before disappearing into an Antaran ship.

To her, the symbol meant nothing, but to Peter, it was a god symbol. He didn't like talking about the symbols, but to him, his wearing one meant he had a soul. He'd been told by everyone that recombinants didn't have souls because their DNA had been recycled and in part, artificially created. The god symbol gave him hope that there was something for recombinants after death. It seemed to comfort and amaze him at the same time.

And she refused to take his hope away. Ever.

She sat down beside him and slid her arms around his waist. Kissing his neck and then his mouth. He smelled like soap and rainwater, a hint of pears on his lips. She loved the feel of his strong hands against her body, wanting only to feel his arms around her, his warmth against her chest, his mouth against her ear—nibbling and whispering her name. And that he loved her.

Memories of making love beside the river rolled back to her. Hot, sweltering night, cooled by the breeze rolling off the river. Clothes clinging, falling away against the cooling sand, her mouth pressed against his. Huff of his breath hot on her neck, his hands awkward and frantic against her skin. Fiery build of sensations as she led him through the experience, her body entwined with his, her fingers tangling in his blond hair, sliding down his back.

But right now, she only wanted to hold him. To love him.

"Peter, I care so much what happens to you. Don't you know that?"

He turned his gaze to her, sad, a touch of anger in his eyes. "I love you, Diana. Why isn't that enough to keep you from returning to the Ku'Tal circuit? That's all I'm asking."

She laid her head against his shoulder, running her fingers down his back. "It is enough. I'm not taking the Ku'Tal runs. I'm returning to my base-to-surface transports."

His eyes brightened and a smile twitched at the corners of his mouth. "Really? Then you're not going back to Ku'Tal?"

"Only if you don't go to Ballese."

His lips parted, body stiffening, shock evident on his face. In his clear blue eyes. He sighed in frustration and ran a hand through his light blond hair, shaking his head.

"I can't promise that."

"Why not?" she demanded, sitting up. "Isn't it enough that I love you?" She frowned. "What are you planning, Peter?"

The anger returned to his face, sharp, tightening his features. He jerked up from the bed. It creaked, headboard thumping against the wall.

"Don't you understand? I owe him, Diana! I won't let him rot on Ballese! And neither you, Sarge, or UCOE is going stop me!"

He scrambled through the open door into the hallway.

"Peter, wait!" Diana shouted, running after him. "Don't leave like this! Peter!"

He stormed through the busy dining room and out the restaurant's heavy, wooden front doors, Diana rushing after him. But he was too fast.

When she reached the steamy Civilization streets, she lost him in the twilight cascade of colored lights coming to life against the river's steamy dark mirror.

3

HUMID AIR PRESSED against Peter's lungs as he ran through Civilization's streets, the heat and the night rushing in, his throat burning. He struggled to breathe, the tart air thick with ore dust.

All around him in the bustle of mining shift changes, hordes of tired, dusty miners filled the walkways. Purple, green, and blue lights flickered to life, outlining rooftops and walls, pulsating in the heat.

His pulse raced, sweat clinging to his face like a mask.

Gasping for air, he turned a corner and faded into the mass of sweaty miners rushing toward transit stops, hoping Diana hadn't seen him in the chaos of shift change.

Roar of voices and footfalls throbbed in his ears, distant surge of shuttles whisking past, almost drowning out the echo of Diana's clear, sweet voice calling out to him.

Don't go like this! Peter! So much worry in her voice, so much concern sparking through her warm, bright eyes.

Why didn't she understand how much Sting meant to him?

Of all people he'd met, Diana should have understood. But she didn't. And it hurt.

He couldn't face that right now. His going to Ballese wasn't the same as her going to Ku'Tal.

It just wasn't!

He ran until his sides ached, temples throbbing, shops and buildings blurring past on all sides in misty smears of purple and blue. He didn't stop until he'd reached the edge of a transit platform.

Frantic, he glanced behind him, fearing Diana, Mimi, and Sarge would all be waiting there to tell him everything would be okay, to gloss over what happened, sweep it all away so he'd just forget about Sting.

It wouldn't be okay.

Not like this. Not with the Antarans still out there gaining ground, holding Sting and so many other recombinants as their prisoners.

And...he'd never forget about Sting. Ever.

The night began to cool, cutting through the thick, heavy swath of heat blanketing everything. Only strangers lingered on the platform. Shadows clung to the streets, the shuttle track floating above the city as it curved toward the spaceport's distant lights.

Citizens. People with a birthright to walk these streets without fear. Not some reject with recycled, recombined DNA—xDNA—like him.

He bent over to catch his breath. Everything felt so out of control. Even his dreams. And the nightmares. He'd try to stay awake and avoid those horrible nightmares.

Cavernous wells of circuits lighting the bodies in the tubes. In the bubbles. Or the memory of Sting disappearing into the Antaran ship.

He pressed his hands to his face, wanting to scream out his rage and frustration. His fear. He wouldn't sleep tonight. Wouldn't let those images take hold. Wouldn't let the pain pierce his heart and make his chest ache. He gritted his teeth, sweat pouring down the sides of his face.

No! He wouldn't dream tonight! He wouldn't.

When he'd caught his breath, he hurried up the flight of stairs, metal steps singsonging as he ascended the platform. A transit shuttle paused at the gate, door flung wide, bright white light cascading into the night like a search beacon. He slipped into the light and held onto one of the metal poles in the center of the car. On both sides of the rounded, bullet-like shuttle were padded green seats and smooth white walls speckled with flakes of blue, green, and purple. Signs lined the walls above the row of windows. Advertisements for things he didn't understand or recognize. The flashing blue sign above the door blinked the words *shuttle port.*

Maybe at the port he could find a ride to Ballese?

He'd heard Mimi and Diana talk about chartering shuttles from the port all the time. Mimi always said those charters were costing her a fortune. He'd saved nearly every credit Mimi had paid him at the restaurant. Almost two months' worth. And that included the handful of credits Mimi gave him (like every rescued recombinant in her care) for his new life beyond the military. He'd give up every last one for the chance to reach Ballese. And Sting.

Somehow, he'd get there. Some way.

In a few moments, a pleasant female voice warned that the doors were closing. He gripped the shiny silver pole tighter. With a shudder, the transit shuttle whispered away from the platform bound for the gold gleam of the shuttle port in the distance.

The shuttle shot into the track and whooshed along the rails, the gold gleam growing wider until the shuttle shuddered to a stop at the brightly lit shuttle port.

He stepped off the transit. The heat had dissipated. Nightfall deepened, intensified, lights sharp and stretching across the dark outlines and shapes of Civilization's streets and the huge, gleaming lens of the shuttle port that sprawled across the desert.

Ahead, at the end of a long, winding walkway stood a tall metal arch that framed three sets of double doors leading into scorching white light. The doors opened as he approached and stepped inside. Into the cool, conditioned air that smelled recirculated—almost stale —like the training base that orbited Civilization. But the air was so cold. Almost like that frosty white storage room in Mimi's restaurant.

People rushed past him carrying bags and rolling them alongside on wobbly squeaky wheels. It made him grin. Where were all of them going? So free to move about and go wherever they liked. And all the possibilities that must be out there!

Places with trees and green grass like Diana described. Places with deep, wild stretches of water that seemed endless. Icy cold places with white, solid water in mirror-like sheets and soft mounds like the foam inside his pillow.

This shuttle port reminded him of those rooms beyond the gate in the Recombinant Development Center, where he'd achieved consciousness. He'd huddled there at the gate and watched the people at their desks, mesmerized at how they moved around so freely. Like ghosts. How they all disappeared under that green exit sign. And came back!

He loved to watch their expressions and hear them talking to each other as they unwrapped lacy green sandwiches with thick slices of bread frilly with lettuce and bright red tomatoes. And how they slurped bubbly iced drinks in tall glasses. With curvy things Diana called straws.

Had that exit door led them to places like this? Shuttle stops and spaceports that took them to faraway places like Diana's apartment and Mimi's restaurant? Or the planet where they all achieved consciousness? He only knew its name. Earth.

He wandered through the sprawling, bright expanse, white floors shiny against the miles of glass reflecting its white sheen onto every wall, every grey countertop, and every floating display that scrolled information.

The port was busy tonight, so he followed behind the crowds rushing to gates, investigating the different shuttle services and flight availabilities listed on a row of screens that ran along the walkways.

He gasped. Walkways that moved people down the long corridor without them having to take a single step!

He moved closer to the information displays along the wall. So many words and numbers! So many places! And so much to understand, but it was all so confusing. There was so much that was just beyond him.

He felt small and stupid.

The glaring lights gave the long, expansive port a skeletal feel, revealing all its metal rafters, side supports, and its tall, arched ceiling. It reminded Peter of something that hadn't been designed for permanence. Like the shelters at Ku'Tal. Like recombinants and UCOE's five-year maximum life policy. The one that automatically washed out recombinants after five unlikely years at the front.

Like his whole life.

That's why he hadn't used the dresser or trunk in his room at the restaurant. He'd kept everything he had in the duffle bag Ron Kraver, Mimi's lead underground agent, had given him on the shuttle leaving Ku'Tal.

Waiting for everything to shift again. Waiting for it all to change again and send him someplace else. The one certainty in his life was that nothing was permanent.

Ever.

And he hated that most of all, wanting to belong someplace. Wanting to settle in somewhere and live a life.

His black chukkas squeaked against the shiny floor. Ahead, in the long corridor were a handful of brightly colored food vendor stalls tucked between the numbered shuttle gates. Smell of hot coffee and yeasty scent of baking bread floated through the port. He pulled in a warm breath of coffee and yeasty bread until the strong scent of honey wafted toward him.

He froze.

Memories of the front twisted through his brain. Sickening sweet stink of honey filling the air. Like the stench of Antaran biodrones.

He gulped air, breaths coming in gasps.

Surge of biodrones swinging out the treetops.

Talons glinting against the snow.

Can't breathe!

Sweating, he struggled against the haunting memories, the fear trembling through him as he fought to control his breathing. Fought to move.

Slowly.

Let it go, he told himself over and over as he forced his feet to move again.

He ran past the pastries and cookies, his stomach lurching. He couldn't stomach anything sweet now. Not after Ku'Tal

To his right was a stall that sold ice cream. He'd tried ice cream at Mimi's restaurant. A rich strawberry and cream that tasted like a lazy afternoon beside the river.

Behind the counter, a short, pudgy man in a blue apron dipped pale honey ice cream into a cup for a woman.

The scent of honey wafted toward him.

Gagging, Peter turned away and rushed away from the shop. Had to get clear of that hideous smell.

Past another food vendor (nothing sweet this time), at the far end of the shuttle port, stood two or three shipping offices and a series of shuttle gates. A large coffeehouse stood between the offices and the gates with a dozen or so tables. Some booths in a soft blue green color, the chairs and cushions black lined the walls.

But the shipping offices caught his attention.

Maybe he could charter a cargo shuttle to Ballese? Someone that might be willing to fly him in and out of there. For a price.

He had to get there before it was too late for Sting. Before the Antarans killed him.

Peter hurried over to the nearest grey counter. The small office was dark. A black and grey sign hung in the window. *Taus Traders, serving Taus and Sol for all your shipping and charter needs. Terios Wagner, proprietor.* Under the large black and grey sign hung a small white sign. *Inquire after hours at the Black Canary.*

Filing those names in the back of his thoughts, Peter stopped at the other two traders' offices One sign read, Swift Shipping and

Charter, Frederick Swift, owner. Closed. The other trader's office, called One-Stop Shipping and Charter, was dark like the others.

Discouraged, he wandered away, his lack of sleep catching up with him. He headed toward the coffeehouse. Maybe a stiff cup of coffee or two would keep him awake?

Ahead, a loud, tinny-sounding voice filled the corridor. As Peter moved closer, he saw a thin man with dark stringy hair and intense hazel eyes. The man smelled of soap and mint and he wore a long-sleeved oatmeal-colored tunic and faded blue pants. His boots were short brown chukkas, military style. The man held a black, leather-bound book in the air and tapped it with his knuckles. The three people walking ahead of Peter gave the man a wide berth. Most ignored him.

Then Peter saw it. A god symbol!

A gold cross dangled around the man's neck. Peter was transfixed.

Maybe this man could explain more about the god symbols? Where they came from and how someone earned theirs?

How did citizens earn their god symbols? And their souls?

Peter paused to listen to the man's jumble of words and numbers. So many numbers! Most of it made no sense to him. The man pointed a finger at Peter's chest, startling him.

"Have you been saved, young man?" the man shouted in a grating voice.

Saved? He'd been rescued from the military, was that what the man meant? Finally, he nodded.

A grin stretched across the man's smooth face. "Good! Excellent!" Then the man's gaze fell onto Peter's god symbol and the grin faded. "Where's your cross? You're not one of those New Agers with your crystals and chakras and all that, are you?" The man tapped the book in his hand again.

What was that book? Did it explain about the god symbols?

Peter's hand fell to his chest, grabbing hold of his god symbol. "You mean my god symbol?"

"A yin yang?" The man laughed. "That's one name for it, I suppose."

"This one was given to me," Peter answered. "I haven't really earned one yet."

"You can't earn it, kid," the man said with a toothy grin. "Otherwise, nobody'd get into heaven!"

Heaven? Was that where souls came from?

Peter frowned. He'd never heard that term before. Why couldn't he earn a god symbol like others? He ran his thumb across his god symbol and his heart ached.

Had he been given a soul by mistake? Like the same mistake that had created him?

He stepped backward. Did this man know he was a recombinant? Maybe the god symbols really were reserved for citizens?

Peter shifted his weight, the man's unblinking stare unnerving. "Then how does someone receive a god symbol?"

The man waved his book in the air and thumped it with his hand. "Salvation's a gift, kid, you can't earn it. It's a gift for everyone who believes in The Word. I wonder about people like Judas and Herod, of course." The man laughed at his own joke, but Peter didn't understand.

"Judas? Herod?"

"Judas of Iscariot. You say you're saved, yet you don't know about Judas? Gotta bone up on your Bible studies, kid."

"Who is Judas?" Peter asked again, stepping closer. What was this book?

The man slapped the leather cover with his hand again. "He sold out the savior! His best friend and he turns him over to the soldiers to be killed. Now, there's a lesson in forgiveness."

Horrified, Peter stumbled back. Judas sold out his best friend? To the soldiers?

The eerie similarity sent a chill through him. Sting had given him this god symbol and he sold him out. His best friend. His stomach somersaulted.

"What's the matter, kid? It's all right here." The man held out the book to him. "In the Word."

Peter shook his head, stepping backward. He didn't want to touch that book. He didn't want to know what happened to Judas—what became of his soul. He winced.

He'd sold out his soul along with his best friend! What had he done?

The man took off his gold cross and held out the god symbol to Peter. "Here, you look like you could use this, kid." His gaze was soft, almost concerned. "Take it," he said in a sincere voice, "I hope it gives you comfort."

"No! I can't wear that!"

Peter fled from the man.

———

STILL SHAKING, Peter rode the transit around the city a few times, trying to put those horrible things out of his mind. Ahead, the bar district sparkled and gleamed. Then he remembered the shipping company's sign: *inquire at the Black Canary*. Maybe this trader would deal with him? Even getting passage as far as Farnas would be a good start. Then he could hire a shuttle to Ballese from there. Any movement closer to Ballese was worth the effort.

Two rows of small, run-down buildings the color of sand and drenched in thick strands of colorful lights lined both sides of the street. The smell of roasted grain and smoke permeated the air. Miners and traders frequented this street across the river from Mimi's restaurant.

Why hadn't Diana ever taken him here, where the colored lights hung? He remembered the cozy little pub she'd taken him to, with its warm cedar paneling and green plants that hung from the ceiling. She played darts there. It was across the river, too.

He gazed up at the tubes of blue, gold, and purple lights that dripped from the rooftops, clinging to rooftop edges, and outlining the buildings. This was the source of the colored lights, he realized, the ones that glimmered across the river.

The colored lights calmed his panic. He forced Judas and the god symbols out of his head and searched the rows of bars until he found The Black Canary.

The crowded, noisy place overflowed with miners. He weaved through the mass of people until he found his way to the bar. The crowd shifted, smashing him against the press of bodies. He struggled to move to the side where two ladies in short dresses sat on a wooden bench against a bright yellow wall. They drank blue-colored drinks and stared at him, smiling with their red-lipped faces and smoky eyes.

The air burned with hot, spice-laden smoke from the wispy thin coils of colored paper the women held between their lips. The smoke was heady, making him lightheaded.

He smiled politely at them and then ordered a beer. He plinked down a credit and turned toward the crowd, scanning for anyone who might look like the trader, Terios Wagner.

"Looking for someone," one of the red-lipped women asked, grinning at him over her drink.

"Some company?" her friend asked.

The first woman's gaze traveled down his frame, sizing him up for something. He tried not to meet her gaze when it found its way back to his face.

He nodded. "A trader with a route out near Farnas."

She cast a look at her friend. "We'll trade with you," she said.

"Do you go out to Farnas?" he asked, wide-eyed. Maybe there were other traders in Civilization who didn't have their own offices in the shuttle port?

She laid the magenta coil in a glass dish that sat on the faded wood. Reaching into a glittery bag at her side, she held out a handful of small, sparkling blue spheres. "No, but this will take you anywhere you wanna go, honey."

"What's that?" he asked, frowning.

He needed a shuttle ride, not trinkets. Sarge told him about some of the Taus system planets not on the credit system. Perhaps this was another kind of credit?

"These are imagemakers," she purred, sliding closer to him. Her hand reached around behind him and in a moment, slid around his waist. He felt uncomfortable with her touch and slid away from it. "They'll take you anywhere you want to go. First one's free." She held the spheres closer to his face. They smelled tart, almost sour.

"No thanks. I really am in need of a trader—and a good night's sleep."

She stroked the clear plastic bag with long sparkling red fingernails. "These little babies will help you sleep, too. You think about it, okay?" She pecked his cheek with one of those talon-like, red fingernails.

Peter turned back to his beer. He tipped up the glass and drank the cold brew. It tasted a little tart and flat, but he was thirsty.

"Who's the trader?" the other woman asked, a blue coil wedged between her too-white, too square teeth.

"Terios Wagner," Peter answered.

The other woman pointed toward the back of the room, at a man in a grey skull cap and waistcoat.

"See that guy back there?" she asked.

Peter craned his neck to the right. "The man in grey?"

She nodded. "That's Terios. He's the trader you want. He might be able to help."

"Thank you very much," Peter said, smiling. He finished his beer and tunneled through the crowd until he stood beside the man in grey. He tapped the man on the sleeve.

"Excuse me, sir, do you trade near Farnas?"

The man called Terios was thin with a white-blond Van Dyke beard that ringed his mouth. His facial features were sharp and his dark blue eyes were bright, matching his mop of blue curls.

"Get lost," Terios snapped and turned away.

"Sir, please—I'm trying to charter passage to Ballese, but if I could get as far as Farnas, that'd be a big help. I stopped by your office and—"

The man frowned at him. "Look, buddy, I'm not a shuttle service. Charter a flight through the port."

"The sign said to come here after hours. I've got credits to pay, but no one will fly into the hot zone. Can you help me?" He pointed to the two women at the bar. "They said you might be able to help."

"Kalla sent you?"

Peter shrugged. "I didn't get her name."

Terios waved at the woman with the long red fingernails, who nodded at him.

Smiling, the trader put an arm around Peter's shoulder. "Well, if Kalla sent you, then I'll see if I can help. Let's go take a look at some star charts and you can show me where you need to go."

"Thank you so much," said Peter as he followed the man into a back room.

The room was dark.

"Let me find the switch," said Terios, fumbling against the wall until he clicked a button.

Blinding light filled the room. Peter flung his arm across his eyes, but someone shoved him forward. The door locked behind him.

"We'll make this easy on you, son," said Terios. "Give me your credits and we'll call it even."

Confused and still blinded by the bright light, he tried to make out Terios' outline. Peter's eyes burned, tearing from the intense light. Shapes oozed to his left. He turned.

"Forget it," said Peter.

"I was afraid you'd be stubborn about this," said Terios. "Take it."

Someone grabbed his arm and Peter kicked out, catching the man in the side. The kick broke the man's crushing grip and Peter jerked his arm free.

A crack to the chin knocked Peter to the floor, but he rolled away and scrambled to his feet. His eyes still couldn't focus, but he felt the men coming at him again. He threw himself forward, knocking the men over, but needles stabbed into his calf. Convulsing, he dropped to the ground.

"Told you we should have stunned him," said one of the men.

"You should have waited for the imagemaker to take effect first," another voice chastised.

Shadows hung over him. He struggled up from the ground. A fist cracked him in the face, another slamming into his stomach. He tried to rise, but his muscles wouldn't respond.

Another fist smashed against the side of his head. The warm trickle of blood oozed down his face.

A kick to the side.

He gasped, his chest heaving as he wheezed for air. Hands moved all over him, sliding under his shirt, digging into his pockets. He was powerless to stop it. He tried to shout but couldn't even summon his voice.

"Dammit, he's only got a handful of credits!"

A fist raked across his face, cutting his lip.

"Dump him out back," said Terios.

Peter heard the door slam.

Another door creaked open and someone picked him up. Flinging him out into the darkness.

Unable to move yet, he laid there, terrified they'd return, and he couldn't even crawl away.

Slowly, time loosened his seized muscles, allowing him to crawl into the night and hide behind a trash bin. He laid his head against a sunbaked wall, the heat heavy against his chest.

Why had they done that?

They said they'd help him and then they stole his credits. At least, he hadn't brought all of his hard-earned credits along. Exhausted, he dropped his face into his hands.

Citizens didn't make any sense to him. None of this made any sense to him.

LIMPING and hurting from the damage that Terios and his men had inflicted, Peter staggered through Civilization's streets for hours. He couldn't go back to the restaurant looking like this.

He haunted pub doorways and paced the emptying streets until the horizon began to lighten. Exhausted and afraid to dream, he broke into a run to keep himself awake.

Every muscle in his body screamed at the exertion, especially after the beating he'd taken, but he couldn't go to sleep. He couldn't.

He didn't stop running until he reached the solitude of the dark riverbank. He collapsed onto the cool sand. He was so tired. His eyelids drooped and he struggled to keep his focus.

The man with the god symbols returned to his thoughts, reminding him of what he'd done. What else had he sold out? His soul? Had he lost it now?

Had that been the price of walking away from Ku'Tal instead of Sting?

He pulled off the god symbol and held it up to the remnants of the starry night sky. Neon pinks, purples, and blues flickered off the smooth white and black surface of the yin yang.

"Sting," he said with a groan and his voice cracked. "What have I done?"

"You survived."

Peter jerked his head around. "How'd you…"

Sergeant David Temple leaned against a tree beside the riverbank. Sarge smiled. "I figured if I waited here long enough, you'd show up."

"I can't talk to you right now, Sarge," said Peter, turning back to the river. He waved him away.

"But it's the truth, Mitchell. All you did was survive."

Sarge sank down beside him, but Peter couldn't look at him.

"You came back from Ku'Tal. You beat the odds! Sting wanted you to beat those odds. Sure, he wanted more than anything to come with you, but he couldn't make that happen."

Peter jerked his head around, glaring at Sarge. "I'm the one who made the deal! I'm the one who should be on Ballese right now. Not Sting—me. He would have made it out if I'd just done the decent thing and washed out."

"Don't you ever say that again! Do you hear me, Mitchell?" Sarge's voice was taut with anger, pointing a finger at Peter. "You learned how to survive out there. You saved both of us from being killed and you made the deal that would have gotten us out, too. Not Sting, not me—you. That was Sting's way of cleaning the slate."

Peter wiped the tears out of his eyes. "But I miss him, Sarge. And I feel so sick inside I can't stand it." He grabbed hold of Sarge's arms, his chest aching. "I feel so lost. And there are so many things I'm forgetting now. Little things. Like how bright the city's colors are against the dark river. How a thunderstorm sounds or how good the air feels when it sweeps over the transit platform. I'm overlooking everything I used to cherish."

"It's okay, Mitchell...we all do it," said David.

He shook his head. "No! Not a recombinant. I've only been here such a short time. How can I be taking these things for granted so easily? So quickly?" He felt so hot and his head throbbed.

Sarge's eyes looked sad and glassy. "People forget things, it's that simple. We have so much on our minds, so much to remember that we forget the ordinary things around us. We just forget sometimes. It doesn't mean you don't believe in them anymore."

"But I won't forget about Sting, Sarge. I won't. I'll find a way to get him out of there." Peter let go of Sarge's arms and turned toward the river again.

"Washouts are happening sooner now, did you know that?" Sarge's face was grim. "Training time is three months or less now."

"What?" A shiver of fear quivered through Peter's stomach. "Three months?"

"We're getting record numbers of recombinants through the station and half the time to train them. Survival rate has fallen and life expectancy is back to six months."

Sarge studied him, making Peter uncomfortable. The darkness hid the beating he'd taken. Sarge wouldn't see that. Yet.

"But that's not the worst of it."

Peter stared at him. "What do you mean?"

Sarge cleared his throat and stared down at the sand. "The worst part is that none of this is going to matter soon."

"Why?" How could it not matter?

"Because if someone doesn't figure out a way to stop the Antarans, they'll sweep over Civilization within six months." He rubbed his forehead. "They've dug into Ku'Tal again and have landed on Farnas and Karaba."

The thought of Antaran biodrones living beyond Ku'Tal was incomprehensible to him. He felt sicker than ever now. Everything they'd accomplished on Ku'Tal was for nothing now.

"How do we stop them, Sarge?"

Sarge's silence was crippling.

Peter waited for him to snap off a quick and dirty solution, but all that whispered into the darkness was a sigh. A skimmer surged down the river, leaving rivulets of purple, green, and gold lights in its wake.

"Sarge! How do we stop them?"

"Wish I knew, Mitchell," he said finally. "A good place to start though, is to figure out what they want. No one seems to know the answer to that question. And it's hard to figure that out with all the lies they've told. When we know that, then maybe we can stop them."

Peter staggered to his feet, but everything tilted for a moment. He struggled and managed to find his balance point.

"We won't find that out this far from their encampments," he said.

His head felt so light and the river seemed to ooze out of its banks and then return.

"You're right, of course. UCOE needs to go in there and find out the answers. Covert ops, brute force—something! Believe me, Mitchell, if there's any way to go to Ballese, I promise you, I'll do my best to get Sting out of there. That's the best I can offer, though."

"What?" A smile slid across his face. "Then it might be possible?"

"I've heard the brass mentioning Ballese, Peter. Several times. So, it's not completely out of the question."

"That's all I'm asking, Sarge—just the chance to try."

Smiling, Peter leaned back against a tree trunk. The light from the city against his face.

Sarge gasped and scrambled toward him. "Dear God! Mitchell—your face! What happened?"

Again, the river oozed from its banks, wrapping around him, squeezing him, then releasing. Colored lights undulated around him, showering him in sparks. He fought against the blackness enveloping him and the river again returned to its banks. The colored lights dissipated.

It was so hot. He couldn't breathe.

The ground began to rise until Peter found himself lying in the sand. The gritty sand rasped against his face, burning his cheeks. Sarge's hands grabbed him, turning him over.

"Mitchell? Mitchell, answer me!"

He spit sand out of his mouth. "I feel really strange," he muttered.

In a moment, Sarge was cradling his head in his lap.

"What happened?" Sarge insisted. "Tell me what happened."

"Went to—to Black Canary. To get passage to Farnas."

"Oh, Mitchell, you didn't! The Black Canary's the most dangerous bar in that district. You're lucky you weren't shanghaied or poisoned!"

"They said they'd help. Then they took—my credits. Why? Why do citizens say one thing...then do another? Why, Sarge?"

Sarge winced. "I wish I knew, Mitchell."

Again, the river rose from its banks, swirling across the ground toward him. It swelled over him and he was drowning in colored lights.

"Sarge, help me...current's too strong! I'm drowning!"

"You're safe on the bank," Sarge said, his voice steady.

Peter flailed against the thick, black water churning blue and green lights around him, but Sarge held him down.

"Did they make you take something, Mitchell? Something you'd never seen before? A strange drink? A smoke? Anything?"

He remembered the blue spheres and the tartness of his beer. Working hard to form the word, he pursed his lips.

"Imagemaker," he muttered.

"Oh, God...hang on, Mitchell!" His face contorted. "I'll get you some help. Stay with me, okay?"

Peter tried to answer, but he was sinking again, somewhere between the cool sand and the dark, sparkling river.

———

"HIS PULSE IS ERRATIC, what'd you say it was—imagemaker?" The voice echoed in his head and vibrated through his bones.

Diana? He wasn't sure.

"Hold him down, David! Mimi, try again!"

Peter's body was on fire and he struggled against the hot blankets enveloping him, but he couldn't free his hands.

"I'm burning up! Burning up!" He shouted, but heavy weights kept him immobile.

"Diana, his legs," said another voice.

Was that Mimi?

He cried out, hoping someone would hear him and rescue him, but no help came.

Something razor-sharp sliced into his hip and he screamed.

"No, don't wash me out! Please! I won't fight! Please!" He crossed his arms against his chest. "Put the restraint jacket back on, but please don't wash me out!"

A hand fell to his forehead, stroking his hair. "Peter, it's okay. No one's going to hurt you or wash you out. You're safe here."

"Easy, Peter, that was just a little counteraction for imagemaker."

Mimi. "Hang in there. I want to know who did this." Her voice was pinched, teeth gritted.

Another voice echoed through the well of heat. "I never got a chance to ask him." Sarge.

"Sarge, did I fail my training sim? It's too hot. Don't send me back to RDC."

Sarge squeezed his shoulder. "No, Mitchell. You passed, remember? You're in your own bed. This will be over soon, I promise. Hang in there a little longer."

SOMETIME LATER, Peter awoke in his own bed. Sunlight streamed through the blinds and he squinted. At last, he noticed the figure sitting at the end of his bed. Sarge. He wore his training blues. Then Peter remembered that Sarge's medical leave was over today. Peter glanced at the chair by the window. Diana lay curled in a ball beneath a green blanket. She slept soundly.

"I thought we were going to have to take you to the hospital," said Sarge with a wry, but relieved smile. "The counteractant worked. You've been asleep for nearly twenty-four hours."

Yawning, Peter sat up, feeling weak and sick, but he didn't remember dreaming last night.

"Diana's been so worried about you."

"What happened? I remember talking to you at the river and then the ground rose."

"Someone drugged you, Mitchell," said Sarge. "Imagemaker. It's a popular street drug out here. In small doses, it boosts confidence and evens out the personality. Someone must have given you a shitload. You passed out at the river and your skull missed hitting the stone steps by a matter of inches. Do you remember what happened?"

"A woman at the bar must have slipped something into my beer. She tried to sell me the drug, but I told her I was looking for a trader."

Sarge studied him for a moment, his eyes sad. "How long has it been since you've had a decent night's sleep?"

Peter shrugged. He had no idea. The nightmares had been with him for weeks. He almost couldn't remember a time without them.

"I have the nightmares, too, Mitchell. I understand."

Peter's eyes widened. "You, Sarge?"

Sarge's eyes turned glassy. "Ku'Tal will always haunt me."

Peter knew it would stay with him and Sarge forever. And anyone else who'd served there. Did Sting have nightmares on Ballese? That thought made his stomach twist into knots.

"Mitchell, promise me you won't try to charter something to Ballese again," said Sarge, changing the subject.

He stared unblinking at Sarge. He couldn't make that promise.

"Look, I know this has been hard on you." There was an angry edge in Sarge's voice now. "The military's all you've ever known and Sting was family to you. But it's not your fault that Sting didn't come back."

Peter shook his head. "I can't make you a promise that I can't keep."

Sarge reached out and hugged Peter. "Then just promise me you won't sneak off," he said, letting go. "That you'll keep me informed. Okay?"

"All right. I'll promise you that much."

This brought a smile to Sarge's face. "Diana and I will do whatever it takes to help you adjust here. You're family to us, Mitchell. Remember that." Sarge patted his foot. "Now, get some more rest. I've got to get to the base."

"Good luck, Sarge," he mumbled.

Peter tried to keep his eyes open. Couldn't. He slid back underneath the covers and closed his eyes.

A LONG TIME LATER, Peter awoke to the smell of hot soup. He opened his eyes and found a tray sitting on the end of his bed. A creamy red soup. Diana smiled at him from the chair.

"There you are," she said. "I brought you some tomato soup."

How silly he must look to have run off like that last night. "I'm—I'm sorry about what happened, Diana," he said with a sigh.

Diana rose from the chair and sat beside him. She laid her hand on his arm, stroking. "It's all right. I expected too much too soon, Peter. I expected you to be just like every other guy I've known. See, I forget that you started out at twenty-two in this world. I forget that all of this is so new to you, things I take for granted. Your sense of wonder is still one of the things I love the most about you."

He smiled and laid his hand against her face, caressing. "I just need time. I feel like I've been starved to death. Then someone let me wake up in the mess hall and I gorged myself on everything. It's all come at me so fast. And Sting—Diana, I feel so terrible about Sting." His hand fell away from her face.

"Please don't go back to the bar district alone, Peter. You could have been killed."

She sounded like her brother now, but the fear in her pale face sobered him. Her expressive, warm brown eyes were one of the things he loved most about her.

"You have my word," he answered with a smile.

He had no desire to return there.

Diana slid her arms around him and he held her. "I know how hard that must be. I know how I felt when David didn't come back with you. I waited and waited, praying he'd contact me and let me know he was okay. The worst part is the not knowing, isn't it?"

She laid her cheek against his chest, her eyes closing.

"I feel like—Judas," said Peter.

"Judas? What are you talking about?" She pulled back from him, confusion in her eyes.

He rose from the bed and paced unsteadily as he told her about the man with the book and the god symbols.

"Oh, Peter, no. You didn't sell Sting out. You tried to save him. He was the one who took your place. It's not your fault they took him away."

"But it was, Diana!" he shouted. No one understood what happened in that Antaran repository. "I made the deal. I should have gone. But not him. Not Sting." He pulled at the god symbol around his neck. "And this. I can't wear this anymore." He pulled it off and flung it onto the bed. "I didn't know I'd have to sell out my best friend for it."

Diana's warm hands pressed against his shoulders and he sighed, wanting to take her in his arms. These could have been some of the best moments in his life, but not with Sting in those murderers' hands. He slipped away from her touch.

"Diana, please—I can't talk about this right now."

She moved toward him again, taking his hands in hers. "When you're ready, I'm here." She let go of him, reaching for the god symbol. "I'll hold onto this for you."

He nodded. He couldn't even look at it anymore.

Slowly, Diana opened the door and entered the hallway. She closed it quietly behind her. Peter stared at the closed door for a few moments and then exhausted, he sat down heavily on the bed.

Never, in his one year of life, had he felt so alone.

4

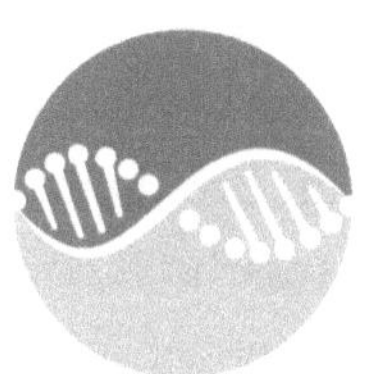

THE SHUTTLE RIDE bounced David against his restraint harness, making him queasy. His training blues felt stiff and unresponsive. He fidgeted with his tie, the air smelling like burnt rubber. After all, it'd been nearly a year since he'd worn this uniform. How different it all looked the shuttle, the base. How different it felt, too.

No matter how he tried to hide it, his unexpected combat tour on Ku'Tal had changed him forever.

There were times when he hated Field Sergeant Galloway. Even now, David wondered if the ruddy-haired soldier had gotten drunk and fallen down the stairs (breaking both his legs) on purpose. Galloway was no longer here, but he'd changed David's life with that little stunt forever. Only days after Galloway's accident, David had been bumped from a *no combat* training commission to field sergeant bound for the front.

He had no choice but to go. He'd signed the contract.

And now, after a six-month tour on Ku'Tal and a month's medical leave, he was back at the base and recommissioned a training sergeant.

With a final, stomach-twisting jolt, the shuttle careened into the base's launch bay and jerked to a stop. David hurried out of the shuttle, into the heat and light and noise of engine burns and constant flow of soldiers, half-expecting to see his little sister, Diana, grinning at him from the pilot's seat. In a short time, she would be, he reminded himself. She was returning to the base very shortly.

David walked slowly through the drafty bay with its burnt smell and scalding lights. Dull grey walls and lines of traffic crisscrossing the composite floors in a network of yellow, red, green, and blue. He studied the faces around him. Strangers stuffed into grey and green and blue uniforms. And most without combat experience.

Even now, that felt odd to say. He had combat experience. It didn't seem possible.

He followed the red lines on the floor, remembering the drills and his first assignment. He and his unit had followed those red lines a thousand times. The air smelled stale and gritty, loud with engine roars and burns. He'd forgotten that.

A unit of recombinants hurried into the launch bay and marched quickly, at their field sergeant's insistent shouting, into an awaiting transport. They were going to Ku'Tal or Farnas—how the front had changed. Their faces were masks of aggression, grins of excitement burning across their young faces. He frowned. How different these new recombinants seemed from those he'd guided through Ku'Tal's swamps over six months ago.

Except for Mitchell and Stingley, David's whole unit was dead now and forgotten—like the thousands and thousands of recombinants that had come before and after them, wave after wave.

How sad that would make Mitchell.

Still, Mitchell had had a bit of luck on his side after all. UCOE would have washed out the sensitive young man in his first week if he'd been in this group. The Recombinant Development Center seemed to be producing soldiers with higher and higher aggression quotients—and they were a helluva lot more unstable.

UCOE had forgotten Mitchell now. To them, Mitchell was just another dead recombinant.

David smiled. He'd assured that designation when he'd switched Mitchell's ID chip with one from a dead recombinant. David thought about the swamps and the Antaran biodrones again.

Maybe this war needed more aggressive soldiers now?

The bloodiness of the Ku'Tal combat was still fresh in his mind and part of him delighted in seeing the recombinants' aggression.

Yes, he'd changed.

He wanted to pay back the Antarans for all the killing and destruction. For all the lies that kept this conflict fresh and bloody and raw.

Mitchell trusted them to keep their word. He trusted everyone, expecting truth, and without fail, he was surprised by lies. If Stingley hadn't switched places with him, Mitchell would have willingly followed them off world—to his death.

Who knew what tortures they'd already inflicted on poor John Stingley? He sighed. If Stingley was even alive. Still, a small part of David hoped that somehow Stingley would survive—if it was possible —to pay back those vicious monsters, the Antaran caregivers.

David moved toward the lift at the end of the bay. He pressed the button and waited, dreading his return to duty. In moments, the lift door slid open, revealing several shuttle techs. They filed off, bound for a shift change.

"Hey, welcome back, Temple!" said one of the shuttle techs that stepped off the lift in a blue flight suit. The tech tapped the shiny gold medal on David's chest. "Nice swag!"

"Yeah, nice buff," said another tech. "Heard your recombinant blew up the munitions depot. And your leadership got you that bling."

"My comrade took it out," David corrected the tech. "I'm just sorry we didn't take out more Antarans with it."

The tech grinned and patted David on the shoulder. "You'll get more for us next time, Temple." He hurried away to a maintenance station in the opposite corner of the bay.

David shuddered. *Dear God, could there be a next time?*

He turned away from the lift, staring out at the recombinants piling into the transport and the techs repairing shuttles. Clang of tools and bang of shuttle doors echoing through the cavernous bay.

They didn't have a clue what was happening out there. Not a clue.

They didn't even realize what was happening within these base walls. The United Countries of Earth had lost part of its humanity with the Recombinant Defense Program. And they'd lost even more when they knowingly sent these recombinants out to fight a war that they had no hope of winning. UCOE was hiding behind the body counts, not even caring when droves of recombinants died for them.

They just made and sent more.

But the memories remained—of mud-covered faces with their empty-eyed stares, bodies torn apart and lying in the swamp like old clothes. Recombinants didn't even get a proper burial. Or have the comfort of the knowledge of an afterlife.

If anything, they were told they had no souls. Because they were recycled.

For a moment, as David watched the doomed recombinants boarding the transport, his body ached with sadness. At best, two or three of them would come back. How terrible Mitchell must have felt that awful day that he and his unit shipped out for Ku'Tal. He understood how Mitchell felt leaving Sting to the mercy of the Antarans, too. He'd learned more about the world from this wide-eyed recombinant's one year of life than he had in all his twenty-nine years.

With a sigh, David turned back toward the lift and slipped inside as the doors were closing. He pressed the lit up seven for the station's top level. He had a meeting with D'Angelo in fifteen minutes. There, he'd find out his next training assignment.

His field commission had expired a month ago and he couldn't have been happier. Still, unease nagged at him. He feared what D'Angelo and UCOE had planned for him.

CAPTAIN THOMAS D'ANGELO sat rigid and intense behind his wide, mahogany desk in the narrow, grey-walled office. Shiny gold captain's spirals crowned his shoulders. UCOE had rewarded the quiet, brooding officer with a promotion. The gold spirals gleamed in the desk's antique finish, its several coats of polyurethane so clear that they captured the entire room in its reflection. David saluted and D'Angelo asked him to be seated.

Seeing D'Angelo across a desk rather than addressing his field commanders at base camp seemed strange. The short man, no more than five foot eight, was lanky with bushy greying hair, but he looked seasoned and his grey, eagle-eyed gaze laser sharp. D'Angelo paid attention to details and made sure he knew what was happening everywhere around him.

"Good to see you back in uniform, Temple," said D'Angelo in a gruff voice, almost a smile on his lined face. "We were mighty proud of you back there on Ku'Tal. Blowing up that munitions depot alone took guts, son. Especially from a first-time field sergeant."

David smiled. "Thank you, sir, but Stingley blew up the depot. I just provided field support."

"Well, you were still in charge of the op. That took guts."

"I was too angry to be scared," said David. "I just wanted to make them pay."

D'Angelo nodded. His brow furrowed and David wondered what older man was remembering. A touch of pain shadowed the man's eyes. D'Angelo had been a military man for a good number of years. He'd seen a lot, but the Antarans seemed to be his personal demon. David had seen that more and more in his correspondences from the captain after he'd come home.

D'Angelo seemed to enjoy the detailed descriptions of his assault on the depot. And there were times when D'Angelo seemed almost envious. David had been so exhausted and heartsick by the end of his tour that he just wanted it all to be over—one way or another. After

Mitchell reached Mimi's safe house intact, David's anger sent him back through the swamps with fistfuls of plasma grenades.

He'd do it again if he had to. It was that simple. It was his one moment of satisfaction throughout the entire tour.

His answer seemed to please D'Angelo. The shorter man leaned across the desk, a smile curving across his face.

"How'd you like to make them pay more, Temple? A lot more than they've ever had to pay in this war." D'Angelo's voice was low and deadly determined.

David thought about John Stingley, the young, curly-haired blond recombinant missing in action, his status making Mitchell sick with guilt. Yes, he'd like to pay them back for what they'd no doubt already done to Sting. For what they'd already done to Mitchell. And him.

"What did you have in mind, sir?"

Steepling his fingers, D'Angelo settled back in his chair as if reeling in a line with the hook he'd just tossed out.

"A series of covert recon missions beyond Ku'Tal are being planned, Temple. A small unit consisting of an officer, a field sergeant, and a team of recombinants. Using bits of the aliens' own bioshielding technology, the recon team would land on Ballese and document just what in the hell those Antarans are plotting."

A cold chill shivered down David's spine. Go to Ballese without another unit to back them up? With no way to call in the cavalry?

He stared down at his gold *bravery under fire* medal. What did D'Angelo see in this shiny gold symbol? He knew what he saw. A lot of luck and exhaustion. He wasn't a hero. He was just fed up with the killing and his unit's heavy casualties.

But Ballese? What was D'Angelo thinking?

"I'll have to think it over, sir." He grimaced, knowing he had little choice. If D'Angelo wanted him on this recon, he would be deployed. It was that simple.

"First one's been away for four weeks and the second one left five days ago, Temple. I plan to lead the third one and I'd like you there as my field sergeant."

David stiffened. An uneasy silence built in the room. Finally, D'Angelo spoke.

"Look, son, I want someone there who's handy with a plasma rifle and who's good with those wild recombinants. And someone who's encountered enough Antarans to know what they may be doing out there. Think it over. I'll expect your answer within the week."

D'Angelo's gaze was unsettling.

For some time, David had suspected a build-up of Antaran forces beyond Ku'Tal, but if D'Angelo was about to risk his own life—on a recon Op—what could be at stake out there?

Just what did D'Angelo expect to find on Ballese?

David squinted at D'Angelo. "Sir, what are you looking for?"

A faraway expression emptied D'Angelo's gaze, his face tightening.

"Evidence. They're making something horrible out there, I can feel it." He gritted his teeth. "Those slimy caregivers promise you safety and all kinds of alluring possibilities, but they're anything but safe. Most dangerous things I've ever encountered." He turned his gaze back to David. "They carted off lots of our recombinants, Temple. Those boys and girls disappeared off the battlefields at regular intervals. I want to know what they're doing with them— before it's too late to stop it. Think it over, Temple. Dismissed."

David rose from the chair, saluted, and hurried out of D'Angelo's office.

Dazed, he wandered down the hallway, day-shine lights warming its grey length that smelled metallic and like stale coffee. He hadn't known about the Antarans' widespread trapping of recombinants on Ku'Tal. His mind spun through the events of that night in the Ku'Tal repository, the broken machinery, the caregivers' almost desperate bargaining with Mitchell.

None of it made sense.

Were they trying to distract Mitchell, keep him occupied with this *trade* so he wouldn't figure out the true nature of that facility?

The caregivers said the place was for the creation of their mindless, tentacled biodrone creatures. For patrolling their perimeters. The caregivers claimed they were protecting the genomes of their people and trying to bring them back from extinction. How much—if any of that—had been true?

Still, David wondered why D'Angelo was so concerned about recombinants. Did the man truly care about their well-being or was it just about the tech? Had to be the tech. He watched D'Angelo send them out like disposable targets for months.

———

DAVID'S OFFICE looked just the way he'd left it nearly eight months ago. Tiny, cramped room with its blue-grey walls and small desk wedged into one corner, his workstation crammed against a sliver of a portal. The door to his right, leading into his small staff apartment, was still locked like he'd left it.

He moved to the door, pressed his thumb to the lock, and opened the door. His bunk was still made, overhead light off, white blanket stretched tight and crisp white sheet folded in sharp corners beneath a bright white pillow—just like he'd left it. Everything seemed to be in order.

He laid his duffle bag on the bed and went back into his office, dreading the barrage of emails that awaited him. Seating himself in front of the workstation, he sighed and turned on the virtual display. As the screen wavered in the air above his desk, he tapped the glowing blue envelope and opened his email.

Throughout the day, he played catch up, wading through months of emails, but he couldn't push D'Angelo's meeting out of his head. D'Angelo hadn't even given him his new training assignment. He'd just dangled a chance at revenge in front of him.

Was the recon mission his only choice?

He rubbed his right arm, the pain and shrapnel only a shadow in his memory. He had no desire to return to Ku'Tal—or God forbid, something worse. There was nothing to think about. He was staying right here. He'd let D'Angelo know tomorrow. For today, he'd get caught up on paperwork. It was only eight months overdue. He glanced at his watch: 1300.

After a quick trip down to mess for lunch, he returned to his office and continued the barrage of paperwork. Emails. Reports. And forms. He groaned. Screens and screens of information to fill out and file.

All because he lived through those months of hell on Ku'Tal.

He flipped through screen after screen, inputting until his hands ached and his eyes burned. When he finally checked the time again, it was 1744. Way past time to knock off and relax. He changed into his sweats and went down to the gym to get his injured right arm back in shape.

THE NEXT MORNING, David rose early. He showered and dressed in his training blues. He stood in front of the latrine mirror. He looked the same, except for a wrinkle or two under the eyes, yet he felt so different inside. Even food tasted different. He'd always loved Mimi's imported ales, but they tasted flat after Ku'Tal and the pasta dish he'd ordered was bland even with the hot sauce. Too many rations, he thought then stepped out of the latrine and into the hallway.

Today was his reintegration interview with the staff shrink. Standard operating procedure, he was told, but the process still worried him. He didn't want to talk about Ku'Tal.

Not with someone who hadn't been there.

The mess hall hadn't filled up with officers yet. Only a handful of UCOE personnel haunted the tables of the brightly lit mess hall. The chairs, tables, and walls were all a soft, safe beige. The room looked as bland as the food, a hint of sage in the stale air. Synthsausage links sizzled on the griddle behind the line as a cook turned them. The juice machine hummed as its reservoir filled slowly with frothy orange-colored water.

He hurried through the line with his pale fried eggs, almost-burnt toast, and bad coffee. The scent of rewarmed coffee and synthsausage clung to his clothes as he carried his tray to a table against a portal and ate quickly.

Still, D'Angelo's proposition nagged at him.

He flexed his right arm, only a trace of stiffness remaining. He'd only been off medical leave for a day or two.

Why had D'Angelo picked his first day back to hit him with a covert recon mission?

It was too soon.

Didn't D'Angelo understand what Ku'Tal had done to him? He rubbed his eyes. How could the man ask him to go back when even he didn't yet understand how that place had affected him?

He took a bite of eggs. They tasted lukewarm and powdery, but he finished them, washing them down with rewarmed, weak black coffee.

Through the portal, David studied the amber curve of Civilization, the planet below the station. It had no name that anyone knew of. It was simply labeled Taus Mining Colony #2. Long ago, the personnel started calling it Civilization after the only mining town on the planet's surface. It was a small place, surprisingly civilized—except for the bar district where the remaining dregs of the Taus system conducted business, some of it even legal. UCOE personnel were warned not to visit bars in that district because some ended up shanghaied into the pirate brigades. Or worse. Mitchell was so lucky to escape that bar only minus his pride and a few credits.

Civilization's familiar silhouette in the portal was reassuring and he thought of Diana, but the sounds of the Ku'Tal front still echoed in his ears. The high-pitched whine of activated cascade mines, the hiss of cold wind across the swamp, the emphatic screeching tick of a sensor grid. If he closed his eyes, they filled his ears and he felt like he was drowning in them.

He stared out the portal, concentrating on the quiet serenity surrounding the base. It soothed his restlessness. He took another sip of coffee.

As he nibbled on his toast, he thought about the other recon missions D'Angelo mentioned. Two other teams were already out there on short-term missions to Ballese.

Had anyone heard from the recon units? Had they even reached Ballese?

D'Angelo told him next to nothing, perhaps on purpose. After his interview, he'd investigate the current status of those missions.

When David finished his food, he dropped the beige tray onto a stack at the end of the table and returned to his office. Plopping into his desk chair, he reopened his mail. He still had a lot of correspondences to send.

In a couple of hours, he left the office for his reintegration interview, but he moved slowly toward the lift, dreading the formality. He had no desire to arrive at the UCOE shrink's office early and detail his plans for reintegrating into a routine he no longer understood. This was the last formality standing between him and getting his life back to normal.

Inside the lift, he punched B08 on the grid and the doors slid shut. The lift lurched sideways and then down. In moments, the doors opened and with reluctance, David stepped out. He plodded down the well-lit hallway, passing two techs from the shuttle bay in their tan coveralls. He smelled a pungent scent that reminded him of rubbing alcohol.

"Hey, Temple, good to see you back," said one of the techs, his tan coveralls smudged with dirt and grime.

"Glad you made it out," the other tech said, a smile on her angular face. Her coveralls were streaked with an oily, rainbow-sheened fluid.

David nodded in thanks and continued down the hallway. At the end of the hall was the Psychological Services Office and the shrink ready to measure his whacko quotient. With a downcast gaze, he knocked on the door.

A young voice told him to enter. He hesitated then opened the door.

Inside, the office was a mirrored layout of his own office, with the sliver of a portal to the left of the workstation desk. Another door off to the right contained the shrink's living quarters. The warm scent of fresh-brewed tea filled the room. On the desk set two silver, wire baskets, each one containing folders. David saw his own file open on the shiny black desk. The shrink was a guy about twenty-five years old with thick brown hair and grey eyes. This guy was younger than he was.

Instantly, David loathed the young man. Here was this—this *kid* who'd probably never even seen digitals of an Antaran, much less gagged on the biodrones' overpowering sweet stench moments before it swung down from the trees. Yet, this guy was supposed to evaluate experiences he knew nothing about and determine whether David was still reintegration material.

"Sergeant Temple," said the shrink, "I'm Nathan Faris. Please, have a seat."

Faris, lanky and about five foot seven, seemed a little nervous as he shook David's hand with a limp grip and then motioned David toward the chair in front of the desk.

David hesitated a moment, but then closed the door and sat down.

"First of all, welcome back to base," Faris began with a thin smile. "How's the arm?"

He rubbed his right arm. "It's a little stiff, but it gets better every day."

"Good, so there's no range of motion loss?"

"None," David answered.

"How did it happen, Sergeant?"

He explained about the munitions depot and how it had collapsed around him when he set off the charges.

"Did you act alone when you blew up the depot, Sergeant, or did you have help?"

Thanks to Mitchell and Stingley, the depot had been wide open. But he couldn't give Mitchell any credit or risk him being discovered as AWOL.

"Private Stingley blew up the depot," he answered stiffly. "I was support on the op."

Faris leaned back in his chair. "Tell me about that day, Sergeant."

"Not much to tell," he said with a sigh. "I'd been separated from the rest of my unit and biodrones were swarming over the landscape. A massive pull-out was underway, so all of our forces were trying to destroy this thing and get to the shuttles. I ran into Stingley at the Antaran munitions depot."

"Please, continue," Faris replied.

"He'd armed every one of his plasma grenades and I helped him shove his way into the hidden facility. He scattered the grenades throughout and we retreated outside. Then we waited for the grenades to go off in succession. Five grenades ripped through that place, bringing down the roof and destroying every piece of equipment in the Antaran depot."

"What happened to Private Stingley?"

A very good question. One he wanted answers to—for Mitchell.

"Biodrones got him," David snapped.

He'd destroyed any means for the Antarans to create more biodrones in that place. If only he'd been able to destroy the depot before the Antarans had escaped with Stingley.

Faris gazed at him for a moment, a pleasant, nonjudgmental look on his face. "Do you feel ready to return to duty?"

"Of course," David answered. He shifted nervously in the chair.

"How has the front changed you?"

David stared at Faris for a moment. "I'm not the same inexperienced sergeant that left here for Ku'Tal."

Faris nodded. "Who are you now?"

"I-I don't know." He hadn't had time to find out. "I know my own mind and I trust my own judgment. I don't fear the enemy as much as I hate them."

Faris rose from his desk and stood in front of David.

"Sergeant, I'm not asking you these questions in order to trap you. I'm here to help you if you're having trouble adjusting. I don't hear difficulties in your voice and what you're telling me sounds reasonable." The shrink sat down in a chair across from him. "The front has changed all of us. That's expected. What I want to know is how we can make your transition back to the station easier?"

He sighed. "The hardest part is surviving."

"Surviving?" Faris asked with a frown. "Please explain."

"You have this horrible hindsight. And you see soldiers going over now that you know won't be coming back. And you see soldiers who won't have a shred of sanity left if they do return. It's like some terrible sixth sense. I wish I didn't know those things, y'know? I'd rather not know who's number's up. I'd rather not think about it at all."

He closed his eyes, fighting back the sting of moisture in his eyes. His chest tightened and he held his breath a moment.

The shrink patted him on the shoulder and moved around to his desk chair again.

"You've adjusted as well as anyone could, Sergeant. Do you have a lot of friends? Any family out this way?"

"Yeah, some friends and a sister out here. I'll be all right. I just need—"

"Some time and to give yourself a break. It's okay to feel how you feel, Sergeant. You saw a lot of death. There's no sense to be made of it, only your reaction to it."

Faris closed his file and placed it in the first wire basket. David squinted, seeing a check mark on the front of the basket. "If you need someone to talk to, please don't hesitate to call on me. For a soldier, it can be hard to talk about combat with people who haven't experienced it. The important thing is not to let it eat you up inside, Sergeant. If it hurts, talk about it."

"I'll do that. I just feel so strange when I talk to personnel that haven't been to the front. They don't know what I've been through. They expect me to be like my old self."

"But you're not your old self," said Faris, motioning at him. "You survived a place that could have killed you thousands of times. And you saw a lot of comrades die. Many soldiers feel guilty because they come home and their friends don't."

David pictured poor Mitchell trying to get through each day, knowing he'd survived and Stingley was probably dead. That guilt was very real and he had no idea how to help Mitchell.

"I have a buddy like that," David answered.

"Please, tell him to get in here and talk to me about it. Guilt has a way of building to critical mass."

Sighing, he shook his head. "He'd never come in." Poor Mitchell. He couldn't come in. David had to do something for him before it was too late.

"Try to convince him, Sergeant. His life may depend on it."

David stood and glanced into the other basket on Faris's desk. This basket was marked with the letters *reeval* and inside it, were a few folders. The top one had a familiar name. Captain Thomas D'Angelo's file lay on top of the pile in the *reeval* basket.

What had happened to D'Angelo on Ku'Tal? Had something far worse happened to him?

Faris rose to his feet and extended his hand to David who shook it.

"Again, welcome back, Sergeant. They will be processing your orders very soon. You'll be back to training recombinants shortly."

"Thanks for your time, Faris."

He turned and entered the hallway, a heavy feeling in his stomach. Was D'Angelo just angry like him or did something darker and broken lurk beneath the man's calm veneer?

Something that might just get a lot of soldiers killed?

5

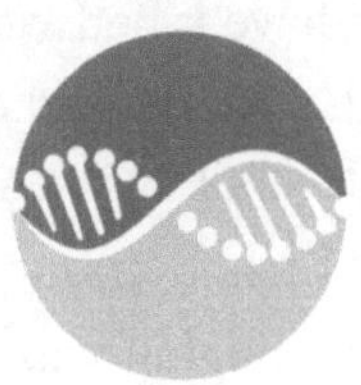

MORNING BROUGHT Peter aches he didn't know he had. He tried to get out of bed. Couldn't. His head throbbed and his ribs hurt with every movement. His grey T-shirt smelled stale with alcohol and blood. He stripped it off and threw it into the chair.

A thin stream of light warmed the dark room. Another hot day in Civilization. If he didn't hurt so badly, he'd have gone for a long walk today. He loved the heat against his skin and seeing the sun bright in the sky. So much of his time had been spent trapped inside facilities and training bases, never seeing the sun. The rest had been spent in a grey place of swamps and pain. Seeing the sun calmed him.

Struggling, he slid to the edge of the bed and rocked himself onto his feet.

The room swayed.

He fought the shift, grabbing hold of the blue curtains. He pulled them open and sunlight filled his room. With an arm cradling his bruised ribs, Peter stumbled back to his bed and collapsed. The sun warmed his face and bare chest.

He draped his arm over his eyes. No traders would go to Ballese and no charters were available. Besides, Sarge'd find out if he did manage to charter a flight. He squinted at the window, the light flickering against the smooth, pale wood floor, and tried to think of another way to help Sting. Mimi had shuttles. He sighed. But he couldn't fly one. What if he asked again about the underground going in? It couldn't hurt. Besides, he was out of plans.

Except for one desperate idea that hung on the edge of his thoughts.

All he needed was a private's uniform to get him back onto the training base. It was a huge risk, but he might just find a unit going to Ballese. If Mimi refused to help again, then he'd have no choice.

He'd get Sting out somehow.

What if he didn't ask to go all the way to Ballese? What if he just accompanied Mimi's shuttle to Karaba? It was halfway along the route to Ballese. Halfway got him closer and maybe he could charter another shuttle? Diana and Mimi's other pilot would let him ride along. He smiled. No one would expect him to disappear from the shuttle.

Satisfied, Peter slept on and off all morning until Diana's presence awoke him.

"How are you feeling today, Peter?" she asked with a smile as she leaned down and kissed his lips. "Hungry? Brought you breakfast."

She set down a plate of eggs and toast for him on the dresser.

"Better," he answered. "But not hungry."

Diana stroked his bare shoulder and he closed his eyes, losing himself in her touch. He reached up and cupped her chin, pulling her close enough to kiss.

"You *are* feeling better," she said, leaning down.

He kissed her, softly, gently.

"I've got to get into the shower," he said finally. "I'm supposed to work at sixteen hundred today."

Diana sat down beside him on the bed, shaking her head. "Sorry, Peter, but you're staying right here. Mimi refuses to let you come back to work yet. She said we'd talk in two days."

His eyes widened. "Two days? I can't lie here for two days!"

"You can and you will, Peter Mitchell." Her hands snapped to her hips. "You almost got yourself killed yesterday. Besides," she said, touching his arm, "you're too weak to even stand."

He sighed. No matter how he rebelled against it, Diana was right. Maybe lying here would give him time to plan his next move? If he had to go back to the base, he needed time to get a uniform before Mimi had all the rescued recombinants' uniforms destroyed. It was a last resort, but it was all he had left if Mimi wouldn't agree to send her underground into Ballese.

"How was Sarge's first day back?"

"He survived," Diana answered. "He said it was hard. Especially seeing personnel ship out for Karaba and Ku'Tal. He said he could tell which ones weren't coming back. He sounded very sad."

Sarge had always cared deeply about his units. Maybe too much. He spent way too much time teaching Peter how to read the sensor grid. On Ku'Tal, Sarge shadowed him, making sure he got through patrols. Most of the time, Sarge tried to hide his concern, but it usually bled through his military facade. Peter admired him. A lot.

He yawned. "I'm glad he got through it. He's got a tough job."

Diana reached out and stroked his hair. "You get some sleep. I'll check on you later."

"I love you," he whispered.

She kissed him on the lips again. "I love you, too, Peter." She left him drifting off to sleep in the warm sunlight.

AN HOUR LATER, Peter struggled out of bed. He hugged the wall until he reached the latrine where he combed his hair and brushed his teeth. He slid a shirt out of the closet and struggled to ease the sleeves over his sore, aching arms.

The room tilted violently and he grabbed hold of the closet door to steady himself. In a moment, the vertigo passed, leaving behind nausea. He scowled at the eggs and toast, turning away to grab his boots.

He shoved his feet into his boots but couldn't fasten them. Finally, he dragged his foot up onto the bed and fastened the chukkas. When the boot felt secure, he slid it off the bed and fastened the other boot strap.

He moved with slow, uncertain steps to the door and staggered into the dark hallway. He made it as far as the back door when Mimi stopped him, a small tray of dirty dishes balanced in her left hand.

"Going somewhere, Peter?"

Peter turned. He studied her petite frame draped in black silk for a moment and then nodded. "Out for a little fresh air."

"Or a city shuttle ride?"

"City shuttle ride?" he asked with a frown.

"I've seen that look on your face before. Last time I saw it, David brought you back in pieces."

Peter leaned against the wall and stared at his feet. "I'm no good here, Mimi. All I do is break things." He shook his head. "I just don't fit in."

Mimi slid her arm around his shoulders and hugged him. "Of course, you fit in, Peter! You think my other employees don't break dishes?"

"Just me," he said with a sigh.

Mimi tilted her tray forward. Dishes and glasses rolled off, crashing to the floor.

Startled, Peter jerked back, watching the shards of glass and plates scatter. His mouth gaped as he stared at her.

"As I said, you're not the only one who breaks dishes, Peter. Besides that, I didn't hire you to wash dishes. I hired you so you could familiarize yourself with the entire kitchen first. After that, I planned to help you learn about the business side of this restaurant. From there, I hoped to put you in an educational certification program where you could earn the certificate of your choice."

He grinned. A certification program! Like the kind Diana and David had taken.

"See," she said with a laugh, "I knew you'd like that. Your aura's calming already. Now, help me pick up this mess."

Unsteadily, he bent down and helped her stack the glass and plate shards onto the tray until they'd gathered all the bits of dishes littering the floor.

"Still need to go out, Peter?" she asked, setting the tray down on the nearby counter.

"That depends," he answered.

Her lips tightened into a thin line. "On what?"

"On whether you'll help me get to Karaba. Maybe from there, I can get Sting out?"

Mimi grabbed his shoulders and shook him. "Listen to me and listen very carefully. Only the military can get to Ballese now. Do you understand what I'm telling you?"

He started to reply, but she shook him again.

"Listen to what I'm saying, Peter. Only. The. Military. I'd give anything in this world to help you find your friend, but it's beyond what I can do. And if you keep this up, you're going to get yourself killed. John Stingley wanted you to live and he'd be furious at you for throwing it away like this."

He gazed at her, his lower lip quivering. "I can't live with the guilt, Mimi," he said in a soft voice. "And I can't stand knowing he's there being tortured."

Mimi held him. "I know it hurts. I had a brother on Ballese. And you look so much like him that it's scary. To this day, I've never known what happened to him. Don't think I didn't want to go in there, I did. Thank God there were people here to hold me back. Even his wife, Connie, told me it was suicide. I know the pain you're going through, Peter, but you can't help Sting now. You can't."

She let him go.

He stared at the broken dishes on Mimi's tray. So many pieces and no way to put them back together again. Like the life he was living.

"I feel so helpless," he said in a hushed voice.

"It's not your fault," said Mimi. "Someday, you'll realize that."

Peter sighed. That day was a long way off. Right now, he only felt miserable.

"Come on, Peter, go back to your room and lie down before you fall down. I give you my word that if I can ever send a shuttle into Ballese, you'll be aboard it. All right?"

"Yes...thanks, Mimi," he answered and plodded with shaky steps back to his room.

6

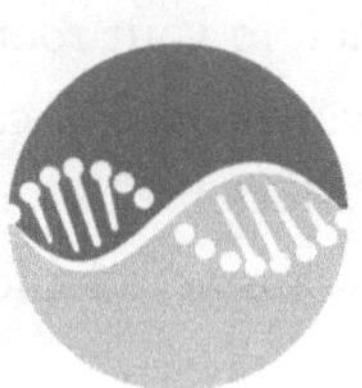

ALL WEEK, David waited for his orders to be cut. D'Angelo wanted an answer about the recon mission, too, but he refused to give the man an answer until he knew the status of the other recon teams. He'd risked his life once already. He wouldn't do it again without a damned good reason.

Before opening the day's email, David checked in with Diana. She smiled back at him from the virtual display as he drank his morning coffee.

"How's Peter today? Back on his feet?"

Diana shook her head. "Mimi won't let him come back to work until tomorrow. He stayed in bed today. I brought him breakfast, but he didn't seem interested in eating it."

"He's lucky he wasn't killed, Diana. What was he thinking to go down in there?"

"That everyone here can be trusted. He didn't even know he was in any danger, David. I talked to him about that. He had no idea. He's got a lot to learn. He doesn't understand the concept of lying unless it's a life-or-death situation."

David sighed. "A hard way to learn a lesson in human nature, but it could have been worse—so much worse. Just keep an eye on him."

"I will, David," she answered.

"I've gotta go now. Have dinner with me Friday? At End of the Line?" David asked.

"I'll make the reservation," she answered.

"Talk to you later," he replied and cleared the connection.

He entered the appointment into his calendar and then started on his paperwork again. He worked all morning and then stopped for lunch.

After Mess, he planted himself in front of his virtual display again, but this time, to do research. He began a slow, thorough search through UCOE archives, hoping to locate progress reports on the other two recon missions D'Angelo mentioned.

Hours of perusing files turned up nothing.

Finally, he sent email to Captain Anderson with a request for status based on D'Angelo's request that he sign onto the next mission. Anderson had coordinated the recon missions and every enlisted soldier involved in a mission was entitled to obtain additional information. Part of the UCOE code and David was grateful.

The response came in less than an hour. He poked the virtual screen with his forefinger and a long message scrolled onto his screen.

Anderson outlined the first recon mission that left the station a month ago. A captain, whose name David didn't recognize, accompanied by eight recombinants and one field sergeant left the Civilization base approximately thirty-nine days ago. Only one status broadcast had ever made it home from Ballese—a garbled request that after augmentation, revealed it was a request to invoke Naharra rules.

David shuddered.

Why would a recon team order another nuclear strike on an entire planet? Nuking Naharra had been a horrendous decision, one that would haunt Earth for generations.

Ballese was still a battleground between UCOE forces and the Antarans. Had there been sufficient provocation? Had enough time to gather the amount of information required to make such a heinous recommendation?

What new kind of Antaran threat lurked on Ballese, the sight of a destroyed Earth colony where thousands died? It was empty. Desolate. Laden with ghosts of the dead and what could have been.

Uneasy, he skipped to the bottom of the message for the mission's status.

One word: *unknown*.

As of eight days ago, all the personnel on that first recon mission were listed as MIA. Missing in action.

Anderson's next message arrived shortly after, describing the second recon mission that left thirteen days ago. Anderson had received two messages from recon team two, but they hadn't been heard from in four days. UCOE feared the worst.

And with good reason, he decided.

That was good enough for him. D'Angelo was on a suicide mission and he wanted no part of it.

ALL WEEK, he checked on the second recon mission, hoping that contact would be reestablished, but the mission team had simply stopped transmitting. He distracted himself with his quest to clear out the mounds of paperwork remaining on his desk. After a quick bite in the mess hall, David returned to his office. Same old weak black coffee and over-cooked pasta. He smiled. Some things never changed. He settled back in his chair and continued reading his backlog of email.

A deafening explosion ripped through the station.

Darkness engulfed him as he was thrown from his chair. His desk slid sideways and smashed into the far wall.

The station pitched and yawed, finally rolling onto its side, and then bobbing back again.

David slammed into the wall then back against the remnants of his desk, picture frames and ceiling falling around him. His shattered computer sputtered with smoke.

In seconds, the red haze of emergency lighting filled his office, followed by the insistent whine of the klaxon.

He struggled to extricate himself from the debris as the station pitched again, pinning him against the far wall.

A hail of broken furniture rained down on him, sliver of portal pressed against his face. He strained to turn his head to protect his face and assess the damage to the station from the portal.

A long trail of debris floated into space where the aft wing of the four-pronged station had been. A chill raked his spine and he squeezed his eyes closed.

Dear God...all those recombinants!

Huge chunks of the base had been gouged out of the station's midsection. He had to get out of here. The station couldn't survive that much damage.

The comm sputtered to life, echoing ominously in the silence. The air was hot with the scent of smoke and burnt electronics. A fine patina of dust clung to his clothes and made his skin itch. He covered his mouth, his throat burning.

"Attention all personnel, please move quickly and orderly to the landing bays for immediate planetside evacuation. Repeat, please move quickly and orderly to the landing bays for immediate planetside evacuation."

The message echoed through his jumbled office as he tried to gain his footing.

Quickly and orderly. They had it half right anyway.

Stabilizers groaned, trying to kick in and level the station as David finally struggled up from the floor.

Pain sliced across his shoulder and into his elbow as he reached the door. The auto-open proximity sensor was dead, so he struggled in the smoky haze to throw the override lever. It clicked uselessly.

"Hull breaches in sections C-18, A-4, C-23. Sealing these

sections in thirty seconds. You have thirty seconds to evacuate. Repeat. You have thirty seconds to evacuate."

The count droned hollowly through the room. David glanced at his door. C-20.

Dammit, they were sealing sections almost next door to him!

He had to get off this floor now.

The room seemed to close in around him, dust and smoke clinging to his hair and clothes. He couldn't breathe. The klaxon's warble throbbed through his chest. He gasped for air.

Frantic, he pounded the lever as the station rocked again, nearly knocking him to the floor. Finally, he grabbed part of his desk chair that lay broken on its side and slammed it against the door.

Again and again, he pummeled the door until it gave way.

He flung the chair aside and staggered into the hazy, red-washed corridor.

The long, smoky hallway loomed at a violent angle as the station rolled onto its side again.

David smashed against the wall, sending sharp pain through his right arm again.

Damn! He'd reinjured it.

Wincing, he hugged the wall as the stabilizers strained to keep the station upright. There was nothing to hold onto, not even a door handle.

"Hull breaches in sections A-3, A-2, and C-19. Sealing these sections in thirty seconds. You have thirty seconds to evacuate. Repeat. You have thirty seconds to evacuate."

The counting rose above the rumbling of the bobbing station until finally, the hallway leveled out again.

Fighting against the pain in his arm, David scrambled to his feet and ran down the hallway toward the nearest access stairwell. He was several decks above the landing bay.

Where was the access stairwell!

"Hull breach in section C-20. Sealing this section in fifteen seconds. You have fifteen seconds to evacuate. Repeat, you have fifteen seconds to evacuate."

"Hey, what happened to thirty seconds!" he shouted.

His chest pounded as each number burned through his chest.

Ahead, in the dim lighting he saw the access stairwell — beginning a slow fade beneath a bulkhead.

"Hull breach in section C-20. Sealing this section in ten seconds. You have ten seconds to evacuate. Repeat. You have ten seconds to evacuate."

"No!" he shouted, pumping his legs.

"Eight...seven...six..."

With every pained step, a light fixture above his head exploded in a shower of sparks and composite.

Sparks rained down as David flung himself under the bulkhead.

He skidded to a stop against the access stairwell door. With his left hand, he grabbed the door release lever and pulled himself up. The lever responded and the door opened. David plunged down the narrow flight of red-washed stairs.

Dust swirled in the red haze as he propelled himself down the stairs, two and three at a time.

Was there enough time to get aboard a shuttle before this thing disintegrated?

Every thirty seconds, the evacuation message resonated through the emptying station that felt more like a buoy bobbing in a hurricane than a training base.

Stabilizers were failing.

Any moment, the station could go belly up, forcing all sections to seal to prevent the frame from buckling and imploding.

Once more, the station tilted. David slammed into the stairs railing and pitched over it, but his grip on the rungs remained. He clung to the railing, pulling himself against it when he felt the stabilizers rumble into action.

The station sling-shot backward, overcompensating, and then

tilted again. The walls groaned, the stairwell shifting into a upside down vertical gallery.

Screams filled the expanse as people fell over railings, plunging into the swirls of red darkness.

David held on until the stabilizers righted the station again. He knew it couldn't keep recovering.

Unfolding himself from the railing, he careened down the stairs toward the landing bay.

When he finally reached the bottom of the stairs, a throng of frenzied people crammed into the landing bay where transports and shuttles waited.

David fought to keep on his feet and not be trampled as the crowd surged toward a transport that had landed.

Fear soured the air. Blaring voices blended into a steady roar as he fought for his place in line.

The station rumbled again as the lower-level stabilizers engaged.

Another transport arrived, swallowing another chunk of the crowd, and dropping out of the bay.

He felt the station shifting beneath his feet and he prayed it would stay together long enough to get the rest of these people off base.

Two more transports arrived and shrieking people clawed at the opening door to get inside. He looked around. The bay was emptying. Maybe they'd all get off the base in time?

The crowd shifted forward, carrying him with it. The open transport door loomed.

The station trembled.

David reached for the door.

It slid shut with a hiss.

Dammit! He'd been four places shy of getting aboard.

The transport lurched forward and disappeared into the darkness.

Another shock rippled through the station, knocking the remaining personnel to the bay floor.

The red line pressed against David's face and he fought not to be smothered as people trampled across his legs and stepped on his back. He crawled through the tangle of people until he struggled to his feet.

Rising in the darkness was another transport. And a shuttle.

"Hull breach in landing bay. Sealing this section in fifteen seconds. You have fifteen seconds to evacuate. Repeat, you have fifteen seconds to evacuate."

This was it. He had to get aboard now or be sealed in this tomb.

"Thirteen...twelve...eleven..."

People flung themselves at the transports, but David ran headlong for the shuttle.

His body slammed into the side as he kicked at the door. With his left hand, he pounded the doors until finally, the hatch opened. He threw himself inside, several others pouring in behind him.

Clawing through the knot of frenzied personnel, he flung himself into a seat and jerked the restraint harness into place. He closed his eyes and prayed to feel that nauseating drop through atmosphere.

Two seconds later, the door closed and the shuttle dropped like a stone into the darkness of space. His stomach rolled into a taut, cold ball and he held his breath.

From the portal, he watched the outer bulkheads seal the landing bay, trapping anyone left behind.

The drop into atmosphere smashed him into his seat, the restraint harness keeping him from being crushed against the shuttle floor. The pain in his arm crept back slowly, as finally, the realization set in. He shuddered.

Antarans had attacked the station orbiting Civilization.

7

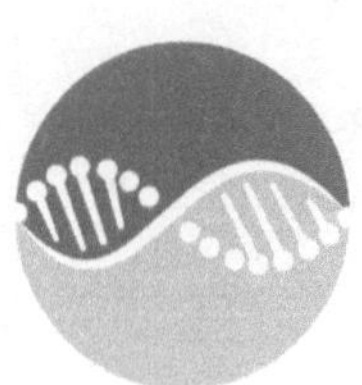

WHEN THE SHOUTING in the restaurant began, Peter rushed out of his room to see what had happened.

Mimi, dressed in black pants and a sparkly black tunic rushed through the room, carrying a stack of white tablecloths. Her servers, dressed in their burgundy tunics and black pants, moved tables out of the room's center. Near the window, Diana gathered pillows from the floors and stacked them in the corners. He hurried over to her.

"Diana, what's going on?"

She turned to him, her face wet with tears and her hands trembling.

"The station was attacked. It's critical, Peter." Her voice was raspy.

"Attacked? By Antaran forces?"

With a shiver, he remembered the biodrones with their spiked talons and how they eviscerated soldiers in seconds.

She shrugged. "There's been no confirmation yet. But people are trapped all through the station and no one can get to them." She sucked in a breath of air.

At last, he understood. Sarge. His stomach clenched. "Where's Sarge?"

She shook her head and the tears welled. She turned away for a moment and wiped her eyes.

"No one's heard a word. There are more casualties than the hospital can handle, so Mimi offered to take some of the overflow here. We're trying to get ready."

"What can I do?" he asked.

"We need to clear the floor and rearrange the tables." Diana pointed to the pillows strewn across the floor.

Sarge always hated sitting on these pillows, preferring the straight-backed chairs in the restaurant's contemporary section. His eyes misted. Sarge was a good guy. He hoped he was okay.

He took Diana's hand and squeezed gently. "He'll be okay, Diana," Peter said softly. "He will. If he can survive Ku'Tal, then he'll survive this, too."

"I hope you're right, Peter."

Peter gave her a comforting hug and then moved toward the pillows, yanking them from the floors. Quickly, he and Diana cleared away the remaining pillows and started scuttling chairs over to a side section of the restaurant. When all the chairs were stowed, he and Diana shifted the tables into rows.

To become makeshift beds.

He watched two men carry boxes of bed linens into the room. There were four boxes in all and the men set them on the nearest table. Mimi descended on the boxes, she and her servers quickly creating beds out of the tables.

Seeing the rows of tables with the faded white linens reminded Peter of the Recombinant Development Center, the rows of cots with recombinants lying wrapped in white restraining jackets. He fought down the memory and went to help Mimi with the tables.

"Thanks, Peter," she said and spread a sheet across the nearest table.

"You're welcome," he answered and gathered an armful of blankets and pillows from the nearest box. Then he followed behind her, laying a folded blanket at the foot and a small pillow at the head. "Any word on Sergeant Temple?"

Mimi glanced over at Diana and shook her head. "No one knows anything about how bad the injuries are. I did hear that the station lost an entire wing. Recombinants barracks. No word on other casualties."

He winced in horror. A whole wing?

That was most of the recombinants aboard the station. How many weeks had those poor recombinants gotten? He'd gotten a whole year, but this group never even got the chance to live.

In a short time, the wail of ambulances echoed outside the restaurant. UCOE soldiers carried in personnel on stretchers and Mimi directed them to tables. At first, Peter hung back from the soldiers, but when he heard the moans of the injured station personnel, he went to the nearest table. He laid a hand against a woman's forehead. Her clothes were torn and her arms and legs were bloodied.

"It's okay," he said to her. "We'll take good care of you. Just relax, you're safe."

He smoothed the hair from her eyes and moved to the next casualty. The man was starting to thrash against the crude splints on his broken legs. He pressed gently against the man's arms, keeping him still.

"You're safe now. You're on Civilization, so don't worry. You're safe." He spoke the mantra over and over to the man in soothing tones until his thrashing stopped.

Peter worked through every patient in the row, calming them and keeping them quiet so they wouldn't reinjure themselves.

Mimi touched his shoulder, grinning.

"Peter, keep talking to them. You're doing a great job. There's a doctor and a few medics that survived the base attack. They're setting up triage here." She patted his hand. "Must be that true purple aura of yours."

His smile hollowed. He didn't believe in Mimi's auras anymore.

From one of the beds, a blood-spattered hand reached out to him. He took hold, noting the young man's rank: a field sergeant. The young sergeant trembled, pain hovering in his glassy brown eyes. His dark hair was plastered to his face. The field sergeant looked younger than Peter which startled him.

"My folks warned me not to come out here," said the young man with a groan.

"You'll be fine," said Peter. He loosened the field sergeant's now-ragged collar.

The young man moaned and clutched Peter's hand tighter. "I'm never going to see them again, am I?"

Peter unbuttoned the young man's uniform shirt to survey the damage. A wound bled at his abdomen. Apply pressure to a bleeding wound. He remembered reading that somewhere. He pressed his left hand against the wound until the young man winced.

"Stay with me until the medics arrive," said Peter, his gaze catching the young man's frightened stare. "I'll keep the pressure steady until a medic arrives. Give me your word, sergeant."

"You-you have it."

Peter kept applying pressure, slowing the bleeding. "Where are you from?" he asked, trying to distract the young man.

"Mars colony," the sergeant answered in a thin, raspy voice.

"Mars? I've never been there. Tell me about it."

The young man talked about his home world in a weak voice, taking some of his attention away from the pain in his gut. Peter listened in amazement, marveling at Mars' red peaks and the bubbles —biospheres, the sergeant had called them—where people lived.

"What do you miss most about Mars, Sergeant?" Peter asked, increasing his pressure to the wound.

The young man was silent for a moment. "My folks," he said finally.

So many generations, Peter thought. All those years of life overwhelmed him.

At last, the doctor and two medics reached the restaurant. Peter caught the doctor's attention, motioning frantically to her. She hurried over, her short dark hair gleaming in the bright lights.

"I've been applying pressure to the wound, but it's still bleeding."

The doctor set her equipment bag on the table and from it, she retrieved a small laser suture. Like the one they'd used to close Peter's shoulder wound last year. How far he'd come in one year.

She plugged the wound with some sort of expanding bandage and then closed the gaping wound carefully, removing the bandage as she closed. As she began to bandage it, Peter patted the sergeant on the shoulder.

"Say hello to your folks for me," he said and moved into the next row.

He started to bend down when he recognized the man in the first row. His heart hammered against his chest, his stomach twisting.

Lieutenant D'Angelo!

His gaze fell to the gold swirls on his shoulder. D'Angelo was a captain now.

Would the officer recognize him?

A gash down the side of D'Angelo's face glittered red and his left arm hung at an odd angle. Broken.

D'Angelo mumbled, his hands clawing at the sheet. Cautiously, Peter stepped toward him.

"...got to get someone in there...find out before—too late...before too late...Temple? Temple!"

"Did you see Sergeant Temple?" Peter asked.

D'Angelo mumbled something that Peter couldn't hear.

"Sir, did you see Sergeant Temple?" he repeated.

"Temple, report to my office," D'Angelo snapped. "I want your decision now."

"Did the Sarge reach a shuttle, sir? Please, it's very important."

D'Angelo began to babble about recombinants and some recon

mission. Sighing, Peter stepped back. D'Angelo couldn't provide any information about Sergeant Temple. Diana would have to wait for the news.

———

FOR HOURS, Peter, Diana, and Mimi assisted medics with patients, shifting them into ambulances or making them comfortable for the night. It was getting late when the restaurant's com chimed. Mimi, her steps slowed with exhaustion, hurried to the entryway, and answered the call.

"Diana!" she shouted and hurried into the dining room. "David's calling for you."

Grinning, Diana raced down the rows of patients toward the entryway. Peter followed. She slid into the chair and Sarge's bruised face appeared on the screen.

"David! We've been worried sick! Where are you? How are you?"

"Whoa, slow down, sis," he said in a weak, raspy voice. "I just got out of emergency. Messed up my arm a bit, but I'm fine. Can you and Peter pick me up?"

"We're on our way. Seeya in a few, David."

Diana cleared the call and then leaped up from the chair. Grabbing Peter's arm, she pulled him toward the door.

Mimi's skimmer sat out front and Diana climbed into the sleek craft. Peter slid in beside her as she pressed her palm against the lock to release the controls. She slid in the ignition card. With a quiver, the skimmer whispered in the midnight shimmer of heat as Diana turned it away from the restaurant. And punched the accelerator. The skimmer surged down a side street and onto a main thoroughfare.

SARGE SAT on a bench outside the hospital, training blues jacket draped across his bandaged arm. Diana slid the skimmer to a halt and clambered out, Peter behind her.

"Sarge! How are you?"

Diana hugged him. "Oh, David, I've been so worried!"

He smiled and held her tightly. "There were a few tense minutes there when I didn't think I'd make it past the bulkheads sealing up the place. It was close, Diana. Really close."

"Sarge, was it an Antaran attack?"

"Help me up," said Sarge, nodding Peter over.

He was stalling. He carried bad news.

Peter slid his arm around Sarge's waist and let him lean on his shoulder to stand. He wasn't in much better shape than Sarge. They walked with slow steps toward the skimmer. Diana opened the skimmer door.

"How big of a force?" Peter asked. "An isolated attack or an advance scout for a major assault?"

Diana stared at Sarge with wide eyes. "He's right, isn't he, David? The Antarans have slipped past Karaba."

More Antaran lies, Peter thought with a scowl. At first, on Ku'Tal they told him they wanted a cease fire. Later, at the repository, they insisted that they only wanted to resurrect their dead.

All of it had been a lie.

Sarge rubbed his face with his good hand. "Everyone's pretty tight-lipped about the attack, but I've been able to piece together a few facts." He gazed at Diana for a moment, his expression pained. "Yeah, Mitchell's right. They're digging in on Ku'Tal. In record numbers again. They've pushed past it to Farnas and Karaba— halfway to Civilization. And now, they've attacked this base. Civilization is a breath away from home system's outer edge."

"Can the base be repaired?" Peter asked.

Sarge sighed. "It'll take months or longer to repair what's left of that station—if it can be repaired."

"But we can't let them know it's disabled, Sarge," said Peter.

That would open Civilization up for the devastation of Ku'Tal or worse—Ballese.

With stiff movements, David slid into the back of the skimmer. Peter climbed in beside him as Diana hurried around to the driver's side and plopped into the seat. She turned around and leaned her chin on the back of the seat, her steady gaze encompassing Sarge then Peter. Peter saw her fear.

Civilization could be Antaris' next target.

"Mitchell's right," Sarge said finally. "Even if the station is crippled, we have to make it look operational. Otherwise, Civilization could be overrun. I've got to locate D'Angelo and find out what the brass is planning."

"He's at the restaurant," said Peter.

Sarge frowned.

"Mimi let the hospital setup a triage station there."

"How was D'Angelo, Mitchell?"

Peter shook his head. "Out of it. He kept babbling about you and some decision."

Sarge stiffened.

"What decision?" Diana asked, a wary glint in her gaze. Diana knew Sarge better than anyone.

"You might as well know that D'Angelo wants me as his field sergeant for a covert recon mission."

Diana didn't blink. "To where?"

He hesitated.

"Where, David?" she insisted, fear rising in her face.

"Ballese," he answered finally in a quiet voice.

Peter gaped at him. Ballese!

"David, you can't!" She slapped the seat with her hands. "You nearly died on Ku'Tal! You've only been back on base one week. One week! How do you get yourself into this much trouble in one week?"

"Take me with you, Sarge," Peter replied.

"You, Peter?" she asked, surprised. Her face paled and all she could do was shake her head.

"Yes. Me." He turned to Sarge. "I lived through Ku'Tal and you know I'm good with the sensor grid."

When he was still at the training base, Sarge worked with him for weeks on the grid until he could translate the Antarans' every shift and every bow echo.

"Peter...no..." Diana could barely get the words out.

"Besides," he said, charging ahead with his argument, "the base lost most of its recombinants. Pass me off as another recombinant, I don't care how! Just get me to Ballese." He grabbed hold of Sarge's good arm. "Sarge, please—before it's too late."

"Oh, no, you don't, Peter Mitchell!" Diana shouted, arms folded against the headrest, glaring at him.

"If I have to go on this mission to Ballese, Mitchell, trust me, I'll want you at my back." David turned his gaze to Diana, shaking his head. "I'm sorry, sis. If I have to go out there, I'll need him watching my flank."

Peter leaned back against the seat, filled with grim satisfaction. One step closer to Ballese. He couldn't look at Diana though. He couldn't bear the hurt look of betrayal in her eyes.

"What are you smiling about?" Sarge asked.

He looked up. To his surprise, Diana was smiling.

"I'm probably going to be the only shuttle pilot available to fly that recon mission."

"No way, Diana!" David shouted, his face flushing. "No way you're flying us into Ballese, you hear me?"

Peter felt a cold chill rake his heart.

"You may not have a choice, David."

She turned around and set the skimmer into motion.

THE SKIMMER SLID to a stop in front of the restaurant and Peter helped Sarge out of the vehicle. Sarge leaned against Peter's shoulder as they moved slowly up the steps and inside. Peter saw a familiar face haunting the kitchen doorway.

Ron Kraver, from the Ku'Tal safe house. He'd been running a safe house out there somewhere. He looked like he hadn't slept in days. If Ron was here in Civilization, then that had to mean that the Antaris Nation had gained more footing in the Taus system.

"What's Ron doing here?" Diana replied, exhaling sharply. "He's supposed to be running the new safe house on Karaba." Her frightened gaze caught Peter's and he nodded.

"Something's happened to the Karaban safe house," Peter said in a half-whisper.

When Sergeant Temple destroyed the munitions depot, the Antarans left Ku'Tal. After that, Diana began flying Ron and the others to Karaba to establish a safe house there. They hadn't gotten very far. No one expected the Antarans to return with an even larger force.

"Mitchell, take me to D'Angelo," said David, his voice growing weary. He needed rest.

"Talk to him tomorrow, Sarge," said Peter.

"Tonight, Mitchell."

"He's incoherent. Besides, you need to sleep."

Sarge protested, but Peter ignored him, leading him into the short hallway that led to his room. He opened the door and eased Sarge onto the bed. Diana was right behind him. She pulled off David's shoes and turned down the thick blue blanket while Peter helped him slide into bed.

"Where will you sleep, Mitchell?" Sarge asked finally.

Peter sighed. He hadn't slept in some time. Tonight would be no different.

"I'll make do, Sarge. There are lots of beds in the dining room now—and those fluffy pillows you hate to sit on. I'll be fine."

He slipped out of the room, allowing Diana a moment to talk to her brother alone. When he reached the kitchen, he found Ron Kraver sipping coffee and rapping his fingers against the stainless-steel countertop. His face was stubbled with two days of beard and his bleary, red-rimmed blue gaze told Peter the man hadn't slept in a while either.

Another insomniac to keep him company.

Peter sat down on a stool and picked up a burgundy coffee cup. He filled it from the nearby pot of coffee. "You look like you were part of the training base casualties," Peter said and took a sip of black Karaban coffee. Mimi only stocked the finest.

Ron looked up from his coffee and offered a faint smile. "I feel like I was. You look familiar to me."

Peter returned his smile. "I'm one of your success stories."

"A recombinant?" Ron asked, his voice soft.

"I was one of the last ones you got out of Ku'Tal before the Antarans pulled out."

At last, recognition filled Ron's eyes. "I remember you. The one Diana Temple was trying to get out. Mitchell, right?"

"Yes, Peter Mitchell."

Ron extended his hand and Peter shook it. "Good to see you still out of uniform and doing well."

"Thanks to you." Peter took another sip of his coffee.

Ron refilled his cup. "I've feared this day for a long time. The Taus system has always been unstable, but today, it fell apart at the seams. I don't know how we'll keep them from pushing through to Civilization."

"By figuring out how they're producing so many biodrones and shutting it down."

"That would mean a one-way trip to Ballese, Mitchell."

He'd heard that line before, yet he'd come back from Ku'Tal. He could come back from Ballese, too.

"Maybe, maybe not. I'm willing to find out."

Ron's smile deepened. "Me, too."

A shadow passed by the kitchen doorway. Peter glanced up from his coffee. Captain D'Angelo was on his feet and talking to Mimi. His face was animated, his voice intense. Peter listened closely.

"...You'd be doing UCOE a great service, Ms. Constantine. We have to act now. There isn't time to wait for repairs and new shuttles to be shipped out here."

"I'm certain we can arrange something. We'll discuss it tomorrow, Captain. For now, you rest."

D'Angelo moved unsteadily past the doorway and back to his makeshift bed. Peter turned and stared at Ron for a moment.

"What was that about?" Ron asked.

"Sounds like D'Angelo just made arrangements to borrow one of Mimi's shuttles."

"What for?"

"For a covert recon mission to Ballese," said Peter.

D'Angelo seemed more preoccupied than he ever remembered him. No, it was more than that. The man seemed almost obsessed.

Peter excused himself and carried his coffee into the dining room. He gathered a few pillows from the corner and propped them against the window. From here, he could see the skimmers racing across the river, leaving behind brightly colored wakes as if little bits of their souls trickled out behind them into the water.

He reached for his god symbol, but then remembered he'd taken it off. It seemed strange not to feel it against his neck.

Only when Sting was safe could he wear it again. Only when Sting was safe.

Diana saw him by the window and hurried over, a pillow in one hand, blanket in the other.

"Hey, lover," she said, dropping down beside him.

"Thought you'd gone home," he said, smiling at her.

"And leave you here like this? Never." She leaned over and kissed him.

She laid a pillow beside his and kicked off her shoes. He settled his body against hers and she snuggled against him, her arm stretched across his chest. He leaned over her, sipping her lips, his arms sliding around her. She returned his kisses as she pulled the blanket over them.

"Thanks for always being here for me," he whispered in her ear.

"And I always will because I love you, Peter."

He smiled. "I love you more. More than you'll ever know, Diana."

He laid his head against her chest and she wrapped her arms around him, but he couldn't close his eyes. He thought of Sting as the room fell quiet and he felt Diana's warm breath against his neck.

Somehow, he'd bring his best buddy home.

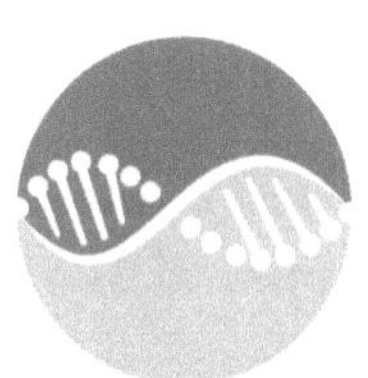

EARLY THE NEXT MORNING, David hobbled out of Mitchell's room and plodded toward the restaurant kitchen. He paused in the dining room for a moment. Only half a dozen patients remained in the table-bed triage unit. He'd heard the noise of them being shifted to the hospital during the night.

Returning to the kitchen, he found Mimi making coffee and scrambling eggs. The scent of browning butter, melting cheddar cheese, and brewing hot coffee made his stomach rumble.

"David, how are you feeling this morning?" Mimi asked. Her strawberry blonde hair swung loose at her neck. She wore a blue robe over Asian-styled blue satin pajamas.

"Much better, thanks," he answered. He stopped at the coffeemaker, grabbed a burgundy cup, and poured himself a cup of coffee. "Where'd Mitchell stay last night?"

She pointed toward the dining room and David poked his head out the doorway. Mitchell lay curled in a ball beside the window.

"He hasn't been asleep long. Two hours, maybe? Diana stayed with him most of the night though."

If he'd been feeling better, David would have insisted on Mitchell keeping his own bunk. Shaking his head, David sipped his coffee.

"Your captain made me an offer last night."

David frowned, turning around. "What do you mean?" D'Angelo didn't seem like the dealing sort—especially with civilians.

"He wants to make use of one of my shuttles for a while, until the base is repaired. The base is setting up operations in a warehouse near the shuttle port."

D'Angelo was going ahead with the recon mission, with or without UCOE support or approval. *Was* it a suicide mission?

"What did you tell him?" he asked, keeping his tone nonchalant.

"I told him we could probably make some sort of arrangement. Why?"

"Because I'm supposed to be his field sergeant on that trip."

Mimi laid down her spatula and set her pan off the heat. She wiped her hands on a plain white apron. "David," she said and moved toward him, "Just make sure that your captain's mockup isn't a one-way trip. Otherwise, he'll take all of you with him."

"Mockup?" David asked, raising an eyebrow. More of Mimi's new age babble?

"A mockup," she repeated, as if he should already know. "A picture he's created in his head of what he wants to happen. Or thinks will happen. Should happen. That man's mockup is screaming *one-way trip*, David. Just so you know."

Why would D'Angelo suddenly go kamikaze? Was it fear? Was it revenge? Or was this just more of Mimi's new age philosophies?

"D'Angelo wants to stop the production of Antaran biodrones," said David. "And I'm all for it."

"Your captain's aura is so far in front of his body, David—it's like he's ready to leave this world. Don't let that man take you with him."

David waved her away. D'Angelo wanted to stop this war just like every other soldier—and recombinant. Where did Mimi get this stuff?

"Somebody's got to go into Ballese and find out what's happening there," he said in a quiet voice. "Discover what those bastards are creating."

She cast a deep stare at him and it felt as if she was looking into his soul.

"David, I've been running my underground operation for a long time and I've learned more about the Antarans than I care to know. One thing I know for sure is that if you step into their territory, you may not leave it."

A chill snaked down David's spine and he stiffened.

What if he was captured like Stingley? What horrible things would they do to him? What had they already done to Stingley?

Nobody knew what the Antarans did on Ballese, nothing beyond the random trickle of horror stories from the destroyed UCOE colony. Maybe the reason they guarded Ballese so closely, closer than any of their other strongholds, was because it was their weakest point? When UCOE nuked Naharra in the hopes of destroying the Antarans, they overlooked Ballese. Naharra had barely been surveyed. Life there had been sparse at best, so nuking it somehow seemed humane compared to worlds like Ballese and Karaba.

But to destroy UCOE's famed jewel and the last hope that some of the colonists had somehow survived—hidden from the Antarans? Well, crushing that last thin hope was just too horrible to consider.

Something the Antaris Nation had counted on.

"Somebody's got to find out what they're doing out there, Mimi. All this time, we've left them alone to create more and more biodrones, build structures, weapons. Hell, they destroyed our colony there! If we don't do something soon, they'll be attacking our Pluto and Jupiter bases from newly acquired Civilization."

Civilization was the nearest planet in the Taus system, with Farnas and Karaba the next closest planets. Ku'Tal had been the outer edge of Taus since the colony on Ballese had been destroyed—and Naharra, the farthest planet in Taus from home system. Naharra had been a dark world for as long as he could remember.

Mimi was silent for a moment. Her eyes filled with tears. It was the first time David had ever seen her cry.

"I had a brother on Ballese, David. Orlando was a system-renowned geneticist, human and alien. Moved there from Io. His wife, Connie was a UCOE council member. She was preparing to leave Io and join him at the colony when the news came."

"I'm so sorry," said David in a hushed voice. He hadn't known anyone at the colony, but that event had haunted him these past seven years.

"Connie's my benefactor," she said, scraping fluffy eggs out of her pan and into a bowl. "She's the one funding my operations here. She and Orlando were appalled by the Council's earliest murmurings about recombinants. Connie voted against it, but the motion still carried. Orlando would be pleased with what Connie's doing."

David stepped over to Mimi and laid a hand against her shoulder. "I'm certain of it. But Mimi, we're coming back. I demand it."

Sniffling, Mimi patted his arm and turned back to her breakfast preparations.

David grabbed another coffee cup, filled it with hot, black coffee, and left her alone. With a coffee cup in each hand, he moved toward Mitchell's sleeping frame slumped against the pillows. After setting down the coffee beside him, he shook Mitchell until his eyes slid open.

"Sarge? What's the matter?" he asked, his voice sleepy but concerned.

"We need to talk," David said and handed him the coffee.

Mitchell drank slowly until the grogginess left his face and eyes.

"You've changed your mind, haven't you?" Mitchell asked.

Every part of his brain screamed yes, but he couldn't tell this troubled young man he couldn't go. Mitchell had so much to lose besides his life. If D'Angelo recognized him, Mitchell would be destroyed as a deserting recombinant. Or worse, returned to the program and sent back out there again. Nothing good awaited them on Ballese either. He was afraid that they *would* find Stingley—

tortured or worse—part of some horrible experiment. Sting and Mitchell had been best friends on the training base and Ku'Tal. He prayed that Mitchell wouldn't have to go through the pain of losing his best friend a second time.

David shook his head. "I should, but I can't. I can't deny you a shot at freeing Stingley. My other reason is selfish. I want you watching my back. You're the only one I trust."

Mitchell grinned. "When do we leave?"

"D'Angelo is coming back today to finalize an arrangement with Mimi. From there, the timetable will be quick, I'm sure. Polish your chukkas, Mitchell. We're shipping out again."

LATER IN THE DAY, D'Angelo arrived, his head bandaged. Mimi, Mitchell, and Diana cleaned the dining room, sanitizing tables and throwing out ruined linens. It would take several days to get everything inspected and ready for operation again. David was forbidden to help, so he sat in a booth with D'Angelo until Mimi could join them.

D'Angelo looked tired, his grey eyes glassy and intense.

"Glad to see you made it out of the station, sir."

D'Angelo nodded. "And you, Sergeant." He was silent for a moment. "Temple, I need your answer."

"About the recon mission? How will you have the personnel now?"

"We'll make do, Sergeant. I'll requisition more recombinants."

David gazed down at his hands, not wanting D'Angelo to see his disgust. D'Angelo requisitioned recombinants like pads of paper. "Most of the station's recombinants were lost, sir. It'll take weeks to requisition more." He hesitated. "Sir, are you opposed to civilian assistance?"

He made a sour face. "Civilians! Not on my shuttle, Sergeant."

"These are former military enlisteds, sir."

Mimi moved toward the booth. "I'm afraid they come with the shuttle, Captain. That's the deal."

D'Angelo's face flushed red and he gritted his teeth, thin lips tight with anger. "I can commandeer that shuttle, Ms. Constantine."

Mimi put her hands on her hips. "And I can blow the thing up. Look, Captain, I'm protecting my investment here. You want my shuttle? You agree to my terms. Kraver's former military. Served on Ku'Tal. Diana Temple flew shuttles in combat conditions."

A palpable silence hung over the table. Frowning, D'Angelo turned his angry gaze to Mimi.

"Either they answer to me or they stay behind," he said, his voice tight with anger.

David smiled.

"Agreed, Captain. How soon do you want her?"

Settling back against the booth, D'Angelo's tension began to fade. "In two days. I'll need to secure a military pilot and the necessary authorizations. After this attack on the base, it shouldn't take long. Should have lots of volunteers." He turned to David. "I'll send a courier over with a list of provisions and equipment we'll need."

"You can have everything delivered directly to the shuttle port, Captain," said Mimi.

With a nod, D'Angelo rose from the booth. David stood, too, and saluted. D'Angelo snapped a salute and hurried out of the restaurant.

So, that was it. They were going to Ballese. He feared that Ku'Tal would pale in comparison to the horrors that awaited them at the destroyed colony.

9

CIVILIZATION'S COLORED lights sparkled in the skimmer wakes as Peter sat on the riverbank, watching the blues and reds deepen to purple. The recon mission departed Civilization tomorrow morning. He had no idea who'd be boarding that shuttle tomorrow. It hurt his heart at the thought of Diana being their pilot. He desperately wanted her safe in Civilization, but with the attack on the base, maybe she was safer with them?

A skimmer rushed past, casting a frothy white wake behind it that glimmered with purple and green lights. What would Sting think of this place, he wondered? Would Sting adjust right away or stumble through Mimi's attempts to turn him into a citizen.

He sighed. Like him.

He lay back in the sand, staring at the indigo blackness that burgeoned with stars. Somewhere in those tangles of lights, Sting probably sat in some dark cell. He hoped.

It terrified him to think that his best buddy might already be dead.

"Hang on, Sting," he mumbled. "It won't be long now."

Peter closed his eyes, forcing himself back to those old datadump images his military headgear used to supply. From his sparse memory, he conjured up that familiar, black-haired woman in her blue dress, hugging him as he went off to war. He moved past her to the memories of his tour on Ku'Tal, the burnt, cloying smell of honey, the white-hot slash of talons against his flesh—the shrill whine of the sensor grid. He'd survived it once.

He'd endure it all again to get Sting out.

"Want some company?"

His eyes snapped open. Diana sat down beside him. She wore a thin, short-sleeved green blouse, khaki shorts, and heavy brown sandals.

"Of course," he answered with a smile, his arms enfolding her.

He was trembling. Her warmth pressed against his chest and arms and he held her tighter. She smelled of rain and vanilla, soft and comforting.

"Peter, you're risking everything, you know that, don't you? Your citizenship—your life. Us."

He kissed her cheek. "I have to, Diana. He'd have done it for me."

"What if D'Angelo figures out who you are?" Her eyes were wide, her voice shaky.

Smiling, he lifted her chin. "When you're a recombinant, there are no *what ifs*, Diana. There are only days passed and opportunities. I'm twenty-three and it's been six weeks since I escaped the military. RDC gave me a year's life expectancy, and I've already lived past that. It's more than I ever expected. It's enough."

Furious, Diana bolted up from the sand. "But it's not enough for me, Peter Mitchell! I love you and I say you deserve a long life. Not just cramming experiences into slivers of time but building them into something over a lifetime. Together. With me."

Peter rose from the sand. "But not at Sting's expense. I can't live with that." He shook his head. "I can't."

He turned away, back toward the river. Wind rose, blowing cool air across his body. He'd forgotten how good the wind felt against his face.

Her hands slid around his waist, caressing his chest. She laid her face against his back. "I know. I just don't want to lose you, okay? I want to spend the rest of my life with you."

He took her hands in his and pressed his cheek against her warm palms. "If you were the captive on Ballese, I'd take on every single biodrone and caregiver there to get you out." He kissed her hands. "I love you, Diana. And I want to spend my forever with you. I just hope that means a long lifetime, not weeks."

She turned him around, his face against hers, and kissed his lips. He kissed her frantically, stroking her neck and face. Entwining her rich brown hair around his fingers. Finally, he clasped her to his chest, the fear taking hold at last—the fear that he might never see her again. He clenched his eyes shut, fighting back a wave of sorrow.

"I just need to hold you for a little while," he said in a quiet, aching voice.

He dropped to his knees, his head against her stomach, arms around her legs, eyes squeezed shut. She held him a moment and then slid down beside him.

Cradling her in his trembling arms, he concentrated on the skimmers and the colored lights. Everything he'd ever dreamed of when he'd slipped past those datadumps was right here, in his arms. This very moment.

Why was it always so fleeting?

She said nothing. She held him until his shaking subsided. When the wave of fear had passed, he let her go. Smiling, he kissed her softly on the lips again.

"Take a transit ride with me through the city?"

She grinned at him and smoothed his light blond hair out of his eyes. "Anywhere you choose, I'll be right beside you."

He took her by the hand and they hurried away from the riverbank.

A transit platform was only a short distance away. They raced through the dark, quiet streets, past the boxy sandstone and rounded terracotta buildings, laughing. Peter let go of her hand when he reached the platform steps. He ran up the steps two at a time. He'd forgotten how alive the shuttle's backdraft made him feel.

He stood as close to the platform edge as he dared, almost leaning out. Diana stood beside him. He and Diana waited until the rattle of the approaching shuttle vibrated across the platform. It radiated through his feet and into his stomach. Peter took hold of her hand and together, they raised their arms high above their heads as the shuttle surged past, a burst of wind flowing across the platform.

Peter shouted as loud and as hard as he could, matching the roar of wind and shuttle. Diana's voice mixed with his, a raw, wild scream.

At last, the shuttle slipped past the platform and he stopped shouting. Diana fell silent. She leaned her face against his shoulder and he put his arms around her.

"Let's walk instead, Diana."

She nodded.

They left the platform behind, walking along Civilization's streets in a wash of purples, blues, and greens. The muggy heat held tight to the sidewalks, turning the colored lights misty. He didn't mind.

Finally, they ducked into the coolness of a pub with green plants hanging from the wooden rafters in a pale, yellowish wood. Throughout the square room with tall ceilings to trap the heat, small round tables dotted the cool, terracotta floor. The air smelled tart with ore and warm with sautéed onions, bright music playing. Diana took him to the red and green and black targets lining one dark corner and showed him how to play darts. He and Diana drank cold ale and threw darts until the pub closed.

As the pub emptied into the streets, Peter led her onto the river path that ended a few blocks from End of the Line. They walked beside the onyx swath of river the rest of the way, arm in arm.

When they finally reached the restaurant, Peter led her down the short hallway to his room.

IT WAS STILL night when his alarm bellowed in the stillness. He jerked up from the bed and stabbed at the clock until the wailing stopped. That sound reminded him of the sensor grid's alarm. It made his skin crawl.

He glanced over at Diana, but only a tangle of sheets lay beside him.

"Diana?" he whispered.

No movement filled the room. Only the ticking of the clock and the soft rasp of his breathing. He glanced over at the chair where Diana had draped her clothes. Gone. He surveyed the floor for her sandals, but they were gone, too.

A knock echoed through the room.

"Yes?" he answered, groggy.

"Peter, David wanted to make sure you were at the shuttle port by 4:30 sharp."

Peter glanced at the clock, 0348 A.M. He had time to dress and slam a few coffees before hitting the transit.

"I'll be out shortly."

He rose from the bed and stumbled into the latrine for a quick shower. He shaved in the shower and brushed his teeth. Drying off quickly, he slipped into a navy pair of trousers and a tan T-shirt. Pulling on his military-issue boots that felt so foreign now, Peter fastened them and hurried out of his room. After combing his wet hair into place, he slipped into the restaurant kitchen for some coffee.

Mimi stood by a counter, pouring coffee into two cups. Her strawberry blond hair was straight against the blowsy white shirt she wore. She wore black leggings and socks.

"God, Peter, you look so much like my brother standing there it's almost frightening."

Peter shrugged and reached for one of the cups. He vaguely remembered Mimi mention she had a brother or two and how much he looked like one of them. Maybe that's why she kept him around breaking dishes and all?

"Thank you," he said and took a big gulp of the black coffee.

"Sugar? Cream?" she asked, holding out a packet of sugar.

He made a sour face. "No, thank you."

"Diana told me to tell you she'd see you at the shuttle port," Mimi replied, opening the sugar packet. She poured it into her coffee and stirred it with a spoon. A generous draught of milk followed, muddying the dark coffee.

His face flushed and he nodded. Mimi knew Diana had stayed the night with him.

"She's your pilot, you know," Mimi added.

Peter sighed. "I was afraid that'd be the case." He took another big drink of coffee.

"D'Angelo couldn't find any combat pilots. They were all injured or killed in the attack on the base. He turned to the secondary list and Diana's name was at the top."

"There's no way I could stop her from flying this mission." He wouldn't even try.

Peter finished off his coffee and reached toward the pot to refill it. The warm liquid smelled of sunlight and campfires. He savored the scent for a moment then took another sip.

Mimi sighed. "If you're going, then she wants to be right there with you."

"Maybe that's best," he said.

He finished off the coffee, setting down the cup, and moved toward Mimi, squeezing her hand.

"Thank you for everything you've tried to do for me, Mimi. Whatever happens, I'll never forget your kindness."

"Take care of yourself out there, Peter Mitchell," she said, ruffling his hair. Her eyes were glassy, brimming with tears. She gripped both his hands in hers, closing her eyes a moment. "Don't lose that true purple, Peter. Not when you've fought so hard for it. Promise me."

He knew what she meant by true purple. Mimi's New-Age-speak about auras and chakras and other stuff had always intrigued him. Sarge scoffed at it, but Peter carried Diana's purple scarf against his heart through his entire tour on Ku-Tal. He came back changed forever. And Mimi insisted his lavender aura had deepened, moving closer to the true purple of a long life.

He hoped she was right.

Mimi turned abruptly toward the dining room. "Your room will be here waiting for you when you return." Her voice cracked.

Without turning around, she slipped into the dark dining room, leaving Peter standing in the glaring kitchen lights.

He took one last look at the place. He wanted to hold onto the image and remember the nights here with Diana. Nights when he'd lived like a citizen, even if he could never truly be one.

"See you soon, Mimi," he called to the darkness, but no one answered as he walked through the dining room.

Mimi's silhouette hung by the picture window that faced east. She stared out the window as if waiting to see their shuttle launch. He'd never seen Mimi that subdued. He hurried through the entryway to the front door. Mimi had unlocked it for him. He closed the heavy restaurant door and stood on the steps as the heat rushed up at him.

Without looking back, he ran down the steps toward the distant transit stop. Its curved silver tracts stretched out in all directions through the city, standing high above it. He raced onto the platform and pressed the glowing green summons button. In less than five minutes, a dusty silver transit shuttle hissed to a stop. He climbed aboard the bullet-shaped cabin and collapsed into a seat. There were two seats on each side of the cabin and a dozen rows or so. The windowed transit doors slid shut and the shuttle whisked him north toward the shuttle port.

It rose quickly in the distance, a silver and white bubble stark against the umber landscape and yellow sky.

When he arrived, he didn't go through the passenger terminal in the front with its three rows of double doors. He walked down the sidewalk, around the silver and glass port, and toward the cargo area where the shuttle would be docked. He'd been down here many times to pick up recombinants and take them back to End of the Line for Mimi.

He walked down a hot, dimly lit white corridor that ended in a maintenance station and a shuttle gate. Sarge, dressed in his green field sergeant's uniform, met him at the station.

"What took you so long, Mitchell?" Sarge asked with a wry smile.

He returned Sarge's smile but said nothing. Sarge's smile faded when he held out the familiar, dull green private's uniform Peter had once worn. This one had the name Thompson on the pocket. He motioned toward a room off the maintenance station.

"Put these on, Mitchell."

Peter inhaled sharply. To have to put that uniform on again...it was something he hoped he'd never have to do again.

"I can't pass you off as a civilian, Mitchell."

"But Sarge, I—"

"You see," said Sarge, "With you calling me *Sarge*, D'Angelo would get suspicious."

Peter hung his head. He was right. He had never called this man anything but Sarge.

"Don't worry, Mitchell," said Sarge, patting him on the shoulder. "Thompson passed away in the makeshift triage. Thanks to Mimi, UCOE doesn't have a record of Thompson's passing yet."

Finally, Peter sighed and took the uniform from Sarge's hands. For Sting, he told himself. For Sting.

He hurried into the dusty white storage room that had a square, grey metal table, and matching shelves on every wall. It smelled tart with chemicals and had a bright light above the shiny white floor that reflected the uniform's dull green back at him as he removed his boots.

Shucking off his tan T-shirt and dark pants, he quickly dressed in the awful recombinants' uniform. It felt cold and stiff against his skin as he put his boots back on and exited the room. Sarge looked him over a moment and then plopped a helmet on his head.

"Just in case, okay? At least until we've lifted off."

Peter nodded. He had no choice if he wanted to reach Ballese and find Sting.

"All right," said Sarge, steering him toward the shuttle gate. "Let's go."

Three other recombinants waited near the shuttle, plasma rifles slung over their shoulders. Sarge pulled a rifle from one of the storage bins and handed it to Peter.

The rifle felt heavy and unfamiliar. He wanted to drop it, remembering those nights of bitter cold, sloshing through half-frozen swamp water in search of biodrones. Fearing cascade mines and caregivers. He shifted the rifle onto one shoulder and let it dangle there. Sarge hung a lanyard with a small sensor grid around Peter's neck.

"Get reacquainted," he whispered and turned away.

If there was one piece of equipment he would never forget how to use, it was the sensor grid. It took him a long time to learn to read it, his frequent failures almost causing his entire unit to washout. He ran his hand over its smooth, flat black surface.

"Thanks, Sarge," he answered.

D'Angelo rose from a crate he'd been sitting on and both Sarge and Peter snapped to attention. That was one military instinct Peter hadn't lost yet either. Recombinants were sent back to RDC for not obeying orders—and that included saluting officers.

"Sergeant, who's the new private?" D'Angelo asked, scrutinizing Peter.

Sweat beaded across Peter's upper lip and forehead. He kept his gaze forward, not daring to look D'Angelo in the eye. Granted, thousands of recombinants had gone through the base over the last month or so. Maybe D'Angelo wouldn't remember him?

"This is Private Thompson, sir," Sarge replied. "He was released last night from the hospital, so I signed him out here, sir."

D'Angelo nodded. "Good work, Sergeant. An extra recombinant will come in handy. Carry on."

Peter and Sarge saluted again and D'Angelo walked away. A little rattled, Peter wiped the sweat from his face, hands shaking.

"You're fine, Mitchell," David whispered. "Everything's okay."

"For now," he answered, watching D'Angelo inspect the techs' work as they fitted the civilian shuttle with military accoutrements like Antaran bioshielding radar jamming equipment.

Sarge gripped his shoulders, squeezing. "Don't worry. Go sit with the other recombinants and get familiar with that grid again. I'm depending on you out there."

"All right, Sarge," Peter answered and shuffled over to where the three recombinants stood.

One recombinant was tall and thin, with short cropped, chestnut hair and brown eyes. He stared blankly at the activities. The other two recombinants were average height, one slightly shorter than Peter's six-foot frame. They were lean and muscled. The light brown-haired recombinant's face was hard and looked cruel, but the black-haired recombinant seemed more apathetic than angry.

"Where'd you come from?"

"Hospital," Peter answered.

The light brown-haired recombinant scowled at him. "You don't look sick to me."

Peter ignored the man's comments.

"You're not in our unit," snapped the tall recombinant.

"I am now," Peter said with a shrug.

The black-haired recombinant nodded at him. "I'm Private Langley."

"Thompson. Good to meet you."

Langley motioned toward the tall recombinant. "This here's Newlin and this is Tanner."

Tanner's eyes narrowed and he stepped toward Peter. "You're odd man out, Thompson. See, I'm point man, Langley's flank, and Newlin's backup. What are you going to do besides get in the way?"

Gritting his teeth, Peter gripped the sensor grid. He'd endured months and months of insults and beatings at Drake's hands when he was still in the military. He wouldn't take that again, especially from a younger recombinant. "I'll match my point skills with yours, Tanner. Best grid reader gets the job."

Tanner burst out laughing. "You think you're hot because you got good scores in the sims?"

"I think I'm hot because I did six months on Ku'Tal and lived to tell about it. When I achieved consciousness at RDC, they gave me a year at best and I'm past that."

A hush fell over the recombinants. "You were at Ku'Tal?" Newlin asked in a hoarse whisper.

Peter nodded. "For six long months."

"Is it like the sims?" Langley asked, pushing past Tanner. "The biodrones, I mean?"

"They're meaner and they'll kill you twice as fast. And there weren't any sims teaching us how to avoid cascade mines. Step on one and a ring of mines blows up around you and your closest friends."

Newlin and Langley seemed mesmerized by Peter's experience, but Tanner seemed annoyed by it. This guy and Drake must have been recycled out of the same xDNA sample, Peter thought with a groan.

Tanner settled back against the shuttle and fiddled with his plasma rifle while Newlin and Langley bombarded Peter with questions.

Peter settled in beside the two recombinants and told them about Ku'Tal. Just as he'd finished telling them about the depot, Diana hurried down the hallway toward the shuttle. Former military officer and Mimi's lead operative, Ron Kraver walked beside her, a tan field pack on his shoulders. Diana wore standard pilot's greys, a thick, drab olive jacket, and black chukkas. Her shiny brown hair was pulled back from her face with her grandmother's purple scarf.

He smiled. He'd know that scarf anywhere. He'd carried it against his heart all through his tour on Ku'Tal with the hope of returning it to her one day.

Her gaze met his and she smiled. He couldn't help but grin.

Tanner gawked at her. He rose from his chair and moved closer, his gaze encompassing her as she stepped past them toward the shuttle.

"What's the matter, Tanner?" said Peter with a hard look. "Haven't you ever seen a woman before?" He sighed, remembering Sting saying those very words to him once, but admiration was very different from leering.

Tanner glared at him and shuffled past toward the other recombinants. Peter plopped down on a work bench.

Had he changed that much?

Before Ku'Tal, he'd have never shot off his mouth to someone who might take his head off. Yet, here he stood, antagonizing a soldier he'd just met. He laid his head against the shuttle's hull and closed his eyes. Maybe he was just tired?

Shortly, someone shook his shoulder. He opened his eyes. Sarge.

"On your feet, private."

D'Angelo stood a few feet away, frowning. Peter jumped up from the work bench and snapped to attention.

"Sorry, Sarge."

"You're going to be sorry if I catch you sleeping again." Sarge cast a wary look at him. He pointed to a stack of crates. "Get these aboard, now!"

"Yes, Sarge," he answered and set down his rifle. Then he shuffled down to the crates to help the other recombinants load them into the hold.

THE SUN ROSE above the landing strips, the umber terrain arid and dusty as the techs announced that the refittings were complete. At Diana's insistence, she and the techs did a walkthrough of the new hardware and the shuttle's systems. She did test fires and system checks until the techs were groaning. Only when she was satisfied did Diana say the craft was ready for flight. Ron checked through all the equipment to make sure everything had been stowed.

"Good work, Ms. Temple. I feel confident this shuttle will reach Ballese intact." D'Angelo.

"I'll get us there in one piece, sir," she said with a nod. "And I'll get us out of there, too. You have my word on that."

D'Angelo smiled. "Ever flown combat drops before, Temple?"

"Just on Civilization," she answered.

She couldn't tell him she'd flown shuttles at Ku'Tal—as part of Mimi's underground operation.

D'Angelo turned to Sarge. "Assemble the troops, Sergeant."

"All right, men, fall in!" Sarge bellowed.

Peter and the others rushed to stand at attention, saluting D'Angelo. Ron Kraver slipped out of the shuttle and stood behind the recombinants, listening.

"At ease."

D'Angelo paced an invisible line, a hand to his left temple. Peter wondered how bad D'Angelo's injuries were from the base attack. Sarge stood stiff and waited for D'Angelo to address them. David held his right arm close to his body, as if protecting the still injured limb.

"This recon mission is taking us into Ballese," D'Angelo began. "Our objective is to locate the major Antaran facilities in operation on Ballese and ascertain their function. We will gather as much intel as we can about the size of their attack force and their munitions. I believe that this intel can help us win this war. Is that understood?"

"Yes, sir," Peter answered in a sharp tone, the other recombinants answering in unison.

"All right then. Climb aboard and strap in. We're lifting off in fifteen minutes. Dismissed."

After saluting, Peter and the other recombinants dispersed. Peter stopped Sarge as he moved toward the shuttle.

"Sarge, how long of a flight are we in for?"

"A good eighteen hours. We'll probably stop on Farnas or Karaba for a refuel."

Peter winced. That meant rations and sleeping in his restraint harness. He wondered how poor Diana would get through eighteen hours of flying. He felt guilty for keeping her up so late last night.

"Diana can't fly eighteen hours with no sleep!"

"Relax, Mitchell," said Sarge in a soft voice. "I'm certified in base-to-surface shuttle flight, so she won't have to fly the whole trip herself."

Peter nodded, satisfied with that.

Sarge motioned him toward the hold. "C'mon, Mitchell, get aboard." He grimaced. "Thompson."

Obeying, Peter retrieved his rifle and plunged inside the dark, narrow shuttle. Restraint harnesses lined both walls. Peter plopped down in the seat farthest from the cockpit and strapped into it. This was a luxury cruise compared to the stark military transports with their bare metal seats and bulky harnesses. Mimi's craft had been a civilian model. The padded seats and harnesses would certainly make the long trip more comfortable.

Three crates had been strapped to the far wall. Enough gear to make camp and stay alive until they'd surveyed Ballese. He leaned his head against the wall and closed his eyes.

Enough gear to help him find Sting.

10

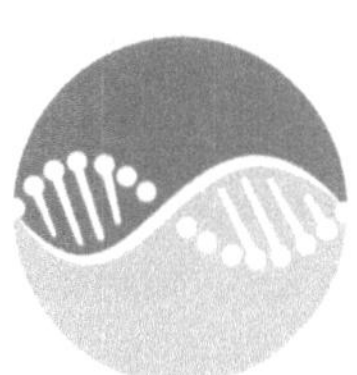

IN THIRTY MINUTES, the shuttle taxied out of the shuttle bay. It lurched down the runway, picking up speed until it lifted off and shot across the landscape.

Peter remembered hearing Diana talk about shuttle flights, something about slingshotting, orbits, and gravity wells. He didn't know enough to understand it all, but the shuttle would slingshot from planet to planet. Whatever that meant. He didn't exactly know what a slingshot was, but Diana said it was the fastest way to travel and the best way to conserve fuel.

All around Peter, the recombinants chattered and laughed, talking about their kill numbers and how many biodrones they'd have by the time they came back. Peter sighed. He'd been created with an abnormally low aggression level—he understood that now. He wasn't like other recombinants, lacking their aggressiveness and love for combat.

What else was he lacking?

It would have gotten him washed out if Sarge and Sting hadn't helped him. He hated the Antaran biodrones, all talons and tentacles, but the caregivers were so much worse. The biodrones did what they'd been programmed to do—kill. But the caregivers...every word they spoke was a lie. Saying anything they could to get him to go with them. On Ku'Tal, Peter never understood what they'd wanted from him and Sting back in that alien repository.

In some ways, Peter knew he had something in common with the Antaran biodrones, being the result of recombined and artificial DNA. Created to fight. UCOE owned the copyrights to his genetic combination, making him property of the government.

The Recombinant Defense Program coded its recombinants to crave combat, to hunger for a kill, but something went wrong with his genetic code. Making him different than the others—so different.

A mistake in his xDNA? Some traits not switched on? Something in his brain turned off by military hardware he didn't know about? He'd heard about the latest recombinants having other hardware in their heads beyond MRCs. Did he have those things too? Something else UCOE never told him.

Regardless, he was an anomaly. Unlike him, these three recombinants were prime examples of the Recombinant Defense Program's ideal soldier. He was an example of recombinants they washed out.

Recycling soldiers from donated and redesigned DNA had stopped masses of citizens from dying—and it kept the war with the Antaris Nation far from Earth. Sitting here now, with plasma rifle and sensor grid in hand, Civilization seemed like a datadump image again. Like a beautiful dream he had one night after slipping past the datadumps. He'd learned to do that early on. He'd taught Sting how, too.

Had he really been there? Had he ever truly escaped the military?

In the back of the shuttle, Peter sat in silence while the other recombinants chattered and laughed. Up front, Diana's voice hung just above the shuttle's vibration as she talked to David and Ron Kraver who sat in the seat nearest the cockpit. Sarge seemed relaxed as he laughed with Diana, but Ron seemed tired. His eyelids drooped and he fought to stay in the conversation. D'Angelo sat in the navigator's chair, pensive and brooding. He'd completely detached himself from everyone in the shuttle. His hand rested against his forehead, rubbing his temple.

Sarge said the man had a bad head injury. *Maybe he wasn't well enough to take this trip?*

Peter fell asleep twice, but nightmares woke him. Newlin walked through the hold, passing out ration packets to the recombinants. He, at last, reached Peter and handed him a silvery packet. It was slightly larger than his hand and very thick.

"Hope you like spaghetti, Thompson."

"Yeah, thanks, Newlin."

Peter pressed the sensor pad on the bottom of the packet, activating the self-heating ration. When the ration packet radiated heat, Peter tore it open and tipped it to his mouth. The tomato sauce tasted powdery, some noodles mushy and others crunchy, but he choked it down. He'd gotten spoiled eating all his meals at Mimi's restaurant. He remembered a time when rations and mess hall food were all he knew.

How far he'd come in his first year of life.

"You don't have any coffee rations over there, do you?" Peter called to Newlin.

"Thompson, catch!" Sarge called from the cockpit.

Peter turned to see a black canister sailing toward him. He caught it. A thermos! He smiled. Mimi's slow-brewed Karaban coffee.

"Thanks, Sarge!" he called and unscrewed the lid. "Is it Karaban?"

"Yeah, so go easy on it."

Peter inhaled the rich coffee smell, savoring it before he poured himself a cup.

"Share the wealth, Thompson," Langley called.

"In a minute," he answered. He took his time with his cup of coffee, only passing the thermos when he'd finished.

WITH COFFEE IN HIS VEINS, Peter remained awake when they reached Farnas. Sarge clambered into the back of the shuttle and waited until someone rapped on the hatch before he released it.

"All right, men, fall in! Let's move it!"

Sarge hurried out into Farnas' tan and brown shuttle bay and waited for Peter and the other recombinants to hit the line. The hangar was old, dusty, and poorly lit, smelling of grain and livestock. Peter snapped to attention and waited for D'Angelo to address them. Ron sat on the hatch stairs and listened.

D'Angelo paced in front of Peter, more nervous than he ever remembered. The man seemed almost distracted.

"You were each chosen to play an important function on this recon team," D'Angelo began, still pacing back and forth. "One of our objectives is to identify the purpose of a large structure that long range scans have pinpointed near the Ballese colony ruins. And to assess the size of the enemy force. We will identify and record the structure's operations and then upload this data to Tactical. This shuttle has been fitted with the alien bioshielded jammer technology, so we should be able to land on Ballese undetected. Your sensor grids have been fitted with the same jammer technology, offering you some protection from being detected while you're wearing one."

Peter's thoughts rushed ahead, trying to figure out how he could slip out of D'Angelo's sight—and Sarge's—long enough to find Sting.

"Due to the attack on the base," D'Angelo continued, "there were no combat pilots available, so we're utilizing a civilian shuttle pilot and a former enlisted man. Diana Temple volunteered to fly us in and out and we're thankful to her for her courage. And to this man who will bravely provide onsite support and backup." He pointed to Ron sitting on the stairs. "You, sir, please stand and state your name."

Ron uneasily rose from the stairs, light brown hair wind-blown. "Ron Kraver, sir. Former weapons programmer. I spent a year on Ku'Tal."

D'Angelo smiled. Like he was pleased with Ron's credentials. "Where are you currently employed, Mr. Kraver?"

Ron sighed. "At the moment, I'm unemployed. Before the war, I was a virtual reality developer. In the gaming and entertainment industries."

With the safe houses on Ku'Tal and Karaba lost, Ron Kraver *was* technically unemployed, but Peter knew how valuable Mimi considered this man. She'd have another position for him when he returned from Ballese. Kraver got him off Ku'Tal, so Peter considered him a friend.

"Thank you very much, Mr. Kraver, for your bravery." D'Angelo kept up his pacing. "We'll land, operate, and depart from the colony ruins. Any questions?"

No one spoke.

"All right then. Dismissed. I'll expect you back here in ten minutes." He pointed a finger at Peter and the other recombinants. "But if any of you has ideas about escaping, forget them. I've given your ID scans to Farnas security, so all four of you are under constant surveillance. Any recombinant left behind will be shot on sight, so make sure you're not late. Dismissed."

Peter sucked in a breath of air and leaned against the shuttle hatch. He no longer had an ID chip in his neck, but he wasn't moving from this spot until they lifted off. He had too much to lose.

AFTER THE SHUTTLE refueled and rechecked and reprovisioned supplies, Peter and the other recombinants strapped into their seats. Ron returned to his seat near the cockpit. D'Angelo settled into the navigator's station again and absorbed himself in a series of charts and maps on his datapad. Sarge took the controls and Diana tilted back the co-pilot's chair. She was asleep in minutes, even despite Sarge's rocky takeoff and bumpy ride up through the atmosphere. She looked so soft and frail. He smiled at the memory of holding her in his arms only a few hours ago.

The shuttle shimmied, its hull growing uncomfortably warm, but

Sarge held onto it, launching the shuttle back on its course for Ballese. He moved up through orbits until the shuttle was flung out of Farnas' orbit. Karaba would be the next planet in the Taus system, an agricultural world.

They were moving closer and closer to its edge, where Ballese stood equidistant between UCOE and Antaris space. Where the ruins of the Ballese colony remained untouched and unburied, decimated over seven years ago. UCOE's forced had managed to keep Farnas and Karaba safe so far. Beyond Ballese was Naharra and the edge of known space. UCOE's first colony.

"Sarge, what's the plan when we land?" Peter called.

"Okay, everybody, listen up!" His voice crackled through the shuttle's com, startling the other recombinants. "The landing site UCOE intelligence chose is on the edge of the colony ruins. That area is totally blacked out and with our radar jamming equipment, the Antarans shouldn't be able to detect our ship. We'll make camp in the ruins where we'll strategize our next move. UCOE doesn't have any information to guide us once we land. Nobody even knows what remains of the colony structures. Efforts over the last seven years to make contact with possible survivors have failed. No human response or movement has ever been detected."

Peter planned to go on a little fact-finding mission of his own, scouting out the Antaran structures and searching for a glimpse of any recombinants or humans. On Ku'Tal, the Antarans had kept the recombinants they captured in the same place they produced their biodrones. For testing. The unidentified facility had to be a biodrone production and research facility. Where he hoped to find Sting.

He remembered the ghost echoes on his sensor grid after he'd located their biodrone production facility on Ku'Tal. He smiled. If he could get Sarge to recalibrate the grid to find recombinant IDs like he did on Ku'Tal, then the sensor grid could lead him right to Sting.

The hours slipped past slowly. D'Angelo fell asleep in his chair, leaving Sarge the only one awake in the cockpit. Even the other recombinants' banter had died down to murmurs. They were falling asleep, too.

"You awake up there, Sarge?"

"I'm awake, Thompson. How you doing back there?"

"I'm all right."

"You sure?"

"I'm fine, Sarge."

"I don't know what we're going to find when we land. No one's ever seen the ruins of Ballese. So many surveillance biodrones landed, but not one ever sent back images—or even sounds. Nobody knows what happened there. Except the other two recon teams that landed ahead of us."

All those scientists, farmers...scholars and families, Peter thought grimly, killed when Antarans overran the planet. And their families back home knew nothing about their fate.

"How far out are we?" he asked.

"About four hours. I'll wake Diana in about three. She can land on anything. My takeoffs are okay, but my landings stink."

He and Peter laughed.

AN HOUR OUTSIDE BALLESE, Sarge woke Diana. Groggy, she struggled to sit up. Peter released his restraint harness and retrieved the thermos from the sleeping recombinants. He laid it in Diana's lap and squeezed her hand.

"Thanks, Peter," she whispered, smiling at him.

He let go and moved back to his seat as Diana poured herself a cup of coffee. With a stretch, she rose to her feet and traded places with Sarge.

"We're about an hour out, Diana."

"Is our radar still clear?" she asked.

"We had some Antaran forces pass over us about two hours ago, but they never even saw us."

Diana glanced over at D'Angelo. "How long has he been asleep?"

"Quite a while," Sarge answered. "We'll wake him before we descend."

What would they descend into, Peter wondered? *Masses of writhing biodrones, talons ready to strike?*

He shuddered, closing his eyes to blot out the memories of Ku'Tal. He tried to think about other things, concentrate on what he'd do when he returned to Civilization. With Sting.

Sarge reached over and shook D'Angelo awake. D'Angelo coughed and shuffled about in his chair.

"Report, Sergeant," he said finally in a weary voice.

"We're about thirty-six minutes outside Ballese, sir," said Sarge.

Diana turned her gaze to the groggy man. "I'm about to start my re-entry sequence, sir."

"Carry on, Ms. Temple. Sergeant, inform the men."

"Attention, unit," Sarge announced.

Recombinants stirred. Ron Kraver stretched and sat up.

"We are beginning our re-entry sequence. In approximately forty-nine minutes, we'll touch down on Ballese, so pay attention and be ready to move on my order. We have no idea what we'll face down there. So be ready. Is that clear? Acknowledge your orders."

"Yes, Sarge," answered voices from the dark shuttle.

"Yes, Sarge," Peter added.

"Check your restraint harnesses and hang on. This will be a rough landing. The landing strips and other facilities have eroded significantly over seven years and we have no idea what might be waiting for us either."

Without warning, the shuttle dropped. Re-entry.

Peter gripped the edge of his seat. The force threw him forward, but the harness held onto him. He grabbed hold of the straps, his hands aching. He clenched his teeth, his stomach knotting.

"Hang on," Diana shouted. "We're almost through!"

The moments trickled by, the straps cutting into his skin.

Abruptly, the drag stopped and the shuttle leveled off.

He was thrown backward into his seat as the craft began to slow. He tried to catch a glimpse of what lay out there through a small porthole behind him, but only blackness swirled past the cockpit. The shuttle lurched again and again, losing its momentum, until it abruptly came to a hard stop.

Stunned, he sat there for a moment.

They were on Ballese. He was finally here.

"Okay, people, move out," Sarge announced. "Get that equipment unloaded quickly and quietly. Radar's clear for now, but be ready with grids and rifles."

Peter didn't have to be told twice. He tore at his harness, pulling himself to his feet. Grabbing his plasma rifle, he slung it over his shoulder and hurried to the hatch door.

It slid open into silent indigo darkness.

He grabbed a crate and carried it outside.

Brisk, cool air buffeted his face, smelling clean like rain and crisp, like a long drink of cold water. He nearly lost his balance and fell out of the shuttle, but he quickly regained his footing and stepped outside.

Grassy landscapes stretched around him in the darkness, the tall, wispy blades looking almost silver. He was mesmerized by the short, squat trees creating lacy violet canopies around them, the corkscrew-like tree branches swirled almost a deep purple against the indigo sky. The half-moon shaped leaves were a soft, silvery lavender. Dotting the landscape as far as he could see, coffee cup-shaped luminescent orange blossoms hung on nearby brush, giving off an eerie glow.

Ahead, beyond the blossoms, the ruins of Earth's first colony here loomed, dark and broken. Like they'd been empty for a lifetime. Buildings had crumbled, streets littered with stone and twisted metal, umber soil, silvery green grass, and tangles of yellow vines reclaiming the dark, burned out spaces.

Over twelve thousand people in the advance colonization party landed here with more than that waiting to join them. Everyone in the advance party perished.

Including Mimi's brother.

He swallowed hard at the stillness. Was this the fate that awaited Civilization, too?

He set down the crate and raced back into the shuttle for another one.

"Hand me another one, Newlin," he called.

Newlin appeared in the threshold, handing down another crate.

Peter took it, setting it on the ground beside the others. Newlin jumped down and together, he and Peter passed the last crate from the shuttle to the ground.

By this time, D'Angelo had disembarked and was using a tan, handheld scanner to assess the ruins.

"We aren't going to camp in there, are we?" Langley asked.

Peter half-expected to see ghosts from the ruins walk past the luminous orange blossoms.

"Fall in," Sarge announced in a harsh whisper.

Peter snapped to attention beside the other recombinants.

Sarge pointed toward the crates. "We're going into the ruins to make camp, so get those crates moving. Tanner, Langley, you take one crate between you. Newlin, Mitchell, take the second. Kraver and I will take the third. Langley, you're on flank. Newlin, you're on point. Move it!"

D'Angelo scrutinized Peter for a moment.

"I'm Thompson, Sarge," said Peter, giving Sarge a wary look.

"Right, sorry, Thompson. Ku'Tal stays with me even now. Get moving!"

Peter gratefully slipped out from under D'Angelo's scrutiny.

Tanner grabbed hold of a crate, Langley picking up the other side. Peter and Newlin retrieved their crate, carrying it toward the scorch marks leading into the ruins. Langley and Tanner brought up the rear, sensor grids swinging from tan lanyards around their necks as they transported their crate.

Ron and Sarge walked in front of them, carrying a crate. Peter's rifle hung taut against his shoulder. He reached up and turned on his sensor grid, silencing the alarm. With his free hand, he scanned the perimeter, waiting for D'Angelo and Diana to take the lead.

D'Angelo finally stepped in front of Peter and Newlin, Diana a few paces behind him. Both carried rifles on their shoulders. Peter walked cautiously, fearing Antaran biodrones would slip down from the trees and gut them.

Not even a whisper of movement rippled across his grid. For that, he was thankful.

The dead city rose ahead, building after building gutted, facades blackened. On the edge of the buildings stood the shadow of a glass greenhouse with most of the windows shattered. Its roof had been splintered into fragments, revealing rows and rows of empty pots. The huge blue water reservoir tank was dry.

He strained to gaze beyond the ruins, surprised to see a dark lake beyond the colony.

Diana lagged behind D'Angelo, her slowed pace moving her closer and closer to Peter until she walked almost beside him. She reached out a hand to him in the darkness. He let the sensor grid fall against his chest and took hold of her hand.

"We'll make it out of here, Diana," he whispered.

She squeezed his hand. "Civilization seems so far away," she whispered.

It was a lifetime away. If they ran into trouble, there was no backup. They could meet the same fate as the colonists had seven years ago. And those two other recon teams that had gone dark.

D'Angelo chose a hollowed-out structure in the middle of the ruins to make camp. Only one side of the brick-like building had been compromised, a deep, jagged fissure cutting across one dark wall. A hole tall enough and wide enough for a single person to step through gaped on the wall opposite the fissure. The inner wall had been partially peeled back to its wooden frame. A strange yellowish grained wood.

A potential weak spot, Peter surmised.

In the stagnant, uneasy darkness, they unpacked bedrolls and foodstuffs. They stacked food and ammunition into a sheltered far corner, while Diana flicked on an ion lantern. Pale yellow light barely affected the building's heavy darkness hanging over them. Besides, they didn't want the light to be seen by Antarans. This was enough light to see their hands in front of their faces.

Peter huddled in a crevice, rifle gripped in his hands, and gazed out into the night. He continued to monitor his sensor grid, not wanting any surprises. What lay beyond that black lake?

Somewhere nearby, according to D'Angelo, there was a biodrone production facility, but how did the missing recombinants fit into Antaran biodrone production? He remembered the caregivers' DNA repository and how they claimed that they needed the recombinant technology to reanimate their people. What was it they'd said to him? Something about searching for recombinants with a combination of loyalty and complexity.

What did that even mean? Most likely another lie.

Peter turned away from the crevice to find D'Angelo staring at him.

"You look familiar, private," he said.

A chill shivered through Peter.

"Sir?"

"I've seen you somewhere before," he said, his voice tight and his eyes wary. D'Angelo squinted, studying him.

"Thompson!" Sarge snapped. "Stop annoying the captain and see to that weapon of yours! It's filthy. I'm putting you on report. Next time, take better care of your equipment."

Peter slipped past D'Angelo, grateful to be out of his line of sight. Still, he felt sick inside. D'Angelo was already chewing on a sliver of memory with his face on it. It would be only a matter of time before the man remembered him.

What then?

From one of the crates, Sarge gathered a handful of radar jammers and with Ron's help, he set them around the camp perimeter in a redundant circuit.

D'Angelo moved toward the far corner of the room where he'd placed his bedroll. He collapsed onto it, rubbing his head.

"Sergeant, set up a sentry schedule. I want round-the-clock watches, so those bastards don't sneak up on us."

"Yes, sir," Sarge answered and turned back to Peter and the other recombinants. "Langley, Tanner, you take the first two-hour watch. Thompson, you and I will take the second. Newlin, you take the third watch solo. That should get us to morning."

Ron stepped over to Sarge. "David, I can stand watch with Newlin."

Sarge smiled at him and laid a hand on his shoulder. "Tomorrow, okay? You're dead on your feet. Get some rest tonight."

"Okay, tomorrow," said Ron. "Maybe by then this place of the dead won't feel quite so haunted." He walked over to an empty, dark spot against the wall and laid out a bedroll.

Langley and Tanner moved toward the front of the building's shell and took up watch positions around the gaping holes. Each recombinant held a sensor grid and a rifle.

Peter gathered his bedroll and pitched it as close to Diana's as he could. Exhausted, he lay down on his stomach, one hand on his rifle, and closed his eyes. He reached out in the darkness to her and his fingers closed around her hand. He smiled when he felt her lips press against his palm.

11

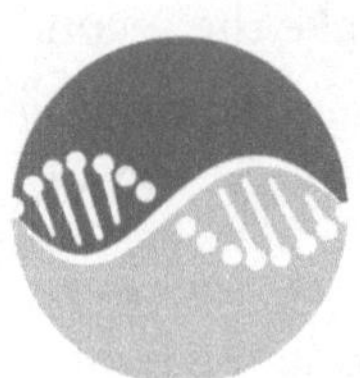

IN TWO HOURS, someone shook Peter's shoulder.

"No, let him go! Let him go!"

"Mitchell," Sarge whispered, "It's me, Sarge. Wake up. It's okay."

His eyes snapped open and he stared wide-eyed at Sarge.

"Sting?"

Sighing, Sarge shook his head. "Sorry, Mitchell. Come on, snap out of it. We're on watch now."

At last, the haze of the nightmare lifted and the man shaking him let go of Sting's features, taking on Sarge's face.

"Give me a minute, please, Sarge," said Peter, his gaze falling from Sarge's face.

Sarge ruffled his hair. "Sure, kid."

He rose from the blackened floor and moved to a hole in the wall. He cradled his plasma rifle in his arms and turned on his grid, scanning.

Peter inhaled sharply and held his breath for a moment or two until the shaking passed. Then he picked up his rifle and his sensor grid and hurried to join Sarge on watch.

Sarge was silent for some time until Peter broke the silence.

"Do you think D'Angelo has figured out who I am?" Peter asked in a whisper.

"Not yet, but I'm afraid he will before we lift off." Sarge said and sighed. "Blast it, I never should have taken you on this mission. It was too risky. I'm so sorry."

"Either way, I'd have found a way here, Sarge."

Sarge laughed. "I have no doubt about that." His face turned somber. "But honestly, do you really think you can find Sting in this expanse?"

"I don't know," said Peter, shaking his head. "But I'll do everything I can to try."

"Peter, you have my word that if I can help you at all, I will. If there's any way to free Sting, I'll assist."

Smiling, he reached out and slapped Peter on the shoulder, but there was pain in Sarge's eyes. Sarge had been there when Sting left with the Antarans. Sarge understood his grief.

He appreciated Sarge's kindness. He meant well, but Peter knew Sarge would also be there to stop him from doing anything not officially sanctioned by D'Angelo. He'd wait though. When Newlin took the third watch, he'd slip out of the building and do a little searching on his own. It was Sting's only chance.

He waited out the two-hour shift. At the end, Sarge was dead on his feet. He dragged himself away from the wall.

"Time to get Newlin to spell us," Sarge muttered.

Peter steered Sarge over to his bedroll. "I'll wake him, Sarge. Get some sleep."

Almost incoherent, Sarge nodded and fell onto his bedroll. He was asleep in moments. Peter quickly shook Newlin awake.

"Newlin, you're on in five."

Newlin nodded, muttered something Peter didn't catch, and sat up. While the man fumbled for his rifle and grid, Peter hurried toward the wall. He slipped over the side and hurried across the dark, empty paved street to the next row of buildings. Four streets were laid out in a grid pattern, uniform and orderly, making it easy to get his bearings even if he didn't recognize any of the destroyed structures. But based on his grid as he scanned the ruins, he could be near the lake shore in five minutes.

He sidestepped broken bits of stone, decaying black tarps, and rusty metal rods as he weaved his way through the rubble. Every time he passed a building, he caught a glimpse of that onyx lake gleaming in the open spaces.

Until he saw the god symbol!

Tucked away in a tiny room off a small white building with a high roof, stood several god symbols. A crossed T, the five-pointed star, a nine-pointed star, a moon and star, a flower, and the half black and half white circle he'd worn hung on the walls. They were each a foot tall.

And there were others that he'd never seen before!

All of them hung on the walls of the long, narrow room with all its benches and a tall wooden stand at the front of the space. It was bathed in velvety darkness, but somehow illuminated with an orange sheen from the foliage that filtered through the breaks and cracks in the walls. And ceiling.

So many god symbols! *What was this place? Could he get his soul back here?*

He reached out a shaking hand to the half white and half black circle. The god symbol that Sting had given him.

He reached up to his neck, forgetting it wasn't there.

Within these walls, he felt a presence. A quiet peace that calmed him somehow as he crept through the space. When he reached the stand in the front, he stood behind it, feeling hollow, but somehow drawn to this spot. He didn't know how to work it though. How to activate the god symbols. How to reclaim his soul.

As a recombinant, he knew he didn't belong in this citizen's place, but something here felt familiar.

Connected.

That's when he felt something raised under his feet. He bent down. A trap door!

With quiet, careful movements, he opened the door, finding steps winding away into thick, total darkness.

Something thrummed through him. A rhythmic hum, like a computer or a machine, drawing him down those dark stairs. He grabbed a glow stick out of his pocket and snapped the base until it glowed gold. With slow movements, he crept down the stairs. Down deep under this small space where the god symbols hung.

Finally, it opened into a pitch-black hallway, long and narrow. Eerily quiet.

He moved forward, slow, careful steps.

Blue lights flipped on above him, revealing a massive metal door ahead. At least it looked like metal. An icy blue and silver hue, cold to the touch. The metal surface lined the walls now and covered the floor, causing his boots to tick softly across the metal.

When he reached the door, a panel beside it opened, revealing black metal indentations. Shaped like a human hand.

What was this place? Was it connected to the god symbols? Did it lead to the better place that citizens always talked about? The place where they kept souls?

A green light surged across the indentations and a computer voice spoke in the silence.

"Welcome, Dr. Constantine. Please submit a genetic scan to access the lab."

Peter frowned. *Dr. Constantine? Was this Mimi's brother's lab?*

Again, the computer voice spoke about a genetic scan.

Peter reached out and laid his hand inside the indentation.

Green lights flashed, grid lines rolling down his fingers, across his hand, and up his arm. In moments, his entire body was flooded with the blue grid lines.

Something pricked his finger.

He tried to jerk his hand back but couldn't.

"Who are you?" he snapped. "Let go of me!"

For another long minute, the scan persisted until finally, everything went dark. And his hand was free. He pulled it back, rubbing his index finger as a sharp throbbing pain pulsed into his wrist.

"Welcome, Dr. Constantine," said the computer voice. "It has been two point nine years since your last visit."

Two point nine years? He'd only achieved consciousness a year ago. Three years was a lifetime! What did it mean?

Metal rasped against metal as the thick, massive door slid open.

Wide-eyed, Peter stepped inside. The door slid shut behind him.

Panicked, he turned, clawing at the door until he noticed the hand indentation on the wall to his right. Chest pounding, he pressed his hand to it and the door rumbled open again. He pulled his hand back and a minute or two later, the door closed again.

His breath slowed and he exhaled a sharp breath. He wasn't trapped.

He turned away from the door to look at the room and he gaped at it.

The cavernous space was unlike anything he'd ever seen before. The walls pulsed with multi-colored lights through channels and grids that covered all three walls. Like printed computer circuits.

He walked toward a rounded hunk of metal pulsing green in the center of the room. Strange symbols gleamed in the walls and glowed across the rounded metal. It was a language he didn't know. The symbols were fluid swirls and curves, flowing together in a diagonal pattern, curving around the metal plate and throughout the room.

The air smelled gritty and dry. And old. So very old that it made his nose burn and his eyes water.

As he reached the metal plate, its center lit blue and a clear cover slid open. A silvery purplish disk, reminding him of a gear with glowing lights and swirls of metal and a clear glittery material on one side. It was about six inches across, its surface polished and shiny.

When he reached toward it, the green light with its grid lines whirred to life, rolling across his body. *Another scan?*

It finished and winked out.

Again, Peter reached toward the strange object and slid it free of the compartment. It lit up on all sides, pulsing with life as he held it up to his face. The rhythmic thrumming was familiar somehow. Comforting. Like he'd held this thing before.

It clung to his hand when he tried to put it back. So, he put it in his pocket. He would take it to Mimi. Maybe she'd know what it was? Since this must have been her brother's lab.

Overhead, all the lights winked out, the entire chamber going dark. He held out the glow stick and moved back toward the door. Off to the right was a small desk and chair, surrounded by computers and lab equipment. Jars and containers and instruments along the adjacent wall. The air smelled warm and sharp, like overheated equipment, like the equipment in the library sometimes smelled like on the training base.

He glanced over at the desk, finding a small grey datapad and an orange hardbound notebook. He took them. Both were small enough to fit in his uniform jacket pockets that were wide and deep.

Turning away, he hurried over to the indentation and pressed his right hand into it. The metal door groaned open and he rushed out into the metal hallway that led toward the winding stairs.

Back at the trap door, Peter climbed out and closed it. Dr. Constantine hid this place well. Or maybe the man had just found it? It didn't look Antaran or like UCOE built it.

It was something else.

Something much, much older. He shuddered. Lifetimes older.

He put the glow stick in his pocket and hurried outside into the night, heading toward the lakeshore.

Behind him glittered the faint orange of those strange blossoms he'd seen by the shuttle. They dotted the landscape like little campfires, making it look as if someone still lived here. He walked beyond the blossoms, toward the thick forest that fanned out around the lake.

At last, he reached the landing. A long wooden dock, broken in several places, jutted into the blackness. The lake was a polished slab of onyx that rippled with small waves lapping at the rocky shoreline.

A faint trace of mildew hung in the air. Peter couldn't see across to the other side of the lake.

But he knew the Antaran facility was out there somewhere. Beyond this lake. And somewhere inside that facility was Sting.

He scanned the shoreline for a boat, finding several still docked there as if someone was coming back for them. He navigated around the ruptures in the dock until he reached the nearest boat. A black rowboat. Untying the mooring on the small boat, he set out across the lake, sensor grid around his neck, rifle in his lap.

The air turned chilly over the lake and Peter shivered as he traversed the slick blackness. He eased the oars gently into the water, moving steadily but quietly. Not even a chirp came from his grid. The air scrubbed his cheeks with cold and his teeth began to chatter, his fingers numbing, but he kept rowing. The boat began to hum against the water, almost singsonging. It reminded him of the images from his datadump headgear, the black-haired woman in the blue dress humming to him from a past he'd never known.

The military tried to substitute images for memories, trying to build their recombinants into more dedicated soldiers. All it had done to Peter was make him ache for his own memories. Regardless of what happened to him now, he had his own memories of Diana and the short time he'd spent on Civilization. But he'd sold his soul when he let Sting take his place here. He had to right that terrible wrong.

At last, shadowy shapes formed on the far side of the lake. The horizon was still dark, sunrise several hours away. As he drifted closer, he scanned a large facility stretched across the landscape. From here, it looked similar to the Antaran biodrone production facility on Ku'Tal, but much larger.

He checked the time. One hour left of Newlin's watch.

Peter steered the boat into a tree-lined cove and tied it off. He climbed over the side and crept through the trees toward the facility. When he was close enough to observe, he watched the building for signs of life.

After a few minutes, his grid began to chirp. He reached down and turned off the sound, but he watched the grid intently. Bow echoes slithered across the grid.

Biodrones.

He turned his gaze back to the facility. It was a tall, square structure with two or three smaller structures connected to it. Like the spokes of a wheel. The domed roof seemed to be made of that same green glass that had enclosed the biodrone facility on Ku'Tal. The two smaller structures flanked the large building on each side.

He recoiled at the sight of biodrones slithering out of the left-hand structure. He counted them...four, five, six...eight biodrones in all.

His mouth went dry. He held his breath as he watched the bow echoes flit across his grid.

For a long while, he watched the biodrones. Finally, he checked his watch. Newlin would go off watch in less than twenty minutes. He had to go back. He hurried back to the boat, climbed inside it, and crouched low as he cycled the oars through the water as softly as he could row.

His rowing picked up speed when he reached the center of the lake. By the time he reached the shores of the ruins, his muscles burned and ached from exertion. He crawled out of the boat and slipped back through the ruins, waiting until he saw Newlin leave his post.

He raced across the street and climbed through the opening. Newlin never heard him slip into his bedroll. He was asleep the moment his head hit the pallet.

TEN MINUTES LATER, Sarge called them to formation. It was still dark outside. Exhausted, Peter dragged himself out of his bedroll and stood at attention. D'Angelo stood before them.

"Scanning reports indicate the large facility across the lake is an Antaran biodrone production facility—as expected. And probably other activities we don't yet know about. We will break up into three-person teams to gather data on the site. The pilot and I will remain behind with the shuttle to run more scans and gather data on the ruins."

Diana frowned. She was not happy about being grounded on this operation.

"Sergeant, assemble the teams."

"All right," Sarge began in an assertive tone. "We'll take a north and south route around the lake where we'll observe the facility until 1200 hours. Then we'll return to camp. Tanner, you're in charge of your unit. You head south. I'll take the second unit and we'll head north. Newlin, Langley, you're with Tanner. Thompson, Kraver, you're with me."

Peter's face fell. He'd hoped to go out with the other recombinants and slip away. That's probably why Sarge made the team assignments the way he did.

"I want light field kits and full ammo complements. Grids on silent. Is that clear?"

"Yes, Sarge," they announced.

"You've got ten minutes to assemble your gear. Get to it."

Peter hurried to the ammunition crate and filled a small field pack with plasma rounds and some plasma grenades. Then he retrieved several rations and a canteen, packing them into his pack. When he was finished, he hurried over to Sarge.

"Ready, Sarge," he said.

"Good. Kraver's just finishing his pack." He squinted suspiciously at Peter. "You look dead. How much sleep did you get?"

Sarge was trying to trick him into an answer. "As much as you did, Sarge," he answered.

In a few minutes, Kraver emerged from the back of the room, field pack on his shoulders, rifle in hand.

"Ready, Kraver?" asked Sarge.

Ron nodded. "As much as I'll ever be."

Sarge motioned Tanner's team into the ruins. They scrambled

over the wall and into the streets beneath a grey sky. He gripped his rifle in both hands and turned to Peter and Ron.

"Let's go."

Leading the way, Sarge rushed across the street and into the next gutted building. The walls were a soft sky blue, crumbling onto a wood floor made from that yellow grained wood again. The remains of furniture scattered through the room rotted and fell apart.

Ron followed, Peter behind him. Sarge scanned the building. Empty.

"Mitchell, you run flank. I'll run point and Ron will run backup."

"Right, Sarge," Peter answered, pleased to be running flank.

"Exactly what are we looking for?" Ron asked, crouching on the floor of the burned-out building.

Sarge pointed to the hazy structure across the lake. It looked like a gear with four wings or spokes intersecting the huge green dome. The building was made from a slick white material that Peter didn't recognize.

"Answers to what they're doing inside that facility." Sarge tapped his sensor grid. "Make sure your grid's on silent mode."

Quickly, Peter and Ron flicked a switch on their grids, silencing them.

"Sarge, how about setting my grid to scan MRCs?" Peter asked in a quiet voice.

Sarge glared at him. "And then you take off alone to find Sting? Forget it."

Peter sighed.

Once more, Sarge scanned. Then he rushed out of the broken building and across to the next one, Ron then Peter following. White walls and whitewashed floors, stained black and filled with holes. From massive amounts of plasma fire, Peter realized.

They slipped through building by building until the lake shore loomed ahead. A line of brush and those purplish frilly trees wound around the lake, so they kept to the brush, scanning constantly.

Peter watched intently for any sign of a bow echo, but so far, the grid was clear. They skirted the lake for several minutes until a ripple spilled across Peter's grid.

"I've got movement," he whispered and they halted.

Something stirred ahead. Peter waited, his heart pounding, his grip tightening on his rifle until finally the bow echo faded into the distance.

"We're clear," he replied.

Sarge visibly relaxed. "Good work, Mitchell."

They waited a moment and then kept moving around the lake.

Several minutes later, they reached the edge of the facility. Sarge pulled out a surveillance scanner from his pack and panned the horizon.

"Got movement in the northeastern quadrant, Sarge," Peter whispered.

"Confirmed," said Ron. "Looks like eight or nine echoes."

Peter watched a series of Antaran biodrones moving toward the facility from the east. Then to his amazement, a dozen humans trailed behind. All looked about the same age, mostly young men, some of them female. They had to be recombinants. Behind them, another eight or nine biodrones followed.

"Prisoners," Peter hissed.

Sarge recorded the footage on the surveillance scanner.

Peter studied the figures, but at this distance, he couldn't make them out.

"Sarge, let me see them, please."

Sarge handed off the scanner and Peter scrutinized each figure, hoping to see Sting among them. The recombinants disappeared into the facility, but shortly, they appeared again in a pen on top of the facility. Several other recombinants joined them. They all still wore their UCOE uniforms.

Maybe Sting was still alive after all?

"What do you see, Mitchell?"

"There's a pen on top of the building. There are lots of recombinants inside."

The pen hung on the edge of that green domed structure. Suddenly, a piece fit together.

Peter fell back on his haunches with a horrible revelation. The DNA repository had been under that green dome on Ku'Tal. If this dome was the repository here, then that meant the Antarans were using recombinant's DNA in their biodrone production.

They didn't want UCOE technology to save their people. They wanted it to infiltrate Earth's military and dismantle it from the inside.

"Sarge...we're in big trouble."

Wide-eyed, Sarge stared at him. "What is it, Mitchell?"

Peter let the scanner sink against his side. He grabbed hold of Sarge's arm. "Do you remember the DNA repository? For the survival of their species?"

Sarge thought for a moment and then nodded. "Under the dome."

"Yeah, under the dome. They're housing the captured recombinants near this dome. What does that tell you?"

"That recombinants are being used in their genetic experiments." He answered.

"To produce more intelligent biodrones?" Ron offered.

Peter shook his head. "No! To produce biodrones that *look* like recombinants."

A palpable silence held them as the realization hit them like cold steel. Dread gripped Peter's stomach.

Was it already too late to save Sting?

"Sarge..." Peter couldn't voice the horrible solution to the problem.

Sarge's face was grim in the predawn greyness. "We'll have to destroy the facility. And recommend that the planet be treated under Naharra rules."

Peter shivered. *What did that mean?* He remembered someone saying Naharra was destroyed by UCOE to prevent the Antaris spread. Would they destroy another planet?

"The colonists are gone and probably most of the recombinants are lost. There's nothing here to save."

Yes, there is, Peter wanted to shout. *Sting's still out there!*

He had to know what happened to him. He had to know. He wouldn't leave Sting here like this.

The caregivers had been very interested in him on Ku'Tal. He knew now that had been an elaborate ploy to trick him aboard their ship. They could have taken a dozen other recombinants at any time off the battlefields. No, they had a purpose in mind for Peter, but something in Sting allowed his best buddy to go in his place. Because of that, he knew there was still a chance he'd be able to rescue Sting.

"Do we report back, Sarge, or wait until 1200?"

"We'll observe them as long as we can," said Sarge. He held out his hand for the scanner and Peter handed it off.

In silence, they scanned the facility, monitoring how long the recombinants remained in the pen. By 1100, the recombinants were still in the pens. Sarge put away the scanner.

"All right, let's get back to camp. D'Angelo will want to hear all about this."

With rifle cradled in his right arm and sensor grid in his left, Sarge led the way south back toward the lake. Ron held tight to his rifle and fell in behind Sarge, while Peter scanned the flank for any surprises.

12

D'ANGELO PACED THE DARK BUILDING, his hand to his head. He mumbled to himself and Diana felt uneasy. His level of distraction had deepened. She wondered about the head injury he'd sustained. Doctors and medics had knitted his broken skull back together, but she wondered about his psyche.

"Those filthy caregivers are behind all of this," said D'Angelo, anger sharp in his voice.

"Caregivers, sir?" she asked.

His pacing increased. "Yes, Ms. Temple—caregivers. They've got to be stopped. Watched them eviscerate two field sergeants right before my eyes. All in the name of the Antaris Nation. Before Ku'Tal. On Naharra. My first tour as a field sergeant. I was next, but our troops overran their facility and they retreated. Too late for poor Williams and Mallory. To the Antarans, we're all a bunch of lab rats, free to be experimented on and discarded."

Diana frowned. That was rich coming from a man who fully supported the Recombinant Defense Program and treated recombinants like paper cups. Still, it was a horrifying story.

"That's horrible. I'm really sorry," said Diana.

He wrung his hands. "Mallory fell for their smooth talk about going home a hero. They promised they'd release us. They promised us no harm would come to us. They strung Mallory all over the floor right after that." He closed his eyes, his hands balling into fists. "Then they took poor Williams, screaming and kicking. They fed him to the biodrones." D'Angelo was trembling now. He went back to wringing his hands, the dry skin rasping and chafing.

"You went through a terrible ordeal."

"Where the hell is Temple? It's almost 1200 hours." D'Angelo paced again, his voice falling to mumbles again.

Diana held the plasma rifle closer to her chest. D'Angelo was losing his grip on sanity—what little he'd had before this mission had even started. They were in for a rough time. She feared for Peter now, terrified D'Angelo would snap out of his madness and remember him.

D'Angelo pulled out the mobile comm and Diana felt her tension draining. Good, he was reporting in to UCOE. That was a good sign that he still had a grip on reality—for now.

His voice hung low in the corner, his words barely audible as he gave UCOE a lengthy report on their situation.

She scanned the open, crumbling walls for movement. Nothing. Jammers were still in place. And flashing red.

Red? Was that right?

"Yes, sir," D'Angelo replied. "The facility is too large for a small force like ours to impact. Affirmative, colonel—too large."

Diana smiled. At last, he recognized how stupid this mission was —and dangerous. Maybe now, they'd get some real support from air or orbital cover, or another unit of soldiers?

"Yes, sir. I understand. I recommend that you launch orbital and surface strike forces immediately and invoke Naharra rules as soon as possible. Yes, sir, there's just nothing left here. It's the only way to stop them, sir. Seventy-two hours? Right. I understand. D'Angelo out."

D'Angelo slid his mobile back into his pocket, an unsettling grin perched on his lined face. Fear welled in the pit of her stomach.

What had he just done?

A soft chirp echoed through the hollow building. Diana looked around for the sound. *Was it malfunctioning equipment?*

Again, something chirped.

"Captain, what's that sound?"

D'Angelo rose from the floor and continued to pace, ignoring her.

The chirp began a staccato beat, long pauses between each note. A cold chill rushed over Diana when she saw D'Angelo's sensor grid lying on a crate. She ran toward it and swept it into her hand.

Three blips on the screen. *biodrones?*

Fear throbbed through her as she grabbed the man's sleeve.

"biodrones, sir, on the grid."

"Not now, Ms. Temple, there's planning to be done. Have to trap those caregivers somehow. Keep them busy until the strike force arrives."

The chirp sharpened, growing louder.

She jerked him to the ground and crouched in front of him as he kept mumbling about caregivers, oblivious to the danger approaching.

The steady beat of the grid intensified, turning into a sharp whine.

A fourth blip appeared on the screen. *Which direction?*

She swiveled the barrel of the plasma rifle, her back to the wall. D'Angelo sat on the ground, muttering.

Swallowing hard, she watched the wall for gold eyes and talons. Her only experience with biodrones had nearly killed her on Ku'Tal.

She shuddered at the memory of those things leaping at her from a shuttle's cargo hold as she'd waited to take off.

Her hands ached from clutching the rifle.

The grid pulse quickened, the pitch growing shriller with the passing seconds.

Something glinted off the wall to her left.

She turned.

Talons scraped over the edge. A biodrone burst through the opening!

Just like darts, she told herself and fired.

The biodrone shrieked, falling into a charred heap against the wall.

She turned again, the grid screaming now.

Three more blips pulsed.

Two biodrones careened over the far wall, spiraling toward her.

Diana fanned the rifle in a long burst, laying down a line of plasma fire that spanned the width of the room. A talon raked across her left shoulder.

Screaming, she whirled, firing.

The dead biodrone fell against her, writhing and scorched. Clutching her shoulder, she kicked it away.

"Diana!"

Peter's voice rang out through the ruins. Relief surged over her.

He leaped over the wall as a biodrone swung down from the rafters. He raised his rifle and fired. The biodrone exploded in a shower of sparks.

He ran to her, catching her as she slumped.

"Where are you hit? Diana, where are you hit?"

Another biodrone scurried over the wall and Peter blasted it into oblivion.

"Diana!"

David launched himself over the wall and ran toward her. Ron Kraver was a few steps behind.

A biodrone scrambled over the wall as Ron cleared it. He dropped to one knee and fired. The biodrone screeched and disintegrated.

Four more biodrones entered the building, but David and Ron dispatched them.

At last, the grid fell silent.

Peter stroked her hair gently as he carried her to the nearest bedroll. David was on her other side, worry gleaming in his kind brown eyes. Gently, Peter peeled back her torn sleeve, revealing a huge gash.

"Diana, I ran as hard as I could, but I—"

She pressed her fingers to his lips. "It's okay. You're here now."

"Are you hit anywhere else, Sis?" David asked.

She shook her head. Only her left shoulder throbbed. She'd be fine though.

"Mitchell?"

Peter turned.

D'Angelo stood behind him, rifle in hand, pointing it at his chest.

"I thought I recognized you, Mitchell. It took me a while, but I finally remembered. According to my records, you were killed on Ku'Tal, yet here you stand in another recombinant's uniform."

Peter stared from D'Angelo to David.

"Explain yourself, Mitchell. Now!"

Peter bowed his head. "I have no explanation, sir."

Only then did David step forward.

"Sir, he didn't act alone. I'm the one who destroyed his MRC chip."

D'Angelo pointed a finger at David. "I'll have you in irons for this, Temple." He turned his gaze to Peter. "And you've earned a one-way tickct back to RDC."

Diana sat up. "Captain, both of these men are standing here on a planet no one else would have followed you to, voluntarily. Peter Mitchell was a free man, yet he risked his freedom to don a private's uniform and follow you here. Isn't their loyalty worth anything to you?"

D'Angelo fell silent for a moment. Diana seized the opportunity. "And besides that, they're here for the same thing you're here for—to destroy those horrible caregivers."

She watched his eyes, waiting for that glassy look to reappear. It took a few moments, but that fevered stare returned and he began to babble about caregivers again.

He walked away, wandering toward his bedroll.

"Diana, what were you talking about?" David asked, dropping down beside her again.

"David, D'Angelo's a few darts short of a bullseye."

"What?"

"He's a few rocks shy of a quarry. All his neurons aren't firing. David, he's crazy obsessed with destroying some sort of caregiver. He's slipped over the edge. Say whatever you can to pacify him, but he's not in his right mind. Mentioning the caregivers sets him off. Every time."

She reached out to Peter who looked stricken. "It'll be okay, Peter. I promise."

He gripped her hand. "Let's dress this wound," he said in a shaky voice.

David squeezed Peter's shoulder. "Hang in there, Mitchell. It's not over yet. I'll get the medic's kit."

Moving past D'Angelo, David retrieved the kit. Peter took the scissors and cut away her sleeve. Then using a disinfectant, he gently swabbed the bleeding gash. He applied a topical antibiotic and then sealed the wound. When that was completed, he wrapped her shoulder with a generous amount of wound wrap that sealed into place.

He offered her a smile. "How's that?"

"Better. Thanks, Peter." She held his hand in hers. "How did you know to do all of that?"

He shrugged, frowning. "I...don't know." He smoothed the hair out of her eyes. "Now, you rest."

She settled back against the bedroll, but D'Angelo's ominous call to UCOE returned to her thoughts.

"David," she began, trying to recall D'Angelo's exact words. "D'Angelo called in our position to UCOE."

"Good, at least someone knows where we are," he answered.

He looked pissed. She couldn't blame him. D'Angelo would get them all killed if he had his way.

Peter cast an uncertain look at him. That wasn't necessarily good news—at least for him.

"He said some odd things, David."

David leaned against the wall. "Like what?"

"He called in orbital strike forces."

David's eyes bulged. "What? Strike forces? Are you sure?"

Diana nodded. "And he invoked Naharra rules. David, what does that mean?"

His mouth fell open, the color draining from his face. He shook his head, his kind brown eyes sharp with fear and shock. She knew that look and it terrified her now.

"Are you sure, sis? One hundred percent sure?"

"Positive, David. I was sitting right beside him when he said it."

Groping for a steadying handhold, David held onto the wall.

"Sarge, what does that mean, invoking Naharra rules?" Peter asked.

He was silent for a long while. Finally, in a scratchy voice he asked, "How much time did he give?"

"Seventy-two hours."

"Sarge, please!" Peter cried. "What are Naharra rules?"

David stared out at the ruins. "To invoke Naharra rules is to acknowledge that all hope of success is lost and an immediate threat to the home system is imminent. The only course of action is to detonate a nuclear device or devices, destroying the planet. Like they did on Naharra." He turned around, his face deathly pale. "In seventy-two hours, UCOE strike forces will swarm over Ballese with nuclear warheads." He dropped his head into his hands. "It didn't work on Naharra and it won't work here, either. D'Angelo's just escalated everything. For nothing."

Diana turned to look at Peter. He cradled his rifle against his chest. He looked sick, his face pale, soft blue eyes so sad.

"Peter, there's still time to find Sting," she replied.

His jaw tightened and he turned away toward the broken wall. He'd lost everything this trip.

"Anybody seen Langley or Newlin?" David asked.

Ron shook his head. "Nope, but I did find this." He held out one of the jammers. Blinking red.

Peter's eyes widened and David gasped.

"David, what's wrong?"

"Someone turned off the jammers," David said, his voice low and worried. He looked up, over at D'Angelo sitting on his bedroll as he stared at a datapad.

"It wasn't me, David," Diana replied.

She shivered. Someone in this group was sabotaging every part of this mission. Was it D'Angelo?

She glanced around for the other recombinants. Or one of them?

FOR HOURS, they kept a lookout for the missing recombinants, but Langley, Tanner, and Newlin never showed.

"That biodrone patrol probably got them," Ron offered as he fished out ration packets from one of the crates.

He activated them and passed them around. Peter refused his.

"Come on, eat up."

"Not hungry, Ron," he said in a soft voice, his gaze trained west where the Antaran facility stood dim and hazy on the horizon.

"Mitchell, you've got to eat."

Peter waved it away. David noticed this time.

"Mitchell, you eat that ration. That's an order."

Glaring, Peter took the ration from Ron and opened it. Slowly, he tipped it to his mouth and ate.

Ron even carried one over to D'Angelo who sat in the corner reviewing charts and mumbling to himself.

"Ration, sir?" Ron asked.

D'Angelo gracefully accepted the packet and continued with his analysis.

At last, Ron handed Diana a packet. She opened it. Beef Stew. With David's help, she sat up and pressed the packet to her lips. The broth was a bit salty and the carrots mushy, but the warm food felt good in her stomach.

"It's Tanner!" Peter shouted from the wall.

Tanner trotted out of a nearby building and staggered into the camp.

"Tanner, report!" David shouted, rushing to the recombinant.

He sagged in David's grasp. David dragged him over to a bedroll and eased him to the floor.

"What happened to Langley and Newlin?" he demanded.

"biodrones."

He wheezed and Ron handed him a canteen. Tanner sucked greedily at the cool water. When he was satisfied, he pulled the canteen from his lips.

"They got us on the way back. Newlin and Langley are dead."

Peter rose from his position, circling Tanner, a wary expression on his face. He scrutinized Tanner, studying his movements, his uniform.

"How close to the facility did you get?" Peter asked, a frown on his face.

"We were almost on top of it," said Tanner, glancing at David. "There was this green dome and a little fenced-in area on top."

"What'd you see there?" Peter demanded, hands clutching his rifle.

Tanner grimaced. "What's your problem, Thompson?"

"I want to know what you saw," he insisted.

Sighing, Tanner sank against the wall. "I saw other recombinants, okay! They were all penned up in there, bunches of them. Made me sick! Like they were cattle or something."

Peter's wary gaze didn't waver. He scowled and finally walked away, back toward the wall and his sentry watch on the facility. The sun was already fading from the yellow sky that was darkening fast to indigo. Already, Diana saw little glimmers of orange dotting the landscape. Those orange-blossomed plants were beginning to glow again.

It would be a long night.

Behind her, D'Angelo continued his mumbling monologue as he

fiddled with an array of star charts on his datapad. Peter brooded at the wall and David, subdued, seemed troubled and deep in thought. Probably blaming himself for D'Angelo recognizing poor Peter.

Pain stabbed at her left shoulder as she turned on her side to get a few hours of sleep. The first watch would begin. She may need to stand watch soon. Now that they'd lost Newlin and Langley.

David and Ron got Tanner a ration and he devoured it fast. Tanner didn't seem terribly upset at the loss of the other two recombinants. Of course, that was probably typical behavior. She kept forgetting that Peter was the anomaly.

He looked so handsome standing there, light blond hair soft and tousled by the wind, his face stubbled with a trace of beard, his pale blue eyes so sad. But he looked tired and something nagged at him. Had to be D'Angelo recognizing him.

But this time, she wouldn't let anyone take him from her again. Ever.

She wanted to go to him, comfort him, but she was too weak. She laid her head down and watched him until her eyes closed.

13

SEVENTY-TWO HOURS. Peter's stomach clenched.

Sting had seventy-two hours to live unless he could somehow get into that facility and get both of them out again.

His eyes stung and he bit his lip, trying to hold it all inside. Furious, he kicked at the wall until the pain quieted him.

No, it wouldn't end like this! He'd find a way in there. *He'd* clear the slate this time. Even if they sent him back to RDC for it.

He turned to see Sarge standing beside him.

"You okay?" Sarge asked.

"Tell me what happens now, Sarge?" he asked. "From here, I go off to RDC for washout and Sting goes up in flames with this planet." He bowed his head. "I've lost everything, haven't I?"

Including his soul.

Anger crept into Sarge's face. "No, you haven't, Mitchell. I won't let it happen. As soon as we lift off from here, I'll contact Mimi and have her send another shuttle to Farnas. We'll smuggle you off this shuttle when we refuel and onto another one. When D'Angelo reports the incident, I'll deny everything and I'll attribute it to his obsession with the caregivers—and the head injury during the training base attack. It'll work, Mitchell. Trust me."

Sarge meant well, but he knew that when even one string hung loose, the entire fabric had a way of completely unraveling. He remembered a night on the training base when four recombinants were sent back to RDC with reclamation orders. Seeing them board that shuttle for the last time had been deeply disturbing.

Now, he faced that same last walk.

"But what about Sting?"

Sighing, Sarge hung his head. "I don't know. We've already lost Langley and Newlin. Mitchell, I don't see how we can get him out. We don't even know where they're holding him in that vast facility."

Sarge had given up too. Peter saw it in his face.

He turned away, staring at the darkening horizon again. "How do you want to do the sentry schedule, Sarge?" he asked, changing the subject.

"You take the first watch. I'll take second. Ron will take third. Tanner the fourth." He turned to the unit—what was left of it. "All right, here's the sentry schedule. Thompson is on first watch. I'll take second. Ron takes third and Tanner fourth. Thompson, you'll take the final watch. Is that understood?"

"Yes, Sarge," Peter answered, calculating his time. He'd sleep for two hours and then when Kraver went on watch, he'd slip out. He'd move his bedroll near an opening in the wall. In the darkness, no one would know he was missing.

PETER TOOK THE FIRST WATCH. Diana slept peacefully beside David, Tanner snoring beyond them. D'Angelo slept fitfully in the far corner. Ron lay against the wall, asleep against his plasma rifle. The night was calm, serene with the orange glowing blossoms and the soft wind moaning through the horribly silent ruins.

Death whispered through the crumbling structures, calling up ghosts of memories and the unsettling uncertainty of what remained in absence of the lives cut short.

He wondered about the people who'd died here. What had the Antarans done to them? Had they been the Antarans' first test subjects? Facing vicious biodrones and horrific genetic mutations? Watching the people they loved torn apart?

Peter shivered at the thought.

While everyone slept, he added grenades, a canteen, plasma charges, and his sensor grid to his field pack. He laid it by his bedroll. When the shift change came between Sarge and Ron, he had to be ready to move.

He forced himself to remain awake even though he was dead on his feet. He'd been operating on two hours sleep and he was exhausted.

At last, his shift ended. He stumbled over to Sarge and gently shook his shoulder until his eyes rolled open.

"You're up, Sarge," he said, yawning.

Sarge rose without a whimper. He grabbed his rifle and moved toward the wall. Peter walked beside him on the way to his bedroll. Sarge patted him on the back.

"Get some sleep, Mitchell. You look terrible."

Nodding, Peter collapsed onto his bedroll and fell asleep.

In less than an hour, nightmares shook him awake. A towering machine regurgitating people, exact copies—over and over. He stood behind the machine, in a blue lab coat and glasses, hands raised, laughing maniacally as he printed more and more copies.

Of himself.

Each more soulless than the last. Swallowed up by the god symbols as they stepped out of the cavernous room with its circuited walls. The machine ground and sputtered smoke, spitting out more and more copies. Faster and faster.

And he just kept laughing. Watching his soul stretch farther and farther until it collapsed into a pillar of smoke.

He cried out and bolted up from the bedroll.

Arms wrapped around him, a hand over his mouth.

"Ssshhh, Mitchell—it's okay," Sarge whispered. "It was just a bad dream. Everything's okay."

He glanced up. Sarge. "What happened?"

"You were shouting. It's okay. Go back to sleep." Sarge eased him back down against the bedroll.

Nodding, Peter lay down and closed his eyes, grateful to let that horrible machine fade from his dreams.

He slept through the next hour, waking when he heard movement. Sarge woke Ron who rose unsteadily from his bedroll and fumbled for his rifle.

Groggy, he seized the opportunity. He snatched up his field pack and rifle and rolled against the wall. Wind blew against his back from the outside as he slid through the opening and dashed across the street.

Toward the room with the god symbols. And then the lake.

PETER HAD NO PLAN. He decided that if he could get into that pen on the roof carrying a grenade, then maybe he could find Sting and escape.

UCOE grenades were small and looked more like rubber balls than explosives. With the jammer technology he carried, they may not notice him climbing the pen wall. After all, he doubted they'd expect a recombinant to break *into* the facility.

He hurried around the northern edge of the lake, sensor grid in hand. To his surprise, no biodrones prowled this side of the lake at night. He kept up his brisk pace. Sarge would be furious at him for this, but with a strike force on its way, he had no choice.

He walked for an hour until he reached the edge of the facility. Crawling into the middle of some tangled yellow brush, he made his way around the side. A tree with yellow leaves and white bark stood very close to the roof, so he hefted himself into it. He hung his rifle and field pack on the highest branch.

Carefully, he removed two grenades and slid them into his pants pockets, opposite the gear thing he'd found in the lab. Slipping his sensor grid around his neck, he cautiously moved across a limb and slid onto the roof. He climbed buttresses, rising higher until he stood in front of the pen.

Empty.

The top of the pen looked like it would electrocute him, so he crept around to the coppery tower that housed the green dome. If he could climb onto the tower rim, then he could roll into the pen without touching the top of the fence.

He slipped twice and nearly fell off the roof, but he held onto the slick green surface, lowering himself slowly until his boots crested the overhang above the pen.

There was no turning back from here.

Closing his eyes, he took a deep breath and slid down the dome, into the pen.

He landed on his left ankle, twisting it badly. He bit back a yelp and crawled to the side. With his back against the wall, he gripped his injured ankle with both hands and sucked in deep breaths to counteract the pain. When the rawness finally subsided, he glanced around.

A door into the facility. The rest was barren dirt.

He limped over to the door. No handle.

He was trapped out here until that door opened. He moved back against the wall and sank down, awaiting sunrise.

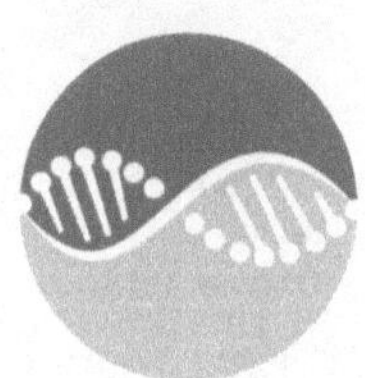

14

DAVID AWOKE to someone urgently shaking his arm. He rubbed his eyes and tried to focus. Ron Kraver knelt beside him.

"I'm awake," David muttered. "What's the matter?"

"It's your sister," he said, his voice low. "She's sick."

Terror welled cold in the pit of his stomach. In the swamps, he'd seen delirium in other soldiers attacked by biodrones. He'd had that delirium, but Mitchell carried him out of the swamps to the safe house. Saved his life. Twice, if he counted the cascade mine incident that had nearly killed him.

He owed Peter everything.

He scrambled up from his bedroll and hurried over to Diana. She groaned, restless in her bedroll. A fine sheen of sweat coated her face and drenched her hair. Gently, he laid his hand to her forehead. She was burning up.

"We need to take down this fever," he said to Ron. "Get the medic's kit. There's got to be some antibiotics in there."

"Right," Ron answered and rushed through the darkness to get the kit.

"Hang in there, kiddo," he said, smiling. "Ron, you got it yet?"

"Yeah, I found it," Ron answered.

David heard the shuffle of his feet in the darkness. In a moment, Ron was kneeling beside him, medic's kit in hand. "Here," he said, handing David an antibiotic-filled syringe and needle.

David swabbed her uninjured arm. This would hurt. He held his breath and then pressed the needle to her upper arm. She jumped, but he and Ron held her steady. When the syringe was empty, he slid out the needle and covered the entry point with a small bandage. He sighed. They could clone a fully functional soldier in three months but couldn't manage a painless needle.

He sat down beside her and stroked her hair. "Don't go anywhere on me, okay, Sis?" He glanced over at Ron. "Who's on watch now?"

"You're up, David," said Ron, "but why don't you let me take it? That way, you can stay with Diana."

"Thanks," he answered. "I'd appreciate that."

Ron slapped him on the shoulder. "Consider it done."

"Get Mitchell to spell you in three hours."

"Right," said Ron, disappearing into the darkness again. David heard the shuffle of his feet and the creak of his rifle.

Diana's labored breathing filled the expanse and David feared it might bring biodrones. She began to shiver, her teeth chattering, as she tossed back and forth on the bedroll. David grabbed a nearby canteen and fumbled through the medic's kit for a cold pack and some old-fashioned aspirin. He tilted her head up, cradling her shoulders as he dropped two aspirin onto her tongue, and put the canteen to her lips.

"Here, kiddo, drink some water and swallow those aspirins." Slowly, he poured water into her mouth until she swallowed. He waited and then poured more. Then he activated the cold pack and laid it against her forehead.

She continued her restless tossing for some time until finally, she began to quiet. Already, the horizon had begun to lighten. The aspirins were bringing down her fever. Maybe the antibiotics would break it quickly?

"Peter, don't go. Peter!"

David mopped her face with a clean scrap of bandage.

"Peter's fine, Sis. He's asleep in the corner."

Again, she called for Peter. David sighed. Of all people to fall for, it had to be one of the most inaccessible men in two systems. Someone who hadn't been built for long-term endurance.

They recycled recombinants every five years because of the mental instabilities brought on by intense combat. Now, David wondered how many like Mitchell had already been washed out. It had been a stroke of luck to have gotten Mitchell out of the military at all. He didn't see how they could be that lucky again, but he knew it would kill Diana to lose that vibrant young man.

He'd never had a brother and he looked on Mitchell as the one he'd never had. He wouldn't let D'Angelo send Mitchell off to RDC for reclamation. He glared at the floor. Reclamation, hell. It was a straight up execution. Euthanasia—like they put pets to sleep with something that stopped their hearts. Still, Mitchell had been lucky so far.

He hoped that luck held one more time.

At last, Diana's breathing softened and she slept peacefully. He crawled back to his bedroll and leaned against the wall, a hand over his eyes as he watched her sleep. She had to get better. He'd never forgive himself if she died out here. It was his fault she was on this mission. She'd have never accepted this job if he—and Mitchell—hadn't been involved. That fact gnawed at him.

He stared out at the dark ruins, unable to get D'Angelo's orders out of his head.

Invoking Naharra rules. Dear God, what the fuck was he thinking? Without even waiting for them to reconnoiter the area. And understand the situation here. D'Angelo hadn't even assessed the facility when he invoked it. He'd done nothing except make camp.

If he lived through this, he vowed to force UCOE into amending the Naharra rules, making sure one person didn't have the power to invoke them without just cause. To call that in so lightly...it made him shudder. But recon teams one and two had sent the same message before losing contact. Recommending that Naharra rules be invoked. No one had been left to complete the process from the first two recon teams.

What had they found here?

Footsteps moved across the room. Ron's sentry duty must be over.

"Mitchell?" Silence. "Mitchell!"

Footsteps ticked toward him as Ron emerged from the darkness again. "Where's Mitchell's bedroll?"

David pointed to the far right-hand corner. "Over there."

Ron hurried toward the corner. David's eyes were closing and he fought to stay awake.

"David," Ron called. "We've got a problem."

David groaned. No! No more problems! He was swimming in problems.

"Just wake him up and get him on sentry."

Ron backed slowly out of the darkness, hands in the air.

Tanner emerged in front of him, a plasma rifle aimed at Ron's chest.

David stumbled to his feet, rifle in hand. A hundred thoughts rushed through his head.

Had Tanner shot Mitchell? Was the poor kid lying over there dead?

His breath caught in his throat, rage swelling in his hands. If Tanner killed Mitchell, he'd tear him limb from limb and feed him to the biodrones.

"Tanner, I order you to put down that rifle," David said in a steady voice.

Tanner's eyes were glazed.

"Tanner, acknowledge your orders."

The expression on Tanner's face remained deadpan as he swiveled the rifle barrel toward David.

15

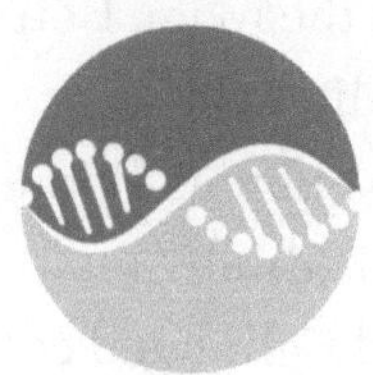

SUNRISE WAS BARELY a splash on the horizon when the Antaran facility door snapped open.

Startled, Peter sprang to his feet, the door missing him by fractions. He watched anxiously as several recombinants filed into the pen. Not wanting to look out of place, he quickly slipped into the tangle of restless recombinants and hobbled across the pen, fear burning his throat.

Desperately, he scanned the faces as he walked around the pen, but none of them was Sting. He didn't recognize any of them.

Peter tried talking to one of the recombinants, but the recombinant growled and shoved him out of his path. Peter tried to address a few other recombinants, but their hostility made him back off.

Dejected, Peter paced the pen, his injured ankle throbbing, and waited for the time when that pen door opened again. This seemed to be an exercise area. It reminded him a little of RDC.

The recombinants kept to themselves, silently plodding around the pen. Some stared out at the lake below and the distant ruins of the Ballese colony. None of them spoke, either. What had the

Antarans done to them? When he looked into their eyes, he saw only emptiness.

He had his back to the sun when the first punch landed, smashing into his right shoulder, knocking him to the ground.

He struggled to his feet as a recombinant came at him. The dark-haired, thick-bodied man coiled his meaty arms around Peter's torso and squeezed him like a python. Peter gasped for air and struggled to break the man's hold.

Finally, he kicked the man in the stomach. The recombinant staggered backward, wheezing.

Two other recombinants pounced on the big man, their fists slamming into the man's face and rib cage. Peter hobbled back against the wall as the entire pen exploded into a raging fight.

They tore at each other like rabid dogs, tearing and gouging, trying to kill each other.

Eventually, two more recombinants came at him.

He backed away, but the wall slammed into his back. They tore into him, pounding him with their fists and clawing at his throat.

Pain burned through his chest. Screaming, he launched himself at the first one, his head smashing into the recombinant's stomach.

The recombinant staggered and fell.

The next recombinant grabbed Peter in a headlock and repeatedly slammed his fist into Peter's stomach.

His stomach lurched, air knocked from his lungs. Wheezing, he kicked the second recombinant backward.

A high-pitched screech rippled through the pen, the sound agonizing.

Peter doubled over and grabbed his ears, the pain unbearable. Miserable, he writhed on the ground, the noise piercing his ears like ice picks.

When the last recombinant had fallen to ground, the horrid sound stopped. Then the door opened.

Recombinants struggled to their feet and stoically entered the facility. Swallowing hard, Peter shoved his sensor grid into his jacket and fell into step with the other recombinants.

Inside, the facility was dark and when the door finally closed, Peter stared into a chasm of cells. His heart sank. How would he find Sting in here? Cells lined one whole wall, but they resembled caves more than anything. It took a while for his eyes to adjust. The recombinants filed through the expanse freely, telling Peter that this area was cut off from the rest of the facility.

Above them, he knew, was the DNA repository for the entire Antaran race. The proximity of this place to the repository was disturbing.

Peter reached into his shirt and flicked on his sensor grid, being careful to turn off the sound. Keeping the device hidden, he gazed down at it. The screen was black with biodrone blips.

A shiver slid down his spine. These weren't recombinants anymore.

They were some sort of biodrone hybrid. His knees felt weak, but he kept walking, following the crowd. And turned off the grid.

When he'd come full circle in the cavern-like holding area, Peter knew he was in with the recombinant-biodrone hybrids. Now, he had to figure out where they kept their test subjects and find a way in there.

How deeply into this facility would he have to travel to find Sting? And risk never surfacing again.

He found a place to sit down and rest his aching body. His rib cage throbbed and blood dripped down his face from the fight in the pen. He wiped it quickly on his sleeve. The other recombinants had similar cuts that bled freely down their faces and arms, but they seemed unconcerned. At least the blood looked human.

Then he thought of Diana and hoped the biodrone slash to her shoulder hadn't made her sick. He also wondered if Sarge had discovered him missing yet. The man would be furious at him for pulling a stunt like this, but with D'Angelo invoking Naharra rules and biodrones ready to swallow them up, he couldn't wait any longer.

Sting was in here somewhere. He felt it. He *would* find him.

In about an hour, a door that had been obscured in shadows opened and two tall, thin creatures entered the chamber. Everything about them seemed thin—almost wispy. Their moss-brown eyes were set high on their heads and closer together than human eyes. Their skin was translucent, their hair white. Peter gritted his teeth, trying to control his anger.

Caregivers.

They moved through the crowd of recombinants, shifting some of them toward the door.

Peter rose from the chair and stood, studying the interchange. It seemed as if they were choosing a group of recombinants for some task—testing, perhaps? He watched blankly as they chose a dozen recombinants. Like sheep, the recombinants followed behind the caregivers who led them out of the chamber. The other recombinants seemed unaffected by the disappearance of so many of the group.

He tried to count them all. There seemed to be about fifty or sixty recombinants milling through the chamber. Peter decided that if the caregivers brought back the others, he'd maneuver himself into the next grouping. He needed to see what lay beyond here. He had a hunch that Sting was above him somewhere, near the DNA repository. He was probably being used somehow to create the recombinant-biodrone hybrids.

Maybe that meant the Antarans still needed him alive?

Peter rose from the chair and continued to traverse the chamber with the other recombinants, not wanting to appear different. They never seemed to tire of their mindless circles through the chamber. Peter suspected this came from the biodrone's simplistic thought processes, judging from the ones he'd encountered.

Real recombinants were boisterous and aggressive, full of life. At their worst, they were volatile and extreme, shouting, fighting, angered easily. They had emotions. They were human. Most craved combat and the prospect delighted them. But these recombinants?

They looked the part, appearing every bit human, but they behaved like biodrones.

They'd be easily spotted.

Then a thought slid into his mind. Were they just prototypes in the process of creating a final model? Were the more advanced prototypes held elsewhere?

What if he displayed those characteristics? He was undoubtedly being watched. Would they take him back to the original specimens for comparison? He smiled. Might be worth a try.

In a short while, a door opened in the side of the chamber. Two crates, crammed with silver food packets slid inside. Recombinants bolted toward it, shoving and beating the others to get close to that crate. There wouldn't be enough for all of them.

Peter threw himself into the middle of the fray but couldn't get through. Finally, he crawled under the others and managed to snatch a ration packet out of the crate. Then he slipped out of the crowd. Recombinants tried to take his ration from him, but he shoved them back, trying to act the part of a half-starved recombinant.

He wasn't even hungry.

Two recombinants slammed into him and he fought them off, sneering at them as he opened the food packet. He poured it into his mouth and finished it before anyone else tried to snatch the packet from him.

He took another beating for managing to get the ration, but he held his own.

After the commotion for the food had died away, the other recombinants returned to their mindless travels around the chamber.

Peter had other ideas.

He picked up rocks twice the size of his fists and carried them to one of the shallow caves, stacking them until he'd created a suitable barrier between him and these mindless recombinant shells. Then he slipped inside his makeshift room and settled against the wall to get some sleep.

Out of sight, out of mind seemed to be the hybrid's method of operation, Peter discovered. When he was hidden behind his wall in one of the dark cell caves, no one approached him.

They literally forgot he was there. Another sign these recombinant-biodrone hybrids were rejects, he finally decided.

Somehow, he had to elevate himself to a new class of recombinant-biodrone hybrid. He settled in and slept, listening for the pen to open again.

THE NEXT MORNING, Peter awoke to find a caregiver standing over him. His first impulse was to recoil, but he forced himself into the part of an aggressive recombinant. He rose up on his haunches, hands poised to fight, and glared at the caregiver.

"Out!" the caregiver shouted, motioning him out of the cave.

"Why?" Peter asked, unblinking.

The startled caregiver staggered back a step and a curious smile touched its face. Peter longed to smash his fist into its smug, narrow face.

A second caregiver arrived and the first one turned to it.

"Advanced reasoning. Our quality control missed a promising hybrid."

The caregiver mumbled something in a language that Peter didn't recognize and then the second one departed. The remaining caregiver gestured more slowly and without threat for Peter to exit his rock-fortress.

"Did you create this?"

Peter nodded.

The caregiver smiled. "Survival skills, too. This is indeed promising."

Again, the caregiver motioned Peter up from the ground.

With reluctance, Peter stood. "Where are you taking me?"

"Where would you like to go?"

He grinned. "Anywhere I can shoot something." Peter hoped he sounded convincing enough.

"Come with me, please, and we'll see what we can arrange."

Still wary, Peter followed, uncertain about what they might arrange. He hoped they wouldn't put his mock bloodthirst to the test.

The caregiver led him to a grey door in the side of the room. A hidden panel in the wall opened and the caregiver pressed a button. The door creaked open. Reluctantly, Peter entered.

The hallway was dark and narrow as he felt the caregiver's ghostly presence beside him. Seeing the caregivers again awoke a thirst for vengeance he never knew he had until now.

Maybe he had more in common with the other recombinants than he ever realized?

The hallway circled around and then veered left until it widened into a sunlit rotunda. Deep green tiles covered the floor. The walls were a soft grey. Caregivers hurried past. More than Peter had ever seen in one place before. The sight of them repulsed him. They spoke nothing but lies and he bristled at their every word.

He followed his caregiver around the rotunda and the caregiver veered right into a hallway. Four shorter hallways jutted off this main hallway, looking like offices.

At the end of the main hallway stood a door and the caregiver opened it. They stepped through into a dark chamber similar to the one he'd just left, but smaller. Another group of recombinants milled around and Peter heard them talking softly to each other. Still, there was that emptiness in their eyes.

Apparently, he'd been moved up the quality scale.

"So, these are supposed to be soldiers?" Peter said with sneer, mimicking his old recombinant enemy, Stephen Drake's attitude. At last, Drake had been good for something besides making Peter's life miserable. Drake was dead now, killed on Ku'Tal, but he'd done a lot of damage to him before that.

The caregiver seemed amused by his comment.

"Do you see a problem with these soldiers?"

"They all look as dumb as stumps. What's wrong with them?"

The caregiver moved toward another door that opened into another outside pen. Peter felt nervous now. What had he gotten himself into with this bloodthirsty act?

The door swiveled open. About a dozen recombinant-biodrone hybrids, looking more like zombies than humans, wandered around the pen. The emptiness in their eyes was alarming. Not even a spark of life glimmered in their gazes.

"What are they?" Peter asked.

"Earlier attempts," said the caregiver, its voice buttery smooth. "Useless now."

The caregiver moved to a small compartment to the left of the door and to Peter's surprise, he pulled a UCOE military-issue plasma pistol from the compartment. Peter's jaw tightened, his stomach clenching. The caregiver armed the pistol and handed it to Peter.

"All right, soldier, you've got your wish. Let's see how effective your skills are with the pistol."

Peter took the pistol, a hundred thoughts rushing through his head. He couldn't shoot these recombinants. He couldn't!

He stared at the weapon, heavy in his palm and tested the weight, whatever he could do to buy some time. He glanced from the anxious caregiver to the pen of recombinants. If he didn't fire the weapon, there was no telling what the caregiver would do.

Would being returned to that first pen be the worst thing they'd do? Or would this caregiver shoot him on the spot?

He pretended to examine the weapon closely. Studying the balance, the sighting, and the safety mechanism.

A dangerous smile curved across the caregiver's face. "Stalling?"

Peter scowled at him. "This could be some sort of trick." He held the weapon up. "You could have this thing set to discharge in my hand."

It was now or never. He had to fire the weapon. Slowly, Peter brought the weapon up, sighting the nearest recombinant. His hand trembled, his palm sweating. He glanced over at the caregiver.

And then it came to him.

"Man, this is just too easy! This isn't combat. I can shoot every one of them without even blinking." He shoved the pistol at the caregiver and walked away. "There's no challenge here. I want the hunt, not just shooting captives. Try me again when you've got a battlefield for me."

He turned away, holding his breath as he walked down the short hallway. The weapon clicked behind him, charging. It was a soft, anxious whine in the silence. Peter's hands shook and he held them tightly against his side, but he kept walking.

The caregiver said nothing and Peter kept up his pace, his heart hammering against his chest. Would the caregiver fire at him? Would it fire?

"Soldier," the caregiver called, the tone clearly a challenge.

Peter stopped. He waited a moment or two then turned. The pistol was aimed at his chest, the caregiver walking slowly toward him.

"Go ahead," said Peter, a wry smile on his face. "Like I said, it's no challenge."

The caregiver pressed the pistol to Peter's temple. He stared at the alien, unblinking, expressionless.

"Seems to me you're wasting resources," said Peter. "Aren't I what you're looking for? Wasn't that why you were so excited?"

The caregiver pulled the weapon away from Peter's head.

"I'll need to compare you with the others," it said. "You are what we're seeking, but I need to be sure."

Would this take him to Sting?

He tried to hold onto his Drake-like sneer.

"What does that mean? I get to wander around with a new bunch of idiot soldiers? When am I going into combat?"

"I'd like to compare you with our control group."

Peter hoped that meant the real live recombinants whose DNA was being used to produce these recombinant-biodrone hybrids.

With the barrel of the pistol, the caregiver motioned Peter back into the hallway. Peter complied this time, following the hallway back through the rotunda and into that long, dark hallway leading him back to the group he'd left.

Sighing, Peter paced the cavernous chamber, intentionally walking against the current of other recombinants who wandered aimlessly.

A recombinant about Peter's height ran into him. Knowing the caregivers were still watching, Peter let out an animal scream and slammed the recombinant out of his way. The recombinant fell and started to come after him, but Peter fell on top of him and pounded the hybrid with his fists. The recombinant crawled away from him.

Peter rose from the ground, the hybrid's blood smearing his hands.

His stomach twisted and he closed his eyes to blot out the image. How could he have done that? This was the last thing he'd wanted to do.

He pressed his hand to his throat, feeling the absence of the god symbol. If it had been there, he would have torn it off. He didn't deserve it. He knew that now.

And now, he could never earn it.

Diana put the god symbol away for him, but he could never wear it again. Not someone who'd sold his soul. And his best friend.

Now, he stood here, pounding a man nearly unconscious in order to convince these appalling caregivers that he was the bloodthirsty creature they were seeking.

His whole body ached as he staggered past the other hybrids. They weren't even remotely concerned that a comrade had just been beaten senseless. Sick, he moved over to the stones he'd stacked and collapsed behind them. Hugging himself, he closed his eyes, trying to erase the image of the hybrid's face he'd bloodied. But it hung there before him. He still felt the contact with the man's face against his hands.

His eyes snapped open and he stared down at his hands, still smudged with blood. Furiously, he rubbed them against his shirt, trying to be rid of the blood and the sensations.

Even when the food packets were shoved through the wall and hybrids lurched toward them like hungry fish, Peter didn't rise from the ground. He curled up on the floor, trying to summon any memory that might shove these horrid ones out of his head.

But all he could summon was Sting standing on the ramp of that alien ship, handing him a god symbol.

He recoiled from the image. God symbols burned through his memory, crosses and stars and half circles. All of them reminded him of his loss. So, this is what it felt like to lose his soul. The emptiness expanded inside him, masking the pain.

Now, he envied the emptiness in those hybrid's eyes.

16

DAVID STOOD VERY STILL, trying not to frighten Tanner into pulling the trigger. How had a recombinant this unstable made it out of RDC?

He'd heard stories before about recombinants turning on their superiors, but RDC had taken steps to eliminate that problem. Apparently not enough.

He glanced at Ron who shrugged in helplessness.

D'Angelo seemed oblivious to the situation. He sat with his charts, mumbling about strikes forces and coordinates.

"Captain, we need some help over here."

No response from D'Angelo.

David took a step back, Ron still beside him.

"Tanner, acknowledge your orders," David said in a sharp voice.

Tanner jerked the rifle from Ron to David, advancing on them. The empty expression on his face was unnerving.

Again, David stepped backward, but his heel smacked against the broken wall of the building. There was nowhere to go now.

"Dammit, Tanner! Acknowledge your orders!"

The blank expression didn't change when Tanner raised the rifle.

Then David remembered Mitchell speculating about the Antarans creating a recombinant-biodrone hybrid and realized he was staring at one.

An ion lantern smashed against the side of Tanner's head and he crumpled. Diana stood behind him, but then collapsed on top of Tanner in a fevered heap.

"Diana!"

He rushed to her, scooping her up and carrying her back to her bedroll.

"Couldn't—let him—shoot you," she huffed, her face drenched with sweat. Her whole body burned with fever. She needed more antibiotics.

He smiled at her, easing her against the bedroll. "You were marvelous, kiddo! Now, you lie still while we get you some more medicine, okay?"

Diana nodded, her eyes closing to slits.

"Ron, get the medic's kit and give her another shot of antibiotics."

"Right," Ron answered and reached for the kit.

Grabbing some cord from one of the crates, David secured Tanner against a broken support column. Then he turned to the grim task of checking on Mitchell.

He moved with slow, uncertain steps toward the dark corner, dreading the moment he would stumble over Mitchell's body.

He swallowed hard. *How would he tell Diana?*

He kept moving until he felt the soft bedroll against his boots. Slowly, he bent down and groped the floor for a sign of Mitchell's body. The bedroll felt dry, no warm, sticky feel of blood. He slid his hands across the bare floor. It, too, felt dry.

"Ron," he called. "When you get a chance, light one of those ion lamps and bring it over here."

"Did you find Mitchell?"

"Just bring the lamp."

Diana moaned softly and he heard Mitchell's name roll off her lips. He prayed Mitchell wasn't lying dead at his feet.

Several, long moments crawled by until he heard Ron moving toward him. Then light filled the corner. Mitchell's bedroll lay scrunched against the wall, almost hanging out of a jagged break in the wall. He stepped through the opening. Nothing.

Anger burned through David's veins. Where the hell was Mitchell?

A cold chill brushed across his skin. He'd gone to the facility alone to search for Sting. He was certain of it.

"Dammit, Mitchell!" David shouted. He turned to Ron. "He's gone to the Antaran facility. Alone."

Ron shook his head. "That's suicide! Are you sure?"

"I'm sure," David answered flatly. "With D'Angelo invoking Naharra rules and Mitchell facing a washout, he probably thought he had to do something right now."

"Then we've lost Mitchell, too?"

David turned to gaze at Diana tossing and turning in her bedroll, mumbling Mitchell's name. A sick feeling burned through his stomach.

How would he ever get Mitchell and Sting out of there before they had to lift off? Was the kid even still alive?

He moved over to Diana and sat down beside her. For her sake, he hoped so.

"What do we do now, David?" Ron asked.

Leaning against the wall, David slid to the floor.

D'Angelo had taken him on a one-way trip all right. They'd lost all the recombinants now and he had the grim task of telling Diana that Peter Mitchell was lost, too. And they only had sixty-some hours at most left.

Unless he could prove D'Angelo incompetent.

If he failed, they'd bring him up on charges. And kill Mitchell if he did manage to find him and get him off Ballese.

He glanced at Diana. She'd never forgive him for losing Mitchell while she was down sick.

He rose from the ground. "Ron, we need to get to D'Angelo's comunit."

"I'm right behind you," Ron answered.

David moved toward D'Angelo.

The man never looked up. He seemed obsessed with his star charts.

David slipped behind D'Angelo who sat on one of the crates and knelt beside the small comunit. His hand fell to the receiver.

D'Angelo whirled around and grabbed David's arm.

"Use of this comunit is for commissioned officers only, soldier. Stand down immediately."

Sighing, David pulled back. It was true.

Only a commissioned officer had access to the comm. It was in àll the regs. D'Angelo wasn't in his right mind, but he knew his regulations cold. And he wouldn't deviate from them.

"Sir, we've got an emergency here. I wanted to call it in and not disturb you."

D'Angelo's eyes narrowed suspiciously as his hand fell to the plasma pistol in his belt. "I said stand down, Sergeant."

Inhaling sharply, David pulled his hand away from the comunit. He stared at D'Angelo and then Ron. There was one avenue left to him. He'd have to relieve D'Angelo and assume command of the unit.

He didn't expect Ron Kraver to act. Ron stepped forward and saluted D'Angelo. "Sir, Lieutenant Ron Kraver, weapons programmer, reporting."

Turning his angry stare away from David, Captain D'Angelo focused on Ron.

"Report, Lieutenant."

Ron hesitated a moment. "Sir, request coordinates for alien targets. With your permission, I will upload the coordinates and the long-range strike parameters via comunit as per regulations."

D'Angelo smiled. "Let the caregivers survive this strike," he muttered and returned his gaze to his star charts. "Proceed, Lieutenant."

Ron saluted again and moved behind D'Angelo who ignored him now. Ron glanced at David and then picked up the comunit headset.

"Base camp requesting secure channel. Over."

Static filled the silence and David waited, hoping D'Angelo wouldn't try to stop Ron when he called off the bomber strike.

"You're secure. Go ahead, base camp."

"Requesting status on strike force. Over."

"Strike force will launch in approximately thirty-six hours. Over."

"Ron, request that the strike force stand down. Cite emergency procedure number five oh two in my name."

Ron frowned. "What's that?" he whispered.

"Just do it."

Nodding, Ron turned to the comunit again.

"Base camp requesting that the strike force stand down based on emergency procedure number five oh two. On Sergeant David Temple's command. Over."

D'Angelo hummed to himself as he shifted to another chart. He mumbled something about caregivers and flicked to the next chart on the screen.

"Request acknowledged. Patching you through to strike force commander. Over."

Ron kept a wary gaze on D'Angelo, but the man seemed to have forgotten about Ron and the comunit now.

Silence clung to the connection.

David shoved his hands into his pocket and fought down his urge to pace.

Static continued, raking down his spine. *What was taking so long?*

Finally, the static fell away.

"This is Strike Force Commander Reynolds requesting further information about emergency procedure five oh two. Over."

Ron turned to David. "What do I say?"

David nodded toward D'Angelo. "Tell them command has been

relieved under that procedure and to request immediate cessation of retaliation until further notice."

"Uh, Reynolds," Ron began, "base camp command has been relieved under procedure five oh two. Request immediate cessation of all retaliations until further notice. Over."

"On whose authority?" Reynolds demanded.

"Sergeant David Temple. Over."

"That's a negative, base camp. Strike force is unable to comply."

Ron's face darkened. "Unacceptable, Reynolds. Situation here is critical! Pilot and commander are incapacitated. Commander was not stable enough to have invoked Naharra rules."

The comunit crackled. "Unable to comply, base camp. Order was locked into system with a high-level security key code. The counter-code must be entered in order to revoke Naharra rules. Over."

Damn! David pounded his fist against his leg. He'd forgotten about the key code. Somehow, he had to get the counter-code from D'Angelo and stop UCOE from nuking Ballese.

"Peter? Peter, where are you?" Diana's fevered voice rose in the silence.

"Ron, sign off," David said and motioned him away from D'Angelo.

"Affirmative, Reynolds. Base camp out."

The connection cleared and Ron shuffled away from D'Angelo. David pulled him out of earshot.

"Okay, listen to me," David said, his voice low. "We've got to get that code from D'Angelo or Mitchell's a dead man. And so is Sting."

Ron nodded. "Tell me what you want me to do."

David pointed at D'Angelo. "D'Angelo thinks you're a lieutenant and his weapons programmer. You might be able to get the code by telling him you're coding the weapons for the assault. He may buy into that. I'm going to need you to do this, Ron, while I go after Mitchell. We've got a little over two and a half days before we get the final warning from UCOE."

"What if he doesn't believe me?"

"You have to convince him. Develop a plan. Convince him you're who you say you are. Talk about the caregivers. Whatever it takes, but get that counter-code or Mitchell and Stingley are history. And so are we."

"All right," said Ron. "I'll put together a series of command functions and discuss it with D'Angelo."

David smiled. "That's good, Ron. You tell him how you need to keep that counter-code safe from the caregivers. Just get that counter-code."

"I'll do my best. You find Mitchell and his buddy."

"Right." He glanced over at Diana sleeping restlessly in her bedroll. "I'll get Diana more antibiotics, but you've got to promise me one more thing."

"I'm listening."

"Whatever you do, do not tell Diana what's happened to Peter or that I went after him. She'd go ballistic." David grabbed Ron's arm. "Promise me, Kraver."

Ron glanced at Diana and then back at David. "Sure. I'll keep my mouth shut and do my best to keep her here."

David glanced over at Tanner lying unconscious on the ground. "We'd better secure Tanner."

Then a strange idea slid into David's head. The Antarans had gotten hold of Tanner and apparently attempted the biodrone hybridization process on an existing recombinant. So, they could control Tanner. The Antarans might not think anything about Tanner re-entering the facility. He grabbed hold of Tanner's arm and started unfastening his uniform.

"Help me get him out of his uniform," said David.

"Why?" Ron asked.

"If the Antarans have already grabbed Mitchell, then they wouldn't think anything about Tanner walking into the facility again. Not after making him a hybrid that they could control."

Ron let go of Tanner. "No way, Temple! I'm not going to help you get yourself killed. Besides that, you're the only pilot we have left."

"Diana will be able to fly us out when the time comes. Besides, I wouldn't be in any danger. I'd get the information and find Mitchell. Then we ship out before the strike force arrives."

"Temple, you're crazier than D'Angelo," said Ron, who handed Tanner's uniform shirt to David. "But there's a kernel of sense in what you're saying. Good luck and be careful."

David smiled and started shucking off his clothes. "You just watch Diana and get that counter-code."

He slipped into Tanner's uniform, grabbed a rifle and a pistol from the ammo crate, and hurried into the predawn greyness.

WITH HIS HEART throbbing in his throat, David weaved through the burned-out structures that were once the proudest moment in the history of Earth's achievements. Now, it was part of a dark and sobering history. Like the Jupiter space station disaster, the Mars Surveyor Point biosphere contamination. All of those horrors lived on in history like the ancient Titanic sinking and the German concentration camps. Every fifty years or so, these past tragedies re-emerged with new information and new generations to mourn them.

A tart, acidic residue clung to the air, burning his throat and nostrils. He covered his nose and hurried through the building. His boots left deep tracks in the dust-covered floors as he ducked behind a wall. Something scratched at the floor then scurried away with the click of tiny claws. He whirled, rifle raised, but the sound rose around him until he couldn't track the movement. David reached into his pocket and retrieved his sensor grid. Setting it on visual only, he studied the grid for a sign of biodrones.

Damn Mitchell anyway for running off like that!

He glanced down at his watch. sixty-one hours until the strike force arrived, thanks to D'Angelo. Somehow, he had to find Mitchell and get out of there before this whole planet burned into a nuclear cinder.

He scanned in all directions. No biodrones blipped on the grid, so he shuffled across the street and into another building.

The ruins felt so quiet and eerie and he swore he felt ghosts stirring in the rubble.

His chest tightened. Twelve thousand people dead. Not even skeletons left.

Whispers clung to the rafters, memories mingling with the dust. He smelled the grit mixing with that stale scent of old houses. Exhaling, he rushed across the last street and headed south, into the thick tangle of forest.

A clean scent scrubbed the air of grit and age and David breathed easier as he crashed through the brush. He swung the grid in a wide arc in front of him, hoping he'd see any biodrones before they saw him.

His thoughts shifted to D'Angelo and he hoped Ron could coax the counter-code out of the unstable man. It would take time to get to Mitchell, but he couldn't return empty-handed.

For Diana, he couldn't.

David walked for a long hour until he emerged on the southern banks of the black, mirror-like lake. The sandy umber shore, partially camouflaged by trees, was bright against the lavender leaves and grey sky. Squiggly trails brushed through the sand and David knew instantly that taloned biodrones had come this way.

He bent down, examining the tentacled tracks, and realized that these prints were relatively fresh. The cool scent of shade filled pockets of silvery grass in the thick forest.

Tanner's uniform felt a little loose and David was thankful. He gripped the rifle, imagining what had been done to the recombinant.

He sighed. And Mitchell.

In the distance, the Antaran facility rose and he moved toward it, his sensor grid beginning to flash an occasional, faint blip. Something lurked in the area. He'd do his best to avoid a confrontation.

FROM THE BRUSH, David watched the facility and waited for a chance to slip inside. A door left open, some opportunity to enter. The facility looked almost like a pyramid with a wing facing east and a wing facing west. A huge green dome crowned the top and on all four sides, David noted the exercise pens that he and Mitchell had seen populated with recombinants.

Exercise pens?

His brain seized on the idea, wondering what lay beneath that dome and why it was flanked on all sides by wire exercise pens.

A faint petroleum scent filled the air. The building's surface was rough and coppery against the yellow sky, as if pocked by weather...or attack. He wondered if the facility had come before or after the assault on the colony. Had the facility been erected here without the colonists even realizing it?

He shivered. Or had they known and trusted the caregivers. The colony came before the Antaris War. It was possible there'd been some trust between them.

He bristled, remembering the dangerous game that Mitchell played with them as he bargained for their lives on Ku'Tal.

David had been delirious with fever and injury that night, so his memories were sketchy.

Still, he remembered two things: that the Antarans had been afraid and that the Ku'Tal facility seemed like some sort of archive. Perhaps the caregivers had been telling the truth about the DNA repository? Perhaps Mitchell with his grenades and plasma rifle had posed more of a threat than any of them had realized?

At some point, David decided, shifting onto his haunches in the brush, something would exit this facility. And when it did, he'd be ready to act. They didn't have much time and there was no telling what had already happened to Mitchell inside this facility. He sighed. Diana would skin him if he came back without Mitchell.

Besides, he wouldn't leave the kid behind. He couldn't.

David's best chance was to blend in with any recombinants that might be outside the facility to exercise.

All morning, the facility remained quiet, not a sign of movement, but in the afternoon, David watched in surprise as several recombinants hurried out a side door. No one accompanied them and they seemed to move freely about the area. Then David saw the ankle cuff on each recombinant and knew that device kept them from escaping.

Probably created pain.

The recombinants began to run in a circle outside the facility. Their daily exercise, he speculated.

Sighing, David laid his grid and rifle in the brush. He had to act.

When the recombinants surged past, he sprang out of the brush at a full run until he was at the end of the line. He kept up with the recombinants' pace as they ran lap after lap around the facility.

He began to sweat, his breath hot and huffing in his throat. He was in excellent physical shape, but the recombinants were approaching his breaking point. He hoped they'd stop before he gave himself away. They each looked so tall and determined, their faces taut, lips pressed together, and cheeks pale.

His own pace was slowing.

Lightheadedness took hold and he felt his body rising. His side ached and his leg muscles burned from the exertion. Just when he thought he'd pass out, the recombinants angled their path toward the facility door.

Relieved, he held onto his pain and followed them into the facility.

17

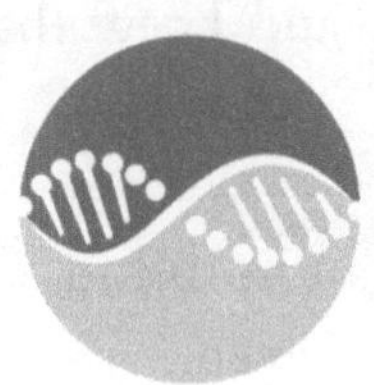

HUNGER BURNED in Diana's stomach. How long had she been asleep?

Groaning, she opened her eyes as sunlight filled the gutted building, hanging in translucent ribbons from the remains of the roof. She studied the room's layout and the heavy layer of dust covering the broken tile floors and cracked foundation underneath. Hints of red and blue and cream bled through the grit and scorched debris. The air smelled so dirty.

Her body felt weak, her limbs barely responding. As she struggled to sit up, the memory of the biodrone attack slipped back again. And the fiery slash to her shoulder.

She shivered, still seeing those empty gold eyes looking right through her.

Behind her, D'Angelo lay in the corner, sleeping fitfully on his bedroll. His muttering echoed through the building and she feared it would bring more biodrones.

She looked around the expanse, expecting to see David and Peter standing guard. Their absence was unsettling. She felt vulnerable now. And a little scared.

Must be out on patrol, she decided.

Ron leaned against the far wall that faced the street, a rifle slung across his shoulder. His head slumped against the broken stonework, his shoulders rising and falling in an even rhythm. He was on watch, but fast asleep. Had the poor guy been the only one on watch all night long, struggling to stay awake?

That made her nervous. *Where were the other recombinants?*

Across from her lay one of them. She thought for a moment—Tanner. He stared at her with a glazed expression that unsettled her. She sat up.

"Ron?" she called.

His shoulders continued to rise and fall.

"Ron?" she said, louder this time.

No response.

The recombinant tried to rise from the ground, but his legs and hands were tied together.

Where were the others?

Diana groped the gritty floor debris until her hand closed around a sizeable stone. She flung it at the wall and it plinked with a sharp report.

Startled, Ron jerked awake, his head snapping up, hands fumbling against his rifle. Bleary-eyed, he swiveled, panning the area for a sign of movement. Finally, he scanned behind him and saw her sitting up.

"Diana!" He hurried toward her and laid a hand against her arm. "Thank God," he said with a weak smile. "All this silence was getting to me."

"When will David and Peter be back from patrol?" she asked.

His gaze softened, his mouth taut. The muscles in his cheeks tightened. She studied him a moment, her heart beating fast now.

Something was terribly wrong.

Her eyes narrowed. "Tell me everything that's happened since I was sick and if you leave out something, I'll know."

Nodding, Ron sat down in front of her. He inhaled sharply.

"You've been asleep for quite a while. And a lot has happened. Let me start with the worst first."

Diana stiffened, bracing herself.

"First, D'Angelo has gone over the edge. You already know he's contacted HQ and invoked Naharra rules. That means a nuclear bombardment of the entire planet."

A chill surged through her at the thought of nuclear warheads raining down on their campsite. She shuddered. Even a civilian out this far knew that was the worst-case scenario.

"Holy hell, I remember now! How long?"

Ron glanced at his watch. "Approximately forty-seven hours from now, the UCOE strike force will be in orbit around Ballese, ready to empty their payloads."

"Then we'd better make sure we're all on that shuttle well before that," she said, unblinking.

Scary, but she could deal with it. They had a shuttle. They'd get out in plenty of time. But it made her sick to think UCOE would destroy another planet. It didn't work the first time and failed to defeat the Antarans. Nuking Naharra had been futile. It made no difference to the Antaris Nation's advance toward home system.

Why would they do something so drastic and irreversible a second time? Everyone knew it was insane!

Correction, not UCOE—D'Angelo. Why would he order this?

He'd probably never had so much as a blemish on his record until now. UCOE had no reason to question his orders. They had no idea that he'd cracked out here.

"That's the plan then...to make it to the shuttle in time." Ron seemed comfortable with that.

They'd get out in time. She'd make certain of it.

"What else happened?" she asked.

Ron's gaze fell away from her face.

"Ron...please, what else?"

"It's Mitchell," he said finally, sighing.

She sucked in a breath, her heart dropping into her stomach. "What about Peter? Ron, please!"

"Mitchell..." Ron snapped a hand to his forehead, frowning. "This is so hard" He sighed.

Her heart smashed against her rib cage and she shuddered, terrified that he was dead—or taken by Antarans. She could barely breathe.

"What's happened to Peter?" she asked again, her voice trembling.

"Yesterday, Mitchell slipped into the Antaran facility between watches. He's been gone about twenty-four hours now. David feared he was in trouble." Ron laid his hand against her arm, squeezing. "Diana, he went in after Mitchell."

Fear pressed against her chest and for a moment, she couldn't pull any air into her lungs.

David and Peter were trapped in that facility with less than forty-eight hours between them and a massive nuclear detonation.

She felt sick. She shook her head, mouth falling open, no words to reply.

"Oh, Peter, no," she whispered finally. "And David?"

Peter's guilt had been too much for him to bear. She thought that time might have healed some of that pain, but Peter's loyalty—and naiveté—blinded him to danger. He and Sting were like brothers and she knew that eventually he'd find a way into that facility.

If only she'd been coherent enough to have stopped him.

"David will find him. Don't you worry." Ron offered a thin smile that disappeared quickly.

Her eyes filled with tears. "But who will find David?"

She smashed her hand into a fist. She would.

Even if she had to ram the shuttle right through that facility, she would get them both out. And with Ron's help, she'd do whatever it took to stall that strike force.

She swallowed hard, shoved her pain to the back of her mind, and grabbed hold of Ron's sleeve.

"All right. David and Peter are in the facility and a strike force is on its way. We have to maneuver the shuttle near the facility and then stall."

Ron nodded. "My thoughts exactly." He pointed to D'Angelo. "The captain has a counter-code that can stop the UCOE attack. We need to get it from him somehow."

A counter-code!

Diana wanted to shriek with joy. She grinned. "That's great news, Ron! How do we get it? Distract him?"

Asking him about the caregivers would be a good place to start.

"Yes, that's it exactly," said Ron. "If we can get him to let down his guard with questions about the caregivers and then hit him with a request for the counter-code, maybe we can get it?"

She turned her attention to D'Angelo and his restless tossing and turning. How would they trick a career military man into revealing a code that he'd been trained to give up his life to protect?

But that code was David and Peter's best chance. For them, she'd try. And keep trying.

Her stomach rumbled painfully. She needed to eat.

"Are there any rations left?" she asked.

Ron smiled. "Of course. I'll get you one."

She nodded at D'Angelo. "Do it loudly, will you? Get him on his feet."

Ron adjusted his rifle over his shoulder and moved to the crates beside D'Angelo's bedroll. She heard clanging and shuffling until D'Angelo's startled voice barked into the expanse.

"That's a good way to attract biodrones, Kraver! Stow that noise."

Ron didn't respond. He turned away quickly and carried a ration over to Diana. She clutched the silver packet, activating the heating reaction in the bottom. When the packet felt warm, she opened it and sniffed, hoping for one of the least offensive rations. Hot cheese scent mixed with the warm starch of noodles.

She smiled. A macaroni and cheese-like substance clumped in the sweating bag.

She blew on the contents until the bag no longer burned her hand. Then she tipped it to her mouth and sucked in a glop of cheese and noodles. The cheese tasted processed and powdered, the noodles overcooked, but right now, it was the best-tasting macaroni and cheese she'd ever had. She devoured the packet's contents, the warmth feeling good in her stomach.

Ron opened a couple of coffee rations and handed her one. It wasn't Karaban with that warm, nutty spice, but it would do.

"Kraver," D'Angelo called, still sounding irritated.

"Captain?"

"How about one of those coffee rations over here?"

Ron located another coffee ration and passed it to D'Angelo who struggled with trembling hands to activate then open the packet. He sat down on one of the crates and still using the other one as a makeshift desk, he called up his star charts on a datapad again. He drank coffee, mumbled to himself, and marked points on the map with swipes of his thick fingers.

Ron returned to Diana. He cast a wary gaze at Tanner and then helped Diana up from the bedroll.

"Over here, to Mitchell's bedroll," he whispered.

With Ron at her elbow, she moved slowly and uncertainly toward the bedroll. When her knees felt like buckling, she sat down on Peter's bedroll. Faint traces of the cedary cologne she'd bought him last week clung to the thick brown material.

Her stomach clenched. *Please, let David and Peter be all right.*

"What's the matter?" she asked Ron. "Why are we whispering and moving all the way over here?"

"That recombinant," said Ron, nodding toward Tanner.

She stared at Tanner lying on his side, a rumpled bedroll beneath him. He struggled against his bonds.

"David and Mitchell both said he's a recombinant-biodrone hybrid. He tried to kill David and me, but you clocked him with an ion lantern."

Diana frowned. *Had she hit him?* She remembered nothing. Just heat and pain.

"Where's Langley and Newlin?" she asked.

"Dead. Tanner came back from patrol alone. We still don't know what happened out there."

"What did Peter think?"

Of everyone here, Peter knew the most about recombinants.

Ron sat down beside her, his voice barely above a whisper. "That the caregivers are trying to hybridize existing recombinants in order to speed up some process that isn't quite working. Yet."

"So, Tanner's a prototype," Diana offered, her mind spinning off possibilities.

"Exactly," said Ron.

She turned her gaze back to the recombinant. The bedroll lay twisted. Empty.

"He's gone!"

Ron scrambled to his feet, but the barrel of a plasma rifle ground into his shoulder blades, forcing him back against the bedroll again. Diana waved her hand, distracting the recombinant, whose dead gaze turned toward her. The rifle barrel swiveled toward her chest.

She braced herself for the charge.

A frenzied scream tore through the burned-out building as D'Angelo leaped at Tanner.

Ron sprang to his feet and launched himself at Tanner.

Diana struggled to stand, but weakness made her sink back against Peter's bedroll. She didn't have the strength to help them.

Tanner cracked Ron in the head with the rifle and he tumbled the ground with a yelp. D'Angelo, teeth gritted, white rage seething in his gaze, was an enraged demon.

He had Tanner in a headlock, the barrel of the plasma rifle swinging wildly. Diana stumbled to her feet and flung herself against the wall as Tanner squeezed off a burst of plasma.

The blast gouged a gaping hole into the corner of the building, scattering crates and incinerating D'Angelo's precious star charts.

Dear God, the comunit!

Fighting against fever and protesting muscles, Diana staggered toward the crates. She threw herself at the brick-sized silver comunit and clasped it to her chest as plasma fire arced above her head. The heat radiated into her injured shoulder and she winced, searching for a pistol. A rifle! A sharp stick!

Anything to stop Tanner.

Slipping the comunit into her jacket pocket, she struggled toward the crates, trying to find a weapon. A lantern—anything! But all the rifles were gone!

Behind one of the now-broken crates, she found part of a lid. She picked it up and stumbled toward the recombinant.

Ron hammered Tanner in the kidney and the recombinant hybrid doubled over with a gasp.

The butt of Tanner's rifle snapped up and slammed into Ron's chin, knocking him unconscious.

She drew back the heavy lid and slammed it against Tanner's body.

Staggering him.

The lid broke into pieces. Useless now. But maybe she could at least get that counter-code? She had to try.

"Captain!" she shouted at D'Angelo. "The counter-code! Please, before the caregivers escape in our shuttle."

D'Angelo's eyes widened, the mixture of fear and anger unmistakable as he sprang at Tanner, pounding his fist against the recombinant's chest over and over, shouting and cursing.

"Captain, please!" she cried. "They're getting away! They'll get hold of the nuclear device. We have to disarm it before they use it against us. Hurry!"

Tanner kicked D'Angelo off him and swung his rifle barrel up from the ground as D'Angelo charged him.

The flash of blue was blinding as it struck D'Angelo in the chest, burning black and red through his side.

He screamed, convulsing, and fell on top of Tanner. Another

blast of plasma discharged and Tanner's body seized.

Thick, dark smoke obscured them as Diana looked away.

She struggled toward D'Angelo. Gently, she turned him over.

He clutched a plasma pistol in his hand, his body still shuddering. The pistol had melted in the blast, D'Angelo's hand fused to it. His intestines protruded from his laid open belly.

Sickened, Diana looked away. He screamed again, his voice abruptly cut off with a sharp, wet wheeze.

He reached out to her, Tanner dead beneath him. She hesitated then gripped his hand as she knelt unsteadily beside him.

"The counter-code, please, sir," she pleaded, her eyes clouded with tears. "Help me stop all of this."

Please don't die! Please don't die.

She gritted her teeth.

No, he couldn't just die and take that counter-code with him. Dammit, he couldn't!

"They're deceivers," D'Angelo gurgled. "Ku'Tal was—a lie. They want to repopulate—us...with their own DNA. Like parasites." His body arced in a wave of pain. He gasped, a cry slipping between his gritted teeth. "Not resurrect—dead race... takeover ours...humans. Stop them." He cried out again, eyes pressed closed. "Stop them!"

Diana gripped his hand in both of hers, letting him know she was still there with him. His teeth chattered and the convulsions deepened.

"Sir, please—I beg you! Give me the counter-code."

"Antaris Nation—must fall," he said, shaking his head once.

He sucked in an agonizing breath, a rattle clicking in his lungs as blood trickled out of his mouth.

"At all costs. Naharra...rules...stand," he said, gurgling.

He drew in a sharp breath, eyes wide and terrified, the rattle thick in his voice. He exhaled with a hiss and his gaze froze. Only a few muffled clicks and a final wheeze filled the growing silence as his hand slid away from hers.

Diana bit her lip, her jaw tightening, panic rising.

What he saw in that last breath, she didn't know, but she hoped it was something beyond his madness.

Reaching down, Diana closed his eyes and laid him down on the charred ground.

"Peace, Captain."

In a moment, Ron was at her side, dazed and unsteady.

"Damn, that's all we needed. D'Angelo becoming a dead hero." He shook his head and turned his gaze to Tanner. "Poor angry Tanner. His buddies were luckier than he was. He probably didn't even know what happened to him."

She gazed at Ron. Blood caked the side of his face and chin, a dark, swelling bruise on the left side. His left eye was beginning to close.

"That needs attention," she said, pointing to his gashed face.

Diana staggered up from the floor and found the medic's kit lying against the far wall. She motioned him away from the bodies. Ron dropped down beside her as she opened the case. Inside, she found topical antibiotics and bandages. Gently, she applied the antibiotics to his face.

He gritted his teeth, wincing, but allowed her to slather on a thick coating of the goopy cream. Then she covered the gash with a wound sealer and closed it with suture bandages.

"Thanks," he said.

Diana slid the comm unit out of her pocket and handed it to him.

"Guess I'd better contact UCOE command and inform them of D'Angelo's death."

Diana shook her head. "All of that noise and those shots are going to attract biodrones. I say we grab the food packets and head for the shuttle. Now. We're not safe here anymore.

A glint touched Ron's eyes. "Good plan. When we're safe inside the shuttle, we'll contact UCOE and tell them about D'Angelo's death. Maybe the lack of officers and the deteriorating circumstances will convince UCOE to rethink the strike on Ballese?"

"I hope so. Let's take anything useful and get out of here."

Ron rose to his feet. "I'm right behind you."

18

THE FIGHT over the morning's rations startled Peter awake.

Fearing an attack, Peter jerked up from the ground and flung himself against the wall, his heart pounding.

Shouts and snarls echoed through the expanse.

He peered slowly over the stone wall he'd erected. Dozens of hybrids tore at each other, gouging faces, kicking, and choking each other. They tangled together in an angry pile, punching and growling. Almost like animals as flashes of silvery food packets bounced from hand to hand and skittered across the ground.

He watched in horrified fascination as the fighting swelled then died down when the rations had been devoured, empty food packets littering the floor.

In moments, the door to the outer pen creaked open and like zombies, the hybrids wandered toward the bright patch of light shining into the cavernous chamber. The scent of cool, clean air blew through, clearing out the stale air and dust. A hint of sweetness in this sour-smelling place.

That made him uneasy. Anxious.

He stepped out from behind the wall and moved toward the crate of food packets. Blood flecked the ground, mingling with the dust. Underneath a crate lid was a food packet. It must have fallen out during the fighting.

Peter grinned at his good fortune and slid out the packet. He tore it open and drank the salty, soupy mixture until the packet was empty. He had no idea what he'd just eaten, but it would keep him going.

Dropping the empty packet into the crate, Peter moved past the opening to the pen. He hurried to the wall where the hallway into the rotunda had been hidden. He pressed his hands against the wall, examining the crevices for a hidden panel or switch. The caregiver hadn't carried any sort of special equipment, so there had to be a switch.

He searched diligently for several minutes, finding only sharp rocks and deep cracks. Finally, his fingers flitted over a smooth, bumpy surface on the wall. With both hands, Peter pried at it until the bump slid back, revealing a lever. He yanked it down and the door opened into the dimly lit hallway.

Grinning, he ducked out of the expanse and into the dark corridor.

The labyrinth of passageways confused and frightened him. He expected biodrones to leap at him at any moment, but he shoved back his fear and kept moving. Were the caregivers watching him even now?

None of that mattered as long as he found Sting.

He rounded one empty curve after another, each one twisting into shadows and thin lighting until, at last, he blundered into the vaulted rotunda, illuminating the floor with a green glow.

Faint traces of honey made him shudder, the fear sharp and growing.

The memory of that scent was palpable and it gnawed at his stomach, his hands trembling now.

Beyond this circular corridor lay the repository. He was certain of it.

He'd spent enough time in the Ku'Tal structure to recognize a lot of similarities to its layout. Granted, the Ku'Tal repository had been a lot smaller, but he recognized similar patterns and hallways. But this structure was much more dangerous. He had no way of knowing if any of these recombinants were real now. They could be the hybrids or worse—caregivers shifting form.

What if he did find Sting and they'd already turned him into one of those mindless, dead-eyed monsters?

He shuddered, hands balling into fists. He'd never forgive himself.

Inhaling sharply, he entered the rotunda, head high, moving with confidence. He had to look like he knew where he was headed. Like he was supposed to be here.

The rotunda's glass ceiling glimmered like a big green sun, casting rivulets of swirled green light across the white floors and white walls. He was surprised that his footsteps made no sound against the hard, white tiles, like they had in the structure on Ku'Tal. The wide-open space seemed to absorb sounds instead of reverberating them against the glass and the walls. On Ku'Tal, every sound had been magnified.

He relaxed a little as he continued around the circular walkway. Avoiding any eye contact with the creatures passing by him.

No caregivers stopped him. He was relieved, but a little surprised. Did the hybrids have free rein to travel the facility or were the caregivers just testing him?

Gathering his nerve, he decided to find out.

He steadied himself as a caregiver sidled toward him. Its blob-like body startled him. The mottled flesh was the color of tarnished, dirty brass and it had a sheen of thin white hair covering its bulbous body. It had four close set, gold eyes all in a row, reminding him of the magnified image of a spider he'd seen in the library at the training base once. They were bright but emotionless, empty. Its gait was quick but jerky, dragging its feet. Four in all.

He hadn't seen caregivers in this form before and it unnerved him. Bracing himself, he looked full on into the creature's eyes. As he kept walking.

The caregiver's gaze encompassed him, but it kept moving without reacting to him in any way. Its eyes were as dead as Drake's had been on Ku'Tal after the biodrones had attacked.

Halfway around the circular walkway, he passed the hallway that a caregiver had taken him down yesterday. Dead-eyed creatures passed him without acknowledgement. He moved past the hallway, into the next one. Two more hallways slipped past. Their empty eyes were disturbing, but he realized that was the one thing the Antarans hadn't been able to recreate.

Emotion. That's how he'd recognize the real recombinants.

A faint rumble emanated through the towering dome's walls.

Peter halted, glancing back at the rotunda with its shiny white floors and walls.

A door in the outer wall opened into the rotunda. He hadn't seen any seams or grooves to indicate doorways, but the wall slid open.

From the opening, a group of eight recombinants marched into the round walkway behind one of the blobby-looking caregivers.

Hybrids? He had to see their eyes to know for sure.

Among those recombinants staggered a thin young man with curly blond hair. His face was shadowed, green eyes dull with despair and exhaustion.

Peter's heart pounded into his throat at those familiar green eyes and curly blond hair.

STING!

His knees shook, his eyes misting. He grabbed hold of the wall to steady himself and then turned around as naturally as he could, moving with quicker strides toward the recombinants. To slip into their group.

Sting.

He bit his lip, fighting back his emotions, the burn of moisture in his eyes. He was still alive!

Relief overwhelmed him and he ached to talk to him, to tell him how sorry he was and how he got here as fast as he could.

The urge to shout at Sting burned through him, but he held it inside. He didn't dare shout or even speak. Calling any attention to himself might bring half the caregivers down on him. And those biodrones.

He was within five feet of Sting when something grabbed his arm, jerking him backward. He fought viciously, but a sharp jolt made his body seize. Flailing, he fell against the wall.

His knees buckled and he collapsed, still shaking. A caregiver stood over him, looking more like the humanoid creatures he remembered from Ku'Tal. It wore a pale, ice green tunic tucked into dark trousers and it held a triangular-shaped object in its hand. Peter quickly realized it was some sort of stunner.

"I didn't expect you to find your way out for several days, but you learn fast." It shook the stunner at him. "We will see how useful you are."

Peter struggled against the caregiver as it took hold of his arms and pulled him up from the floor as Sting moved farther and farther away from him.

No! Sting, no!

Another caregiver, dressed in beige robes assisted the first caregiver. He fought against the stun effect to find his voice, to shout at Sting, but only a strangled, thin moan emerged as the eight recombinants disappeared through another opening in the rotunda's curved outer walls.

19

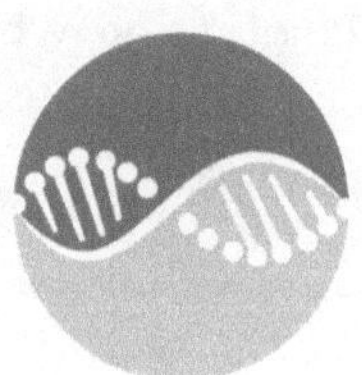

THE SCENT of fresh earth blended with sweat and darkness as the Antaran facility's corridor narrowed, pressing David against the other recombinants. He'd made it inside!

Recombinants pushed and shoved, some arguing, others cursing. He tried to block the blows but couldn't lift his arms wedged in like this.

Movement through the narrow corridor was slow, but in a few moments, bright light filtered into the corridor. Relieved, he stumbled out of the darkness and into a bunk room. A wall closed behind them.

Inside, striated black and grey rock covered the walls, the floors bright white tile. Nearby, water trickled.

His boots clicked in sharp raps across the tile. The room was narrow, but long, allowing about a couple dozen people to be together without inciting claustrophobia or a desire to murder everyone in the vicinity.

A row of bunk beds, stacked three to a column, stretched across and around the room. White sheets and white blankets against dirty iron-like metal. Off to his left, a pale white light illuminated the latrine fixtures. To his right were three small, round tables made from a strange yellow wood that seated about six or eight people. David inhaled sharply and glanced around for a sign of Mitchell.

The recombinants moved to their own bunks or huddled around the tables. The soft hum of conversations filled the room.

He wandered the perimeter, searching for a way out. To his surprise, there were no doors. When all the recombinants seemed to have settled in, he stopped beside what appeared to be an empty bunk and claimed it. His body longed to curl up under the scratchy white blanket and go to sleep, but he had work to do.

Trying not to draw attention, he plopped down on the bunk and surveyed the entire space. From this vantage point, he could study the other recombinants without drawing unwanted attention. Or pissing one of them off—which would turn into a fight. The blanket smelled like dry wool, its texture rough like sandstone.

He peered at the others, trying to gauge if they were recombinants or hybrids like Peter had described, but dammit, he just couldn't tell. Some of the recombinants searched the wall for a way out while others fell asleep on their bunks. A few others gathered in the corner, their faces taut with determination.

He knew that look. They were plotting an escape.

But his eyes were quickly closing and he couldn't hold back his exhaustion any longer. He laid his head against the rock-hard pillow, giving in to sleep for a short nap.

Later, he awoke to the sharp raps of footsteps scurrying across the tile floor.

What now?

He opened his eyes, craning his neck toward the sounds.

A door in the side of the wall slid open and one of those hideous, mottled caretakers slithered into the room. It looked humanoid, wearing a forest green tunic that fastened at its left shoulder and dark trousers. The recombinants in the corner dispersed, moving silently out of the caregiver's reach. The caregiver turned back to the hallway and motioned them into the half-light.

Eight recombinants thundered down the hallway and into this bunk room.

He bolted up from the bed when his gaze fell onto an almost gaunt young man with curly blond hair and bleary green eyes. Much of the passion and exuberance had left that once-young face that had withstood Ku'Tal and so much more than that. Sting looked like a shell of the recombinant he remembered, but he was thrilled to see him alive.

Private John Stingley. He'd managed to survive even here.

It sapped every bit of David's patience to wait until the caregiver left. Fidgeting, he sat with his back against the cold stone, watching Sting fall facedown onto his bunk and slip instantly into sleep. The caregiver started a slow walk around the room.

He decided not to look so prominent, so he slid onto his stomach and buried his face into the smelly, dry wool of the blanket that nearly choked him as he feigned exhaustion.

In a moment or two, he felt a presence hanging over his bunk, but he pretended to slip into sleep, his breath heavier and drawn out. Time seemed to freeze and a hundred thoughts filled him, dread heavy against his chest, but he kept his face against that scratchy blanket.

Finally, the presence dissipated, click of boots across tile.

He opened an eye. The caregiver inspected the latrine and around the tables before it slipped out of the chamber.

When he was certain the caregiver had gone, he bolted up from the heavy blanket, his face and neck damp with sweat. He ran a hand across his forehead and leaned back against the wall. The cool stone felt good against his overheated skin. He glanced across at Sting's bunk, but it was empty.

Dammit! Had he dreamed seeing Sting?

Scratching his head, he gazed around the room until a shadow moved in the latrine. In a few moments, Sting plodded out, his green UCOE uniform shirt hanging open. His cheeks were hollow and hopelessness burned in the young man's eyes. Sting's strong spirit was finally starting to wither.

Sting shuffled up from the bunk.

"Stingley," he called in a soft voice.

Sting looked up, his gaze scanning the room for the voice.

David hurried toward him. "Stingley!" he said, his voice rising. He grabbed Sting by the arms and pulled him into a tight hug.

Stepping back, Sting stared at him for a moment, confusion on his pale face.

"Don't you know me?" David demanded, slapping his chest with his hands.

Sting squinted. "Sarge?" he muttered finally, shock glimmering in his eyes.

David nodded.

"Sarge!" he screeched, throwing his arms around David and wildly pounding him on the back. "Holy shit! Sarge!" Finally, he let go, scrutinizing David. "You're the best sight I've seen in a long time, Sarge." Grinning, he poked David in the ribs. "Damn, it's good to see you, but what the hell are you doing here? How?"

David shook his head, silencing Sting. He nodded toward the empty tables and moved with casual steps through the room. There was no telling who or what was listening to them. Or watching them.

Sting waited and then followed.

The alcove of tables seemed cold and damp, the light shadowy and dim, only a thin bar of light, recessed into the rock, ran the circumference of the room. It had gone out near the three tables in the corner. The chairs were straight-backed and made from an amber-colored wood he hadn't seen before.

Folding his arms against his chest, he sat down at the far table. He waited until Sting finally entered the small room and sat down across from him. He leaned forward, palms on the tabletop.

"So, what's the story, Sarge?" Sting asked in a sharp whisper. "How'd you get here?"

"Long story," he muttered. "Ask me later. But I'm here for two reasons. The second one's to get you out of here."

Sting frowned. "What's the first reason?"

David sighed and dropped his head into his hands. Every time he thought about it, his stomach twisted into a nervous knot. There was no telling what had already happened to him.

"Mitchell."

Sting's mouth fell open, his eyes bulging. "Pete's here, too?" He didn't seem to believe the words as they came out of his mouth, but David could see how desperately Sting wanted to see his best buddy.

David nodded. "He came here to get you out. We all tried to stop him, but he wouldn't be stopped, Stingley."

No words came out of Sting's mouth. He just gaped at David, shaking his head, his eyes welling with tears. "Pete's really here? For-for me?"

Overcome by emotion, Sting turned away, running a hand through his hair. His bottom lip quivered as he wiped his sleeve across his eyes. Only then did he turn back to David.

"Where is he, Sarge?"

David shrugged. If only he knew the answer to that question. "Somewhere inside this place. He's been gone awhile, so I came after him."

"In here?" Anger swept across Sting's face and he pounded the table with his fist. "Damn it, what did Pete think he was doing? One of us got out and he's throwing it all away! He's made Ku'Tal pointless now."

Sighing, David reached out and patted Sting on the shoulder. "Sting, to Mitchell, Ku'Tal was pointless unless you and he both got out. He couldn't handle the guilt, knowing he was free when you were here being tortured."

Sting's eyes were emerald flames. "I did this for him," he said through gritted teeth. "So, he could do what I couldn't. Damn him." He pounded the table again. "Damn him!"

"It's too late for anger. We've got to think logically and find him somehow. They'll eat him alive in here."

Snapping out of the chair, Sting paced the floor. "Of course, they'll eat him alive in here! It's what they do, Sarge!" He whirled around, splaying his hands. Angry red scars striped his forearms. "Everything they said was a lie," he said, his voice a distant whisper. "They've only taken skin samples from me so far, but I'm slated for droning in about a week."

Sting's voice quivered and he paused as if trying to regain his composure. He fell down on his knees beside David's chair and whispered in his ear. "They're building an army we won't see until it turns on us. Soldiers that look human, but they're much, much hungrier for the kill—like a biodrone." He thumped his chest. "And we're the blueprint, Sarge."

A heaviness sat on David's chest. So, it was true. The Antarans were trying to send their biodrones into UCOE's forces disguised as recombinants. How much of this had D'Angelo already known? He shuddered. Maybe *that* was his reason for Naharra rules?

"Listen to me carefully, Stingley," said David, unable to contain his urgency. He leaned forward. "In less than forty eight hours, a strike force is going to nuke this entire planet to hell. We've gotta find Mitchell and get out of here before that happens." He sat back in his chair.

A wicked grin spread across Sting's face. "Let me live to see the day—and take out a few caregivers on my way out."

"Okay, Sting, where could Mitchell be? Where do we look?"

Stingley planted himself in the chair again. "Depends on how he got inside."

"Mitchell's smart," said David. "He would have tried to blend into a group of recombinants."

David glanced down at the rich, amber wood, smooth and cool against his fingertips as he drummed on the table, trying to remember their day on patrol, what they saw that day. That would give him a clue about how Mitchell got inside. He remembered seeing the green dome and the recombinants in a pen outside the dome.

"The dome," said David. "Why are there recombinants in pens outside the dome?"

"The lab's inside the dome," he said with a shrug. "Those pens are exercise/experiment areas where they observe the new hybrids. They also weed out the hybrids in there."

"Weed out?"

Sting nodded. "The ones that look and behave like biodrones are destroyed—they'd be too obvious to the military."

That made sense, David decided. Even if UCOE knew about the plan, they could never be sure about their own recombinants. The hybrids had to fool UCOE forces or the whole plan was pointless.

"The remaining ones," Sting continued, "are put into a bigger group of hybrids that have some chance of being trained for combat. From those, the caregivers test them and see if they're clever enough to fool someone that they're recombinants if requested to speak and react—and kill."

David shuddered. RDC still had difficulty finding the right mix of aggression and conscience. These hybrids were at least half biodrones. They had no conscience.

"The ones that pass that test are put up against a real recombinant. The loser generally dies during the test or shortly after." Sting stared at David for a moment, concern shining in his kind green eyes. "Pete slipped into this place through that pen, didn't he?"

"At least I think so," said David, sighing. Mitchell had been totally preoccupied by the dome and the pen. He had to have gone through there.

"Look, Sarge, Pete's no fool! He's not like the rest of us, but he has the same instincts even if he refuses to give in to them. He hates those bastards as much as I do. I know Pete. He'd enjoy tricking them."

"Would there be another way?"

Stingley shook his head. "The only other way would be in here, with the captured recombinants. I'd have seen him."

"Somehow, we've got to maneuver ourselves toward the group of hybrids."

"Toward the hybrids," Sting muttered, deep in thought and pacing again. "Let me think about that for a minute."

David smiled. The Stingley he remembered was starting to resurface again. It had been pushed down by the Antarans, but slowly, it was coming back.

He was so relieved.

"Think, Sting. What brings these two groups together?"

Sting continued to pace until finally, he turned around. "The one thing that brings recombinants and hybrids together is when the Antarans pit them against each other. They like to test their creations against the real thing. If we want to get close to him, we'll have to defeat a hybrid when they're tested."

Frowning, David rose from the chair. He didn't like the sound of that. He had no desire to fight biodrones. Human or Antaran, it didn't matter. They were still mindless biodrones that killed on command. But he'd face them if it meant a chance to get to Mitchell.

20

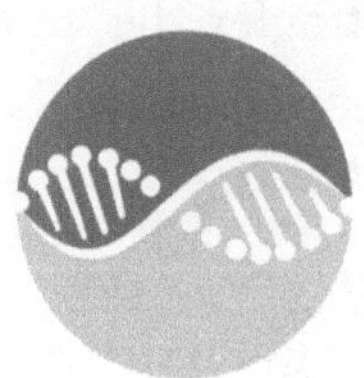

WITH A STUNNER POISED at his neck, Peter moved out of the rotunda and into a wide, well-populated hallway. The walls shimmered dove grey and the green tiles had given way to slick, silver tiles. The air smelled recycled and tart. Around him, several caregivers passed through the corridor.

His chukkas clomped against the floor, but the caregiver behind him made no sound. Peter's pace slowed, the tiles making his progress cumbersome, but the stunner continued to hover near his neck. The air felt warm and that comforted him. He'd grown tired of the dank, cavernous rooms he'd been trapped in for a while. The hybrids didn't seem to notice temperature differences.

He envied them that trait. He hated to be cold.

But all he could think about was Sting. His best friend was still alive! It wasn't too late to save him.

The stunner poked Peter in the head and his pace quickened despite the tile floor. He sighed.

How would he escape this caregiver? Was it too late for both of them now?

Caregivers filled the corridor, some dressed in brightly colored tunics yellows and greens and orange and dark trousers while others wore strange tan and white robes. Their milky skin and white hair made them all look alike.

He remembered their incredible ability to adapt rapidly to their surroundings. How they changed form to suit the situation. He thought about attacking the caregiver when they were out of this main section, but that might bring him even more trouble.

No, he'd have to be patient and move through their system. If the caregiver believed he was a promising hybrid, then he'd have to keep playing that part. He had no choice if he wanted to rescue Sting.

"Where are we going?" Peter asked finally.

"To testing. It's just beyond the lab."

Testing? He glared, wanting to reach behind him and twist the caregiver's head off.

"Where's the lab?"

"We passed it in the rotunda."

That's where Sting had gone, Peter realized. Somehow, he had to get in there. "You mean that dome room?"

"Yes, the dome room."

Peter bristled at the caregiver's snide inflections. As if Peter was too stupid to understand what the dome room was or even where to find it. He clenched his hands into fists.

"Is that where I'll end up?" Peter asked, craning his neck to see the caregiver.

"It is possible," said the caregiver, unblinking. "Depends on your preliminary testing."

The hallway ended in a T, the right turn curving off somewhere in an ice-blue wash of light. The left turn ended at a green metal door. He stiffened and waited for the caregiver to point left or right. He halted at the end and studied both directions. The caregiver stood there for some time before it nudged him left, toward the green metal door.

He refused.

The caregiver turned a knob on the device. "At this level, there might be brain damage. You'd have to be destroyed then."

He bit his lip and reluctantly, he entered the left hallway.

He stumbled once but regained his footing. When he reached the green door, he stopped and waited.

"Enter," said the caregiver.

"You first," Peter replied, glaring.

The stunner swept toward him, but Peter lunged out of the way. He grabbed the caregiver's arm and tried to take the scanner, but the caregiver kicked at his legs.

Fury filled Peter, at all the injustices the caregivers had done to him and the other recombinants, at the lies, the broken promises.

All we want is to bring our race back from the dead, said the Antarans. *We still need recombinants to recover from extinction. We need you alive*, they said. They promised to withdraw from Ku'Tal if they got their key to their genetic repository. The bargain he'd made with them to save Sarge and Sting.

All of it was lies. They were experimenting on recombinants here. Killing them. Like they'd probably killed the other recon teams. And the colony.

He slammed the caregiver against the wall twice until the small, triangular stunner skittered across the floor.

He dove for the stunner.

If it worked on hybrids, then it would work on a caregiver—he hoped.

He whirled around, stunner in hand, but the caregiver lurched toward him with a small silver device in its hand.

The device was a two-inch silver spike rushing toward his throat.

His finger hit a button on the stunner as he shoved it at the caregiver, catching the caregiver in the cheek.

Violent convulsions rolled through the creature. The spike fell out of its hand, plinking against the silver tile as it collapsed onto the floor.

Abruptly, the caregiver stopped seizing and fell silent. Smoke drifted up from its still body and almost instantly, the body began to disintegrate.

Peter, stunner still in hand, gawked at the pile of clothes lying in the hallway. *How had that just happened? What had he done?*

Panicked, he gathered up the clothing, the only evidence of the caregiver's accident, and ran down the hallway.

When he reached the T in the hallway, he didn't turn back the way he came. Instead, he kept running straight ahead and swerved around a curve that led into a long, empty hallway. The tiles were green, the walls translucent white. A thin stream of white light burned across the top of the right-hand wall.

What would happen to him now when they found out he'd killed a caregiver?

The answer burned in the pit of his stomach and he squirmed against it. They'd destroy him. They had no use for a hybrid that turned on its creators. UCOE's answer to uncontrollable recombinants was to wash them out.

What would he do now?

Ahead, the corridor branched out into four directions and Peter ran harder, hoping he wouldn't encounter another caregiver in this long hallway.

No place to hide.

As he reached the intersection, the tick of footsteps echoed against tile.

He rushed into the nearest turn. The hallway had doors on both sides and the first one to his right was ajar. He glanced inside.

A small storage room.

He flung himself inside and closed the door. A small silver plate was affixed to the wall. Curious, he touched it and ice blue lights swelled overhead.

He leaned against the door, his chest heaving, and tried to think through the situation. They'd find him any moment.

He waited, terrified, as footsteps clamored past the room. Shortly, another set thundered past until the quiet swallowed them up, too.

Moments ticked past, his heart throbbing in his throat, his limbs frozen in fear.

The hallway settled into the quiet, only the soft hum of the lights and his own breathing whispered through the room.

When his breathing began to slow, he turned his attention to the storeroom. It was a narrow room with metal shelving on both sides. What appeared to be cleaning equipment hung on the far wall. Brooms, dusters, squeegees, cleaning rags. The shelves contained all sorts of items, including a stack of shimmery, net-like coats and crystal-clear goggles. Gloves of the same shimmery material were stacked beside the coats.

At last, he realized his good fortune. This wasn't any storeroom. This was the one for the dome lab. It was too close to the rotunda not to be.

He grinned. All he needed was a little diversion.

He looked around the room for some help.

The two plasma grenades from his pack were still in his pants pockets, but those were only for a last resort. If he had to, he'd blow open a hole in the facility and walk out, but only if he had to use them. He patted his pocket, feeling their familiar bulk. He couldn't use them until he'd found Sting.

Then, anything was fair game.

The storeroom held lots of malleable, glass-like items: beakers and test tubes, lots of scientific equipment he didn't recognize.

He walked slowly past the metal shelves, studying everything there.

On the shelving to his left, he found bottles of chemicals. The print on them wasn't anything Peter recognized. It was labeled in the blocky, slopey script of the Antaris language—whatever that was. Nevertheless, the chemicals looked dangerous.

He smiled and patted his pants pockets. And hopefully flammable.

He glanced down at the caregiver's clothes in his hands. The clothes smelled tart and smoky. He tossed them behind one of the shelves, hoping they wouldn't be seen.

His gaze flicked from the chemicals to his pocket. The chemicals would likely cause a nice explosion and require some effort to put out the fire, giving him time to reach the lab—and Sting.

If he was fast, he could get into the lab and find his way into the hallways leading to the hybrid pens. From there, the grenades would open a door into the wilderness.

All he needed now was the diversion.

He slid one of the grenades out of his pocket and stared at it for a moment, studying the activator. One twist and it would activate a ten second timer. That was enough time for him to get clear of the blast.

He didn't have a choice. He had to use one of the grenades now.

Cautiously, he opened the door and turned, his fingers against the activator. Sarge told him once that these plasma grenades also had a frequency pairing switch, allowing them to mimic a cascade mine. The first grenade would explode and a nearby one would detonate seconds later because of a frequency emitted by the first grenade. The grenades had to be fairly close to one another.

Peter opened the bottom of the grenade, searching for a sign of the switch. There it was, easily accessed. He flipped the pairing switch.

A hand clamped onto his arm. The grenade fell from his hands, rolling under one of the shelves in the storeroom.

He turned.

A caregiver!

"I'm afraid we have a bad situation here," said the caregiver, dragging him out of the storeroom.

The caregivers' grey robes billowed but didn't slow down the creature's reflexes.

He fought, but he couldn't break the caregiver's grip on his arm. The caregiver threw him against the wall.

Sharp pain surged through his body, spiking again when he hit the floor. Dazed, he lay there, trying to stop the world from spinning.

"As I said," the caregiver continued, "the situation is bad. You were a promising hybrid, but I fear you will turn on us again. That leaves us with one alternative. Field testing."

Again, the caregiver grabbed hold of his arm, pulling him into that long, empty hallway again.

He dragged Peter, the green tiles smacking against his knees and palms, through the intersection of other hallways, finally taking a sharp right turn. There at the end of the hallway was a red door.

Peter struggled.

Something told him this was the end of the line for a hybrid. He couldn't go in there. If he did, he'd never come out again.

Was this what all those recombinants who'd washed out faced at the end of their shuttle trip back to RDC?

Here, the washout process would be much more painful.

He kicked at the caregiver's legs and it stumbled, crashing against the wall. He kicked it again until the caregiver's hold on his arm slipped.

Scrambling up from the tile, he pivoted, his aching legs unresponsive.

He should have expected the stab of a stunner against his neck, but it took him by surprise.

His body seized, trembling and shaking. He collapsed, unable to take control of his legs.

He had to escape! Had to run—move—somehow!

The caregiver clamped its hand on his arm again and the dragging resumed.

His head bounced against the tiles, sending spikes of pain into his neck and across his temples.

Awkwardly, he clawed at the tile, trying to find a handhold, but he couldn't close his hands.

Ignoring him, the caregiver pressed its palm to a recessed gold plate on the wall and the red door whined open.

Unable to gain control of his spasming muscles, Peter couldn't react. Couldn't stop the caregiver from dragging him inside.

21

IT TOOK Diana and Ron only a few minutes to gather up the remaining equipment, thanks to Tanner and D'Angelo riddling the building with plasma fire.

Diana retrieved a plasma rifle and flipped the strap over her head. Despite the biodrone attack, it took only a moment to get used to the heavy weapon against her right shoulder and she quickly found her balance point. She grabbed one of the field packs and crammed it full with rations. She glanced up to see Ron filling another pack with rations.

"That's the last of them," said Ron, hefting the pack onto his shoulders.

Diana swung the heavy pack up onto her back. She staggered a moment under the weight, finally adjusting it so the load point was spread evenly across her shoulders and hips—and away from her tender left shoulder. At last, she straightened up, both hands curling around the rifle.

Something skittered over the wall.

"Biodrones!" Diana shouted, dropping to one knee.

Ron whirled, plasma fire arcing.

Something screeched and fell off the wall, charred and smoking.

A shadow obscured the shafts of light coming through the roof.

Cold fear gripped her stomach.

She jerked the rifle upward and fired until a black, quivering mass dropped from the rafters not two feet from her.

Four more biodrones glided over the wall, talons rasping across the broken floor.

Ron fired two bursts, dropping one.

Diana obliterated one that rushed at Ron, leaving behind a greasy dark slick on the floor.

Two others surged at Diana and she sprayed a burst of plasma at the break in the wall.

The biodrones disintegrated.

"Let's get out of here!" Ron shouted, motioning Diana toward the back of the building.

Diana moved behind Ron, pack heavy against her body. She paused for an instant, freezing an image of the building in her mind.

David's backpack strewn across the burned and busted floor, Peter's empty bedroll tangled into a heap in the far corner. D'Angelo laid out with hands folded on his own bedroll, Tanner lying stiff beside him.

She sucked down the sob that threatened to bubble up in her throat. *David and Peter were safe*, she told herself. They'd escape this place. They wouldn't end up like Tanner...or D'Angelo.

Ron blasted another biodrone that dropped down from the rafter.

Startled, Diana snapped out of her misery. Ron squeezed her right shoulder.

"Look, they'll be all right. We won't leave here without them. I give you my word." He smiled reassuringly at her. "Hey, I'm a master at last-minute military pull-outs, Diana. I wrote the book *and* the fucking series! I may be writing a new chapter with this one, but we won't leave your brother and Mitchell behind."

"Thanks, Ron," she said.

A biodrone flung itself into the building and careened toward them. Diana fried it with two quick bursts of plasma.

"Let's get out of here," she said and scurried out of the building, Ron beside her.

BIODRONES PURSUED them through the brush. Several times, they retreated behind trees and bushes to eliminate a growing number of biodrones massing behind them.

A flash of gold jagged past and Diana drew a bead, firing.

The biodrone collapsed, screeching, and fell silent. Two more slithered up behind it.

The rifle beeped. Charge empty.

Diana reached into the front pocket of her field pack, finding another cartridge.

"Keep cool," she muttered to herself, the gold eyes skittering toward her.

Her fingers closed on the full cartridge, ejecting the spent one with a flick. She slammed full cartridge into the chamber.

Brush shifted. Talons scritched. Gold eyes met hers, talons ripping past her face.

She threw herself backward, scrambling away from the mass of writhing talons.

"Ron!"

She jerked the rifle barrel up.

The biodrone leaped.

She swung the rifle as hard as she could.

It connected with the biodrone's head, knocking it sideways to the ground.

Ron tore through the brush, aiming. Plasma fire erupted, destroying the biodrone.

Diana got to her feet and they ran for cover in a ring of trees.

biodrones surged after them, two and three at a time, but she and

Ron worked together, laying down arcs of plasma fire that eliminated the biodrones quickly and then they picked off the stragglers.

After a few minutes, no more biodrones emerged from the wilds behind them.

"Let's go!" Diana cried.

Together, she and Ron ran out of the ring of trees in the direction of the shuttle. It took some backtracking and relying on gut feelings, but they made their way through the foliage and back to the shuttle.

A surge of relief washed over her when she saw the battered, grey shuttle, but her relief faded at the glint of gold that crested the shuttle's nose and rushed toward them.

A dozen or more biodrones filled her line of sight. From the other direction.

They'd been flanked!

Ron pushed her toward a fallen tree. They ducked down, balancing their rifles. The biodrones were too close to the shuttle to fire. They'd have to get closer before she could shoot them.

Her palms began to sweat, her mouth going dry.

She glanced at Ron. A sheen of sweat clung to his pale face. He licked his lips as he squinted and drew a bead on the nearest biodrone. She took aim at the one behind it.

"Wait for it," Ron said in a steady voice. "We can't risk hitting the shuttle."

"You say when and that second biodrone's toast," Diana answered, her stomach knotting.

The moments dragged by, the empty gold eyes sliding closer. Ron waited in silence until the first biodrone was less than four feet from them.

"Fire!"

Diana's first burst of plasma cut down the biodrone she'd sighted. The first biodrone fell to Ron's plasma fire.

Ron destroyed the main force while Diana scoped for the biodrones that came at them from other sides. She balanced the rifle as high as she could, destroying every biodrone that came toward them.

Still, she knew that they couldn't keep this up all day. One of them had to get to the shuttle door and open it. With one of them inside, the other could make a break for the shuttle. The biodrones couldn't penetrate a shuttle.

She turned to stare at the shuttle, measuring the distance. Ten meters at the most.

With rifle and heavy pack, she was a lot slower, but with Ron covering her, she could make it.

She rose to her feet.

"Ron, cover me!"

He turned, a look of confusion on his face. "What? Cover you?"

She stepped over the log and ran headlong across the large clearing toward the shuttle.

"Diana, don't! It's too far!"

Ron flung himself over the log, running behind her. He shot down five or six biodrones by the time she'd reached the hatch. She slammed her hand against the lock panel, her fingers flying over the number pad. Red letters flashed, "Access Denied!"

"No!" she shouted.

Four more biodrones fell, Ron closing the distance between them.

Two biodrones slid out of the brush and skittered toward his back.

"Ron, two on your six!"

Ron dropped to the ground and rolled sideways. He raised the rifle, firing, and dropped the two pursuing biodrones.

Diana raised her rifle and took out two more biodrones coming at Ron. He scrambled to his feet, Diana destroying another biodrone before it overtook him. He broke into another run toward the shuttle.

She inhaled sharply, held her breath, and slowly typed the number code into the number pad.

Seconds rushed past.

The door slid open.

Slamming his back against the shuttle's hull, Ron turned and fired. Diana took out two more biodrones that slithered around the nose. She jumped into the shuttle and lunged for the hatch controls. Ron fell backward into the shuttle, firing off quick bursts of plasma.

biodrones screeched and burned.

With a quick flick of a button, the hatch slid closed.

biodrones threw themselves at the hatch, but the opening faded to a crack and then shut tight.

Diana collapsed against the wall, her chest heaving. Ron fought for breath.

"That was a—dumb move, Diana," Ron shouted, but he was too out of breath to convey much anger.

"Maybe so," she replied, "but I couldn't stand being out there any longer."

Talons raked across the hatch.

Nodding, Ron closed his eyes and settled back against the hull. They sat across from each other, without saying a word, biodrones clawing at the shuttle. She wished they'd go away, but knowing they couldn't get through the shuttle's exterior wall made their scritching noises easier to bear. She tried to block out the noise.

In a few minutes, Ron rose from the shuttle floor and dug through his pack, finally retrieving the comm unit. He turned it on and requested a secure channel.

"Recon team three to Commander Reynolds. Over."

Static rose above the determined clawing of the biodrones against the hull.

"Reynolds here, recon three. Over."

"Sir, it is my sad duty to report that Captain D'Angelo has been killed in the line of fire. Request further orders and a freeze on present hostile actions directed toward Ballese. Over."

Diana reached into her pack and located a couple of coffee rations. She tossed one to Ron who mouthed thank you as he waited for Reynold's response.

"Recon three, we are unable to comply with your freeze request. Actions are already in motion. Over."

Ron sighed. He was silent for a moment then a smile came to his face.

"Sir, since I am acting commander of this mission until Sergeant Temple returns, I request a re-evaluation of all pending directives issued from this camp. Over."

Would that work, Diana wondered? She didn't know UCOE regulations, but Ron did. *Would Reynolds comply?*

Static filled the dark shuttle. She gripped the coffee ration tightly, waiting to heat it until she heard Reynolds's reply.

"Recon three, I've checked with HQ and as acting commander, you are within your rights to make such a request. The variables will be run against the current scenario and outcomes re-evaluated. I will contact you when this has been completed. Over."

"Affirmative, Reynolds. Recon three out."

Ron collapsed against the hull, a relieved sigh escaping through his gritted teeth.

"How much time did you just buy us?" Diana asked.

"No more than three or four hours, but that might be enough."

For David and Peter's sake, she hoped it would be enough.

Ron glanced over at her as he heated and opened his coffee ration. He grimaced as he drank deeply from the packet.

"All right, we've got less than thirty hours until the strike force arrives," said Ron, rubbing his forehead. "I say when the time comes, we stall them with our departure from the planet's surface. They'll contact us before they're in range and tell us we have to launch."

"I can handle that part," she said with a smile.

She'd stalled a few launches in her time. It was amazing what sorts of unexpected mechanical problems emerged before takeoff.

They drank their bitter coffee in silence, the ever-present sound of biodrones clawing mindlessly at the shuttle filling the silence. What they needed now was a plan. A way to get David and Peter out of there.

She wondered if the first two recon missions had ended up in that forbidding facility across the lake. What had happened to their crews? They hadn't invoked Naharra rules, only recommended it. What sort of reports had they sent back to UCOE?

But D'Angelo made that request so quickly, so easily. There hadn't been any second guessing or indecision. Without hesitation, he believed it was the right thing to do. Or maybe he was just completely out of his mind.

She wanted to understand why.

She gazed out a portal, at the tangles of yellowish vegetation, at the exotic, bright orange-blossom bushes that gleamed at night. Other foliage was green and earth-like (no doubt cultivated by the Ballese colonists). She'd even seen a few maple trees growing near the colony.

Other vegetation, like the delicate, swirled branches of a tree she'd never seen before, created intricate lattice overhangs, the thin, swirled branches plum-colored. The leaves were silvery lilac and grew in half-moons along the branches. Even the grass had a silvery sheen to it. She'd first thought it was due to their night landing, but seeing it in daylight, the grass still looked silver. It was denser than earth grass, but the blades were longer, wispier.

"I'm worried, Ron," Diana said finally. "Even with the Antarans' bioshielding technology, the biodrones knew where we were last. The caregivers will find us, too."

"Too bad we're not going to be here," said Ron, rising to his feet.

Part of her felt like giving up. Time was trickling away, even with Ron's re-evaluation request. She could do nothing to help her brother, no way to even find him. It seemed so hopeless, yet she had to believe that they would escape that facility.

She was also angry at Peter, she realized for the first time. David wouldn't be in there if Peter hadn't foolishly entered that facility. She sighed. *Still, what could he have done?* D'Angelo recognized him, figured out he was an AWOL recombinant. Had the man already reported everything to UCOE? With no one to help him devise a plan and fearing what D'Angelo might do next, Peter entered the facility.

It wasn't his fault, she decided.

Nevertheless, time was running out. She prayed they were both safe.

Ron moved to the cockpit and flicked on the computer system. He turned toward her. "Ready to run your preflight?" he asked.

She frowned as she stood and moved into the cockpit, coffee ration in hand. "Preflight?"

"Yeah, we've got to move, you know that, Diana."

He was right. They couldn't stay here now that the biodrones had found the shuttle. The only smart thing to do was land the shuttle as close to the Antaran facility as she could and still maintain room for a hasty departure.

"All right, let's do it," she said, flopping into the pilot's chair.

Ron slid into the co-pilot's chair. She read off readings and he checked them against the computer system. When she finished, she gripped the stick, eager to leave this clearing.

"Well?"

He nodded. "Everything checks out."

"Excellent! We'll do a test fire and find another hiding place, someplace the caregivers won't see it, and someplace their radar systems won't locate it immediately."

She went through the systems ignition and engage procedures, watching the displays as each system winked online. She monitored the readings carefully as the propulsion system went through a test fire.

"Everything checks out, Diana."

Diana reached for her restraint harness. "Strap in. We're moving closer."

The stick vibrated as she turned the shuttle back toward the long strip of grass behind her. It was a tight turn, tree limbs and brush raking across the hull, but she brought the nose around.

She held her breath for a moment and then lit the engines. Exhaling, she hit the throttle.

22

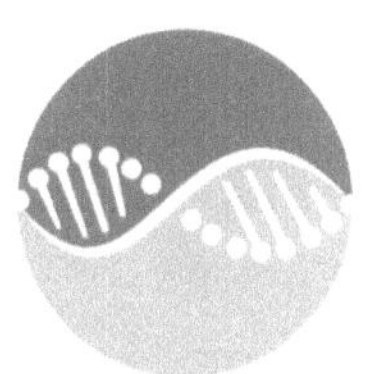

UNABLE TO SIT STILL, David wandered through the chilly, dark bunk room, his thoughts stuck on Mitchell. Sting didn't say a word but continued his own pacing. To David's relief, the old fire in his eyes had returned. He had a goal again—and a chance to escape.

Apparently, that was enough for Sting.

The other recombinants either paced like him, arms folded, or they huddled in groups, talking softly as if someone might hear them. The strip of blue-white light that ran around the tops of the walls seemed dimmer today and the temperature had fallen a few degrees. David found the poor lighting and the chill uncomfortable. He folded his arms against his chest and made a wide circle through the room.

He wondered how Diana and the others were doing. D'Angelo seemed to have gone inside himself, leaving the entire crew to fend for itself. But with Tanner more biodrone than recombinant now and the other two missing, D'Angelo no longer had a crew to command.

He grinned. If he knew his sister, she was moving mountains on her side, buying them more time in any way she could. If she could have stormed this facility herself, she'd have done it by now. He smiled, pitying Tanner and even D'Angelo if the captain got in her way. Diana got things done and chances were that D'Angelo, if he possessed even a sliver of sanity, was learning this the hard way.

From his years of service in Mimi's recombinant underground, Ron was used to moving quickly on short amounts of time and with little resources. He also was a dead shot with a plasma rifle. Had the chops to back up his weapons programming, too. He'd be there to back Diana up when she needed it.

And she'd need it.

Sting poked David in the arm.

"Sarge, they'll be hauling some of us out for testing sometime today. They're always running some kind of tests on us."

Sting laid his hand against his right forearm, rubbing it absent-mindedly as he spoke. David remembered the angry red slashes. Sting had gone through a lot here.

"The comparison tests are the worst," he continued, "and they've been a lot more frequent these past few weeks."

"Comparison tests?" David asked with a frown.

"Yeah, when they take us out and compare us to their hybrids. It's more of a performance test. And if we move outside the boundaries, they stun us. The hybrid always tries to kill us, of course, so they're pretty predictable." He grinned, that familiar twinkle in his eyes. "We just have to outwit it. You trained us well, Sarge. So far, I haven't had trouble out-maneuvering them."

"Do you have any weapons?"

Sting cackled, bringing a smile to David's face. That had once been a familiar sound on base. How much things had changed?

"No weapons for us, but the hybrids carry UCOE-issue plasma rifles." He scratched his head for a moment. "That part can be a little tricky, but it's not like you and the hybrid start off face-to-face. They have to do a little tracking first."

"I hope Mitchell made it that far, Sting," said David, unable to conceal his worry.

Mitchell was too trusting, so gullible at times. The young man's near-fatal excursion into Civilization's bar district was the latest example still fresh in his mind.

"If Pete's lucky, Sarge, that's where he'll be. If he was unlucky enough to have fallen in with the rejects..."

Sting's sentence trailed off and David was grateful not to hear the rest.

"So, one of us may be paired with Mitchell?" David asked and resumed his pacing. Sting walked beside him.

Sting nodded. "Not a big deal. We just let him look like's he's winning and then run for the boundary. We get stunned and end up back here and Pete gets a passing mark."

"Okay," he said as they did another slow lap around the room. "So, we assume they think Mitchell has shown promise because he displays intelligence and they've put him in with the test group?"

Sting stopped abruptly. "Damn," he said with a sigh. "I forgot one other possibility, Sarge." He gazed at David, fear shining in his eyes. "If they're threatened by Pete, then they may put him in the field trials. It's happened before—with other hybrids. Those prick caregivers like to brag about their hybrids, bet on them and shit, so we hear a lot of their talk."

David frowned. "Field trials? What's that?"

"They send out a few rejects—or anyone they're trying to get rid of quickly—and let their most promising hybrid units hunt them down. Through a maze of cages."

Cold fear spread through David.

Sting's voice fell to a whisper. "I heard that the caregivers captured a couple of UCOE recon teams this month. Sent them one-by-one against a unit of their best hybrids. None of them survived."

He stared unblinking at Sting. At last, he knew the fate of the recon teams.

Why didn't UCOE send in a bigger force to find out? A force that small was a straight up suicide run.

Then he understood.

D'Angelo had been in charge of those missions. The man had

probably been losing ground mentally for months and months—or longer. He was used to sending recombinants to their deaths, expecting them not to come back. He'd begun to treat UCOE personnel similarly.

David thought of Diana out there, sick and injured with that mad man and a captured hybrid, Ron Kraver her only ally. He shivered.

"You okay, Sarge?" Sting asked, concern in his gaze.

He nodded finally.

The door to their chamber clanged open and four caregivers slithered inside, strange, silver devices poised in their paper-white hands. Three of them had multiple legs and digits, wearing tan robes and other thin, speckled fabric coverings. One of them had a more humanoid appearance.

David bristled, glaring at them.

Hostility charged the room, recombinants staring with clenched fists and narrowed eyes. Even Sting's stance stiffened, his hands balling into fists at his side. He gritted his teeth, muscles tightening into a grimace. The emotion in his eyes was unmistakable—hatred.

"Easy, Sting," David whispered through clenched teeth. "Hold it in."

Sting cast a sideways glance at David and then snapped a quick nod at him. He stood his ground, but his gaze never left the caregivers as they skittered through the room, studying every recombinant.

Sting took a defiant step toward them. David tried to stop him, but then realized that he was trying to stand out so they'd choose him. David slipped a few steps forward, so he'd be chosen along with Sting. If anybody was going up against Mitchell, he wanted it to be Sting or him.

A caregiver in thin, cream-colored robes, moved through the room. Its pale, icy gaze connected with Sting's hard-edged stare for a moment, but it quickly flipped its attention to David.

He stared unflinching at this creature, unwilling to drop his gaze. It became a contest, but David refused to look away. He would not give in, wouldn't give it the satisfaction.

"Your defiance is futile," said the caregiver, a smug expression in its too high, too widely set eyes. Its skin looked almost liquid it was so white and clear. Almost like a squid or an octopus—an insult to both.

"So is your attempt to subjugate us," David said, the smile on his face matching the caregiver's smugness.

The caregiver glanced down at David's arm. David fought down his surprise. He didn't have any scars there.

Would they know he wasn't a recombinant?

The caregiver grabbed hold and shoved up his sleeve. The skin on his arms was pristine. The caregiver's lips tried to mimic David's smile, but twisted instead into something malevolent.

"You talk high for an untested recombinant," said the caregiver, his voice velvety smooth.

Sting stepped forward. "Not all of us were groomed for the front." David felt Sting's anger bubbling up in his words, but Sting kept control of it. "Some of us were trained to serve generals and at tactical, but our level of defiance is constant."

The caregiver cast an uncertain look at David and then pulled him forward. "I want this one today," said the caregiver loudly as he showed off his choice. "Our UCOE general. That will give us time to setup a few DNA samplings. I wouldn't think about sending hybrids out there without a little higher-class DNA." The caregiver poked David in the chest. "We'll see how our general performs against our best."

Sting's hands trembled from the tight fists he tapped against his leg. His rage was moments from surfacing.

"You bastards," Sting said in a low growl.

The caregiver whirled, stunner extended, cream-colored robes billowing around it.

"And—this one," it said with a stutter. "The one with the big mouth."

The caregiver stepped so close to Sting that he was nearly standing on Sting's toes. Its robes fluttered, settling around it. Sting's nose nearly touched the caregiver's thin almost recessed nose.

But Sting stood his ground and didn't recoil. His fierce glare remained. He looked deeply into its four gold eyes with more animosity than David had ever seen from the even-tempered young man—a rare quality in a recombinant.

"I want to be there when UCOE beats you guys into the ground."

"UCOE?" Some scratchy, quivering sound emanated from the caregiver and David realized it was laughter. "Children playing at war." The caregiver stepped back, something akin to amusement in its large eyes. "We conquered our first world when Earth wasn't even habitable yet."

David held back the urge to spit on this arrogant creature.

"They fight admirably...I commend them on that," said the caregiver by the door. "I am amazed at how far they have come in such a short evolutionary span. But inevitably, children."

Its tunic shimmered grey and it wore dark trousers like one of the other, more humanoid caregivers. The ones that looked more octopus than human wore the paler tan or cream-colored robes. David wondered if the robes were part of a hierarchy.

The cream-robed caregiver cast a stern glare at the caregiver in the grey tunic. "Nikoam, you were not asked to speak."

The caregiver called Nikoam gave a quick nod and averted its gaze. "Yes, Tevihu."

The cream-robed caregiver called Tevihu turned back to Sting, a tightness in its face that hadn't been there before.

Hmmm, dissension among the ranks? David smirked.

"This is a game of holdout at best," said Tevihu. "We'll wait for the proper moment to strike again and then the Taus system will be ours. We are infinitely patient. From there, we'll soon have its neighbor. Sol—as you call it?"

David trained his gaze on Nikoam and the caregiver didn't disappoint. It gave a slight shake of its head.

All along, David thought these caregivers acted as one cohesive unit, but seeing this caregiver's skepticism gave David hope. Or was it defiance? Perhaps their cohesive unit was crumbling? Or were there other dissenters?

Tevihu motioned at the other three caregivers. "Take these two along with two others—I don't care who—to the lab." He turned and pointed at David. "I want samples taken from this one and then take them out for testing. Nikoam, you are in charge, but first, I want a word with you."

Two caregivers grabbed hold of Sting then David, shuffling them toward the door. Sting cast an amused look at David. The young recombinant had found the turn of events as surprising as David had.

THE CAREGIVERS LED DAVID, Sting, and two other recombinants outside the door and turned left into a large, dark freight lift that smelled like grease and heat. It groaned and shook, carrying them up four flights. Abruptly, it opened into a green glass-like rotunda that cooled the space beneath its greenish tinged light.

An acidic smell clung to the air as David stepped out of the lift, Sting behind him. David glanced up at the large green dome overhead. Light filtered through it, naturally illuminating the area in a wash of pale green light.

Several research stations lined the walls, each with a desk light, desk, and worktable, all made of a pale grey polymer-like material, corners softened with curves and simple lines. Every station was occupied, white-haired, octopus-like caregivers completely absorbed in their work. Beakers clinked, someone coughed, a burner hissed on with a wink of orange. Some caregivers wore robes. Other more humanoid ones wore trousers.

David frowned. There was something different about these humanoid caregivers. Something besides job or station separating them from the more biodrone-looking caregivers.

He needed to figure out what that was. And exploit it.

In the center of the room stood four or five examination tables. A half-moon of glass-like cabinets formed a partial barrier around it. The creatures reached through the glass like substance that parted each time they removed a clear container. One of the tables was occupied, a sheet shrouding what lay beneath. David swallowed hard at the human shape beneath the sheet.

Please, don't let that be Mitchell, he chanted in his head, casting an uncertain look at Sting who shook it off.

Tevihu strode toward David, but Nikoam stepped forward, taking hold of David's arm. "You'll be mine for this test," said Nikoam, casting a look at Tevihu whose face pinched. A faint whiff of sweetness touched the air then dissipated.

Another caregiver pointed a stunner at Sting and motioned him toward one of the tables.

"All right, take it easy," said Sting, who turned toward the tables.

Nikoam led David toward the farthest table, but David stopped in front of the sheet. The stale, iron scent of dried human blood mixed with germicide, something sweet, and death. David scrunched his nose. He had to make sure Mitchell wasn't under that sheet. Before Nikoam could stop him, David peeled back the sheet.

A blond man lay there, his scalp peeled back exposing an empty brain cavity. David swallowed his panic and dropped the sheet. Weak in the knees, he exhaled sharply and looked away. It wasn't Peter.

"I'm sorry you had to see that," said Nikoam. "You weren't meant to." He glared around the room, his voice rising. "Someone did not do their job this day."

It took David a moment to catch his breath. "Is that my destiny here?" he asked finally.

"No," said Nikoam. "This hybrid was so violent after its creation that it had to be destroyed on the spot. We are analyzing its brain chemistry and genetic combination. We don't want a repeat of this type of hybrid."

David shuddered, wondering if these aliens could out-human the humans at creating the perfect, advanced human killing machine. Both sides were trying. And failing. Miserably.

Nikoam took hold of David's arm again. It was then that David realized that Nikoam hadn't drawn its stunner. It was still clipped to the caregiver's trouser pocket. David glanced at the other caregivers escorting recombinants to the tables and each one gripped a stunner.

"You're not afraid of us, are you?"

Nikoam shook its head, its white bangs drooping into its large, round gold eyes. Almost childlike. So strange against the empty-eyed, vacuous stares of the other caregivers. It picked up a shimmery, translucent lab coat off the table and enfolded itself in it. Next, it plunged its hands into the matching gloves. The lab coat and gloves flickered for a moment, green light illuminating their matrices. Afterward, glimmers flowed across the fabric. Some sort of protective clothing, David realized.

Or some sort of neural network maybe?

"Despite your aggression, you are all too frightened. Besides, there is no need to foist a weapon at you unless warranted." Nikoam touched the tabletop. "Please remove your uniform and lie down on the table."

David hesitated.

Nikoam stared at him quizzically. "Modesty? That's not in my experience with Earth's recombinants."

He cringed at his mistake. Now, he'd flagged himself as different to the Antarans.

"I don't know what you mean by modesty," he answered quickly. "I just want to know what's going to happen to me on that table first."

"Ah, I understand. Still such a strong fear reaction," said Nikoam. "I need to examine you and take a few tissue samples."

Swallowing his pride, David peeled off Tanner's uniform. He unfastened his boots and stepped out of them. In T-shirt and dark blue boxers, he sat shivering on the table and swung his feet up, lying on his back.

Above him loomed that massive green dome and he concentrated his gaze on it while Nikoam's cold hands slid across his chest and down his legs, lights passing across his body.

Measuring? Copying?

The caregiver picked up an instrument and pressed it to David's stomach. It vibrated softly, deepening until his stomach churned. His stomach lurched and he fought to keep from puking.

As quickly as the nausea began, it disappeared when Nikoam shut off the instrument.

His body stiffened against the next procedure.

Nikoam took hold of his arms and fastened them against the table with straps. His feet were strapped down next and his breath quickened. The next procedure would be a lot more painful.

It was, too. A series of red-light pinpoints pricked his skin like needles, from his legs to his chin. He jumped with each contact until finally something gouged his chin and stopped.

Four more procedures followed, each one confusing and progressively more painful. Then Nikoam, with what looked like a laser scalpel in its hands, gently laid a hand against David's left arm. "This test is the most painful. It will only last a few seconds though."

White hot agony sliced into his left forearm. He swallowed the cry of pain and clawed at the table with his right hand. He pounded the table with his right foot, desperate for the burning pain to disappear. After a few year-long moments, the pain disappeared, replaced by dull throbbing.

He shuddered, his breath ragged as he tried to shake off the pain. Looking down at his left arm, he saw the throbbing scarlet slash.

"The tissue samplings are always the worst. It will feel much better in a day or so."

David groaned. He didn't have a day or so. He had about twenty-five or so hours to find Mitchell and get out of here.

Nikoam reached for some gauze and sealant. "I will bandage it for you."

After the gash had been sealed and bandaged, David was allowed to get dressed. He struggled with his aching left arm to redress himself. When he'd finally gotten on his boots, he cradled the painful arm against his stomach.

Someone shouted.

He glanced up. The first table.

Sting lay on it, his face contorted, Tevihu hanging over him with the laser scalpel. Tevihu seemed to be enjoying the testing and was making it far more painful than necessary.

"When the others are finished, we will take you out to the field-testing area." Nikoam turned and left David for a few moments, making the rounds to the other tables.

Again, Sting cried out, the sound unnerving. Filling David with rage.

He grimaced. With his left arm messed up, he'd have difficulty defeating a hybrid. Still, maybe it would be Mitchell.

Sting screamed once more before it was all over.

Smug-looking, Tevihu walked away, a sick look of satiation on its face. He had no idea if these bastards had any emotions at all, but it was clear that they were monsters.

Moments after Tevihu's departure, Nikoam was at Sting's table, bandaging his arms. David struck the table with his fist. Sting couldn't field test these hybrids with both his arms gouged with that laser tool. That sonofabitch did that on purpose.

Rising unsteadily, David got off the table, careful to avoid the dead hybrid that lay under the sheet, and hurried over to Sting.

Sting's breathing was labored, his eyes squeezed closed. David reached down and squeezed Sting's shoulder. Nikoam moved away from the table toward the next recombinant.

"Hang in there, Stingley," said David in his best confident voice. "It's almost over."

Sting opened his eyes slowly and offered a ghost of a smile. "Thank you, Sarge."

David gazed down at Sting's bandaged arms. Already, they had reddened with his blood.

"What did that bastard do to you?"

David helped him up from the table and back into his uniform. "It's all part of the testing, Sarge," he answered in a thin, ragged voice. "The tissue sample is minor. They just inflict these gashes for the hybrids. To hone their animal instincts. Smell of blood or some shit like that."

Honing animal instincts?

Horrified, David leaned against the table.

These things looked exactly like human recombinants, but they hunted and fed like wild animals.

"Sarge, that's not the worst of it."

What could be worse than that? He turned his gaze back to Stingley.

"I'm fairly bright as far as recombinants go. I can watch somebody do something once and then do it myself, I know how to read and do math—all the basics. But even I know that if they send a shitload of these hybrids into the military, UCOE will destroy every one of its own recombinants to prevent contamination. Or infiltration. Am I right, Sarge?"

David winced. And the Antarans were counting on that.

Destroying all of UCOE's recombinants meant falling back on reserve human forces. In very, very short supply. For more than a decade, Earth had been trying to rebuild and retool its most advanced tech, including the unmanned flying biodrones after the Antaris Nation quickly rendered all of Earth's tech useless. Nothing the scientists threw at these creatures made a difference against their self-repairing, self-replicating technologies.

Would Earth be forced back into fighting this conflict like it had on the battlefields of the twentieth century?

Earth would re-engineer more secure recombinants with clean DNA and faster cloning processes, but all of that took time. Time that Earth no longer had.

By then, billions would die as the Taus system fell.

Would we even have enough forces to fight them on our own doorstep?

"Damn, Stingley, you're right."

"I hate the Recombinant Defense Program, Sarge," said Stingley, sadness edging his words. "All I ever wanted was to be a hero. But I never realized, until Pete came along, that there were whole worlds out there. Within reach." He laid his hand against his chest. "*My* reach. But you know what, Sarge, it still makes me feel kinda sick inside to think it'll all go away. At least in the program, I had a chance for moments on those worlds. Without that program..." His voice trailed off, his head bowed. He sighed. "Without it, I'd never have existed at all."

David's chest ached. Stingley spoke truth. Mitchell spoke truth. But who was right?

Maybe in concept, the Recombinant Defense Program wasn't as evil as he'd come to view it? It needed to be restructured, needed to give these soldiers lives after the war, allow them to leave the military or be retrained into civilian jobs. Hell, even let them buy or earn their way out of service. It was high tech slavery after all. But he'd seen too much. He'd never support washouts and destroying recombinants. Never again.

They weren't machines. They were as human as he was. Maybe more so, considering how much more alive they seemed than their creators and handlers. If he lived through this, he'd visit Mimi Constantine's backer and petition for a better approach, a better way to help the recombinants and UCOE.

There had to be a better way. He'd do his best to find it.

When Nikoam finished bandaging the fourth recombinant's arms, Tevihu and the other two caregivers returned, stunners extended. Nikoam moved toward David who anchored Sting on his feet. Sting was a little wobbly, his face as white as the caregiver's slick, milky-white skin.

"He's a little under the weather."

Nikoam clicked its tongue in disapproval. "They will send him out regardless. Perhaps you would..." Nikoam searched for a word. "Shadow him?"

David grinned. Nikoam was the first caregiver he hadn't wanted to choke to death. He almost liked this one.

"Thanks, I will shadow him."

Nikoam moved toward a set of double doors across the room that David hadn't noticed.

He slid his arm around Sting's waist and helped him stay on his feet. Out of the corner of his eye, he spotted Tevihu rushing toward them from the right. Sting was his charge and he would do his best to make things harder on Sting.

David shifted Sting to his left side, putting himself between the young recombinant and Tevihu. To his surprise, Nikoam moved to his right side.

"This way, to the next phase of testing," said Nikoam, sliding closer to David.

David smiled. Moving between him and Tevihu. Shielding them both.

Tevihu tried to maneuver past Nikoam, but the caregiver stopped in front of him, asking questions about procedures and testing scores as he nodded David toward the doors with a flick of his white mane of hair.

David opened the double doors and slipped Sting outside. Beyond those doors, another group of caregivers awaited them.

Behind him, he heard the sharp crack of metal against skin. He glanced back into the lab. Nikoam clutched its face and Tevihu raged at it. Amber liquid stained Nikoam's face, dripping onto the shimmery lab coat and tunic that sparked green with every drop. David had never seen a caregiver's blood before.

Why had Nikoam stuck its neck out for him and Sting?

Gritting his teeth, he turned back to steady Sting through the tall wire gate ahead that led into something called a comparison test pen.

Before he left this place, he'd have a private conversation with caregiver Tevihu.

With fists and some explosives.

He walked down a long, umber dirt path leading through an open gate into a fenced-in, wooded area. Trees here were short and spindly against a yellow sky, thin ghostly grey and pink shadow-like clouds streaming past like jet trails. Tree leaves weren't green here. Most were sallow and orange or purple and leathery, but paper-thin, and others silvery yellow, shaped like tiny half-moons. None of it provided much cover. The air smelled mossy and dank, traces of chemicals he didn't recognize making it almost gritty with every inhale, like the oxygen fought to enter his lungs.

The grit and chemical tinge dissipated as he moved away from the facility.

Then he saw a red maple tree. Planted by colonists, he realized. Something so familiar. He wanted to run toward it and climb into its branches, like he had as a kid back on Earth.

Robed caregivers in cream and brown stood on both sides of the gate, hands against their stunners. David ignored them, instead concentrating on the cool wind against his face and fresh air comforting his lungs, the grittiness receding. The air smelled almost tart as the yellowy silver grasses fanned out around them.

The change of scenery put eased the tension in Sting's face, the pained grimace fading. He stared up at the sky and inhaled sharply, looking almost relaxed.

David knew they'd be facing the equivalent of wild animals out in this cleaner air and strange vegetation. He couldn't let it obscure his thinking. Or give them false hope.

He shook Sting.

"Concentrate on what's coming, Stingley," he snapped.

"Yes, Sarge," Sting replied in a strong voice, the faraway look in his eyes gone. "They'll give the signal and we have to fade into the woods and elude or defeat the hybrids until the caregivers call time."

"When will that be?"

Sting sighed, shrugging. "Depends on their mood."

David and Sting stepped through the gate and stood beside the other two recombinants, one black-haired and the other brown-haired. David crouched beside Sting, watching his face as he waited for some sort of signal. Some sort of attack to begin.

23

THE WHIR of machinery overpowered any other sounds in the steamy room. Peter, barely coherent after the stunning, struggled to regain consciousness as the caregiver dragged him through sweltering heat. Grating covered both walls, creating a cage on both sides, and in front of them, large turbines spun, the sound a soft clicking.

Steam rose, misting the air. Ventilation ducts twisted across the ceiling, hissing. A large fan on one end clattered, whup whupping against the ka-chunk, ka-chunk and click of machinery. The air smelled of oil and heat, warm tiles slick and fogged with condensation as he slid over them.

Several people pounded the grates with rhythmic thumps all around him, their faces shadowed.

Only after he'd passed the turbines did he hear the low-voiced, intense chant. It was one word and he strained to decipher it. Finally, the word became clear, rising free of the ka-chunk of turbines and whupping of fans.

Chase!

He glanced up, seeing a line of bulky hybrids on each side behind the cages, each one pounding the grating with their palms. Their hungry gazes burned in the heat as they watched his every move. Their chant sent a wave of terror through him, a chill prickling his skin despite the heat. They awaited the release of some helpless creature to hunt, like one of those desert rodents he'd saved from that asshole Drake trying to stomp it back on Civilization.

Today, *he* was the desert rodent.

Desperate, he kicked at the caregiver, but the lithe alien was just out of his range. Those frenzied hybrids would tear him apart if the caregiver released him into their cages. When the caregiver stopped, he'd act. Otherwise, he might not get another chance.

At the end of the wall of climate control equipment was a small green door. The caregiver halted.

Peter propelled himself to his feet and lunged at the caregiver. It stepped backward, the small door sliding open. A chute! Peter fell headfirst into the chute and careened into darkness.

He screamed, trying to find a handhold, but the slick surface offered him nothing but more momentum.

Flailing, he grabbed at the sides, above him, behind him, trying to stop any way he could, but the muggy passageway twisted and looped until finally, light grew at the end of the tunnel. He was falling toward it.

Screaming, he pitched headlong into a large bin.

Voices rose in layers around him, hungry, snarling at him from all sides. The pounding against the grates was violent now, the tempo accelerating, intensifying.

His heart beat faster to match the frenzied rhythm.

Disoriented, Peter staggered out of the bin, grateful he was still safe from the hybrids.

A hybrid bludgeoned the grating behind him.

He jumped, startled, and stepped away. He staggered back only to have another hybrid screaming and beating the grated metal plate beside him.

The heat was unbearable. He gasped for air.

He glanced around in the dim red haze and realized that he'd landed in a big cage. On all sides, the frenzied cadence echoed, resonating into his bones.

Chase! Chase! Chase!

He thrust his hands to his ears. *Can't think! Can't breathe!*

The roar filled his head, clouding his reasoning. He couldn't think straight!

The chute was the only way out. He hunched over, trying to drown out the noise.

Above the din, something creaked and groaned, a lull in the overpowering roar.

Peter glanced up. Ahead, a half-door slid open, revealing a maze of grated corridors.

Crazed shouting and banging rose around him again.

Terrified, Peter plunged underneath the gate and scrambled through the passage.

Footsteps thundered around him, shouts and excitement growing chaotic in the dark heat. Chasing him.

Gasping frantically for air, Peter launched himself through one turn then the next, desperate to be rid of the noise.

He hit a dead-end only to be surrounded on three sides by agitated, ravenous hybrids behind the grates.

Twisting around, he surged back into the maze.

Every turn was met by a gang of shouting, furious hybrids.

Peter ran harder, scurrying with as much speed as he could until up ahead, his steps slowed as the maze branched off into three possible directions. He bounded into the crossroad and stopped.

All three routes led to a gate—and then into a swarm of hybrids. He'd last about two minutes.

Behind him, another gate fell, trapping him.

He threw himself against it, pounding and shouting, but the gate wouldn't budge.

No! He turned, his back against the gate. *Every direction led to death.*

His chest heaved as he struggled for air in the heat.

Terrified, he edged closer to the crossroad, studying the number of hybrids in each pen. All three of those pens were death for him. He couldn't fight off all of those hybrids alone.

There was no way out.

He thought about Diana lying sick on her bedroll and D'Angelo's stern gaze memorizing his face as an escaped recombinant. After this, there wouldn't be anything to report to UCOE.

He winced.

Poor Diana would wonder for the rest of her days what had happened to him out here, blaming herself. He knew that from experience, from worrying about the fate of his best friend. Sting.

He gritted his teeth. *No! He refused to be herded to his death.*

Dammit, he didn't have time to die right now! Not with Sting so close and time running out.

He gazed around the maze again. He'd investigated the tunnels in every direction—almost.

He craned his neck to look above him.

A thin grate covered a tube above his head. He grinned. The way out.

With his fists, he beat on the grating until it popped open. Delirious with relief, he hooked his fingers into the grating wall and pulled himself up into the tube.

Angry shouts and desperate pounding erupted on all sides as Peter climbed out of the maze.

They tried to dislodge him. Shaking the structure with his every move, threatening to knock him off at any moment.

He rode out the unsteady waves of pounding, crawling through the tube and onto a catwalk about five meters above the hybrids. Where he could stand up.

He walked over the top of the caged hybrids as he traced the catwalk around the building. Up here, the heat nearly knocked him out. He wheezed, moving slower. Finally, he dropped to his knees and crawled along the catwalk. His hair was sopping wet, uniform soaked and heavy, sagging against his frame. He kept moving, finally stopping at a lone window in the corner of the room.

It was his only way out of here.

He pulled off his uniform shirt and discarded the undershirt, quickly putting back on the uniform shirt. Taking a quick moment to catch his breath, Peter leaned against the wall and twisted the soaked undershirt around his right fist. The window was too high to kick.

Rising to his feet, Peter cocked his fist and slammed it against the window.

Pain gouged his knuckles and surged down his arm. He sucked in a breath as he examined the window's surface. Below him, the screams and taunts continued. He held his breath, drew back his fist, and propelled it into the glass again. It cracked, chips of glass breaking free as he kept pounding it until the crack widened. Deepened.

One more hit and it'd give way.

He closed his eyes, exhaled, and smashed his fist into the window. Bones broke in his hand. He felt them crack as the window shattered. He swallowed the scream, the pain in his hand agonizing.

Leaning against the wall, he struggled to shove the pain away.

Please, just long enough to get through this window.

Out of habit, he reached for the god symbol around his neck, to gather a little courage, but remembered he'd given it to Diana.

With his left elbow, he knocked away the jagged glass teeth on the bottom edge of the window. Cradling his broken hand against his shirt, Peter climbed through the window. He scrambled for a foothold but found none. Only the rush of wind and the curve of the roof. He looked down. He was three stories off the ground.

The fall would kill him.

Below him, the staccato rhythm against the grate was driving him mad. He'd take his chances outside, he decided, and stood on the window's edge to see what lay above him.

He grinned. The dome. With its repository of precious Antaran DNA.

He struggled out the window and crawled onto a curved overhang, pausing to let the cool air soothe his scalded lungs and evaluate the structures on the roof. When his breathing grew easier, he traced a path.

He'd have to slither across this overhang and from there, a narrow ledge nestled against the edge of the building. He'd be able to traverse the ledge.

Then he saw it. One of those huge ventilation fans with a duct that would take him inside the dome.

Flopping onto his belly, his throbbing right hand extended to anchor him, Peter crawled across the overhang.

It seemed to go on forever.

He hugged the stone, his cheek rasping against it with every forward movement. At last, the solitude of wind and trees calmed his furiously beating heart. He laid his head against the cool overhang, amazed and grateful that he'd escaped that cage.

He looked out at the horizon. He'd lost track of the time now. *Would he see the shuttle streaking across the sky, stranding him here forever?*

No, not while Diana Temple piloted that shuttle.

He imagined her seated with arms folded in the pilot's seat, refusing to take off until he returned. She'd be so furious at him when he got back. He sighed. If he got back. But he refused to return without Sting.

For several more nerve-wracking minutes, Peter crawled across the overhang until he reached the narrow ledge. The pain in his hand was excruciating as he gripped the rough stone and skirted across the ledge. The oily tiles had slicked the bottoms of his boots, he realized, as he fought to keep his footing. It made it difficult to slide his feet across the ledge and not fall, but he moved with slow, deliberate steps.

At last, the ledge ended, allowing Peter to wedge himself into a narrow niche and climb onto the dome. He patted the thick glass with his left hand, remembering the depot on Ku'Tal. Everything the

Antarans cared about lay beneath this dome, and that included their DNA repository.

He had one grenade left.

Maybe in the chaos he could find Sting and escape? It was all he had left. He was out of ideas.

He hurried around the dome and found the ventilation shaft. The fan gyrated in a quiet, even rhythm. In front of it was another grated panel, like the one that had gotten him out of the maze below.

It took only a couple of kicks to unhinge it.

Peter shoved it out of the way and lowered himself into the duct.

Air streamed through the opening, so cool he just wanted to lie there and let it blow over him. When his chest stopped heaving, he crawled away from the enclosed fan until he found the wall vents. Several led inside the facility's inner rotunda. Peering inside, he saw a series of lab stations throughout the room below.

He crawled around the rotunda until he found a vent directly beside the repository. Below the vent, stood a tall grey and glass cabinet. Tall enough to cut his vertical drop in half.

Scurrying quickly, Peter shimmied back through the duct and out onto the roof again. He removed the last grenade from his pants pocket.

Opening the bottom of the grenade, he tripped the frequency pairing switch and replaced the cover. When it went off, it would set off the first one he'd dropped.

He laid his torn, bloody undershirt against the bottom edge of the dome. Then he laid the grenade in the folds of the undershirt. That would hold it in place long enough.

Reaching down, he turned on the activator and ran back toward the fan and its grate. He plunged into the duct and slithered as quickly through it as he could, counting the seconds in his head.

Just as he counted to ten, he'd reached the first wall vent. Covering his face with his hands, he turned away from the vent.

A deafening explosion ripped through the dome. Thick glass shattered and rained down on the lab stations below.

Caregivers shrieked and ran, something shrill pinging.

Smoke rolled into the duct. He held his breath as the fan sucked it out quickly. When the smoke cleared, he crawled through the duct toward the vent into the repository.

Ten seconds later, the first grenade that he'd paired and dropped in the storeroom detonated.

The entire building shook, quaking under the stress as bottles of chemicals exploded in succession.

Peter was thrown against the vent that gave under his weight. It dropped out of the ceiling.

He rolled out of the vent and slammed against the cabinet.

Ribs cracked. He bit back a scream and lowered himself to the ground.

Heavy, black smoke filled the room.

He covered his nose and mouth with his hand and hobbled toward the repository in the center of the room.

A translucent barrier that wrapped around the edges of the repository's climate-controlled room had cracked open. Unable to close around the repository.

From floor to ceiling, drawers containing Antaran DNA lined the walls. The heat from the fire would cause the repository to close and lock.

Unless he stopped it.

The clear repository doors activated and slowly rolled toward each other to shield the repository.

Peter grabbed a thick metal bar that lay on the floor and wedged it between the repository doors, preventing them from closing.

Then he saw the door override switch. And its three keys.

On Ku'Tal, he remembered seeing the caregivers each close the repository protective doors with keys placed in the control panel. There had been three on Ku'Tal.

An orange warning light winked beside the switch, its three keys in their slots. Ready to be turned. Forcing those doors to close.

Peter heard the doors grinding against the metal bar. It was easily removed. The doors' mechanism groaned as it tried to close and couldn't. That alarm would bring a herd of caregivers to these doors.

He reached up to the control panel and snatched the three keys out of the override switch. All three hung on a single, long chain-like lanyard. The warning light went out and the doors stopped straining against the metal bar.

Without these keys, they couldn't close the doors. All their DNA would be lost.

He slipped the keys around his neck and limped away from the repository doors. He got as far as the top of the cabinet when footsteps pounded across the floor.

"Tevihu—by the cabinet."

"You, stop!"

Peter leaped at the vent, clearing the edge. The whine of a charging plasma rifle filtered into the duct. He surged forward.

Plasma fire cut through the duct.

He was almost to the grated panel when a blast ripped through the duct and slammed into his shoulder. He was thrown backward, almost blacking out.

It took a moment or two for his vision to clear, but when the dizziness subsided, he crawled back toward the grating, grabbing the hand holds. Using his legs and his broken hand, he climbed upward, out of the duct. He rolled out onto the roof and collapsed.

"Forgive me, Sting," he whispered into the acrid smoke, his hand against the repository keys hanging around his neck. "Guess we're not going home this tour. I took it as far as I could, buddy."

24

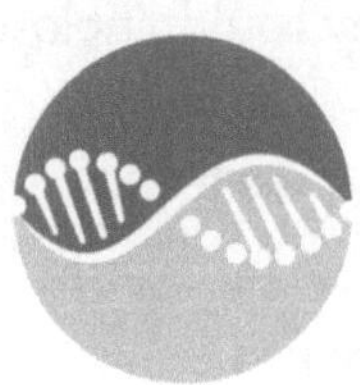

A WHISTLE BLEW and Sting tapped David on the shoulder as he lumbered toward the woods.

"They're coming," Sting whispered. "Hurry."

David followed, the two other recombinants close behind. They reached the cool shadows of sallow, spindly trees as raucous shouts and animal cries rang out.

Footsteps pounded through the thick grass. Four hybrids against four recombinants. At least, the odds were even.

"This way," Sting hissed, jerking David around a squat, gnarled stand of trees grown together into a thick trunk.

Sting's steps were uneven and he bit his lip, rubbing his arms. The gauze had reddened more since Nikoam had bandaged them.

They rushed over a small hill and through a narrow ditch. Smell of damp leaves hung in the air, a small puddle of water clinging to the edge of the ditch.

David side-stepped it.

At the other side of the ditch, Sting stopped. He glanced at the ground.

"What are you looking for?"

"Sticks," Sting whispered. "Find some sticks."

They collected several fallen tree limbs. Sting plunged each one into the ground, jagged ends up. At last, David understood. They'd put a bunch of spikes here and lure a hybrid into the ditch.

When they'd stuck a dozen into the ground, Sting stalked off to the right, David following.

In the distance, someone screamed, the sound making David's stomach ache. He shuddered.

"Hybrids one, recombinants nothing," Sting said, his voice grim.

"How do you know?"

Sting didn't answer.

They circled back, reaching the line of trees again. Sting paused.

"Okay, there's only three of us and four of them. We've got to even this up a bit, Sarge."

David offered a brief smile. "Then let's lure a couple into the ditch."

Sting nodded. "It's our best chance."

"How'd you know to do that thing with the sticks?"

The expression on his face lightened. "Stupid caregivers keep sending the same recombinants out against different hybrids. We've learned how to use this area against them."

A hybrid surged out of the woods toward them.

"Run!" Sting shouted, turning toward the hill.

David sprinted ahead. Trees raced past him, blurring to yellows and silver until he reached the hillside.

He jumped into the ditch just to the side of the sticks and circled around them. Sting was a couple steps behind David, but Sting leaped the sticks, barely clearing them.

In moments, the hybrid lumbered over the hillside after Stingley, falling onto the jagged tree limbs.

The hybrid screamed, writhing against the projectiles piercing its body. Amber blood mixed with damp, silvery leaves and the hybrid fell silent.

Sting moved toward the hybrid and grabbed hold of its arms.

"It doesn't have a weapon," David said with a hiss.

Sting frowned. "Then help me stash it out of the way."

David grabbed its feet and they carried it into a thick stand of trees where they left it.

"More sticks?" David asked.

Sting nodded. "By the time the hybrids are wise to us, it'll be too late."

He and Sting worked together, gathering more broken tree limbs. David chose the sturdiest ones and did his best to splinter the ends. Quickly, they plunged the sticks into the soft ground of the ditch. When the rows of spikes were in place, David led them through the trees and onto the grassy field.

The other recombinant bolted across the grass, trying desperately to outrun two hybrids. David flung himself out of the trees, waving and shouting.

"Hey, this way!"

The black-haired recombinant veered toward him. David shoved him into the woods.

"Turn west and circle back. Don't stop!"

"Thanks for the help," the recombinant said, out of breath from running. He turned and disappeared through the trees.

David and Sting waited until the hybrids saw them. They ran east. David leaped the sticks, Sting flopping nearly on top of him. They scrambled to their feet when the hybrids crested the hillside.

The first one sailed into the ditch, catching the sharp sticks full force. The muffled cry was quickly extinguished. The other hybrid tried to stop on the edge of the hill, but slipped. It fell, dazed, to the ground, missing the sticks.

Sting attacked, pounding the hybrid until he'd knocked it unconscious.

The last hybrid came out of nowhere. It swarmed over Sting, its human form deadlier with its partial biodrone physiology. Its thick hands closed around Sting's throat, trying to crush his windpipe.

David threw himself at the hybrid, jerking its head back, gouging its ribs.

The hybrid struggled, but its heavy grip held tight to Sting's throat. Sting gasped and wheezed, his face turning blue.

Furious, David broad-sided the hybrid. The blow nearly knocked him out, but it was enough to cause the hybrid to lose its footing. It slipped into the ditch, breaking its hold on Sting's throat.

Sting rubbed his throat, gulping down breaths of air. David jerked him out of the ditch and they ran through the trees again.

Sting wheezed for air, his steps slowed, but David dragged him forward. They hurried up an incline and arrived back on the field again, near the gate.

An explosion rumbled through the facility.

The green dome shattered, hunks of glass pelting the yellow grass. Sting snatched a fist-sized piece from the ground.

Caregivers panicked.

They ran from the gate toward the facility. Sting grinned at the opportunity. He staggered to the gate and hefted himself over. The gate was normally guarded by caregivers, so there was no stun field to stop them.

David slipped over the gate behind Sting and they ran for the lakeshore.

A second blast shook the facility. Thick, black smoke billowed up from the ruined dome.

David stopped short of the water. "Stingley," he cried. "What could have caused an explosion in there?"

Sting frowned. "Maybe something blew up in the lab?" He scoffed. "Although, they only seem to be experimenting on recombinants in there."

"We've got to get some weapons and go back inside." He remembered leaving his rifle outside. "Sting, this way," he motioned.

He led Sting through tangles of brush until he found the little thicket he'd hid inside. He'd watched the recombinants from this scruffy line of brush. Quickly, he crawled inside, emerging with his field pack and his rifle, both untouched. David rummaged through the pack, finding a grenade and some more plasma charges. Then his fingers closed on a plasma pistol. He tucked it into his belt.

He handed the rifle to Stingley.

"You're better with this than I am, Stingley," he said.

Sting's eyes glazed at the sight of the weapon. What Stingley might have given for a weapon all this time. His fingers closed gingerly around the barrel, holding the rifle with great respect as he studied it intensely.

He looked up at David, grinning. "Military issue, auto-lock Stupor 180D plasma rifle—standard issue," he said in a loving tone. "I've missed these babies." He clicked the charge into the chamber and slung the strap over his shoulder. The rifle rested naturally against his right hip as if it was another appendage.

"Whenever you're ready, Stingley," said David, suppressing a laugh.

David saw the appreciation for the rifle light up Sting's eyes. Stingley had always been attracted to the hardware, especially the rifles. During training at the base and under David's command on Ku'Tal. He'd appreciated good craftsmanship and David had always given him high marks for maintaining his weapons. And his marksmanship. Whereas Mitchell would have preferred to let his rifle degrade in some corner.

"The explosion in the lab is the perfect diversion, Sarge," said Stingley. "Don't know what happened, but it should give us some time to get in there and find Pete in all the chaos."

David locked a clip into his plasma pistol. "Hope so, Sting. We're running out of time." He nodded them back toward the facility. "Let's go."

"Lead on, Sarge," said Sting.

They emerged from the brush, retracing steps through the wild foliage, the tang of tree sap mixing with the acrid smoke hazing the air. David was glad for the smoke because it shrouded their movements. David edged around the fenced testing area, moving around the gate. That's when Stingley let out a whoop.

"Sarge! Look! On the roof!"

David squinted. The greasy billows of smoke made it difficult to see. He stared, unblinking, until finally a shadowy shape took solid form.

Mitchell. Lying against the edge of the dome, his body wracked with coughs.

David grinned, waves of relief washing over him. Maybe they'd make it out of here after all?

"Let's go!" David shouted.

They surged past the gate, moving around to the side of the building. Sting edged past David, taking the lead, and David let him. Stingley had been here long enough to know the facility layout. He'd trust Sting's judgment. The quicker they got to Mitchell and got him off that roof, the sooner they'd lift off. Hopefully, ahead of D'Angelo's strike force—which was probably, at best, five hours outside Ballese.

Sting moved toward a stack of crates and boxes that leaned against a recessed area of the facility. Slinging his rifle over his shoulder, he started stacking crates.

David moved to help him. Together, they created a pyramid of boxes. When it was high enough to reach a low overhang, Sting hefted himself onto the first crate and stair-stepped them until he could see above the overhang.

"It's clear, Sarge," he said.

David motioned him forward.

Sting laid his palms flush against the top of the overhang and held his breath, like he was gearing up for the pain that would follow. The gauze on his forearms was dirty now and blood covered the bandages.

Muffling a cry of pain, Sting thrust himself up onto the overhang. He crouched, his back against the facility wall, and motioned David up.

The heavy crates held David's weight as he climbed to the top.

The top wobbled a bit, but he weathered the movement as he grabbed hold of the overhang. With a groan, he vaulted onto it.

David's hand fell to the plasma pistol at his belt and he drew it, scanning for company. When no one materialized, he motioned Sting around the overhang and up to a higher section of roof.

First David then Sting climbed onto a flat section of roof that ran behind the dome. It'd be a stretch, but they could reach the narrow section of roof that held the ventilation equipment. That slim part of the roof also framed the north side of the dome, but the ventilation equipment would shield them from sight.

At least long enough to aim their weapons.

The rooftop seemed clear. They should be able to get to Mitchell easily and climb down the way they came. But the longer it took, the more organized the caregivers inside became.

They had to get Mitchell out. Now.

David crouched, pistol in hand, and rushed across the roof. He felt Sting behind him.

They were halfway across the expanse when three caregivers climbed onto the roof from the far side, stunners in hand. All three wore ice blue tunics and dark trousers.

Security force?

David dropped to the ground, his gaze searching frantically for a place to hide. No pipes or shafts protruded from the smooth slab of roof.

There was no place to hide.

"Halt!" one of the caregivers shouted, stunner aimed.

Sting swiveled his rifle barrel and squeezed off a shot.

The blue burst cut down the first caregiver. The other one tried to draw another weapon, but Sting's next shot dropped the second caregiver. The third ran toward the edge of the roof, but Sting took it out, too.

Scrambling up from the ground, David surged across the rest of the roof, stopping beside a service ladder. Sting started to vault up the ladder, but David thrust an arm out, blocking him.

"I'll go first."

Sting's face darkened, his eyes narrowing. "That's my best friend up there."

"That's why I'm going first," David answered. "So, you don't run across that roof and get yourself killed trying to get to him." He pointed at the blood-soaked gauze on Sting's forearms. "Besides, you're weak from Tevihu's sampling. I'll go first and you follow."

Sighing, Sting bowed his head, his gaze on his injured arms. "You're right, Sarge. I'll run flank."

David patted him on the shoulder. "We're almost home, Sting."

Sting grinned at the word *home*, that Stingley sparkle returning. "And Pete, too," he said, nodding David forward.

Grabbing hold of the rungs, pistol poised, David cautiously ascended the ladder. Sting remained two rungs behind. When David neared the top, he peered over.

To his right, a ventilation fan's motor clacked and ticked, the fan blade and cage blown wide open. Thick black smoke spilled out from the ducts, rising into the air.

Maybe Diana will see the smoke as a signal and fire up the shuttle?

He, Sting, Mitchell, and now, this small group of recombinants would meet her at the shuttle and blast out of here ahead of the strike force. He glanced skyward, almost expecting to see the shadows of UCOE bombers swooping low for the drop. D'Angelo had no intention of rescuing recombinants, but David wouldn't give him any choice.

He'd make certain they were on the shuttle with the recon team.

"Sarge, what are you waiting for?" Sting demanded in a sharp whisper.

He was anxious to see Mitchell again, too. By now, Mitchell was like a brother to him.

David scurried across the roof, ducking behind the remnants of the fan. No caregivers rushed at him.

He panned the horizon. No one to stop them.

Finally, he waved Sting across. The recombinant crouched low, rifle across his chest, and slipped behind the fan housing, his back against it. He gripped the rifle in both hands and scanned for enemies.

"Looks clear," said Sting.

"We'll circle around on both sides of the fan. I'll take west, you take east. We'll meet at the dome and get Mitchell down."

"Affirmative, Sarge," said Sting.

He slipped around the fan housing and crept behind the length of the duct.

David pivoted around the fan housing and through the billow of smoke. As he stepped through, he saw Mitchell clinging to the edge of the roof, a robed caregiver hanging over him, shouting.

Mitchell's shoulder was blackened and blood seeped down the remains of his uniform sleeve. His eyelids drooped, pain radiating in his face. He looked ready to pass out.

David gripped the pistol. If Mitchell lost consciousness, he'd tumble to his death.

He raised the pistol, aiming at the caregiver.

Then he balked. What if he missed and hit Mitchell?

Dammit, he had to get closer. Gritting his teeth, he dropped down to crawl around the dome edge.

Behind the caregiver.

25

AT THE NEW LANDING SITE, Diana stretched and sat up. Some sleep—what little she got—in the pilot's seat made her sore and stiff. Her gaze drifted out the cockpit. To her surprise, the green dome was smoking. Heavy black smoke curled out, filling the yellow sky.

"Ron, look!"

Yawning, Ron sat up in the co-pilot's chair and stared bleary-eyed out the cockpit.

"What's happening in there?" he replied, casting a worried gaze at Diana. "I hope nothing's gone wrong."

"Maybe David and Peter have shaken the place up a bit," she said with a forced smile, but inside, she was terrified.

A thousand terrible thoughts entered her mind and mutated into even worse things. Were they both still alive? Did they find Sting alive? Could they escape that horrid place?

"Let's just hope the Antarans are on the defensive and we're winning."

"How much time left?"

They'd been sitting here for hours, less than a half kilometer from the facility, waiting and hoping to somehow help. Never had Diana felt so helpless. But all she could do was sit and wait.

Ron sighed.

"How much, Ron?"

"Two hours and six minutes."

Her heart skipped a beat. Two hours?

"How long before Commander Reynolds contacts us?"

"When they're less than two hours out. Reynolds will advise us to pull out. The second warning will follow an hour later. The final warning will come when they're fifteen minutes from attack formation. If we're not pulling out by that point, we'll be caught in the backlash, Diana. We've got to be away by then. Unless, by some miracle, they stand down after re-evaluation."

Diana's gaze drifted back to the smoke rising from the facility. She hoped David and Peter were already on their way out. With Sting.

She winced. *But they'd make their way to the shuttle—where they originally landed.* Somehow, she had to show them the new location. Without attracting a million biodrones.

"I want to do some fly-bys of our last location. In case David is there." She felt terrible moving the shuttle, but there hadn't been any choice. She couldn't risk those biodrones damaging the shuttle.

"That's a good idea," said Ron, his gaze darted to the darkened instrument panels. "Will you still have enough fuel to reach Karaba?"

She sighed. She didn't have a lot of fuel to spare, but even if she had to tell it jokes to keep it going, she'd get this damned ship to Karaba.

"We have to have enough," she answered.

Stiffly, she rose from the chair and stretched. "You want a coffee ration?" She wanted to be wide awake.

"Sure," Ron answered.

Diana fumbled through the dark hull until she found the food crate. She rummaged through the packets until she located the smaller sized drink ration packets. She grabbed two and moved back to the cockpit. Handing the packet to Ron, she stared out at the smoke thickening in the air.

What was happening in there?

"Thanks, Diana," he answered.

She stood behind the seats and activated the self-heating packet. When warmth radiated from it, she tore it open and drank. It tasted weak and reheated, but it would keep her awake. That was most important. She didn't even miss the sugar. After fighting biodrones, she was beginning to share Peter's aversion to sugar and anything sweet-smelling.

"I wonder what caused that explosion," she said, not expecting an answer.

"Could be anything," Ron muttered. "I just hope it was something that's gone wrong for the Antarans."

And not for David and Peter. Or Sting.

Ron left that part unspoken, although from the look on his face, she knew he was thinking the same thing.

Had David and Peter led the recombinants in a failed rebellion? Were they hopelessly trapped now, about to share the fate of the Antarans when UCOE finally invoked Naharra rules?

After the coffee, Diana paced in the back of the shuttle, her gaze falling to the seat Peter had sat in and bit her lip.

Where is he right now? Is he hurt? Has he even found Sting?

Peter had been through so much. And she loved him with all her heart. She prayed he and David were safe. Her eyes stung with moisture as she sat down in Peter's chair, remembering how his arms felt around her, his lips pressed against hers. That intoxicating, unfailing sense of wonder. She smiled. One of the things she loved most about him.

But she feared he wouldn't come back this time.

Ever since David left her half-delirious at the camp, a horrible thought had nagged at the back of her brain.

What if she had to leave David behind? Or Peter?

She didn't want to make that decision. Her bottom lip quivered, eyes stinging.

No! She couldn't leave them here. She wouldn't.

A dull chime bleated through the silent hull.

"Comm!" Ron shouted.

Diana bolted out of the seat and scrambled into the pilot's chair.

Sweat dotted Ron's upper lip as his hand closed on the receiver. Inhaling sharply, he brought it to his mouth. "This is Recon three. Over."

"Commander Reynolds. We are three hours out from Ballese. Better assemble your team and get out of there. Over."

Ron cleared his throat. "What about the reevaluation of Naharra rules?"

Static crackled. They waited.

"Right, Recon three. Reeval was performed. Naharra rules prevail. I'd suggest getting your team aboard now. Over."

"Affirmative, Commander. We'll begin pull out procedures as soon as we have the rest of our team aboard. Over."

"We'll contact you in an hour. Reynolds out."

The connection went dead, the static echoing through the shuttle.

Diana slumped against her chair, shoulders heavy, her gaze on Ron.

"It's starting," she said in a soft voice. "We've got three hours to find them."

Ron reached for the restraint harness. "Then shouldn't we get airborne?"

She nodded. "If David and Peter are out there, I'll find them."

She snapped her restraint harness across her shoulders and her legs. Then she turned on the shuttle's computer systems. When everything checked out, she engaged the engines.

From the air, she could find them.

"You starting with our original landing site?"

"No," she answered. "I'll skim the southern edge of the lake and then over the ruins. From there, our first shuttle location. That should cover the path David and Peter might take from the facility."

Ron nodded. "Then let's see what's out there."

Grabbing the stick, Diana maneuvered the shuttle down the makeshift runway and hit the throttle. With a jolt, the shuttle lifted into the air.

26

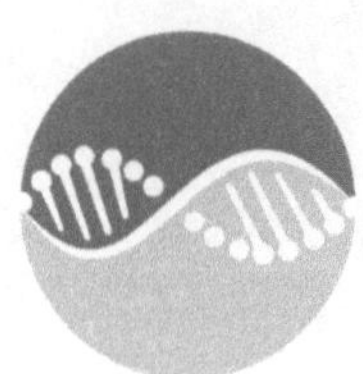

SOMEONE COUGHED BEHIND PETER. He craned his neck, pain shooting down his injured shoulder and slamming into his side. He stifled a groan, the air shimmering as he fought to retain consciousness. He glanced around, but he was alone.

The air smelled like burnt cloth and coppery blood. He glanced down at his blackened clothes, blood streaking his shirt and pants.

His blood.

At the edge of his hazy vision, something moved. His gaze darted.

A caregiver crawled out of the air duct, its cream-colored robes blackened with soot, singed, and torn at the edges. Its pinched, pasty face was smudged with ash, its white stringy hair burned and wild. Its row of four ice gold eyes looked glacial as they narrowed. It held some sort of fist-sized device in its hand that Peter didn't recognize.

Slipping the three repository keys from around his neck, Peter dangled them over the edge of the roof. If the caregiver got too close, he'd fling them as hard and as far as he could throw them.

"You!" it screeched, three rows of tiny, sharp teeth pressed together.

It thrust a small silvery disk at him, poking it close to his face. The hum of energy from it crackled and he felt it from the short distance between them.

This thing was a weapon. Much deadlier than a stunner. He braced himself for the confrontation.

When the caregiver reached the edge of the dome, Peter rolled onto his stomach, his left arm extended over the edge, keys dangling.

"That's far enough," he shouted with such authority that the caregiver stopped, staring in surprise at him.

"We gave you life," said the caregiver in dulcet tones. "Is this how you repay your benefactors?"

Peter's gaze narrowed. He was in too much pain to play games. He'd heard that argument so many times at RDC and at the base. After hearing that canned speech a few times, even he didn't believe it. These creatures still thought he was a hybrid of their creation, but the sentiment was the same.

And it stunk.

"I didn't ask for life, so I owe you nothing," Peter said with a growl.

Another sharp pain radiated through his bones and he shuddered, pushing back the groan on his lips. He could barely move, but he wouldn't let this caregiver know that.

The caregiver seemed taken aback by Peter's response.

"So, you feel no loyalty to us at all?" The caregiver edged forward, but Peter shook his arm, jangling the keys. The caregiver froze, its gaze locked onto the repository keys.

"None," said Peter, a smile twitching at the corner of his lips. "You've done nothing but try and kill me."

As long as the caregivers mistook him for a hybrid, he'd keep playing their stupid little game.

He shook the keys again for effect and the caregiver winced.

"Perhaps, then, we could come to some—arrangement?"

Another slide forward.

Peter laughed bitterly.

"The only arrangement we're going to reach is one of us dying on this roof. You know it and I know it. But remember one thing." He pointed at the caregiver's disk-shaped weapon. "You fire that thing and I release these keys. By the time you find them, the smoke will have long destroyed all the DNA in your repository. Remember that."

The layers of diplomacy were peeling away, angry desperation winding the caregiver tighter and tighter. Peter knew if he kept frustrating it, it would lash out at him.

Setting it off kilter might be his best chance at escape.

"What will it take for me to get those keys?" A pleasant smile angled across the caregiver's face.

Peter held his tongue, a thousand angry replies rising in his mouth. He had to think this through. What could he request that the caregiver might attempt to supply? Then it came to him.

Sting. He grinned. Why hadn't he thought of it before?

"You've got a recombinant locked up inside," Peter began.

The roof took a sudden dip and Peter grabbed at the edge to steady himself.

Smoke coiled around him, the caregiver sparkling.

He pressed his forehead against the warm roof, fighting to regain equilibrium. Finally, his vision cleared.

The caregiver seemed closer.

"What are you talking about, a recombinant?"

"Do you want these keys or not?" Peter shouted.

The caregiver nodded hurriedly.

Peter paused, sharp pains sliding in waves through his shoulder and rib cage. He groaned. "All right," he continued, catching his breath. "The recombinant. His name's Stingley. Bring him here."

"Why do you want a recom—"

"Do it!" Peter shouted, cutting him off. "I want to hand off these keys to a neutral party! I know how precious those recombinants are to you caregivers." *Let it think he was jealous.* "Besides, Stingley's got a big mouth." His face was a mask of sweat. He wanted to wipe it away, but his right arm was in too much pain. And he didn't dare pull in his left hand.

The caregiver smiled.

"You bring Stingley," Peter continued, surprised by how weak his voice was getting. "I'll give him the keys in exchange for you turning your back while I slip off this roof."

That complacent smile appeared on the caregivers' face, the one all caregivers got when they thought they'd won. He'd seen it many times on Ku'Tal. He returned the smile with as much defiance as he could summon.

Just bring Sting here, you bastard. See just how much you've won.

The caregiver disappeared into the duct. Peter drew his left hand back and laid the keys beside him. With his left hand, he searched his pockets for a weapon. Anything to use against this caregiver.

His pockets were empty. If only he had another grenade.

Only a few minutes later, not even enough time to climb in and out of the duct, the caregiver returned.

Peter grabbed hold of the keys and dangled them over the roof's edge again.

"I've arranged for this recombinant to be brought up here."

Yeah, right.

He struggled up from the ground, his legs wobbly as he stood up to the caregiver. He kept the keys extended.

"Then we'll just wait for him to show."

The caregiver cast nervous glances into the smoky haze of the ruined dome. Every moment that Peter stalled, the more smoke and heat filled the repository, threatening to ignite the entire room in flames. That chemical fire he'd caused with that second grenade was still burning.

Their repository was running out of time. And so was he.

"Please," said the caregiver through gritted teeth. "Give me those keys. The repository must survive. It must! We haven't had enough time to reanimate the samples yet." All the anger and malice bled from the caregiver's face. "Please. Give me the keys."

The silver weapon leveled at Peter's chest. Peter sucked in a hard breath of smoky air.

"The recombinant isn't coming, is he?" he said.

Slowly, the caregiver shook its head and took a step forward. Peter slid back.

From the broken dome, something grabbed his foot. He crashed against the roof, a scream tearing from his throat when his injured shoulder made contact. His grip loosened on the keys, nearly letting them drop, but he held onto them.

He kicked at the hand clamped around his ankle until it released him, a crash resounding below.

When he looked up, the silver disk was again leveled at his chest. The caregiver leaned toward him, other hand outstretched.

"You have two seconds to give me those keys. Or I kill you."

Peter tightened his grip on the chain holding the keys. He had one chance here. He had to do this right.

He mimicked a look of defeat, hanging his head. Then slowly, hesitantly, he pulled his hand back from over the roof. He held out the keys.

The caregiver snatched hold of the chain, but Peter didn't let go. He jerked the chain toward him. An explosion erupted between them.

Something slammed into his chest.

The caregiver lost its footing, fell on top of him.

Peter rolled, barely grabbing hold of the roof's edge, but the caregiver careened over the side. It fell three stories, slamming into a network of ducts and ventilation fans.

It took Peter's last breath of strength to heft himself back onto the edge of the roof. His body dangled half on half off, fire coursing through his nerves. He screamed, shaking from the unbearable pain.

Couldn't move. Couldn't save himself now.

He moaned, drained, everything going dark.

This was it. End of the line.

27

DAVID EDGED CLOSER to the ruined dome, closer to Mitchell and the robed caregiver. He crouched beside the open grate in the ventilation duct. Black smoke continued to pour out, nearly choking him. He fought down an urge to cough and turned away from the gritty smoke.

Climbing.

From this vantage point, he recognized the caregiver. He frowned, his body stiffening. Tevihu. David still remembered Tevihu's delight as he gouged Sting's forearms with that laser scalpel. He wanted to smash his fist into Tevihu's pasty, oblong face.

With new resolve, he leveled the pistol at Tevihu, drawing a bead on the back of its head. He wouldn't get a second shot.

The caregiver bent down.

David squinted. *What was it doing?*

He rubbed his eyes, acrid smoke irritating. Obscuring his vision.

Peter held out some keys to Tevihu.

What's Mitchell gotten in the middle of, he wondered, muzzle of his pistol still trained on Tevihu's head.

Like a hungry dog, Tevihu snatched at the chain in Mitchell's hand.

David tried to squeeze off a shot, but Tevihu was just too close to Mitchell.

He cursed under his breath. If he fired, he'd hit them both.

Stifling a cough, he moved closer, treading quietly along the edge of the dome.

Mitchell yanked the chain backward and Tevihu lost its balance. With Mitchell's assistance, Tevihu pitched over the side of the building. To David's horror, Mitchell lost his balance and slid off the edge.

"Mitchell!" he shouted, his voice hoarse and broken.

With clumsy steps around the dome's edge, David stumbled toward Mitchell.

With an agonized shout, Mitchell managed to pull himself back onto the roof's edge. He collapsed on his side, trembling with pain, his blood staining the roof.

"Mitchell!" David cried. "Dear God...Mitchell."

He knelt beside the young recombinant and slid the pistol into his belt. Horrified, he examined the burns on Mitchell's upper chest and shoulder. The weapon had discharged into Mitchell's chest. It had been so close, almost point-blank.

The wound was bad.

He laid a hand against Mitchell's neck and Mitchell lurched, his eyes snapping open.

"It's okay, Mitchell. It's me, Sarge. You're safe now. "

Peter offered a faint smile that fell into a pained grimace. His back arched from a wave of pain and David gripped his forearm.

"Sarge," he said, a gravelly cough rumbling in his throat, his eyes welling with tears. "I—I saw him, but I couldn't...find him. Too many places—not enough time." His voice was anguished. Defeated.

Tears slid down the side of his face and David's chest ached.

"I failed him, Sarge," Mitchell whispered in a raw voice, swallowing a sob.

"No, you didn't," said Sarge with a smile. He brushed the blond hair out of Mitchell's light blue eyes. "I found Sting. He's just a few steps away."

David wasn't sure Mitchell even heard his voice as the young recombinant slumped against the roof. Fear rose bitter in his mouth as he pressed his fingers to Mitchell's neck, seeking a pulse.

It was thready. Damn. Mitchell couldn't die on him now. Not with Sting right behind him. He couldn't!

"Mitchell?" No response. "Mitchell!"

Sting appeared beside a tangle of ducts and debris, rifle cradled in both hands. When he saw Mitchell on the roof's overhang, he hurried around the ducts and the dome.

"Pete! Oh, God—Pete!"

He collapsed beside Mitchell, rolling him onto his back. Sting pulled open the remains of Mitchell's shirt. The blistered, charred skin beneath made Sting look away.

"Aw, dammit, Pete! What'd you go and do to yourself?"

He wiped his eyes and pressed his ear to Mitchell's chest. After a moment or two, his body went slack.

"He's still alive," Sting said, out of breath.

"He needs a medic," David replied.

He wanted to scream. Where in hell would he find a medic with a strike force on the way?

Sting's unwavering gaze studied Mitchell. "We've got to get him off this roof somehow and take care of this. It's bad."

"Where?" David demanded, glancing around for more caregivers.

"Anywhere but here, Sarge," he said, shades of the Stingley he knew on Ku'Tal.

David scanned the horizon. They were too far from the shuttle. If they could get Mitchell off the roof, they might make it to the lake. Take a boat across to the ruined colony. From there, he'd get Mitchell to a bedroll and the medic's kit while he and Diana went for the shuttle. It was the best they could do.

If D'Angelo hadn't already evacuated in the shuttle.

He smiled, dismissing the thought. Diana wouldn't leave without them. He knew his sister. No, the camp in the ruins was their best hope. He'd distract Captain D'Angelo long enough to get Mitchell help.

"All right," said David, turning his gaze back to Stingley. "We're going to take him across the lake to the ruins. The recon camp is there. It's Mitchell's best chance. "

"What happens from there?" Sting asked, his green-eyed gaze encompassing David.

"We'll stabilize Mitchell as best we can and then get him aboard the shuttle."

He grinned, hoping to reassure Sting they had a chance to survive this place. He had no idea how much time they had left, but as long as they were all still breathing, there was still time left to escape.

"We'll get out of here before the strike force attacks, Stingley," David added.

After slinging his rifle across his back, Sting gently slid his arms underneath Mitchell's arms.

"Let's get moving then," he said. "Help me lift him."

David took hold of Mitchell's legs.

"On a three count."

"Right," said Sting with a grunt, rising to his feet.

David counted to three and they hefted Mitchell up in tandem.

Mitchell screamed.

Sting's face contorted at Mitchell's pain. He leaned down close to Mitchell's face.

"Easy, Pete, we'll get you some help. Just stay with me, okay?"

No response from Mitchell. Not even an eyelid flicker.

Fear trembled through David as they hurried around the ruined dome and behind the ventilation ducts. The roof leveled out here, allowing them a clear view of the lower part of the roof.

They reached the ladder without interference.

David studied it for a moment, trying to figure out the best way to get Mitchell down.

"I'll go down first," he said finally.

David struggled to hold onto Mitchell's feet as he descended the ladder. Sting started down a few rungs after him, one hand gripping the ladder, the other arm holding onto Mitchell who moaned with every step.

A pair of pearly white hands reached up, taking hold of Mitchell.

Startled, David jerked his gaze around.

Caregiver!

"Sarge, look out!"

Stingley tried to shift Mitchell's feet to get to his rifle as David fumbled for his pistol.

Nikoam leaned into view, stepping out from behind the fans.

"It's all right," said Nikoam, holding out its hands. "Let me help. Please."

"Sarge, no!" Stingley snarled, teeth gritted, eyes filled with hate.

David shook his head. "It's okay, Stingley," he said in a reassuring tone, his gaze watching Nikoam's every move. "This one's different."

He turned toward the caregiver.

"Thank you," David said finally and accepted Nikoam's assistance.

With Nikoam supporting Mitchell's dead weight, David and Sting got him onto the long stretch of roof that ended in a small alcove behind the building. Nikoam helped them carry Mitchell to the end of the roof. David climbed down onto a crate. When he was balanced on the stack, Nikoam and Sting lowered Mitchell's unconscious body down to him.

Sting climbed down to the next box beyond David, Nikoam stopping beside David. The two of them lifted Mitchell down to Sting. With Mitchell in his arms, Sting stepped onto solid ground at last, David and Nikoam behind him.

David turned as a silver disk pressed against his temple.

He froze.

Dammit! Nikoam had tricked them. Why'd he trust any of these aliens? Why!

"I trusted you," David growled.

"Move forward please," said Nikoam, its voice pleasant despite the weapon. David wondered how pleasant Nikoam would be with a plasma rifle shoved up its ass. "The injured one first."

Sting scowled at Nikoam, but obeyed, carrying Mitchell around the side of the building.

"This isn't over," Sting growled, his voice deadly quiet.

The huge gathering of caretakers startled David. They had evacuated the building and were busy carrying out whatever could be saved. Their smudged faces were ashen and dour as they sorted through piles of rescued equipment and belongings.

"Keep walking please," said Nikoam, a hand on David's shoulder. "Do not stop."

Nikoam led the three of them past the gathering. Several caregivers looked up, but their gazes didn't linger. They returned quickly to their tasks. Only then did David realize what Nikoam was doing. They wouldn't have gotten past all these caregivers without Nikoam's intervention. He felt bad for judging this caregiver now.

"How did you know?" he said in a hoarse whisper.

What looked like a smile stretched across Nikoam's milky, translucent face as they moved toward the gate into the testing pens.

"I went to find Tevihu and saw the man you carry. I knew he was no more a hybrid than you are one of the captured recombinants."

"How?" David asked.

"There hasn't been a hybrid that clever since this program began," said Nikoam. "And your arms were pristine, not a single sample taken. Very unlikely here."

They left the other caregivers behind as the gate loomed. The air smelled of chemicals and heat, the sweet smell of new growth lost in the smoke. Even the rich yellow and silver of the trees had turned grey with ash and smoke.

"Yet you helped us." Sting said, surprise in his bright green eyes.

Nikoam tilted its head in a nod. "I've gathered as much of the genetic samples from the repository as I could."

David stiffened. As long as Antaran DNA survived, the Antarans would still need recombinants to harvest their technology.

"Not from soldiers. Civilians—like I was once," said Nikoam. "They are safe in a vault now. Safe from the others."

Nikoam exhaled sharply, shaking its head. Its creamy gold eyes misted. In a moment, the weapon slid away from David's head.

"We've all lost our way. We were to care for our people, nothing more. Not take lands and lives for those we're trying to bring back from extinction. Or build armies of destruction. This wasn't what the skies wanted of us. Or the stars."

David sighed, running a hand over his sweaty face. "But this won't stop them."

Nikoam nodded. "It won't. But without this facility, your technology is lost to us. The Nation will swarm. There's nothing I can do. I'm sorry. Many of us with small voices never wanted this." He motioned with flailing limbs toward the trees. "I've released all the recombinants into the woods—toward the lake. Without them, some of my people will turn back. Others will fight for control. And the circle will turn again. Go."

Nikoam's weapon fell away from David's shoulder. He started to turn away but felt compelled to turn back. The strike force weighed heavily on his mind now. Nikoam deserved the same chance they'd been given.

"Nikoam," he said. "Take survival gear, lots of food and water, and go into your vault. Don't wait. It's important."

Nikoam frowned, a slight shake of its head and parting of its thin lips as a shadow of confusion slid across its flawless features.

"Trust me," said David. "There's more darkness coming."

"I will do as you say," said Nikoam.

Turning away again, David hurried behind Sting through the woods. The lake wasn't far.

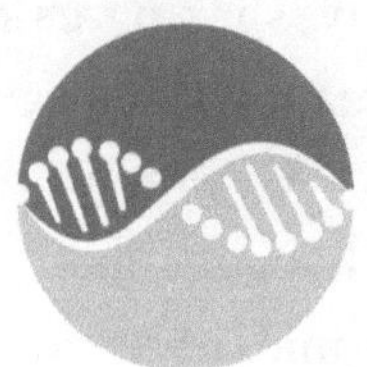

THE SHUTTLE GLIDED through the veil of smoke obscuring the facility and the grounds around it. A fire burned through it, layering the sky with swaths of greasy, black smoke.

Diana coaxed the sleek shuttle into a gentle circle over the forest. No one emerged from the trees or onto the footpaths. Next, she swerved over the ruins, hoping to see David and Peter moving toward the camp site.

She circled twice, but no one moved through the rubble or along the umber footpaths winding out of the silvery yellow trees surrounding the ruins.

Her gaze kept falling to the ship's chronometer. Time trickled away with every pass over the ruins, fuel needle trembling. Ron's gaze was riveted on the horizon, darting to every trace of movement below. An impenetrable black cloud, growing tall like a thunderhead, hung over the facility, the haze obscuring much of the forest and limiting their visibility. She wanted to fly over the facility, to see how badly it was damaged, but that would be too dangerous. Even if the caregivers didn't see her, the thick smoke would make maneuvering difficult.

"Where are they?" Diana cried in exasperation. She shook a hand at the darkening forest. "How will we ever find them in this mess?"

"We'll find them," said Ron, his tone insistent. "We have no choice. Can you fly any lower?"

She shook her head. "Not with the visibility this poor."

Her stomach twisted, nerves taut like overstressed wires. Reynolds would be calling soon, warning that the strike force was an hour outside of Ballese.

David and Peter, where are you?

Her gaze drifted to the fuel gauge. Not critical yet. Still enough to get them to Karaba. Or Farnas. She didn't care as long as they could refuel. Farnas didn't have the facilities that Karaba had, but there were a few crop-export shuttle stations where she could land and refuel.

Fuel was the least of her worries.

She continued her vigil, risking the decreasing visibility to fly lower over the area of forest and grasslands they'd covered on foot. And around the dark ruins dotting the planet.

She wondered how the Ballese colonists died. No one had ever spoken about it. Did they fight for their colony until the last colonist fell to the biodrones? Or did they surrender? Nothing was known about the Antarans back then. No one had ever seen them before either. The people of Ballese—like Naharra—had been the first contact. Judging by the piles of stone and debris below, they didn't live long enough to convey anything to home system.

"I remember the silence best," said Diana, her gaze still on the ruins.

Ron squinted at her, frowning. "What?"

"The ruins. What do you remember?" she asked.

"Those biodrones sneaking up on us," he answered. Then he pointed toward what looked like a leveled greenhouse. "I think I'll remember the dead plants in the greenhouse. To see so many dead plants on a world with such thick vegetation..."

The ruins looked like a bombed-out neighborhood. Like some of the old, abandoned neighborhoods on Earth and Lunar colony. Back home on Earth, there were some cities with whole sections completely empty. After the pollution got too heavy in the northeast.

The comm unit beeped. Her stomach twisted in a knot. She hesitated a moment then reached out to the shuttle control panel and received the call.

"Recon three. Over."

"Recon three, you're still on surface?" Reynolds sounded startled. "Visitors are an hour away from delivering their greeting. How many minutes until your departure?"

How many can we have, she wanted to ask.

"Unknown, Commander. Awaiting the imminent return of the rest of our team. Over."

She glanced at Ron who nodded at her.

"Recon three, I hope you realize just how important this visitor is and how affecting its greeting will be. Over."

Sighing, Diana leaned back in her seat. "That's why I am anxiously awaiting the return of our team. All of them. You'll just have to give us more time to retrieve them. Over."

"More time?" sputtered Reynolds. "There is no more time. Recall your people immediately."

Diana gritted her teeth. *Oh, wow, why didn't she think of that?* She'd just locate the recall button right away and magically whisk David and Peter back to the shuttle And Sting. No problem.

She was so tired of these military ultimatums.

"Now, you listen to me, Commander," Diana began, her tone sharp, her voice rising, "until these last members of our team reach this shuttle, we can't leave. They trusted me to get them here safely and I won't leave them to die down here while I flee to safety. Do you understand that? I will not leave them behind. So, unless you have a magic recall button that will instantly bring the rest of my team back here, we can't leave. Over!"

A heavy silence hung in the air as she waited for a response.

Ron's head was bowed, thumb and index finger pressed against his forehead as he rubbed his brow.

She'd gone too far. She knew it. But she didn't care. No one was going to make her leave her brother behind—or the man she loved. And Sting. They would all be aboard this shuttle or Reynolds would have to kill them all.

"You've got thirty more minutes, Recon three. Over."

"I've got as much time as it takes to bring them back," she answered. "We won't be leaving until then. Over."

Diana didn't wait for Reynold's response. She reached down and cleared the connection.

When she looked up, Ron was grinning at her.

"What?" she demanded.

"All this time, I've been trying that military tact they taught us in boot camp." He spread his hands. "I should have let you talk to Reynolds a long time ago. We could have avoided all of this maneuvering."

Diana winced. "I probably shouldn't have talked to him like that, but it's ridiculous." She gestured at the thickening haze. "Does he think we're enjoying ourselves down here? Having a grand holiday with everything trying to kill us and biodrones trying to eat us? Like we want to stay here and be blown to bits."

She bit her lip, her fears surfacing. This time, her voice was soft and pained.

"I'm afraid David and Peter won't be coming back, Ron."

He reached over and squeezed her shoulder. "David's as stubborn as you are. He'll come back. With Mitchell and Sting."

Her eyes filled with tears, remembering Peter's arms around her and those first nights at her apartment when they'd lain arm in arm on the sofa watching old movies, something Peter had never seen before, and sipping wine. How she loved to watch his child-like wonder at everything: his first walk in the rain, his first taste of ice cream. Making love to him. Now, she'd never feel the same about a rain shower. Those short little bursts of rain on Civilization made her heart race and she wanted to run through the puddles. And dance. Even the rush of the city shuttle past the stop made her heart race with joy.

Because of Peter.

She wanted to re-experience every single moment of the world again through his eyes. Beside him. He deserved the chance to live and she needed him. But without Sting, Peter would never be whole again. It hurt that she hadn't been enough to save him, but she knew that now.

And she understood.

"Mitchell's determined," Ron added. He'd seen her face and he was trying to reassure her. "He'll be here with his buddy if it's within his power, Diana."

She pulled in a heavy breath and wiped away the tears collecting in the corners of her eyes. Reynolds would leave them alone until it was that last warning, but she didn't care. She'd stay until—

Maybe, in all the confusion of the fire and the approaching attack, the three of them had escaped?

It was her best hope right now. Their only hope. And Reynolds could go to hell.

She was staying until the very end.

29

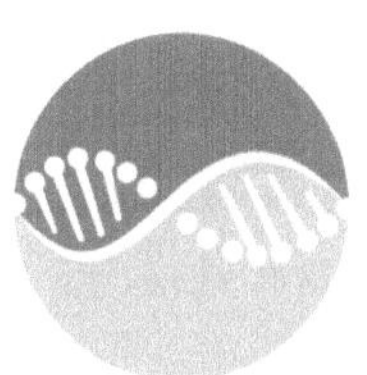

THE LAKE MATERIALIZED out of the pitch-black smoke like dark, polished onyx. David and Sting choked and wheezed as they hurried around the shoreline in search of a boat. Sting saw one, the last one. It was a long, thin rowboat made of amber-colored wood. It looked seaworthy. Two recombinants fumbled with the mooring rope. Sting laid Mitchell down on the shore and ran after the recombinants. David crouched beside Mitchell, trying to shield him from the smoke.

Sting grabbed hold of the first recombinant, jerking him out of the boat. He shoved the second recombinant backward, shouting at them until they stood still and listened to him. In moments, Sting and the other recombinants dragged the rowboat down the shore toward Mitchell.

"Looks like we're going to get you to a medic after all," David said, leaning down to Mitchell's ear. "Diana's going to skin me when she sees you though. And then you."

"Sarge!" Stingley called. "There room on that shuttle for more recombinants?"

David nodded. "Of course. All of them." He sighed. If they ever found it again.

That famous grin sprouted on Stingley's face as he motioned the first recombinant into the boat. Then he bent down and hefted Mitchell from the ground. Mitchell groaned. He stepped around the first recombinant, moving to the back of the boat where he laid Mitchell down carefully on the bottom of the boat. He sat beside Mitchell, a hand on his chest as David climbed in next, the second recombinant smashing in beside the first recombinant.

Grabbing hold of the oars, David pumped his arms, straining against the weight, and the boat lurched slowly away from the shore. Like an apparition, the Antaran facility faded into the crisp grey smoke settling around it like a shroud. These Antarans had no idea they had only a few hours to live.

At least he'd warned Nikoam, but he felt no guilt in watching those other bastards roasting their balls from orbit.

The rowboat crawled through the smooth, silky currents that rustled the lake's silky black fabric. Oars slapped against dark waters with an uneven rhythm as the boat glided across the lake.

To the south, five or six recombinants threaded their way through the woods. Headed toward the ruins. When they caught up to the boat, he'd get them aboard the shuttle.

To new identities and new lives. *Yes, they'd earned it.*

He glanced down at Mitchell's restless form trembling on the bottom of the boat. Sting's hand kneaded Mitchell's good shoulder, trying to ease the pain. Mitchell had no idea Stingley was even there.

"He's got fever," Sting mumbled, poking David in the shoulder.

His face was a mask of worry, mouth pinched, eyebrows pressing downward, those pale green eyes glassy. Mitchell was a brother to Sting and he knew Sting would do anything and everything to save him.

"We're not far from the camp, Sting. There's a medic's kit at the site. Some painkillers and antibiotics will help him while we treat those wounds."

Hopefully aboard the shuttle, he thought.

Sting cast an uneasy glance at David.

Was he worrying too much? No, he had good reason to worry. He didn't know which one was crazier, D'Angelo or Tanner. No, his money was on D'Angelo. Thankfully, Kraver was there to distract D'Angelo with protocol. Regardless, Diana could handle both of them—crazy or not.

The other two recombinants were quiet for some time before the brown-haired one nearest David spoke.

"So, there's really a shuttle over here?" he said, hazel eyes wide-eyed. "A way off this horrible rock?"

David nodded. "UCOE sent us in on recon. And things here are about to get messy, so we need to get to that shuttle quickly." He noted the young man's name on his pocket. Jensen.

"That fire in the lab saved our asses," said the farthest recombinant. He was lanky and dark-skinned, his hair thick and black. His sable eyes looked bright, almost wild in the smoky air.

"What started it?" Sting asked.

The brown-haired recombinant called Jensen shrugged. He was, shorter and stockier than the other one.

"From what little I heard," Jensen replied, "it wasn't an accident. The caregivers were pretty rabid about the whole thing. Then a bunch of them stormed into our chamber, waving weapons and shouting. Screaming about some crazy recombinant blowing up stuff. I thought they were going to kill all of us for a minute there."

David smirked. *Had to be Mitchell.* "I think that was Mitchell's handiwork."

"That's my boy!" Sting shouted, grinning as he patted Mitchell's uninjured shoulder.

"Yeah! Go recombinants!" cried the black-haired recombinant.

David caught a glimpse of his name as the recombinant gestured furiously with a fist pump. Strader.

"Then that other caregiver came in and shouted something about a repository," said Strader. "They all scattered fast after that. Then one of them just opened the far door into the hallway, motioning us all out into the training yard."

Jensen shook his head, still visibly confused by the whole incident. "Yeah, it just pushed us outside and motioned to the trees." He grinned. "I didn't wait to be told twice."

"We went straight for the lake," Strader mumbled. He looked exhausted. The caregivers seemed to work the recombinants constantly. Much worse than any military drills.

David glanced back at Sting, who'd suddenly gotten quiet. He was as exhausted as Strader and Jensen, but David knew he'd hold on until Mitchell was safe. Stingley's loyalty was unfaltering.

"Stingley, you okay back there?"

A pause.

"Yeah, Sarge, I'm fine." His voice was raspy and thinner now.

David's arms ached from rowing. He felt the boat slowing. Strader tapped him on the arm.

"Take a break," he said. "I'll row us in. Sarge."

David stared at Strader a moment, realizing he wasn't like the other recombinants. Another anomaly. The Antarans had hand-picked him, too.

Something clicked into place.

There was a reserved sense of gentleness across the board in the recombinants he'd seen in the Antaran facility. And a sense of camaraderie. Loyalty. Mitchell had displayed that amply to them and then Sting showed it when he sacrificed himself for Mitchell.

It was that gentleness and loyalty combined with the will to fight and survive that the Antarans wanted. They wanted to temper their biodrones' rawness with this refined sense of support. And teamwork. To allow their biodrone hybrids to blend better into UCOE units undetected.

Probably deeper. He had no idea how deeply they'd already infiltrated Earth's military forces.

And that thought terrified him.

Finally, he gave up the oars to Strader, trading places in the rowboat. He rubbed his sore, blistered hands that throbbed and ached.

Strader quickly developed an even rhythm and the boat slipped smoothly across the rest of the distance. After fifteen minutes or so, the rowboat finally nudged the muddy shoreline.

Struggling to his feet, Sting fought to lift Mitchell out of the boat. David waited until Strader had climbed out before he moved back to help Sting. He took hold of Mitchell's legs and they lifted him up from the bottom of the boat.

"You, two, keep watch," said David. "Sing out if you see any movement. biodrones may be around."

Strader stiffened and exchanged an uneasy glance with Jensen.

"Wish I had my grid," Strader mumbled. "And my rifle."

David pulled the pistol from his belt. He extended it to Jensen. "Here. It's the best I can do."

Strader's eyes lit with relief. "Excellent. Thanks, Sarge."

David led them across the silent, empty streets, through rubble-strewn buildings, a little church so eerily quiet and strangely serene. They walked past some ruined flats and decaying skimmers, some in the middle of the streets. Like the end had come suddenly and without warning.

Along the backside of the street that ran toward the lake, he recognized the building where the recon camp had been. Off to the right. Where the western border of the colony ended.

A chill raked his skin. The building...the camp looked deserted.

His mouth went dry, cold fear gripping his gut.

His pace quickened as they crossed the last street. He straddled the broken wall, into the building where they'd made camp.

Walls were pocked, burned and smoking. From a shitload of plasma fire—recent plasma fire.

Sting and Strader lifted Mitchell over the wall and David led them over to Mitchell's tangled bedroll slumped against the wall.

Sting was beside him, straightening the bedroll. David laid Mitchell down, hearing the rasp in his breathing.

"Stay with him, Sting."

He turned toward the corner where they'd kept supplies.

And found D'Angelo's stiff body lying still beside Tanner. Their faces were grey. Gazes frozen.

What the hell happened here?

Diana and Kraver had gone to the shuttle. That's where they were and right now, he refused to believe otherwise.

He'd deal with that next. For now, Mitchell needed antibiotics, fluids, and treatment. He fumbled through crates, finding water purifier tablets and four empty canteens. He snatched them from the crate.

"Jensen, Strader, fall in!"

They complied.

"Take these and get some lake water." He thrust the canteens and purifier tablets at them.

With a nod, they turned and slipped over the wall.

David returned to the crates. The medic's kit wasn't there. He searched the floor until he found it against the back wall.

"Got the kit," he called to Sting, rushing back to Mitchell.

His ragged breathing echoed through the building, making David nervous.

"Mitchell, I won't let you die on me, you hear me?" David said to him.

He yanked open the lid of the kit, rummaging through until he found liquid painkiller and antibiotic wound sealant. David handed the painkiller to Stingley.

Stingley uncovered the microneedle on the painkiller accelerant and slid up Mitchell's right sleeve. Sting found the vein in the crook of his arm and pressed the microneedle against it, delivering a measured dose of meds. He sat back on his heels, waiting for the narcotic to take effect. In a few moments, Mitchell's breathing became softer, less labored. But they'd have to watch his breathing closely with painkiller in his system.

Only then did David peel open Mitchell's burned, bloody shirt.

He cleaned the wound as best he could and then applied wound sealant. He emptied the entire can of sealant spray on Mitchell's battered chest, watching as the thin sealant skin formed across the injuries, expanding into bleeders, and covering burns. It would at least stop any bleeding and keep Mitchell's wounds free of any more contaminants until they got him to a medical facility. It was the best he could do. He prayed the young man hung on until they reached Karaba.

"Is he going to make it, Sarge?" Sting asked, glassy eyed, his gaze darting from Mitchell to David.

"He damned well better, Sting," David said in a soft voice. "Diana will kill me if he doesn't."

Sting found another bedroll and laid it across Mitchell like a blanket.

"biodrones!" Jensen.

David jerked up from the ground.

Sting was already on his feet, running to the wall, rifle swiveling into his hands. He fired a burst of plasma as Jensen and Strader leaped over the wall.

A string of biodrones barreled across the street toward them.

Jensen turned, pistol flashing.

David searched through D'Angelo's things, finding the captain's pistol. He glanced up. Tanner's rifle lay beside him. He snapped it up, sweeping it into his arms.

"Strader!" he called.

Strader turned and David waved the pistol.

The black-haired recombinant darted toward him, snatching the pistol, and returned to the wall.

David rushed back to Mitchell and crouched there, ready to smoke any biodrone that flipped down from the rafters or over that wall toward them.

Talons skittered above him. He looked up, rifle raised.

A gold gleam flickered in the rafters.

He fired.

A biodrone screeched, falling from the roof, and splattering against the ground. It lay still.

"Sarge, behind you!"

Sting pivoted, an arc of plasma scouring the far corner. Two blackened forms collapsed.

Strader fired at the wall and a biodrone disintegrated.

Movement, like the sound of a hundred rats in the wall, scritched behind David.

Horrified, he turned.

More talons than he could count tore at a section of rotting wood. Struggling to get through to them from the adjacent building.

His heart throbbed in his throat and he gripped the rifle.

He couldn't count the number of glowing gold eyes flashing at him through the crumbling wood planks.

30

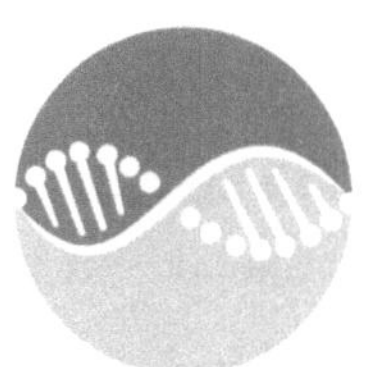

FOUR MORE TIMES, Diana swept low over the umber and silver footpaths snaking through the forest, the shuttle whispering through swaths of grey and black smoke choking the landscape. She followed the path that she and the recon team had taken into the ruins.

She smiled. Where she and Peter had carried crates and held hands in the darkness when D'Angelo wasn't watching. Where they'd made camp.

She skirted the edge of the lake, slipping over the ruins and then into the forest again.

"It's getting too difficult to see," she said, the smoke obscuring most of the landscape now.

"Can you fly lower?" Ron asked.

"I don't dare fly much lower," she answered. "Not with so much smoke around." Still, she had little choice but to fly under the smoke. "But I'll try. And I'll keep flying this circuit until I have to land somewhere."

Again, she veered over the foliage and turned back toward the lake. As the shuttle neared the edge of that glassy black lake, Diana caught a flash of blue.

"Ron!" she shouted. "Did you see that?"

He shook his head. "What? See what?"

Frantically, she scanned the horizon, searching for another flash of blue. Like lightning.

Somewhere off to her right, two blue blooms of light arced through the smoke.

"Plasma fire!" Ron shouted. He pointed to the right.

"That came from the ruins!"

Diana's heart leaped into her throat, chest pounding as she banked the shuttle right over the lake and headed toward the ruins.

Plasma fire meant biodrones. She grinned. And people shooting at them. But at that location it had to be David! And Peter!

"Ron, get more rifles," she said, trying to keep her voice steady.

She flew as low as she dared. Off to her left, six or eight soldiers ran down the street. Following her, she realized. Recombinants!

Ahead, a massive volley of blue flashes erupted, illuminating the shell of the building where they'd made camp.

Where D'Angelo's body still lay in the debris.

She glanced at the chronometer. Twenty-eight minutes until the strike force dropped into orbit around Ballese. Twenty-eight minutes until the orbital bombers armed their warheads and counted down for the drop.

"Set it down as close as you can to that building," Ron replied, rising from his seat.

She heard him checking rifles behind her.

Letting up on the throttle, Diana coaxed the shuttle down slowly in the middle of the deserted street.

In moments, someone began pounding on the hatch.

Ron opened the hatch a crack, seeing seven desperate recombinants. He thrust open the hatch and they scrambled into the shuttle, nearly knocking him over.

"Strap in and don't get in the way!" he shouted at them, closing the hatch again.

The silence in the shuttle was palpable as their labored breaths quieted.

Diana hurried out of her restraint harness and raced to the hatch. Ron thrust a rifle at her and she tossed the strap over her head.

"Ready?" he asked, gripping his rifle.

She took a deep breath and nodded.

Please be out there, David and Peter. I'll never forgive you if you're not!

"Ready," she answered. "I'll stay close to the hatch. Don't want any of those biodrones hitching a ride."

She remembered too well on Ku'Tal how three had hidden in the cargo hold and nearly killed her.

Ron closed his eyes a moment, as if gathered his thoughts, his actions. With a deep breath, he shoved open the hatch.

He jumped down, Diana behind him, standing guard. She closed the hatch as Ron raced toward the abandoned camp site.

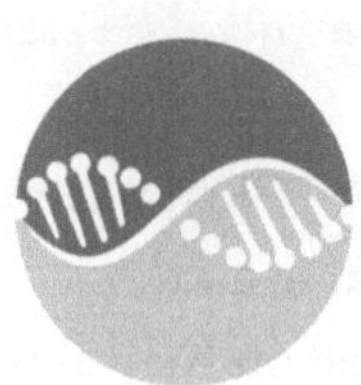

CLAWS RAKED ACROSS WOODEN BEAMS, gnawing, frantic and murderous. Growing louder as plasma fire arced through the building's crumbling shell.

The smell of burnt syrupy sweetness was cloying. It made David gag.

He and Sting grabbed the edges of Mitchell's bedroll and dragged it away from the wall, recombinants firing at biodrones still skittering through the breaks in the wall. All around them, smashed and burned remnants of the biojammers littered the broken floor. The ones they'd set up on arrival.

Useless now.

"On the right, Jensen!" Strader shouted.

Jensen dropped to the floor, tumbling left. Strader squeezed off a shot. Taking down another biodrone.

Jensen scrabbled to his feet. Turned. Fired. Two more biodrones swung down from the smoking rafters. They dropped against the floor, dead and smoking.

Strader stumbled backward. Whipping around the barrel of his rifle, he caught another biodrone in the head.

It hit the floor.

Jensen fired, splattering it against the wall.

Sting ripped Mitchell off the bedroll and stood him on his feet. He held Mitchell against his shoulder with one arm, rifle poised in the other.

"We've got to make a break for it," Sting said with a snarl.

"To where?" Strader cried, apprehension tightening his features.

David aimed at the wall of burrowing biodrones as Jensen and Strader scrambled over beside him.

"Sarge, whadda we do?" Strader asked with wide eyes. "We can't hold off that many!"

"They'll eviscerate us!" Jensen shouted, gripping his rife against his chest.

The grim reality hit David hard. They had nowhere to go. Nowhere to escape this army of ravenous killing machines.

He backed away from the wall.

Couldn't fire at them. And remove the last remaining slivers of wood holding back a massive force from exploding into the building.

He motioned Sting and the others toward the outer wall. Toward the street. No matter what they did, they couldn't stay here.

It was a death trap now.

"Jensen, Strader," he said in the calmest voice he could muster. "Help Stingley get Mitchell over that wall."

"To where?" Sting asked, starting to sound a little rattled.

David sighed. The lake. Biodrones don't swim. Maybe the water would hold them off long enough to find the shuttle?

How long could they tread water?

Without a bunker, defending any point on land would become their tomb.

"Over the wall. Now! Move it!" David ordered. "Head toward the lake."

Strader and Jensen rushed to the wall.

Lifting Mitchell through the opening and out into the colony's broken streets.

David winced. Lined with dark, burned out, and empty buildings, these streets were the perfect place for ambushes now.

Like they'd been when Antarans attacked the colony.

David followed the recombinants over the wall. His gaze never wavered from the burrowing biodrones whittling away the far wall.

He swallowed hard, his palms damp.

He glanced over his shoulder. Jensen and Strader were over, Sting shuffling Mitchell between them as they hurried into the streets.

The biodrones would be through any minute. They were microns from breaking through.

He had to give Mitchell and Sting, the other recombinants some time. Some distance to reach the lake.

Moments later, the first biodrone broke through, lurching toward David.

Aiming carefully, he squeezed off a shot, dropping the gnarled creature in a puddle of amber.

He kept moving backward toward the wall. Toward the opening. Toward the lake.

Two more biodrones surged through, the wall starting to crumble.

"Come on, baby," David muttered, rifle raised. "Hold just a little longer."

Three shots crackled through the building. Two biodrones fell.

He felt the break in the wall at his back. And turned. Swung one leg over.

A talon careened down from the rafter, catching him in the back.

He tumbled off the wall and into the floor. The rifle slipped out of his hands.

Pain snaked down his back as he lunged for rifle that clattered against the broken tile.

Three biodrones skittered toward him, talons raised. Another one at his back.

Damn.

He snapped the rifle barrel up as biodrones plunged on top of him.

He screamed, razor-sharp talons everywhere. And pumped the trigger.

Blast of blue fire blinded him, heat singing his face. But he kept firing.

Its bulbous head ruptured, spewing yellow fluid into the air. It slumped over.

Another plasma burst took down the one tearing at his legs.

He turned and pressed the rifle barrel against the last one's head and fired.

It exploded in a shower of talons and yellow spray.

Something grabbed him and dragged him over the wall.

He turned, barrel raised, teeth gritted.

Sting and Ron! Diana had to be with him!

They dragged him away from the building.

Shadows fell, plasma arced—a door slammed shut.

He craned his neck, glancing behind him at the crisp black shadow hunkered in the middle of the long, broken street.

The shuttle. He grinned, wanting to bust out laughing. Diana had landed it in the fucking street!

"Diana!" he shouted. "Diana!"

She was beside him now, eyes filled with tears, holding his hand as Ron and Sting carried him toward the shuttle. She squeezed his hand.

"Oh, David! I thought they'd killed you!" she cried.

He coughed, holding her hand as tight as he could. "It's worse than it looks," he said. "But we're all going home this time." He sighed, shaking his head. Feeling a little sick inside. "No. We're not. We lost Newlin, Langley, and Tanner—and D'Angelo."

It made him sad. They hadn't deserved this fate. That was on D'Angelo.

"I feel bad leaving his corpse behind," Ron replied.

David nodded. "I do, too. But the guy wasn't in his right mind before this op. UCOE should never have let him return to duty after Ku'Tal. Or the attack on the base."

"Agreed," said Diana, turning away from him. She reached out and squeezed Sting's arm. "So good to see you alive, Sting," she said.

Sting smiled, green eyes brightening. "Good to be alive," he answered in a weary voice. "And leaving this hell hole."

"Peter's been making himself sick for weeks over what happened to you," she told him in a soft voice. "Now, both of you are free."

"Can't tell you how great that word *free* sounds right now," said Sting in a quiet voice. "Thanks to Pete—and Sarge here. Well, all of you. Thank you."

David patted his shoulder.

The hatch loomed and David turned, Jensen clambering inside, Strader behind him. Diana and Ron shuffled in behind them, Sting dragging David inside and slamming the hatch behind him.

Most of the seats were full of recombinants. He noticed the black-haired recombinant that he and Sting were paired with in the training pens. Strapped in beside Peter who was still unconscious.

David smiled and waved at him. He grinned, nodding as he strapped into a seat.

Sting walked up and down the rows of seats, counting softly. "Looks like we've got everybody they were holding. We're good, Sarge."

In the streets, biodrones swarmed through dark buildings, out of treetops, up from trenches, shuffling in a writhing wave of talons and gold eyes toward the shuttle.

The shuttle lurched, biodrones pounding the hull.

"I'll get the rest strapped in," Ron called to Diana. "Get. Us. Out of here!"

"Gladly," she shouted and vaulted into the pilot's chair.

Sting threw himself into the seat beside Mitchell's unconscious form strapped into his restraint harness. He put his arm around Mitchell's shoulders, keeping him from getting tossed around on lift off. Mitchell's head hung down, his weight held in place by the harness.

David dropped into the co-pilot's seat, Ron in the navigator's chair, both of them strapping into harnesses.

Diana switched on the computer and fired the engines. Outside, biodrones caught by the engine blasts shrieked and fell away.

The shuttle lurched and shook. biodrones pounded it, claws scritching against the hull. The sound made her skin crawl.

She grappled with the throttle, shoving it backward, and fired both engines.

Using the street as a runway, the shuttle lurched down the broken pavement. Running over masses of biodrones.

Shaking, the shuttle lifted, shooting up and over the ruined buildings. It soared through the smoke into clear yellow skies. Leaving behind the burning Antaran facility and a swelling army of biodrones.

The comm unit blinked as the shuttle accelerated, climbing toward atmosphere as Diana prepared to slingshot them out of this gravity well.

On course for Farnas. With all these additional recombinants, they'd never make Karaba.

"We'll never make Karaba," Diana muttered.

David smiled. Diana had already handled that issue. "I know. Farnas it is."

They'd refuel on Farnas. The mining and agricultural world was rural and sparsely populated. They minded their own business and kept out of other people's issues. Like rescuing recombinants. And military business. That would be a big help when they landed with this assortment of soldiers. And asked for a medic.

Diana punched through the atmosphere and dropped into orbit. Force against the hull increased as they slingshot around Ballese. The shuttle rumbled and shook until finally, it leveled out.

Only then did she let out the breath she'd been holding and answer the comm unit.

"Recon three. Over."

"Recon three, this is your final—"

"Relax, commander," she said in a tired, annoyed voice. "All personnel are aboard and we're leaving orbit. It's all yours. We're out of here. Over."

"About damned time, Recon three."

"Yes," Diana snapped. "About damned time. We only had the entire Antaris Nation on top of us, commander. It's not like this planet's going anywhere, so chill the hell out. Plenty of time to drop your stupid warheads and destroy another habitable planet. Gotta be billions still left in the goldilocks zone, right? Or maybe we'll just make more. Recon three out."

David and Ron were laughing long before she cut the connection.

THE SHUTTLE BARELY REACHED FARNAS.

It touched down on the runway and limped into a small open-air bay on the edge of the Farnasan wheat fields, a small farming cooperative and refueling station co-existing with civilians and the military. Farther inland were the mines in the rolling hills beyond the grain fields. Much colder at the poles.

Climbing out of the shuttle, Diana paused to stare at the winding rows of feathery, golden stalks of wheat that burned against the fiery orange sun sinking behind Farnas' rolling red hills. She breathed in the calm, clean air, relieved to be away from that horrible black smoke on Ballese. And an army of taloned biodrones.

Two pale blue moon slivers hung on the edge of its velvet green horizon, a calm night creeping in on kittens' feet. Wind carried the nutty scent of grain and acrid smell of shuttle fuel as she stepped out onto the quiet tarmac.

Peter needed a medic. He was badly injured. David probably needed stitches along with Sting and all the other recombinants aboard.

She found the pudgy dark-haired stationmaster walking the runway with a datapad. He wore a red shirt, field blues, and short black boots, a thick beard framing his face. He had a tanned face, deep lines cracking his forehead and curving around his mouth as he spoke.

"Can I help you?" he asked.

"Please," she said, her voice a little shaky. "I need a medic—fast. We have several injured that need immediate attention."

"I sent an urgent call for a medic," he said, tapping the datapad with his index finger. "Don't worry, there's one already on the way."

She smiled at him. "Thank you. I'll be at the shuttle."

She hurried back to the shuttle where several recombinants stood outside, looking a little lost and confused. They'd been carried off by Antarans and probably didn't realize they weren't going back to the military. Anxiety burned in their eyes, the uncertainty in their faces as they wandered around the tarmac. No doubt wondering what would happen to them next.

She smiled. Ron and Mimi would know just where to take them when they reached Civilization. Far from UCOE's reach. They'd been through enough.

She climbed back into the shuttle. Peter was unconscious on the floor, a bedroll beneath him. David was sitting beside him on another bedroll, staring at Peter. Sting crouched beside Peter, worry shining in his green eyes, hands fidgeting against the dirty, bloodied bandages on his forearms.

"How's Peter?" she asked.

David and Sting looked at her, but neither said a word. Even David looked worried. She reached out and stroked Peter's ashen face and soft blond hair filled with soot.

In a short time, someone rapped on the hatch.

"Did someone call for medical assistance?"

A thirty-something woman with honey-blonde hair and grey eyes stepped inside. She wore a blowsy green smock and close-fitting tan pants. A large black case hung on her shoulder.

"Yes," Diana said, rising from the floor. She hurried to the hatch and ushered the medic inside. "Over here. We've got lots of injured."

She knelt beside David and set down her kit.

David pointed toward Peter. "Please, he's in more need than I am."

She scrutinized him a moment then turned to Peter. Sting laid open Peter's shirt, revealing the wound still layered in sealant.

Frowning, the medic went to work, some sort of crisis mode taking over. She carefully removed the layer of sealant, scowling at what lay beneath. She injected him with something and then attended to the chest wound, cleansing as she examined it.

Next, she opened small packages and removed thin layers of what looked like synthetic skin. Using small forceps, she applied the layers across Peter's chest.

When she finished with his chest, she moved to the shoulder wound. Cutting away the shirt, she cleaned the wound and applied more of that synthetic skin. She resealed the wound and wrapped his chest and shoulder. Finally, she cleaned and sealed the scoured, raw knuckles on his right hand and set it in a hard, purple cast.

Diana smiled. True purple. She remembered how he'd first reacted to her purple scarf. He'd never seen the color purple before and had been enchanted by it. And her.

"Why purple?" Diana asked.

The medic glanced up at her, shrugging. "No reason. It was just the first color I grabbed. But it suits him."

Diana reached over and brushed a lock of blond hair out of Peter's eyes. She'd never think about him without that deep, true purple color coming to mind.

After Peter was comfortable, the medic sealed gashes on David's legs, arms, and back. Then she changed and dressed the wounds on Sting's forearms. She went to each recombinant, patching up gashes and treating burns. Bandaging bloodied forearms. She put a blue cast on one recombinant's foot. And green on another one's left hand.

When the medic had treated the last recombinant, Diana paid

the woman for her services (a good bit more for her silence) and the medic left without asking any questions. Or filing any paperwork on her datapad.

A half hour later, Ron and Strader returned with a mountain of sacks filled with real, hot food and several containers of fresh brewed coffee. She grinned. Karaban, her favorite.

The recombinants devoured the food, including Sting, but he never left Peter's side. David picked at his food, washing it down with the hot coffee.

Diana ran through a complete systems' check, doing a thorough walk-through outside to make sure those biodrones hadn't damaged the hull. She needed to make sure the fuel indicators were accurate and that the tank was full. Satisfied with her numbers, she checked engines and the rest of her systems.

When everyone was strapped in, including Peter, she lifted off Farnas. Headed toward Civilization.

Home, she thought. *With David, Peter, and Sting. At last.*

32

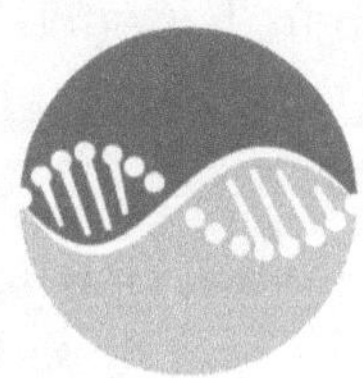

COOL BLACKNESS GAVE way to soft, dove-grey pain. Peter groaned at the tendrils of pain coiling down his shoulder and spiking through his chest.

That's when he realized he was still alive.

Groggy from what appeared to be drugs, he struggled to open his eyes. Part of him was afraid to see what lay beyond the fog of pain and painkillers, fearing the bleakness of the smoking Antaran facility would take shape around him.

In the distance, plates rattled. Soft murmurs filled the room.

Gathering his courage, Peter opened his eyes to slits.

The familiar outlines of his room behind the restaurant took shape. He choked up. He was back on Civilization.

No caregivers, no biodrones—no recombinant hybrids trying to kill him. And no military bunk room surrounding him. Just his own tiny room and his soft bed. He never thought he'd see this room again.

"I think he's awake," said a voice. Diana?

"Diana?" he mumbled, his voice hoarse and tight.

A hand squeezed his. He opened his eyes wider.

There at the foot of his bed sat Private John Stingley, his green eyes watery and bright.

Peter's chest tightened and he bit his lip, overwhelmed by the sight of his best friend.

"Sting!"

He struggled to sit up but was too weak. He fought the weakness again and this time, Diana's hands were at his back, shoving pillows behind him. Tears filled his eyes and he blinked them away as he reached out, fearing Sting was an apparition.

His hand fell against Sting's arm and he clutched his best friend's wrist.

"Sting, is it really you?"

Sting slid closer. "Pete!" He stared at Peter for several quiet moments. "Never thought I'd see you again."

The two young men stared at each for a long moment until finally, Sting and Peter threw their arms around each other. Sting clasped Peter to his chest. Holding him tight.

"Why'd you do it, Pete?" He demanded, voice breaking. "You could've lost everything coming in after me like that! Why?"

Sting let him go.

Peter sighed, his gaze falling to the blanket draped across him. "You gave up everything to take my place. That should have been me there—not you, Sting."

"It's over now," he said in a hushed voice. "Let it go."

"I can't," Peter said, pain in his voice. "You deserved better than that, Sting. You're the best friend I've ever had. I couldn't be here... couldn't be free like this without sharing it with you." He stared down at his hands, afraid to look Sting in the eye now.

"Can't believe you risked everything for me like that," said Sting, a grin on his face now, tears threading down his face. "But I'm so glad you did. You mean the world to me, Pete." He reached out and ruffled Peter's hair which brought a smile to Peter's face.

Sarge rose unsteadily from a chair in the corner and stood by the bed. He looked terrible, cuts marring his face, his arms and hands bandaged.

"Sarge, what had happened?" Peter asked.

He winced at all of Sarge's bandages. He had no idea what happened to the man. He'd missed most of the events after he'd passed out on top of the Antaran facility.

"It's a long story, Mitchell," he said with a smirk. "I'll tell you later. You get some rest. I've got to report in at the base. They've relocated it to Civilization. Indefinitely."

"Can't that wait, David?" Diana asked, hands on her hips.

He shook his head. "I've got to give a report on what happened on the recon, explain about D'Angelo and all. They're going to fortify here. They think an Antaran counterattack is imminent—after what happened on Ballese. They'll want to debrief you and Kraver, too, sis."

Sarge reached down and squeezed Peter's arm. "I'll see you tomorrow, Mitchell. You're going to have to help me find Stingley some work. Now that he's a civilian."

"Will do. Bet Sting breaks less dishes than I do," said Peter, smiling, and everyone laughed.

Diana helped Sarge out into the hallway and then the room was quiet. Just him and Sting.

"Got something for you, Pete," said Sting, grinning as he plopped beside him on the bed. He leaned back against the headboard and slipped something out of his pocket. He dropped it into Peter's hand.

Peter picked it up. The god symbol Sting had given him before! The one he'd flung off and Diana kept for him.

He bowed his head. Ashamed. "I can't take this, Sting," he said, wincing as he held out to him. "I'm a—a traitor. Like Judas."

Sting frowned. "Who? Pete, listen—you didn't sell me out. You saved me. Twice. I'd have gone out trying to be a hero on Ku'Tal if I hadn't had you in my unit. And now, because of you, I'm going to be able to celebrate a birthday, a real birthday. Tomorrow." His green eyes sparkled. "My second."

A smile touched Peter's face as he slipped the god symbol over his head. It was cold against his neck.

"Happy Birthday, Sting," he said, the ache in his chest gone now.

"As soon as you're on your feet, I've got a list of things I wanna do."

Peter laughed. He could only imagine what John Stingley had on this list of his. "Like what?"

Sting pointed out the window. "For starters, I want to see those colored lights you're always babbling about. And eat here—at this restaurant. You and me, buddy!"

It would be good to see those colored lights again, Peter thought as Sting chattered on about the things he wanted to do. The sound of his voice was familiar and comforting. He glanced over Sting's shoulder, grinning at the cot beside his bed. He and Sting would be sharing this small room. Like back at the training base. And in camp on Ku'Tal.

For the first time, Peter felt at ease. When his wounds healed, he'd take Sting down to the river and show him the colored lights. Then he'd take him on a shuttle ride through the city. He smiled. And then he'd take Diana on a shuttle ride, just the two of them. Knowing that Sting was safe, back here at the restaurant would finally give him the peace that he craved.

He put his arm around Sting's shoulders and hugged him again. His best buddy was at his side again.

That's when he realized that the one thing he suddenly had was an abundance of time. Time to do and be and dream, all at the same time. Something he'd never had before.

33

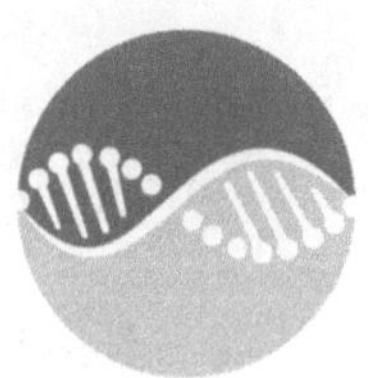

BENEATH B'HA'LLEES' dark skies, bombers swarmed overhead as six caregivers dragged the body of caregiver Tevihu through the dusky, burned out colony streets, an army of biodrones surrounding them. Guarding them.

The burned air smoked with grit, filtered out quickly from Antaran lungs as they dragged tentacled appendages through the crumbled buildings.

Closer now. It wasn't far.

Behind Tevihu's body, two caregivers in brown robes dragged the alien corpse behind them. Three others in cream-colored robes and one caregiver in green.

Green lights sparked across their robes, flashing in geometric patterns as everyone spoke at once.

Hurry, Grand Kefu! There's not much time!

It's not far. Hurry!

There! Turn toward the forest!

In the wash of green light, they slid down the awkward human stairs that led into a vault. Kefu was first, green tunic flickering with lights, as the caregiver slid down each step with a thump and hissed into the vault.

Kefu watched as the remaining caregivers and biodrones lurched into the dark space and closed the heavy vault door behind them. They rolled the alien body across the floor and slumped it against a crate, its arms and legs stiff. Eyes empty. Tevihu's body slumped beside the alien, viscous and grey.

Kefu gritted its three rows of tiny teeth, tentacles curling into knots as it stared at the human. Dead, its shell left behind to stink like on the battlefields of N'ha'Rah and B'ha'Llees. Where the aliens dropped devastating weapons, raining fire across N'ha'Rah. Buildings imploded, others shattered, and others were simply—blown away. It killed a lot of the Antaris Nation, but many still survived.

Including the repository on Ku'Tal. Much of it brought here.

And like N'ha'Rah and Ku'Tal, some of their genetic material would survive this assault, too. Brought here by biodrones and caregivers.

To shelter. And wait.

Kefu crouched between the bodies as the caregivers gathered around them in a circle. The vault door locked behind them. With only portable equipment, the task would take a lot more time.

It couldn't be helped.

But Kefu was patient. So very patient to enact his revenge. And take back the technology stolen from the Nation by these alien scum. Stolen from N'ha'Rah, from the forerunners that gave rise to the Antaris Nation. By the human cleric, Orlando Constantine.

Kefu would find what Constantine stole, take the components back, and restart the ancient machine that had given them life. And power over death. That star-haired human that had killed Tevihu had been such a close match to Constantine.

They must find that one again. Scan its DNA for the codes and ciphers—and the blueprints to the weapon. And the machine. Were those things alive? In the genetic code? All of this technology belonged to the forerunners.

To the Antaris Nation!

The humans were using other technology to create their soldiers. Lesser, inferior technology. They hadn't used the machine. At least not yet. Nevertheless, Kefu vowed to get it all back. And make the aliens pay.

With blood and death like they'd never seen before.

Begin, Kefu demanded through the neural network that connected all caregivers with the Nation. It watched as the green orbs floated above Tevihu and the alien corpse. The network hummed, knitting, capturing, and blending codes together—alien and Antaran. Traversing the fork that had split the two long, long ago.

The first explosion rocked the entire vault. Throwing all of the caregivers against the hard, grey floor.

As orbs of light throbbed and undulated above the corpses.

Charging. Copying. Exchanging. Repairing...

By the time a second explosion ignited above them, the orbs had become one large orb. Hovering between the corpses.

Kefu reached out to the first orb, taking it into two tentacles. The caregiver lifted it above the alien's chest, reading the word there.

D'Angelo.

With a huff of breath, Kefu slammed the orb against the alien's stiff body. It engulfed the corpse with pulsating green lights that filled every muscle and vein. Every bone and patch of skin.

Until a matrix of green light engulfed the alien form.

A third explosion rocked the planet.

The vault shifted, pushing caregivers against the far wall. The two corpses rolled toward the wall, falling in a heap on top of each other.

Kefu fought to stand upright, watching as the alien corpse's chest rose and fell, the orbs breathing life into it.

In a few moments, the smooth-skinned alien sat up. It swiveled its head toward Kefu, its eyes losing their dead stare, looking almost glassy now.

Kefu was pleased.

Tevihu, do you hear us?

The green matrix lighting the alien pulsed and raced with bright white light a moment.

Tevihu hears, Grand Kefu. From this human! But how?

From the last of the forerunner's machine. But the multitude needs the pieces that cleric, Constantine, took from N'ha'Rah and hid.

The alien, D'Angelo rose to its feet.

Why not in my singularity? My form? Tevihu demanded. *Not in this weak, isolated aberration!*

In time, Tevihu. When we recover the cleric. And find the machine.

But the cleric ceases to exist! Tevihu shouted. *Remember? We killed it on N'ha'Rah!*

The original, but not its copy. We must find this copy and destroy it before it reassembles the machines and uses them against us.

Where is this copy? Tevihu demanded.

It defeated you above the repository.

I remember! But that was just another of their recombinants. Tevihu brought a frown to the alien face.

Copy or not, Kefu said through the neural network, *we have scanned it. The multitude will find it again.* Its scratchy laugh reverberated through the vault. *That is, your singularity will find it, Tevihu.*

Are you sending my singularity toward the aliens, Kefu? His voice hungered with vengeance.

Yes. In time. When it's safe to leave B'ha'Llees.

Tevihu pulled the human's legs up and into a sitting position. Having so few limbs was disconcerting, but the caregiver would practice. After it pulled as much from the alien's brain as it could recover.

Tevihu would find those aliens that did this. And kill all of them.

Except for the cleric's copy.

No, that one, Tevihu would torture first. After making it take the caregivers to all three pieces of the forerunner's machine.

For now, the human's ways had to be learned. Only then would Tevihu take the fight to them.

As Captain D'Angelo.

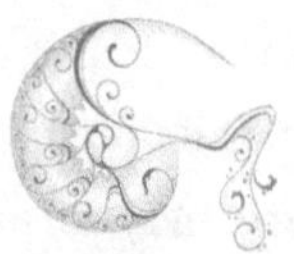

The End of **HELIX: Experiencing True Purple, Book 2**
The story continues in...
SPLICE: Experiencing True Purple, Book 3
FORTHCOMING!

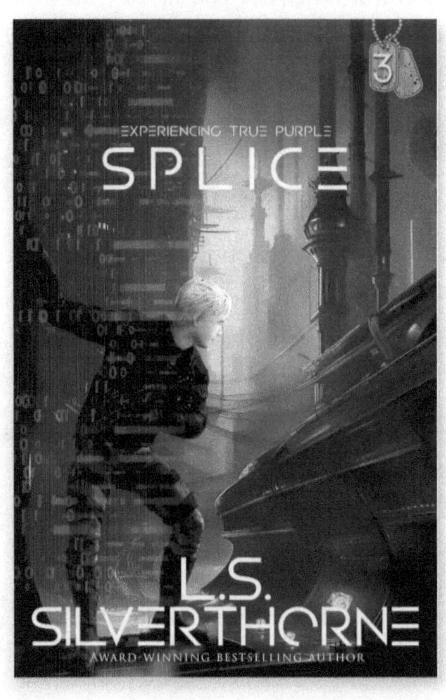

Novels by L.S. Silverthorne

Experiencing True Purple series:
RECOMBINANT, Book 1
HELIX, Book 2
SPLICE, Book 3

Standalone:
REDISCOVERY

Writing as Lisa Silverthorne

A Game of Lost Souls series:
Contemporary Romantasy
THE CINDERELLA HOUR
THE PRINCE CHARMING HOUR
THE EVER AFTER HOUR
THE FALLEN HEARTS SEASON
THE RISING SPIRITS SEASON
THE ETERNAL SOULS SEASON
THE ROYAL WEDDING HOUR
THE HEAVENLY HONEYMOON HOUR
THE DIVINE NEWLYWEDS SHOW
THE CELESTIAL COUPLES SHOW
THE ENOCHIAN APOCALYPSE SHOW
THE ANGELIC ANNIVERSARY SHOW
THE PERDITION PICTURE SHOW
Complete Series!

Curse and Crown series:

Epic Court Intrigue Romantasy
THORN & BLADE
STORM & STEEL

The Spiral series:
Dark Contemporary Fantasy
BETWEEN
REPRISE
AVENGE

The Resurrectionist Papers
Paranormal Romystery
GRAVE RECKONING

Standalones:
ISABEL'S TEARS
LANDFALL
PACIFIC BLUE TATTOO

Short Story Collections
THE SOUND OF ANGELS
THE MAGIC OF ORDINARY THINGS
TIMELESS
WINTER'S EMBRACE

FORTHCOMING!

Experiencing True Purple series:
Cipher, Book 4
Renascence, Book 5 (Series End)

Writing as Lisa Silverthorne

Curse and Crown series:
Flame & Dagger, Book Three (2026)
Frost & Foil, Book Four
Curse & Crown, Book Five (Series End)

The Spiral series:
Ruin, Book 4
Descent, Book 5 (Series End)

The Resurrectionist Papers:
Corpses Delicti (2026)
Stiffed Again

ABOUT THE AUTHOR

LISA SILVERTHORNE, an award-winning author, has published over 30 novels and 150 short stories and novelettes in many genres. She is the author of *A Game of Lost Souls, Experiencing True Purple, The Spiral, The Resurrectionist Papers,* and *Curse and Crown.*

Before you go, you are invited to please leave a **review of this book**!

Reviews are a wonderful way to help an author and share your thoughts with other readers, so **please post yours,** in as many places as possible!

 **ONLINE STORE!**
For Ebook Bundles, book swag, and beautiful
Special Edition *hardcovers (coming soon), visit:*
LisaSilverthorneBooks.com